Nelson DeMille was born in New York City in 1943. He grew up on Long Island and graduated from Hofstra University with a degree of Political Science and History. After serving as an infantry officer in Vietnam, where he was decorated three times, DeMille worked as a journalist and short story writer. He wrote his first major novel, *By the Rivers of Babylon*, in 1978 and has gone on to write many other international bestsellers, with sales of over 55 million copies in 24 languages. He lives on Long Island.

For more information on Nelson DeMille, go to:
www.nelsondemille.net.

ALSO BY NELSON DEMILLE

NELSON DEMILLE

THE QUEST

sphere

SPHERE

First published in 2013 by Center Street, a division of
Hachette Book Group, Inc.
First published in Great Britain in 2013 by Sphere
This paperback edition published by Sphere in 2014

A CIP catalogue record for this book
is available from the British Library.

ISBN 978-0-7515-5326-0

Printed and bound in Great Britain by
Clays Ltd, St Ives plc

Papers used by Sphere are from well-managed forests
and other responsible sources

MIX
Paper from
responsible sources
FSC® C104740
www.fsc.org

Sphere
An imprint of
Little, Brown Book Group
100 Victoria Embankment
London EC4Y 0DY

An Hachette UK Company
www.hachette.co.uk

www.littlebrown.co.uk

To My Three Creative Geniuses —
Lauren, Alex, & James

AUTHOR'S NOTE

An earlier version of this book was published almost forty years ago, and when I wrote *The Quest*, the historical events that take place in this book – the Ethiopian revolution and civil war – were recent history. The old emperor, Haile Selassie, known as the Lion of Judah, had been deposed and died in captivity, and Ethiopia was plunged in chaos.

As a history and political science major in college, and as a news junkie all my life, Ethiopia interested me as an ancient isolated, almost biblical civilization that was being dragged bloodily into the twentieth century. Also, according to family history, some of my Italian forebears had fought with the Italian Army when Italy invaded Ethiopia in 1895, and again when Mussolini invaded in 1936. Thus, my interest in this country was piqued by that family history, and I thought a novel set against this background of a three-thousand-year-old royal dynasty coming to an end at the hands of Marxist revolutionaries would make for a great epic story in the vein of *Doctor Zhivago*, which I had recently read. Now, forty years later, I see that this story of war, love, and loss is timeless.

There is always some literary license taken when writing a novel, but the historical events in this story happened – or at least happened according to the news media of the day whose reporting was my main source of information as I was writing *The Quest*. I did take some license with the terrain and geography for the sake of drama, but the country I described in 1975 was still very much uncharted and dangerous – a perfect setting for an adventure into the heart of darkness.

PART I

Ethiopia, September 1974

'What is it?
The phantom of a Cup which comes and goes?'
'Nay, monk! What phantom?' answered Perceval.
'The Cup, the Cup itself, from which our Lord
Drank at the last sad supper with his own.
This, from the blessed land of Aromat ...
Arimathaean Joseph, journeying brought
To Glastonbury ...
And there awhile it bode; and if a man
Could touch or see it, he was heal'd at once,
By faith, of all his ills. But then the times
Grew to such evil that the Holy Cup
Was caught away to Heaven and disappear'd.'

— Alfred, Lord Tennyson,
'The Holy Grail'

CHAPTER 1

The elderly Italian priest crouched in the corner of his cell and covered himself with his straw pallet. Outside, screaming artillery shells exploded into the soft African earth, and shrapnel splattered off the stone walls of his prison. Now and then, a shell air-burst overhead and hot metal shards pierced the corrugated metal roof.

The old priest curled into a tighter ball and drew the pitifully thin pallet closer. The shelling stopped abruptly. The old man relaxed. He called out to his jailers, in Italian, 'Why are they bombing us? Who is doing this thing?'

But he received no answer. The older Ethiopians, the ones who spoke Italian, had gradually disappeared over the years, and he heard less and less of his native tongue through the stone walls. In fact, he realized he hadn't heard a word of it in almost five years. He shouted in snatches of Amharic, then Tigregna. 'What is it? What is happening?' But there was no answer. They never answered him. To them, he was more dead than the ripening bodies that lay in the courtyard. When you ask questions for forty years and no one answers, it can only mean that you are dead. But he knew they dared not answer. One had answered, once, when he first entered his cell. Was it forty years now? Perhaps it was less.

3

The years were hard to follow. He could not even remember the man who had answered, except for the skull. His jailers had given him the skull of the one who had answered him. The skull was his cup. He remembered the man and his kindness each time he drank. And the jailers remembered when they filled his cup; they remembered not to speak to him. But he asked anyway. He called out again. 'Why is there war? Will you release me?'

He stared at the iron door on the far wall. It had closed on a young man in 1936, when Ethiopia was an Italian colony, and the door had not opened since. Only the small pass-through at the bottom of the iron door was ever used. His sustenance came in and his waste went out once a day through that small portal. A window, no larger than a big book – really just a missing stone – above eye level, let in light, sounds, and air.

His only possessions in the cell, aside from his tattered *shamma*, were a washbasin, a pair of dull scissors that he used to cut his hair and nails, and a Holy Bible, written in Italian, which they had let him keep when he was first imprisoned. If it weren't for his Bible, he knew, he would have gone mad many years ago. He had read the holy book perhaps a hundred, two hundred times, and though his eyesight was growing weaker, he knew every word by heart. The Old and New Testaments brought him comfort and escape, and kept his mind from dying, and kept his soul nourished.

The old man thought of the young man who walked through the iron door in 1936. He knew every detail of the young man's face and every movement of his body. At night, he spoke to the young man and asked him many things about their native Sicily. And he knew the young man so well that he even knew what went on inside his mind and how he felt and where he went to school and the village he came from and how old his father was. The young man never got older, of course, and his stories were always the same. But his was the only face the old man knew well enough to remember. He had seen that young face in the mirror for the last time close to forty years ago and not again since, except in his mind's eye. He wept.

The old priest dried his tears on his dirty native *shamma* and lay back against his cell wall and breathed deeply. His mind eventually came back to the present.

Wars had ebbed and flowed around his small prison and he imagined that the world had changed considerably in his absence from it. Jailers got old and died. Young soldiers grew old as they paraded through the years in the courtyard of the small fortress outside. When he was younger, he was able to hang from the sill of the window much longer. But now he could no longer gather the energy to pull himself up for more than a few minutes a day.

The shelling had jarred loose many things in his mind. He knew that his imprisonment was at its end; if the explosions did not kill him, then the guards would, because he knew they had standing orders to kill him if they could no longer continue to guarantee his incarceration in this place. And now he could hear the sounds of fleeing garrison soldiers. And the jailers would soon open that never-opened door and do their duty. But he held nothing against them. Those were their orders and he forgave them. But it did not matter if they or the explosions killed him. His own body was failing him anyway. He was dying. There was famine in the land and the food had been poor for over a year.

His lungs made a liquid sound when he coughed. Death was here. Inside his cell and outside his cell.

The old man's biggest regret, he thought, was that he would die in ignorance — that as a consequence of the two score years of being held in darkness, he knew less than the simplest peasant did about his world. He did not regret the dying — that held no special terror for him — but the thought of dying without knowing what the world had come to in his absence was a peculiarly sad thing. But then again, his calling was not of this world, but of the next, and it should have made no difference what the world had come to. Still, it would have been nice to know just a little something of the affairs of men. He could not help wondering about his friends, about his family, about the world leaders of his day.

He wrapped the *shamma* around himself more tightly. The sun was fading from his window and a chill wind blew down from the highlands. A small lizard, its tail partly severed by a piece of shrapnel, climbed awkwardly up the wall near his head. Outside in the stillness, he could hear the soldiers speaking in Amharic about who would have to kill him if it became necessary.

Like so many other imprisoned and condemned men and women, like the martyred saints, the thing that had sustained him through his ordeal was the very thing that had condemned him in the first place. And what had condemned *him* was his knowledge of a secret thing. And the knowledge of that secret thing comforted him and nourished him and he would gladly have traded forty more years of his life, if he had them to trade, for one more look at the thing that he had seen. Such was his faith. The years in prison saddened him because they meant that the world had not yet learned of this thing. For if the world knew, then there would be no more reason for his solitary confinement.

He often wished they had killed him then, and spared him this living death for forty years. But he was a priest, and those who had captured him, the monks, and those who had imprisoned him, the soldiers of the emperor, were Coptic Christians, and so they had spared his life. But the monks had warned the soldiers never to speak to the priest, for any reason, or death would come to them. The monks had also told the soldiers that they had leave to kill the priest if his imprisonment and silence could not be guaranteed. And now, he thought, that day had surely come. And he welcomed it. He would soon be with his heavenly father.

Suddenly the artillery began again. He could hear its thump and crash as it walked around the walls of the small fortress. Eventually the artillery spotter made his corrections, and the rounds began to land more accurately within the walls of the compound. The sounds of secondary explosions — stockpiled petrol and ammunition — drowned out the sounds of the incoming artillery. Outside his window, the old priest could hear men screaming in pain. A nearby explosion shook the tiny cell and the lizard lost its grip and fell beside him. The deafening explosions numbed his brain and blotted out every awareness except that of the lizard. The reptile was trying to coordinate its partially severed halves, thrashing around on the reverberating mud floor, and he felt sorry for the creature. And it occurred to him that the soldiers might abandon the garrison and leave him here to die of thirst and hunger.

A shock wave lifted a section of corrugated metal off the roof and sent it sailing into the purple twilight. A piece of spent shrapnel found him and slapped him hotly across his cheek, causing him to yell out in pain. The old man could hear the sounds of excited shouts outside his iron door. The door moved almost imperceptibly. The old man stared at it. It moved again. He could hear its rusty stubbornness over the roar of the fiery hell outside. But forty years was a long time and it would not yield. There were more shouts and then quiet. Slowly, the pass-through at the base of the unyielding cell door slid open. They were coming for him. He clutched his Bible to his chest.

A long, gaunt Ethiopian slithered through the pass-through onto the mud floor and the old man was reminded of the lizard. The Ethiopian rose to his feet, looked at him, then drew a curved sword from his belt. In the half-light, the old priest could see his fine features. He was undoubtedly an Amhara from Hamitic stock. His hooked nose and high cheekbones made him look almost Semitic, but the tight, black hair and dusky skin revealed him as a descendant of Ham. With his scimitar in his hand and his *shamma*, he looked very biblical, and the old priest thought that this was as it should be, although he could not say why.

The old priest rose, carrying his Bible, and his knees shook so badly he could barely stand. His mouth, he noticed, was quite dry now. He surprised the Ethiopian by deliberately walking across the small cell toward him. It was better to die quickly and to die well. A chase around the cell with upraised arms to ward off the blows of the scimitar would have been grotesque.

The Ethiopian hesitated, not wanting to do his duty in the final analysis and wondering now if perhaps he could circumvent it. But having drawn the short straw, he had become the executioner. What to do? The old priest knelt and crossed himself. The

Ethiopian, a Christian of the ancient Coptic Church, began to shake. He spoke in bad Italian. 'Father. Forgive me.'

'Yes,' said the old priest, and he prayed for both of them in snatches of long-forgotten Latin. Tears welled in his eyes as he kissed his Bible.

A shot rang out above the dwindling sounds of artillery outside and he heard a cry. Another shot, then the sounds of automatic rifle fire.

The soldier said in Italian, 'The Gallas are here.'

He sounded frightened, thought the old man, and well he should be. The priest remembered the Gallas, the tribal people who were as merciless as the ancient Huns. They mutilated their prisoners before they killed them.

The priest looked up at the soldier holding his scimitar and saw that he was shaking in fear. The old priest yelled at him, 'Do it!'

But the soldier dropped his scimitar, then drew an ancient pistol from his belt and backed away toward the door, listening for sounds outside.

The soldier seemed indecisive, thought the priest, torn between staying in the relative safety of the cell or going out to be with his comrades, and to meet the Gallas, who were now within the fortress. The soldier was also torn between killing the old priest or letting him live, which could cost him his own life if his commander discovered what he had done – or failed to do.

The old priest decided that he preferred a quick and merciful death at the hands of this soldier; the Gallas would not be quick or merciful. He stood and said to the soldier in Amharic, 'Do it. Quickly.' He pointed to his heart.

The soldier stood frozen, but then raised his pistol. His hand shook so badly that when he fired, the bullet went high and splattered off the stone behind the old man's head.

The old priest had suffered enough, and the strange emotion of anger rose inside him. Here he was, after close to forty years in solitary imprisonment, and all he had wanted in his last moments was to die well and to die quickly, without losing his faith, like so many others did in those last seconds. But a well-meaning and inept executioner had prolonged his agony and he felt his faith slipping. He screamed, 'Do it!'

He stared down the barrel of the gun and saw it spit another flame at him. And he thought of the thing that had condemned him. And the vision of that thing glowed like the fire from the gun, all golden and blinding – bright like the sun. Then everything went black.

He awoke to the miracle of being alive. The roof was mostly gone and he could see pinpoints of starlight against the sky. A bluish moon cast shadows across the floor, which was strewn with timbers and stone. Everything was unearthly still. Even the insects had abandoned the fortress.

He looked and felt around for his Bible, but could not find it in the rubble, and thought perhaps the soldier had taken it.

The old man crawled toward the door, then carefully out the pass-through. The soldier lay naked outside the door, and he saw that the man's genitals had been hacked off. The stripping, the mutilation; this was the mark of the Galla tribesmen. They might still be near.

The old man rose unsteadily. In the courtyard, naked bodies

lay in the blue moonlight. His insides burned, but he felt well otherwise. It was hard to feel anything but well, walking now under the sky and taking more than five paces in any one direction.

A cool breeze picked up swirls of rubble dust, and he could smell the burned earth and the death around him. The damaged concrete buildings gleamed white in the moonlight like broken teeth. He shivered and tucked his arms in his *shamma*. His body was cold and clammy. He became aware that his *shamma* was caked with dried blood, sticking to his skin, and he moved more slowly so as not to open the wound.

It had been forty years, but he remembered the way and walked to the main gates. They lay open. He walked through them, as he'd done in dreams five thousand times, and he was free.

CHAPTER 2

The Jeep bounced slowly over the rutted track, and its filtered headlights picked out the path between the tight jungle growth. In the distance, artillery boomed and illuminated the black sky, like flashes of distant lightning.

Frank Purcell gripped the wheel and peered hard into the distorted shadows of gnarled trees and twisting vines. He hit the brakes, then shut off the hard-idling engine and killed the headlights. Henry Mercado, in the passenger seat, asked, 'What's the matter?'

Purcell held up his hand for silence.

Mercado peered nervously into the encroaching jungle. Every shadow seemed to move. He cocked his silver-haired head and listened, then looked out of the corners of his eyes into the darkness, but he could see nothing.

From the back of the open-sided vehicle, on the floor among the supplies and photographic equipment, came a soft feminine voice. 'Is everything all right?'

Mercado turned around in his seat. 'Yes, fine.'

'Then why are we stopped?'

'Good question.' He whispered, 'Why are we stopped, Frank?'

Purcell said nothing. He started the engine and threw the Jeep into gear. The four-wheel-drive dug into the track and they lurched forward. He moved the Jeep faster and the bouncing became rougher. Mercado held on to his seat. In the back, Vivian uncurled her slender body and sat up, grabbing on to whatever she could find in the dark.

They drove on for a few minutes. Suddenly, Purcell yanked the wheel to the right, and the Jeep crashed through a thicket of high brush and broke into a clearing.

Vivian said, 'What the hell are you doing? Frank?'

In the middle of the clearing, gleaming white in the full-risen moon, were the ruins of an Italian mineral bath spa. A strange, anomalous legacy from the Italian occupation, the spa was built in ancient Roman style and sat crumbling like some Caesar's bath in another time and place.

Purcell pointed the Jeep toward the largest of the buildings and accelerated. The stuccoed structure grew bigger as the vehicle bounced across the field of high grass.

The Jeep hit the broad front steps of the building, found traction, and climbed. It sailed between two fluted columns, across the smooth stone portico, and through the front opening, coming to rest in the center of the main lobby of what had been the hotel part of the spa. Purcell cut the engine and headlights. Night creatures became quiet, then started their senseless, cacophonous noises again.

The moon shone blue-white through the destroyed vaulted ceiling and lit the pseudo-Roman chamber with an ethereal glow. Huge crumbling frescoes of classical bath scenes adorned every wall. Purcell wiped his face with his sweating palm.

Mercado caught his breath. 'What was that all about?'

Purcell shrugged.

Vivian regained her composure and laughed mockingly from the back of the Jeep. 'I think the brave man just lost his nerve in the dark jungle.' Her accent was mostly British with a mixture of exotic pronunciations. Mercado had told him that her mother tongue was unknown and her ancestry was equally obscure, though she carried a Swiss passport with the surname of Smith. 'A woman of mystery,' Mercado had said to Purcell, who'd replied, 'They're all a mystery.'

Mercado jumped from the Jeep and stretched. 'We're out of the jungle, but not out of the woods.' Mercado's own voice had that curious mid-Atlantic accent, common to people who have traveled between the British Isles and North America all their lives. His mother was English and his father a Spaniard – thus the surname – though he'd spent most of his youth in boarding schools in Switzerland, and spoke French, German, and Italian like a native.

Frank Purcell cupped a cigarette in his hand and lit it. In the glow of the match he looked older than his thirty-odd years. Lines worked their way around his mouth and his brown-black eyes. Gray was sprinkled through his shaggy black hair and he looked tired. He slumped back in his seat and exhaled a long stream of smoke. 'What is this place, exactly?'

Mercado was pacing around over the mosaic floor of the huge lobby. 'Roman baths. What do they look like?'

'Roman baths.'

'Well, there you are, then. Bloody Fascists built them as part of their civilizing mission back in '36. I did a story on them, as I recall. You'll find them in the most unlikely places. Come on, then. If the mineral springs are still flowing, we'll have a nice bath.'

Purcell stepped stiffly out of the Jeep. 'Keep your voice lower, Henry.'

'Can't very well keep it low if I'm over here and you're over there, can I, Frank? Come along. Let's explore.'

Vivian joined Mercado at the entrance of a colonnade that led to an interior courtyard. Purcell walked slowly over the rubble-strewn floor. Five years in Indochina as a war correspondent had expunged any fascination he might have once had for ruins. The last ruins he had gone out of his way to see were the ancient city of Angkor Wat in Cambodia, and that side trip had cost him a year in a Khmer Rouge prison camp. That year would remain a very big part of his life. He'd lost there, among other things, any illusions he might have had about his fellow man.

He joined Mercado and Vivian as they walked slowly down the moonlit colonnade. A statue of Neptune with upraised trident stood in the middle of the walkway and they had to go around him. The colonnade made a ninety-degree turn, and as they rounded the corner they could hear the gentle lapping of water.

'We're in luck,' said Mercado. 'I can smell the sulphur. The baths should be up ahead.'

Vivian stepped onto a low marble bench and peered across the courtyard. 'Yes, I see the steam. There, behind those trees.'

They walked across the courtyard toward a line of eucalyptus trees. The large expanse, once paved in white stone, was overgrown with lichens and grass. A two-faced Janus rose up out of a thicket of hedges and projected a monstrous moonshadow through which they passed quickly. The courtyard was surrounded by the colonnade, and vines had grown over most of the columns. Broken statuary of Roman gods and goddesses dotted the yard. The impression was of one of those fantasy paintings of Rome as it may have looked in the Dark Ages, with shepherds and flocks passing through great columned imperial buildings overgrown with vegetation.

They walked by a dry fountain in a melancholy garden and passed between two eucalyptus trees. In front of them was a stone balustrade that led to a curved staircase, and they descended the crumbling steps. At the bottom was a pool about forty meters square. Sulphurous fumes made the air almost unbreathable.

They approached the pool. It looked black, but the moon touched its gently moving ripples with highlights. A huge stone fish spit a never-ending supply of mineral water into the ever-demanding pool. The sound of the falling water echoed off the bathhouse on the far side of the pool.

'It stinks,' announced Purcell.

'Oh,' said Mercado. 'You Yanks. Everything must smell like underarm deodorant to you. These baths are an ancient European tradition. These and the roads are the only good things Mussolini did for this country.'

'The roads stink, too,' said Purcell, stretching his muscular frame.

Vivian had peeled off her khakis. She stood naked at the edge of the pool, her milk-white skin shining in the moonlight, like fine, rubbed alabaster.

Purcell regarded her for a few seconds. In the three-day cross-country jaunt out of Addis Ababa, he had seen her naked at every bath stop. At first he was taken aback by her lack of modesty, but she had insisted on being treated with no special considerations.

Mercado sat on a mossy marble bench and began to pull off his boots. Purcell sat next to him, his eyes darting toward Vivian from time to time. He reckoned her age at no more than twenty-five, so she had been only about sixteen when he was stepping off the plane into the maelstrom that was Saigon's Tan Son Nhut Airport in 1965. He felt old in her presence. Who was she? he wondered. Her features were mostly Caucasian and her skin was like milk, but her eyes were definitely almonds and her jet black hair was long, straight, and thick like an East Asian, or maybe a Native American. But those almond eyes – they were dark green. Purcell wondered if such a combination was genetically possible.

Vivian held up her arms and inhaled the fumes. 'It does stink, though, Henry.'

'It's refreshing and salubrious. Breathe it in.'

She breathed. 'Graviora quaedam sunt remedia periculis.'

Purcell stared at Vivian. There was no mistaking that that was Latin. This was a new language in Vivian's repertoire. He asked Mercado, 'What did she say?'

Mercado looked up from tugging at his boot. 'Huh? Oh. "The cure is worse than the disease,"' he answered as he pulled off his boot.

Purcell didn't respond.

Mercado said, 'Don't go feeling all inadequate. She doesn't know the language. Just a phrase or two. She's just showing off.'

'For whom?'

'For me, of course.'

Purcell pulled off his boots and looked at Vivian, who was sitting on her haunches and testing the water with her fingers.

She called out, 'It's warm.'

17

Mercado slipped off his shorts and padded toward the edge of the pool. His body, Purcell noticed, was showing the signs of age. How old could he be? He was here in Ethiopia during the Italian invasion in 1935, so he had to be at least sixty. Purcell looked at Vivian, then back at Mercado, wondering what their relationship was, if any. He slipped off his shorts and stood near Mercado.

Vivian, a few feet away, rose to her feet, stood on her toes, and stretched her arms in the air. She shouted to the sky, 'There's hell, there's darkness, there is the sulphurous pit; burning, scalding, stench, consumption!' She fell forward and the black, warm mineral waters closed quietly around her.

Mercado hunched down and touched the water. 'That was Shakespeare, Frank. King Lear's description of a vagina, actually.'

'I hope that wasn't his pickup line.'

Mercado laughed.

Purcell dove in and swam. The warm water smelled like rotten eggs, but it was not unpleasant after a time. He could feel the fatigue run out of his body, but the heat made his mind groggy.

Mercado lowered his big bulk into the water, then began to swim.

Purcell floated on his back and drifted. He felt good for the first time in days. Maybe weeks. He let the pool currents take him, and the rising steam lulled him. In the distance, he could hear Vivian cavorting, and her shrieks of animal joy echoed off the surrounding structures. Purcell wanted to tell her to be more quiet, but it didn't matter somehow. He noticed that his member was stiff. He rolled over and swam toward a stone platform in the middle of the pool. The platform was awash in a few inches of water, and he climbed onto it and lay on his back, then closed his eyes.

Mercado bobbed up beside him. 'Are you alive, Frank?'

Purcell opened his eyes. He could see Mercado's face through the steam. 'Tell her to pipe down,' he said groggily. 'She'll have every Galla in the province here.'

'What? Oh. She's sleeping by the poolside, Frank. I told her before. Were you dreaming?'

He looked at his watch. A full hour had slipped by.

'Let's get back to the Jeep. I'm worried about the gear.'

'Right.' Purcell turned and swam with steady even strokes toward the side of the sulphur pool and climbed out. He noticed Vivian sleeping, curled like a fetus by the edge of the pool. She was still naked.

Mercado looked around. 'I'm sure there's a freshwater spring around somewhere. Probably in the bathhouse over there.'

'I'd rather get out of here, Henry. We've taken enough chances.'

'You're right, of course, but we smell.'

Purcell sat on the lichen-covered marble bench and wiped himself with his bush jacket. Mercado sat next to him. The older man's close nakedness made Purcell uneasy.

Mercado pressed some water out of his thick gray hair, then nodded toward the naked, sleeping Vivian and asked, 'Does she make you ... uncomfortable?'

Purcell shrugged. Mercado had not offered to define his relationship with the young lady, and Purcell didn't know if he cared. But he *was* curious. He had the habitual and professional curiosity of a newsman, not the personal curiosity of a meddler. Back in Addis, he had agreed to drive Henry Mercado and Vivian Smith to the northwest where the civil war was the hottest, and he hadn't asked for much in return. But now he figured Mercado owed him. 'Who is she?'

It was Mercado's turn to shrug. 'Don't know, really.'

'I thought she was your photographer.'

'She is. But I met her only a few months ago. At the Hilton in Addis. Don't know if she can photograph or not. We've taken scads of pictures, but nothing's been developed yet. Don't even know if she uses film, to be honest with you.' He laughed.

Purcell smiled. The moon was below the main building now and a pleasant darkness enveloped the spa. A soft evening breeze carried the scent of tropical flowers, and a feeling very near inner peace filled him. He wondered if he was getting Indochina out of his system. Apropos of that, he asked Mercado, 'You were in jail, weren't you?'

'Not jail, old man. We political prisoners don't call it jail. If you're going to talk about it, use the correct term, for Christ's sake. The *camps*. Sounds better. More dignified.'

'Still sounds like shit.'

Mercado continued, 'That it should have happened to me was more ironic, since I was a little pink in those days myself.'

'What days?'

'After the war. The Russians grabbed me in East Berlin. January of 1946. All I was doing was photographing a damned food line. Never understood it. There were food lines all over Europe in the winter of 1946. But I guess there weren't supposed to be any in the workers' paradise. And the damned Russkies had been in charge there for only – what? About nine months? Hard to erect a Socialist paradise in only nine months. That's what I told them. Don't take it personally, chaps, I said. You beat the Huns fair and square. So what if they have to stand on bread lines? Good for the little Nazis. You see? But they didn't quite get my point.'

Purcell nodded absently.

Mercado continued, 'I had Reuters send all the press clippings I had written since the Spanish Civil War in 1936. All my best anti-Fascist stuff. I even had a lot of nice things to say about the brave Red Army in some of those pieces. I don't know if the bastards even saw my articles. All I know is that I was bundled off to Siberia. Didn't get out until 1950 because of some prisoner exchange. And not so much as an apology, mind you. One day I was 168AM382. Next day I was Henry Mercado again, Reuters correspondent, back in London, with a nice bit of back pay coming. Four years, Frank. And was it cold. Oh my, was it cold. Four years for snapping a picture. And me a nice pink Cambridge boy. Fabian Society and all that. Workers of the world, unite.'

Again, Purcell did not respond.

Mercado asked, 'How many years did you do, Frank? A year in Cambo? Well, we can't compare it in years alone, can we? Hell is hell, and when you're there, it's an eternity, isn't it? Especially with an open-ended sentence. You can't even count off the days you have left.'

Purcell nodded.

Mercado asked rhetorically, 'What are you to them? Nothing. Do they let you know that your wife has died? Certainly not.

They don't even know themselves, probably, that you have a wife. They don't know anything about you, except that you are I68AM382, and that you must work. So what if your wife is dying of pneumonia and penicillin is like gold and a woman by herself can't—'

Mercado stopped abruptly, and a look of weariness came into his watery blue eyes. He said in a low, hoarse voice, 'Bloody Reds. Bloody Nazis. Bloody politicians. Don't believe in any of them, Frank. That's good advice from an older man. They all want your body and your soul. The body's not important, but the soul is. And that belongs to God when He calls for it.'

'Henry, no religion, please.'

'Sorry. I'm a believer, you know. Those priests in the camps. The Russian Orthodox priests. Had a few Baptist ministers, too. Some Catholic priests, some rabbis. I was in a camp with a lot of religious people. Some of them had been there since the 1920s. They kept me alive, Frank. They *had* something.'

'Lizards and centipedes kept me alive in Cambodia.' Purcell pulled on his pants and stood. 'Let's get moving.' He walked away from Henry Mercado.

Vivian had been awakened by their conversation, and she moved past Purcell in the darkness. He could hear the soft sounds of whispering as she spoke to Mercado. The words were lost, but the tone was soothing. Poor Henry, Purcell thought, the grizzled old newsman having a teary moment in front of a woman half his age.

They dressed and headed back toward the hotel lobby in the darkness. Mercado, who seemed to be feeling better, said, 'I'll give this place three stars.'

Suddenly the northern sky was illuminated so brightly that all three stopped in their tracks and crouched.

They looked up and could see star shells bursting in the night sky. An infantry attack had begun somewhere in the hills to the north and one side or the other had sent up these artificial suns to light the way. Automatic weapons fire could be heard now and green and red tracer rounds crisscrossed the hills. The deep, throaty sounds of muffled artillery rolled down into the spa complex, and explosions lit up the low mountain range like a thousand campfires.

Purcell stared at the close-by hills. He could see illumination flares pop and float to earth on their parachutes. Even after all the years in Indochina, the sights and sounds of battle awed him. He stood mesmerized as the hills lit up and sent a crescendo of sound through the night air. It was as though it were a light and sound show, a mixed-media symphony played only for him.

Mercado asked, 'Who is killing whom tonight?'

'Does it matter?'

'No, I suppose not. As long as it isn't us.' Mercado suggested, 'We should stay here tonight.'

Vivian agreed, and Purcell said, 'All right. We've found the armies. In the morning we'll go see who won the battle.'

They continued on and entered the main building. The Jeep stood in the middle of the lobby looking very exposed. Purcell glanced around for a place to move the vehicle and spend the night. He noticed that one corner of the roofless lobby remained dark when the illumination flares burst. Between the Jeep and the dark corner was some rubble from the ceiling, but it was not an impossible task to get the Jeep through it. He stepped up to the vehicle and began pushing, not wanting to start the engine and create noise. Vivian jumped behind the wheel and Mercado helped Purcell push.

As their Jeep approached the patch of blackness in the far corner, an illumination flare lit up the lobby, and they saw standing in front of them a man holding a skull.

CHAPTER 3

They laid him on a sleeping bag between the Jeep and the dark corner, and Vivian fed him cold soup out of a can. Purcell threw the skull out a window.

The man's *shamma* was in tatters, so they covered his shaking body with their only blanket. In the dark corner, they did not see the dried blood on the *shamma*.

They could not make out what or who he was. So many Ethiopians were light-skinned, with straight noses and Semitic-Hamitic features, and many wore beards like this man.

Mercado leaned over and asked in Amharic, 'Who are you?'

He responded in Amharic, 'Weha.' Water.

Mercado gave him water from a canteen, then took a flashlight from the Jeep and shined it in the man's face. 'He's not an Ethiopian. Not an Amhara, anyway. Maybe an Arab from Eritrea. I know a little—'

'Italiano,' said the old man.

There was a long silence.

Mercado crouched next to him and spoke slowly in Italian. 'Who are you? Where do you come from? Are you ill?'

The old man closed his eyes and did not respond.

Purcell took the flashlight from Mercado, knelt beside the old man, and stared down at him. The man's beard was unkempt and his skin hadn't seen sunlight in years. Purcell took the old man's hand from under the blanket. The hand was filthy, but the skin was soft. 'I think he's been locked away for a while.'

Mercado nodded in the darkness.

The old man opened his eyes again, and Vivian spooned more soup into his toothless mouth. 'He's in terrible shape, poor old man.'

The old man was trying to speak, but his lips trembled and only small sounds came out. Finally, he spoke in slow Italian. Vivian sat close to Purcell and whispered the translation into his ear as she continued to spoon-feed him. 'He says he is wounded in the stomach.'

Purcell took the can and spoon from Vivian and laid them down. The old man protested. 'Tell him he can't eat until we've seen the wound.'

Mercado pulled down the blanket and tore aside the *shamma*. He turned on the flashlight again. A large mass of coagulated gore covered the man's stomach. He spoke to the old man. 'How did this happen? What made this wound?'

The man made a small shrug. 'A bullet, perhaps. Maybe the artillery.'

Mercado said to Vivian and Purcell, 'We'll have a look at it in the morning. There's nothing we can do now. Let him sleep.'

Purcell thought a moment. 'He may be dead in the morning, Henry. Then we'll never know. Talk to him.'

'I can see why you were put up for a Pulitzer, Frank. Let the old duffer rest.'

'There's all eternity for him to rest.'

'Don't write him off like that,' said Vivian.

The old man moved his head from side to side as if trying to follow the conversation.

Mercado looked at him. 'He seems alert enough, doesn't he? Let's get his name and all that – just in case.'

'Proceed,' said Purcell.

Vivian moved next to Purcell again and put her head beside his.

Mercado began in Italian, 'We cannot give you more to eat because of the stomach wound. Now you must rest and sleep. But first, tell us your name.'

The old man nodded. A thin smile played across his lips. 'You are good people.' He asked, 'Who are you?'

Mercado replied, 'Journalists.'

'Yes? You are here for the war?'

'Yes,' Mercado replied, 'for the war.'

The old man asked, 'Americano? Inglese?'

Mercado replied, 'Both.'

The old man smiled and said, 'Good people.'

Mercado laid his hand on the old man's arm and asked, 'What is your name, please?'

'I am – I am Giuseppe Armano. I am a priest.'

A long silence hung in the darkness. Outside, the sounds of battle died slowly, indicating that everyone was satisfied with the night's carnage. Occasionally a flare burst overhead and gently floated to earth, and as it fell, the crisscrossed steel reinforcing rods of the collapsed concrete ceiling cast their peculiar grid shadows over the floor, and the room was bathed in blue-white luminescence. But the small corner of the big chamber remained in shadow.

Mercado took the old priest's hand and squeezed it. 'Father. What has happened to you?'

The old priest winced in pain and did not respond.

Mercado gripped the priest's hand tighter. 'Father. Can you talk?'

'Yes ... yes, I can. I must talk. I think I am dying.'

'No. No. You're fine. You'll be—'

'Be still and let me speak.' The old priestly authority came through his weak voice. 'Put my head up.' Mercado slid a piece of stone under the sleeping bag. 'There. Good.' The old priest knew when he was in the presence of a believer and again became the leader of the flock — a flock of one. Vivian moistened his lips with a wet handkerchief.

He drew a deep breath and began, 'My name is Father Giuseppe Armano and I am a priest of the order of Saint Francis. My parish is in the village of Berini in Sicily. I have spent the last ... I think, forty years, since 1936 ... what year is this?'

'It is 1974, Father.'

'Yes. Since 1936, almost forty years. I have been in a prison. To the east of here.'

'Forty years?' Mercado exchanged a look with Purcell. 'Forty years? Why? Why have you been in prison forty years?'

'They kept me from the world. To protect the secret. But they would not kill me because I, too, am a priest. But they are the old believers. The Copts. They have the sacred blood and the ...' His voice trailed off and he lay still, staring up at the sky.

Mercado said to the priest, 'Go on. Slowly. Go slowly.'

'Yes ... you must go to Berini and tell them what has happened to me. Giuseppe Armano. They will remember. I have a family there. A brother. Two sisters. Could they be alive?' Tears welled up in the old priest's eyes, but he insisted on continuing. He spoke more quickly now. 'I left my village in 1935. August. It was a hot day. A man came and said I was in the army. Il Duce needed priests for his army. So we went ... some other priests, too ... and many young boys. We walked in the sun and reached Alcamo. There was a train for us in Alcamo and then a boat from Palermo. I had never been on a train or boat and I was frightened of the train, but not so much of the boat. And the boys, peasants like myself, some were frightened, but most were excited. And we sailed in the boat to Reggio. And there was a train in Reggio and we went north to Rome ...' He lay back and licked his dry lips. Vivian moistened them again as she translated for Purcell.

The old man smiled and nodded at the kindness. He again refused Mercado's offer to sleep. 'I am very sick. You must let me finish. I feel the burning in my belly.'

'It's just the food, Father. It has made the acid. You understand?'

'I understand that I am dying. Be silent. What is your name?'

'Henry Mercado.'

'Henry ... good. So we went to Rome, Henry. All my life, I wished to go to Rome. Now I was in Rome. What a city ... have you seen it? Everyone should go to Rome before he dies ... You are a Catholic, Henry?'

'Well, yes, sort of. Yes.'

'Good.' The priest stayed silent awhile, then continued. 'We were taken to the Vatican ... all the priests from Sicily ... there were twelve of us, I remember ... to the Vatican, some place in the

Vatican. A small building near the Sistine Chapel. There was a cardinal there dressed all in white. He did not give his name and I remembered thinking that this was ill-mannered, but what was I going to say to a cardinal of the Sacred College? We sat in chairs of fine fabric and we listened. The cardinal told us we would go with Mussolini's army. Go to war in Ethiopia. We listened sadly, but no one spoke. The cardinal showed us an envelope, a beautiful envelope of hard paper, colored like butter. On the envelope was the seal of His Holiness ... the ring of the fisherman ... ' The old priest stopped, and Vivian finished her translation.

Purcell thought he had passed out, but then he opened his eyes and asked, 'Who sits on the throne of Saint Peter, now? How many since Pius?'

'Three, since Pius, Father,' Mercado replied.

Purcell said to Mercado, 'The guy is near dead and he wants to know who his boss is. Listen, Henry, he is going to ask you a thousand irrelevant questions. Get him back to the story, please.'

'He is telling the story in his own way, Frank. The man has suffered. You and I know how he has suffered. These questions are important to him.'

Vivian put her hand on Purcell's arm and said softly, 'Let Henry handle it.'

Purcell grunted. Mercado spoke again in Italian. 'After Pius XI was Pius XII. Then John XXIII. You would have liked him, Father. A good man. He died eleven years ago. Now Paul VI sits on the throne of Saint Peter. A good man also,' he added.

The old priest made noises that sounded like quiet weeping. When he spoke again, his voice was husky. 'Yes. All good men, I am sure. And Il Duce? Is he still alive?'

Mercado replied, 'There was a war. In Europe. Mussolini was killed. Europe is at peace now.'

'Yes. A war. I could see it coming, even in Berini. We could see it.'

Mercado asked, 'Father, did you see what was in the envelope? The one the cardinal showed you?'

'The envelope . . . ?' He paused. 'Yes. There was an envelope for each priest. The cardinal told us we must keep the envelope in our possession always. Never, never must it leave our person . . . we were never to mention the envelope to anyone. Not even to the officers. The cardinal explained that when a priest dies in the army, all his possessions are given to another priest. So the envelope would always be in the hands of those who were sworn . . . we had to take an oath . . . sworn never to open it . . . but we would know when to open it. This cardinal with no name said that as a further precaution, the message on the inside was written in Latin, so if someone else should open it, he would have difficulty with the words. My Latin was bad and I remembered being ashamed of that. Latin is not used so much by a country priest. Only in the Mass. You understand? But the letter was in Latin, so that if it was opened by error, it would no doubt be taken to a priest for translation. This cardinal said that if we ever came upon the letter in that way, we were to say we had to take the letter and study it. Then we were to make a false translation on paper and burn the letter.' The priest breathed heavily, then moaned.

Vivian finished translating for Purcell, then said, 'This is getting interesting.' She suggested, 'Henry, push him just a little.'

'In his own way,' Mercado answered flatly. 'He will get it all out.'

The priest moaned again. Vivian put her hand on his sweaty forehead. 'He has fever, Henry. Isn't there anything we can do?'

'I'm afraid not. If he holds out till morning, we can make Gondar in a few hours. There's an English missionary hospital there.'

Purcell reminded them, 'Prince Joshua's army and the Provisional government army are less than an hour away – in those hills. I wouldn't try it now, but in the morning, maybe. They should have a surgeon.'

Mercado thought a moment, then replied, 'I don't know. He is obviously a fugitive of some sort. When we find out from whom, then we can decide where to bring him.'

'Right. But push him just a little, Henry,' he said, mimicking Vivian's words.

Mercado turned his attention back to the priest and asked him, 'Father? Can you continue?'

'Yes. What are you talking about? I cannot go to Gondar.'

Mercado told him, 'We will take you to an English hospital in the morning. Continue, if you feel—'

'Yes. I must finish it. The envelope ... he told us that we were on no account to open it, unless, when we got to Ethiopia, we should see in the jungles a black monastery. Black like coal, made of black stone, he said. Hidden ... in the jungles. There was none like it in all of Ethiopia, he said. It was the monastery of the old believers ... the Coptics. And in this black monastery was a reliquary and within that reliquary was the relic of a saint, he told us. An important saint. A saint of the time of Jesus, he told us ... The relic of the saint was so important that His Holiness himself wanted very much to have the relic carried back to Rome where it belonged, in the true church of Jesus Christ. In the Church of Saint Peter.'

Vivian translated for Purcell, who commented, 'Don't they have enough stuff in the Vatican?'

Mercado leaned closer to the priest. 'Which saint? What kind of relic? A lock of hair? A bone? A piece of a garment?'

The priest laughed. 'It was not the relic of a saint at all. Can you imagine such a thing? A cardinal of the Sacred College lying to a flock of rustic priests ... Yes, we were well chosen to follow and serve with the Italian infantry. We asked no such questions as you ask now, Henry. We were simple country priests. We had strong legs and strong hearts and strong backs for the infantry. And we asked no questions of the cardinal who spoke to us in the shadow of the Basilica of Saint Peter, a man who had no name himself, but who spoke in the name of His Holiness. One priest, though, a young man ... he asked why we should take a relic from a Christian country, even though it was not a Catholic country. It was a good question, was it not? But the cardinal said the relic belonged in Rome. That priest did not go to Ethiopia with us.' The old priest laughed softly, then let out a long groan and lay back.

Purcell listened to Vivian's translation and said, 'It sounds to me like Father Armano actually saw this relic – or whatever it was.'

Mercado nodded.

Purcell continued, 'And probably tried to grab it for the pope, as per orders. And that's what got him in the slammer for forty years.'

Again, Mercado nodded and said, 'That's a possible explanation of what he's saying.'

'There may be a good story here, Henry.'

Mercado looked at the priest, who was now sleeping, or unconscious, and said, 'This may be the end of the story.'

'Wake him,' suggested Purcell.

'No,' said Vivian. 'Let him sleep.'

Purcell and Mercado exchanged glances, knowing that the priest might never wake up.

But Mercado said, 'If it's meant to be that we should hear the rest of this man's story, then it will be.'

'I envy you your faith, Henry,' said Purcell.

Vivian looked at the priest and said, 'He's traveled a long road to meet us and he'll finish his story when he awakens.'

Purcell saw no way to argue with the illogic of Mercado's faith and Vivian's mysticism, so he nodded and said, 'We'll post a watch to listen for Gallas and to see if the old man wakes up, or dies.'

'You're a very practical man,' observed Vivian. She added, 'All brain and no heart.'

'Thank you,' said Purcell.

Mercado volunteered for the first watch, and Purcell and Vivian lay down on two sleeping bags.

The two armies in the hills seemed to have lost their enthusiasm for the battle, though now and then a burst of machine-gun fire split the night air.

Purcell stared up at the black sky, thinking about the priest's story, and about Henry Mercado. Mercado, he thought, knew something or deduced something from what the priest had said.

Purcell also thought about Vivian, lying beside him, and he pictured her naked, standing beside the sulphur pool.

He thought back a few days to when he'd met her and Henry

Mercado in the Hilton bar in Addis Ababa. It had seemed like a chance meeting, and maybe it was, just as meeting the priest in this godforsaken place was totally unexpected. And yet ... well, Vivian would say it was fate and destiny, and Henry would say it was God's will.

A parachute flare burst overhead and lit up the sky. He stared at it awhile, then closed his eyes to preserve his night vision, and drifted off into a restless sleep.

CHAPTER 4

They took turns sitting up with the sleeping priest, listening for signs of death and sounds of danger.

At about three in the morning, Purcell woke Vivian and informed her that the priest was awake and wanted to speak.

She wondered if Purcell had woken the priest, and she said to him, 'Let him rest.'

'He wants to speak, Vivian.'

She looked at Father Armano, who was awake and did seem to want to speak. She shook Mercado's shoulder and informed him, 'Father Armano is awake.'

Mercado moved toward the priest and knelt beside him. 'How are you feeling, Father?'

'There is a burning in my belly. I need water.'

'No. It is a wound of the stomach. You cannot have water.'

Vivian said, 'Give him a little, Henry. He'll die of dehydration otherwise, won't he?'

Mercado turned to Purcell in the darkness. 'Frank?'

'She's right.'

Vivian gave him a half canteen cup of water. The old priest spit up most of it, and Purcell saw it was tinged with red.

Purcell said, 'It's going to be close. Talk to him, Henry.'

'Yes, all right. Father, do you want to—?'

'Yes, I will continue.' He took a deep breath and said, 'In Rome … the cardinal … the relic …' He thought awhile, then spoke slowly. 'So he told us to go with Il Duce's army. Go to Ethiopia, he said. There will be war in Ethiopia soon. And then he warned us – the black monastery was guarded by monks of the old believers. They had a military order … like the Knights of Malta, or the Templars. The cardinal did not know all there was to know of this. But he knew they would guard this relic with their lives. That much he knew.'

Vivian translated for Purcell, who asked, 'How can he remember this after forty years?'

Mercado replied, 'He has thought of little else in that prison.'

Purcell nodded, but said, 'Still … he may be hallucinating or his memory has played tricks on him.'

Vivian replied, 'He sounds rational to me.'

Mercado said to the priest, 'Please go on, Father.'

Father Armano nodded vigorously, as though he knew he was in a race with death, and he needed to unburden himself of this secret that burned in him like the fire in his stomach.

He said, 'The cardinal told us to go carefully, to go only with soldiers, and if we should find this black monastery, go into it. Avoid bloodshed if you can, he told us. But you must move quickly, he said, because the monks would spirit the relic away through underground passages if they thought they were being overpowered. He spoke as if he knew something of this.' Father Armano needed more water, and Purcell took the canteen and poured it slowly around his lips as Vivian translated.

The priest asked to be propped up so they sat him against the wall in the corner. He began talking without prompting. 'So, a bold priest asked, "How will we know what to look for and what to do when we enter the monastery?" And the cardinal said, "The words of His Holiness are in the envelope, and if you should ever arrive at your destination, you will open the envelope and you will know all."'

Father Armano paused, and a faraway look came into his eyes. At first Purcell thought he was dying, but the priest smiled and continued. 'Then something happened which I will never forget. His Holiness himself came into the small room where we sat with the cardinal. He spoke with the cardinal and we could hear him address the cardinal by his Christian name. He called him Eugenio. So now the cardinal with no name had a name we could use in our heads when we thought of him. But we could not call him Eugenio, could we?' The priest asked for some time to rest.

Mercado seemed to be thinking, and Purcell asked him, 'Do you know who this Cardinal Eugenio could be?'

'No . . .'

Purcell asked, 'How many cardinals would there be living in Rome at that time? And how many do you think were named Eugenio?'

Mercado replied, 'I wasn't a believer in those days and cared not at all for cardinals . . . but there was one who was secretary of state for Pius XI . . . Eugenio Pacelli.'

'Sounds familiar for some reason.'

'He assumed another name in 1939. Pius XII.'

'That sounds more familiar.'

Vivian pondered this information. 'But we don't know for sure . . .'

'No,' said Mercado. 'We'll have to go to the Italian Library when we get back to Addis.'

The old priest was following some words. Mercado turned to him. 'If I showed you a picture of this cardinal as he looked in 1935, would you—'

'Yes. Of course. I could not forget that face.'

Realizing that Father Armano might not live long enough to see a photograph, Mercado asked, 'Was this cardinal tall, thin? Aquiline nose? Light-complexioned?' He added a few more details.

'That could be him. Yes.'

Mercado leaned closer to Father Armano and asked, 'And did His Holiness say anything to you?'

'Yes. He came right up to us. We were standing, of course. He seemed a kind man. He even tried to speak in the Sicilian dialect. He spoke it with a bad accent, but no one laughed, of course. He spoke of humility and obedience ... he spoke of duty and he spoke of the Church, the true Church. He said we should treat the priests of the Ethiopian church with respect, but also with firmness ... He did not mention the envelopes. The cardinal still had them on his person. His Holiness seemed not to know of the mission sometimes, but other times he seemed to know. The words were general. You understand? He blessed us and left. The cardinal then gave everyone an envelope and also we took an oath of secrecy. I am still bound by that oath, but I must tell you all that happened, so I am breaking my oath. It is of no impor- tance after such a long time ... And we made the oath under false ...' His voice trailed off.

Mercado touched his arm and said, 'It's all right, Father—'

'Yes. Yes. Let me finish. So, we were taken to the Piazza Venezia. There was a military procession there. Tanks, cannons, trucks. I had never seen such things. It seemed that all Italy was in uniform. And he was there, also. The new Caesar, Il Duce. He stood like Caesar on a balcony. I did not like that man. He was too much with guns and the talk of war. And the king was there too. Victor Emmanuel. A decent man. Is he ...?'

'Dead. There are no more kings, Father. Go on.'

'Yes. Dead. Everyone is dead. Forty years is a long time. Yes ... I must finish. In the piazza they had the ceremony of the blessing of the guns. They put us to work, the priests from Sicily. We helped with the blessing. Then His Holiness arrived. He blessed the guns also. I did not like this. His Holiness stood with the king and Mussolini. Then came the cardinal, Eugenio. I was close to them. They spoke very intently. All the parade was going by for them, and the soldiers marched, but they paid no attention. I did not like the looks in their eyes. I was that close. Perhaps I imagined all this later ... in the prison. The looks in their eyes, I mean. Perhaps they were talking about something else. Who knows? But I felt then, or maybe later, that they were talking about the thing ...' His voice cracked and he stopped speaking.

Purcell picked up the canteen, but Mercado grabbed his arm. 'You'll kill him, Frank.'

'If he doesn't have a bad stomach wound, we're killing him with dehydration. If it's bad, then he's dead anyway. We can't get him to a doctor for hours.'

Mercado nodded.

Purcell emptied the canteen over the old priest's mouth, saying to Mercado, 'Keep him on track, Henry. The monastery.'

Mercado said, 'I'm starting to feel guilty about pushing a dying priest to stick to the facts and give us a good story.'

Purcell replied, 'The whole point of the Catholic religion is guilt.'

Mercado ignored him and asked Father Armano, 'Would you like to rest?'

'No. I must finish.' Father Armano continued, 'The next day I was brought to an infantry battalion. The soldiers were all peasants from my province in Sicily. We went to a boat and the boat sailed for many days. And we sailed through Egypt and we could see Egypt on both sides of the canal. The boat went to Masawa, in Eritrea. You know the place? This was the new Caesar's African empire. He called us his legions. "Go to Africa," he said, "and make Ethiopia Italian." In Masawa our engineers were building the harbor. Ships arrived with soldiers and tanks ... there was going to be a war. A fool could see that. The army marched to Asmara. It rained every day. But then the dry season began ... The governor of Eritrea assembled the army in front of his palace. He read us a telegram from Il Duce. "Avanti! I order you to begin the advance." Then a general – I cannot recall his name – he read a proclamation. He spoke of the new Fascist Italy and of sacrifice. The bishop of Asmara rang the church bells and everyone sang the Fascist anthem, "Youth." Everyone seemed happy on the outside. But on the inside, there was much sadness. I know this because the soldiers came to me and told me they were sad. We marched on Ethiopia. At first it was not so bad, except for the heat and the fatigue. In the early part of October we entered Adowa. There was little fighting. But then we marched out of Adowa and the army of the Ethiopians began to fight. So, this

Ethiopian emperor was a brave man. Haile Selassie – they called him the King of Kings. The Conquering Lion of Judah. Descended from King Solomon and the Queen of Sheba, they said. A descendant of the House of David. A brave man. He led his army with his own person, while our new Caesar sat in Rome. I am sure this man is dead, no? He must have died in battle.'

'No,' said Mercado, 'the emperor escaped to England, then returned to Ethiopia when the British drove out the Italians. He is still alive, but a very old man now.'

Purcell wondered if Father Armano could follow all this, but the priest said, 'So, they are not all dead, then. Good. Someone lives from my time. This emperor was a brave man. His army was ill-equipped, but they fought like lions against our tanks and planes. But we won that war. That much I could see before my imprisonment.'

'Yes,' Mercado said, 'you won that war. But you lost the big one afterwards. The one with the Americans and the English. Italy fought with Germany.'

'With Germany? Insanity. Which war is this one, then?'

Mercado was pulled in two directions. On one hand, he wanted to put the old priest's mind to rest about all that had transpired in forty years. He actually enjoyed telling it to him. But on the other hand, there was the priest's own story, which had to be finished.

He glanced at Purcell, who now seemed resigned to the priest's recounting of all he remembered of the past and all his questions about the present. Mercado said to Father Armano, 'It is a civil war, Father. Ethiopia now owns the old Italian colony of Eritrea. Some Eritreans, mostly the Muslims, want independence. They are fighting the Ethiopians. Inside Ethiopia itself, there are Christians and Muslims who no longer want the emperor. Mostly it is the army that no longer wants Haile Selassie as emperor, and they have arrested him, but he is well. He lives in his palace under house arrest. There are some Royalist forces who still fight the army. There are others who want neither the army nor the emperor. It is a very confused war and there is much unhappiness in this land. Also, there is famine. Famine for two years now.'

'Yes, I know of the famine.' He asked, 'And the Gallas? I heard you mention them. They are not to be trusted. In the last war, they took advantage of the fighting and killed many on both sides. They love fighting. They love it when there is strife in the land.' There was actual anger in the old priest's gentle voice. He said, 'It was the Gallas who attacked the place where I was imprisoned ... they killed everyone ...'

Henry Mercado remembered the Gallas very well – fierce tribesmen with no loyalty beyond their clans. He said to the priest, 'Yes. I remember from the last war. I was here then. I am from your time, too, Father.'

The old priest nodded and said, 'You must not fall into their hands.' He looked at Vivian.

Mercado did not respond, but the priest's warning awakened old and bad memories of that colonial war, and especially of the Gallas. Between 1936 and 1940, they fought the Ethiopian partisans who still carried on the fight against the Italians, and when the British took Ethiopia from the Italians in 1941, the Gallas harassed the retreating Italians as well as the advancing British and the reemerging Ethiopian partisan forces. Wherever there was a clash of arms, the Gallas heard it and rode to it on their

43

horses. This was how they lived; on military plunder. And they didn't know a white flag or a press card when they saw one. In quiet times, they stayed in the Danakil Desert, near Eritrea, or the Ogaden Desert, near Somalia. But when the dogs of war were let loose, as now, thought Mercado, they were all over the countryside, as though someone had shaken a beehive, and the famine had made them more fierce and more predatory than usual.

Mercado had suspected and the priest had confirmed that the Gallas were in the area, that the battle in the hills between Prince Joshua's Royalist forces and the army forces of the Provisional government had drawn them like sharks to the smell of blood. They would sit in a place just like this spa and wait patiently for stragglers from one or the other army. Or if an army was badly beaten and retreating, they would attack the whole force. Yes, Mercado remembered them well. They butchered more than one beaten Ethiopian army and never spared the Western reporters who were with the army, and the Azebe Gallas, who populated this region, and who were neither Muslim nor Christian but pagan, were the worst of a bad lot. They hated the indigenous Amhara passionately, but they saved their most creative torture and death for Westerners.

The priest was sleeping again, and Mercado's mind went back to the first weeks of the Italian invasion, which he had covered for *The Times* of London. He'd had the misfortune to be with the Amharic Prince Mulugeta in February 1936, at a place called Mount Aradam, a place historically and topographically like Masada, where the Israelites made their last stand against the Romans, and where the prince was making his last stand against the new Roman legions of Mussolini. Prince Mulugeta's force of seventy thousand was being systematically destroyed by the Italians as the days dragged on. Mercado was with the prince at his headquarters, and with them was a British Army advisor with the evocative name of Burgoyne and a strange Cuban-American soldier of fortune named Captain Del Valle.

The prince, Mercado remembered, was weeping in his tent at the news that his son had been mutilated and killed by Azebe Gallas at the edge of the battle, and he decided to go down to the foot of Mount Aradam to find his son's corpse. Mercado, Burgoyne, and Del Valle, young and foolhardy and playing the part of Kiplingesque Europeans, volunteered to go with him and his staff. When they got to the area where the scouts — supposedly Gallas loyal to the prince — had said the body was located, they themselves were surrounded by Gallas. The Gallas would have butchered them all, except that a flight of Italian Air Force planes swooped down on them and began machine-gunning the whole area, killing not only the Ethiopians but also the Gallas. Prince Mulugeta was killed and so was most of his staff. Del Valle and Burgoyne were killed also. The surviving Gallas stripped and castrated all the bodies, and Mercado escaped only by stripping himself and smearing blood over his body so that he looked to any passing Galla as though he had already been killed and mutilated.

Mercado suspected, thinking back on it, that the whole thing had been an elaborate trap, perhaps with Italian connivance. But that was another time. The place was the same, however. They were not too far from Mount Aradam, where Mercado had lain naked, trying very much to look dead.

He took a deep breath, then looked at Father Armano, who was awake, and asked him, 'Were you at Mount Aradam?'

'Yes. I was there. It was a few weeks before I was captured. It was the biggest slaughter yet. Thousands. I was made very busy in those weeks.'

Mercado thought it was a stunning coincidence that he and this priest were at the same battle almost forty years ago. But maybe not. Priests, reporters, and vultures were attracted to death; they all had work to do.

Purcell lit another cigarette. A false dawn lit the eastern sky outside the gaping windows. He said to Mercado, 'People die at dawn more frequently than other times. Ask him to finish.'

'Yes. All right. I was just remembering Aradam.'

'Remember it in your memoirs.'

'Don't be insensitive, Frank,' said Vivian.

Mercado looked at Father Armano. 'Would you like to continue, Father?'

'Yes. Let me make an end of it. So, you asked about Aradam. Yes. The mountain was drenched in blood and the Gallas came afterwards and slaughtered the fleeing army of Ethiopia. And General Badoglio tried to make common cause with the Gallas because there were many Italian units, like my own battalion, that were weak and exposed to the Gallas, and the Gallas were bought with food and clothes by the Italian generals. But the Gallas were treacherous; they massacred small Italian units that were weakened by the fighting. My battalion – perhaps four hundred men remained out of a thousand – was told to march to Lake Tana at the source of the Blue Nile. The Gallas harassed us as we moved, and the remnants of the Ethiopian army harassed us, and the

Gallas also attacked the Ethiopians. Was there ever so much bloodshed in such a confused, senseless manner? Everyone was like the shark and the vulture. They attacked the weak and the sick at every opportunity. I buried boys who had been baptized in my church. But we arrived at Lake Tana and made a camp, with the lake at our backs, so we could go no further.'

Father Armano fell silent, and Mercado had no doubt the old man was not so much remembering as he was reliving that terrible battle and its aftermath.

After a full minute, Father Armano continued. 'Now, the battalion commander was a young captain – all the senior officers were dead – and we had perhaps two hundred men left. And this young captain sent a patrol into the jungle to see what was there. Ten men he sent and only five came back. These five said they were ambushed in the jungle by Gallas. The Gallas captured two or three of the five missing men. The returning patrol said they could hear the screams of the men as they were being tortured … and the men of the patrol also told of seeing a high black wall in the jungle. Black like coal. It was like a fort, they said, but they could see a cross coming from a tower within the walls, so perhaps it was a monastery. I asked the captain if I could go back and find the bodies of the lost soldiers. He said no, but I said it was my duty as the priest of the battalion and he conceded to my wish. Also, I wished to see this black wall and the tower in the jungle … but I said nothing of this.'

Vivian translated for Purcell, who commented, 'This guy had balls.'

'Actually,' said Mercado, 'he had orders from the pope, and he had his faith.'

Vivian added, 'And he knew he had found what he was looking for.'

Father Armano looked at his three benefactors as though he knew what they were saying, and he nodded, then continued. 'So with the five soldiers who had survived the ambush, and who were not happy to go back, and five others, we returned to the place of the ambush. The soldiers we were looking for were dead, of course. The ones who had been captured alive – three of them – had been tied to trees by the Gallas and castrated. I gave the last rites and we buried them all.'

Father Armano stayed silent awhile, then said, 'So now I had to make a decision ... I had to know ... so I opened the envelope that was with me since Rome, and I read the words ... and I had to read the words in Latin again and again to be certain ...'

Mercado asked, 'What did the letter say?'

The priest shook his head, drew a long breath, and continued, 'So now I imposed upon the leader of this patrol, a young sergeant, whose name I only remember as Giovanni, to show me the place of the black walls that he had seen. He asked my forgiveness and he refused. So then I told him and the men of the patrol of my mission to find the black monastery ... I showed them the letter with the seal of the Holy Father and I told them that the Holy Father himself had asked me to do this ... that within the monastery was a sacred object of the time of Jesus ... I promised them that if we found this monastery and the sacred relic, I would petition the Holy Father to bring them home and they would receive great honors ... Perhaps I promised too much, but they spoke among themselves and agreed, so we set off into the jungle.'

Father Armano stared into the darkness awhile. 'It was a long distance and took many days and we were lost, too, I think. The sergeant was not sure. I felt that the Ethiopians or the Gallas were following ... Please, some water.'

Vivian gave it to him as she translated for Purcell. The dark hour before the dawn had come and gone and now the sky began to lighten again.

'We can move in about a half hour,' announced Purcell.

Mercado said, 'We can leave now. We need to get him to Gondar.'

Purcell replied, 'He needs to finish his story, Henry. He's left us hanging.'

Mercado was again torn, but there were no good choices.

Vivian said, 'I agree with Henry.'

'Well,' said Purcell, 'I don't. And it's my Jeep.' He added, to soften his words, 'It's not only about the monastery. Father Armano wants us to tell his people and the world what happened to him – if he dies.'

Mercado said, 'It's actually about the monastery and the relic. But you make a point, Frank.'

The priest had sat himself up higher in the corner. In the dawning light, his features began to materialize, and he was no longer the shadow of a voice. They stared at him as their eyes became accustomed to the gray light. The priest looked like death, but his eyes were much brighter than they should have been, and his face – what they could see through the dirt and the beard – was rosy. But the rosiness, Purcell knew, was the fever, and the brightness of the eyes was also the fever, and perhaps a little madness too.

Mercado wiped the priest's forehead. 'Father. We will be moving shortly.'

The priest nodded, then said, 'But I must first finish.'

Purcell looked at him. He had become real all of a sudden. The voice had a body. Purcell became melancholy and felt a great sadness, not only for the priest but also for himself. He saw himself as he was in the prison camp. The priest's bearded face brought it back, and he felt uncomfortable with that face. It was the face of all suffering. Indochina had settled into his brain again and he could not cope with it so early in the morning.

The priest breathed softly and continued. 'So, we came upon it. In a deep jungle valley. In a million years you would not find it, but this sergeant was a good soldier, and having found it once by accident, he remembered how to find it again. A rock. A tree. A stream. You see? So we approached the black place. The jungle came up to the walls of the place, and hid it from view, but a tree had fallen and exposed some of the wall. We walked in a circle through the jungle and around the wall, which was of black stone, with a shine like glass, and it was constructed in the old style of the monasteries and had no gate or door.'

Father Armano asked for more water on his face, and Vivian washed him with a wet handkerchief. Purcell was briefly touched by her compassion; he could see why old Henry had taken a liking to her.

Father Armano said, 'We came around to the place from which we started. There was now a basket there on a rope, as in the old style of the monasteries of the Dark Ages. The basket was not there before, so we took this as a sign of hospitality. We called up to the walls, but no one answered. The basket was large and so we climbed into it … all of us. It was made of reeds, but it was strong. And we all fit – eleven – and the basket began to rise.'

He stopped, took a long, deep breath, then went on. 'The men were somewhat uneasy, but we could see crosses cut into the black stone so we knew it was a Christian place and we were not so much afraid, though I remembered the words of the cardinal about the monks. The basket came to rest at the top of the wall. There was no one there. The basket had been raised with a device of stones and gears and it was not necessary to stand by it once it was started. You understand? So we were alone on top of the wall … We climbed out of the basket, over the parapet, and stepped onto a walk.'

The priest's face contorted and he grabbed his stomach with both hands.

Vivian knelt beside him and said in Italian, 'You must lie down and rest.'

Mercado said, 'He's actually better off sitting up. That's why he sat up in the first place.'

Vivian said, 'We need to get him to the hospital. Now.'

Purcell suggested, 'Ask *him* what he wants to do.'

Mercado asked Father Armano, and the priest replied, 'I need to finish this … I am … near the end …'

Mercado nodded.

Father Armano took a deep breath and spit blood into his beard. He stayed silent for a time, then began. 'Within the walls of the monastery lay beautiful buildings of the black stone and green gardens and blue ponds and fountains. The men were very happy at the sight and asked me many questions, which I could not answer. But I told the sergeant, Giovanni, about the monks and he ordered his men to keep their rifles at the ready. We called down into the monastery, but only the echoes of our own voices answered us. Now everyone was troubled again. But we found wooden steps to the ground. We walked with caution like a patrol because we were uneasy. We called out again, but only our own voices answered, and the echoes made us more uneasy, so we did not call out again, but walked quietly. We walked to the main building ... a church. The doors of the church were covered with polished silver and they blinded us in the sunlight. On the doors were the signs of the early Christians ... fish, lambs, palms. We entered the church. Inside, we observed that the roof was made of a substance like glass, but not glass. A stone, perhaps alabaster, and it let in the sunlight and the church was bathed in a glow that made my head swim and hurt my eyes. I had never seen such a thing and I am sure there is not such a thing, even in Rome.' He laid his head back in the corner and closed his eyes.

Purcell, Mercado, and Vivian watched him closely in the dim light. Mercado asked, 'Are we doing the right thing? Or are we killing him?'

Purcell said, 'I think he's accepted death, so we need to accept it.'

Vivian concurred and added, 'He wants the world to know his story ... and his fate.'

Purcell agreed, 'That's what we do best. So I think we need to wake him.'

Mercado hesitated, then crouched and shook the priest gently.

The priest opened his eyes slowly. He said, 'I can see you all now. This woman is very beautiful. She should not be traveling like this.'

Purcell informed him, 'Women do whatever men do these days, Father.' But no one translated.

The priest took a deep breath. 'So, now we make an end of it. And listen closely.' He pressed his eyes with his shaky hands. 'So we walked through the strange light of the church and into an adjoining building. A bigger place it seemed, but perhaps it was the darkness that made it look so. It was a building of many columns. We walked in the darkness, and the soldiers had removed their helmets because they were in a church, but they did not sling their rifles on their shoulders, but held them ready. Though it made no difference. In a second, every column produced a robed monk. It was over in a second or two. Everyone was clubbed to the ground and not a shot was fired. There was very little noise . . .'

Father Armano seemed to be failing, but he was determined to go on and spoke quickly. 'I wore on my helmet a large cross which was the army regulation. So perhaps this is what saved me. The others were clubbed again and taken away. I remember seeing this, although I was stunned by the blow. But you see, I had left my helmet on, as it was not required of me to remove a head covering in church. You understand? So the steel absorbed the blow and God saved me. The monks dragged me away and put me in a cell.'

The priest suddenly became rigid, and his face turned pale. His gums bit into his bearded lip, then the pain passed and he exhaled, drew a long breath, and said something in Latin that Mercado recognized as the Lord's Prayer. He finished the prayer, then he picked up his story in Italian. 'A monk's cell . . . not a prison . . . they cared for me . . . two or three of the Coptic monks spoke some Italian . . . so I said to them . . . I said, "I have come to see the sacred relic ..." and one who spoke Italian answered, "If you have come to see it, you will see it." But he also said, "Those who see it may never speak of it." I agreed to this, though I did not understand that I had sealed my fate ...'

Purcell waited for Vivian's translation, then commented, 'I think he understood that.'

And in fact, Father Armano added, 'But perhaps I did understand ... though when I saw the sacred relic, it did not matter ...'

Mercado asked Father Armano, almost casually, 'What was it, Father? What did they show you?'

The priest stayed silent for some time, then said, 'So ... so they brought me to it, and I saw it ... and it was the thing that was written in the letter ... and I fell to my knees and prayed, and the monks prayed with me ... and the pain of the blow to my head vanished ... and my soul was at peace.'

Father Armano smiled and closed his eyes, as though reliving the peace that had filled him then. His body shook, then he lay motionless.

Mercado felt for a heartbeat and Purcell felt for a pulse. They looked at each other, and Mercado said, 'Dead.'

They waited for more light so they could bury him.

Vivian remained at the priest's side, holding his hand, which was still warm. She felt something — his fingers tightening the grip on her hand. 'Henry.'

'Yes?'

'He's ... squeezing my hand.'

'Rigor mortis. Let go, Vivian.'

She tried to pull her hand out of the priest's grip, but he held tightly. She pressed her cheek on his forehead which was still burning with fever. 'Henry ... he's alive.'

'No—'

The priest suddenly opened his eyes and stared up at the sunlight coming through the open ceiling.

Purcell quickly gave him water and they knelt beside him. Mercado said, 'Father – can you speak?'

He nodded, then said in a weak voice, 'I have seen it ... it was very bright. It was the sun in Berini. I went home ... it was so beautiful ...'

No one responded.

'My sister, Anna ... you must go to her and tell her. She wishes to hear from you.'

Mercado said, 'We will go to her.'

He nodded, then seemed to remember what he needed them to know. He licked his cracked lips and spoke. 'So then ... I was taken into the jungle and given over to some soldiers of the emperor's army. I thought I was being released ... being exchanged, perhaps, for Ethiopian prisoners who were held by our army ... but I was taken to a local ras, a prince named Theodore who kept a small garrison in the jungle ...' He paused in thought, then continued, 'That was almost forty years ago. And last night I walked out of that fortress.' Father Armano looked at Mercado, Purcell, and Vivian and said, 'So now you know it, and I can rest in peace. You must go to Berini and tell them what happened to Giuseppe Armano. And go also to the Vatican. Tell them I found the black monastery ... and saw the relic.'

Purcell felt that he had missed something in the story or the translation. He looked at Vivian, but she only shrugged.

Mercado asked, 'Father, what was in the monastery?'

Father Armano looked up. 'You will never find it. And you should not look for it.'

'What was it that you saw?'

Father Armano did not reply directly, but said, 'My head was bleeding from the blow of the club. The iron helmet took the blow, but still I cut my head somehow. They touched some of it to my head and the pain was gone and the wound healed immediately ... and the monks said I was one of the blessed. One who believed ...'

Purcell listened to the translation and said, 'Maybe he didn't understand the question, Henry.'

Mercado let out a breath of exasperation. 'Frank—' He turned to the priest. 'Please tell us what it was, Father.'

The priest smiled. 'Of course you want to know what it was. But it has caused so much suffering already. It is blessed and cursed at the same time. Cursed, not of itself, but cursed because of the greed and treachery of men. It should stay where it is. It is meant to stay hidden until men become less evil ... The monks said this to me.'

'What *was* it?' asked Mercado firmly.

He asked for water. Vivian gave him all he wanted, and he drank too much of it, but no one stopped him. The priest closed his eyes, then said in a soft voice, 'The Holy Grail ... the sacred vessel which Christ himself used at the Last Supper ... It is filled with his most precious blood. It can heal mortal wounds and calm troubled souls. If you believe. And the lance that the Roman soldier, Longinus, used to pierce the side of our Lord ... it hangs above the Grail, and the lance drips a never-ending flow of blood into the Grail. I have seen this, and I have experienced this miracle.' He looked at Mercado. 'Do you believe this, Henry?'

Mercado did not reply.

The priest said, in a surprisingly clear voice, 'If you find it, you will believe in it. But I would advise you to leave here. Go to Rome, to the Vatican, and tell them I found it, and that it is safe where it was. And then forget all that I have said.' He asked, 'Will you do this?'

No one replied.

'And go to Berini.' Father Armano blessed them, then recited the Lord's Prayer in Latin and closed his eyes.

The sun was yellow now and small birds, nesting in the cavernous lobby ceiling, flew around the ruined vaults overhead and made morning noises at the new sun.

They knelt around the old priest and spoke to him, but he did not answer, and within the next quarter hour he died peacefully.

Vivian bent over and kissed the old priest's cold forehead.

CHAPTER 5

Henry Mercado retrieved a short spade from the Jeep, and Frank Purcell carried the body of the dead priest, wrapped in the blanket, into the courtyard of the spa.

Vivian chose a spot in the overgrown garden near the dry fountain, and Purcell dug a grave deep enough to keep the jackals from the body.

Purcell, Mercado, and Vivian lowered the body into the grave and took turns filling it with the red African earth. When they were done, Mercado said a short prayer over the grave.

Vivian wiped her sweating face, then picked up her camera and took photographs of the unmarked grave and the surrounding ruins. They had agreed not to make notes of this encounter, in case they or their notebooks fell into the wrong hands, and Purcell wasn't sure Vivian should be taking pictures, but he said nothing. She said, 'We can show these to his family.' She added, 'They may want to bring the body home.'

Purcell didn't think that after forty years there was anyone in Berini who would want to do that. But it was possible, and nice of Vivian to think of it.

Mercado looked at the grave, then said to his companions, 'I somehow feel that we killed him with our prodding ... and all that water ...'

Purcell replied, 'He was a dead man when we found him, Henry.' He added, 'We did what he wanted us to do. We listened to him.' He reminded Mercado, 'He wanted us to let his people know what happened to him. And we'll do that.'

Vivian sat on a stone garden bench and stared at the grave. She said, 'He also wanted us to know about the black monastery ... and the Grail. He wanted us to go to Rome ... the Vatican, and tell them that Father Giuseppe Armano had found what they sent him to find.'

Purcell glanced at Mercado and he was sure they were both thinking the same thing: They weren't going to break this story to the Vatican. At least not now. In fact, Father Armano himself had suggested that the Grail was safe where it was, meaning leave it there.

Mercado sat beside Vivian, looked around at the crumbling faux-Roman spa, and said, 'This is a fitting place to bury him.' He asked, 'Well, what do we think about what Father Armano said?'

No one replied, and Mercado prompted, 'About the black monastery ... and the Holy Grail?'

Purcell lit a cigarette. 'Well ... I think his story was basically true ... I mean about the cardinal, the pope, his war experiences, and the monastery. But he sort of lost me with the Lance of Longinus dripping blood into the Holy Grail.'

Mercado thought a moment, then nodded and said, 'I'm supposed to be the believer, but ... you know, in the Gulag, there was a prisoner who said he'd been sent there for trying to kill Stalin. But he was actually there for pilfering state property – twenty years. But you see, he needed a crime big enough to fit the sentence, instead of the other way around.'

No one responded, so Mercado continued. 'We don't know what Father Armano did to spend forty years in a cell. But I think he convinced himself that he was there because he'd seen what he wasn't supposed to see.'

Vivian said, 'But his story was so full of *detail*.'

Mercado said to her, 'Vivian, if you had forty years to work on a story, you would get the details down quite well.' He added, 'He wasn't actually lying to us. He had just deluded himself to the point where it became truth in his own mind.'

Purcell wiped his face with his sleeve. The sun was a brutal yellow now. He asked Mercado, 'Where do you think the story became delusional?'

Mercado shrugged, then replied, 'Maybe after the Lake Tana part. Maybe he had been captured by the Ethiopian army and they put him in jail as a prisoner of war.'

Purcell asked, 'But why lock him up for forty years? The war with the Italians ended within a year.'

Again Mercado shrugged and replied, 'I don't know ... the local ras, Prince Theodore, had captured an Italian enemy ... a priest who they didn't want to kill ... so they threw him in jail and forgot about him.'

Purcell pointed out, 'But when the Italians won the war, the prince would have given Father Armano to them to curry favor, or for a price. Instead, they kept him locked in solitary confinement for four decades. Why?'

Mercado conceded, 'I suppose it is possible that Father Armano did find and enter this black monastery, and maybe the monks did kill the Italian soldiers who were with Father Armano, and that's why the monks handed him over to the Ethiopian prince and had him put away for life – so he couldn't reveal what they'd done, or reveal the location of the monastery.' He added, 'They silenced a witness without killing him. Yes, I can see that happening if the witness was a priest.'

Purcell suggested, 'So maybe what the priest said is all true – except for the part about the Holy Grail and the lance dripping blood.'

Mercado replied, 'That's very possible.'

Purcell asked, 'So should we look for this black monastery?'

'It would be a dangerous undertaking,' said Mercado.

'But,' said Purcell, 'worth the risk if we're actually looking for the Holy Grail.'

'Yes,' agreed Mercado, 'but the Holy Grail does not actually exist, Frank. It is a legend. A myth.'

'I thought you were a true believer, Henry.'

'I am. But I don't believe in medieval myths. I believe in God.'

Vivian was looking at Mercado thoughtfully and said to him, 'I think, Henry, that you're not so sure of what you're saying.'

'I am sure.'

Purcell speculated, 'Maybe you're trying to cut us out of the deal, Henry. Or cut *me* out, and take your photographer along to look for the black monastery.'

Mercado looked offended and said, 'You've been in the sun too long.'

'Look, Henry,' said Purcell, 'you and I and Vivian all believe every word of Father Armano's story, including him finding the Holy Grail in the monastery. But the problem is the Grail itself.

The priest saw it, but is it actually *the* Grail? The cup used by Christ at the Last Supper? Or is it something that the monks *think* is the Holy Grail?'

Mercado nodded. 'That's the most logical conclusion.' He asked rhetorically, 'How many false relics are there in the Catholic Church?' He answered his own question: 'Probably hundreds. Such as a piece of the true cross. The nails used to crucify Christ. A piece of his robe. That is what the priest saw – a false relic.'

'Correct,' agreed Purcell. 'But what we need to decide is whether or not we want to look for this black monastery, and the so-called Holy Grail. Is that enough of a story to risk our lives for?' He added, 'Don't forget what happened to ...' He nodded toward the grave.

Mercado glanced at the fresh earth, but didn't reply.

Vivian reminded them, 'Father Armano said that the sacred blood healed his wound.'

Purcell explained, 'If you believe strongly enough, you can experience a psychosomatic healing of the body, and certainly of the mind. We all know this.'

'Well ... yes ...' replied Vivian. 'But he also described the Lance of Longinus dripping a never-ending supply of blood into the Grail.'

'Well, you got me there, Vivian.'

She continued, 'And apparently the Vatican believes in this – if you believe that part of Father Armano's story. And I do.'

Purcell pointed out, 'The Vatican does not necessarily believe that the Holy Grail even exists, or that it somehow wound up in Ethiopia. But they decided to take advantage of the Italian invasion of Ethiopia and send a bunch of priests here with the army to check out something they heard or read – and while they were at it, grab anything they could find.'

Mercado agreed and said, 'The Italian army looted a great number of religious artifacts from Ethiopia.' He further informed them, 'The steles sitting in front of the Italian Foreign Ministry in Rome were taken from the ancient Ethiopian capital of Axum.' He added, 'The Ethiopians want them back.'

'The spoils of war,' Purcell said, 'go to the victors.'

Mercado agreed. 'Europe, the Vatican, the British Museum are filled with objects looted from the rest of the world. But those days are over, so even if we decide to look for this relic, and we find it, we have no right to try to … take it.'

Purcell said, 'You're getting ahead of yourself, Henry. We're not sure we're going to look for it. And if we do look for it and we find it, what we're going to do is take a few photos and write about it – not steal it.'

Mercado clarified, 'We don't believe it is the actual cup used by Christ at the Last Supper, and we could not prove that in any case. And we most definitely do not believe it has any mystical powers, contrary to legend. But the priest's story – the Vatican, the cardinal, the pope, the monastery, the monks, the Grail, and the lance – are the stuff of a great news story.' He added, 'A human interest story. The dying priest who has been imprisoned since the Italian invasion—'

'Correct, but we couldn't write only about what the dying priest told us and then not report that we followed up by looking for the black monastery.' Purcell added, 'We'd look like all those journalists sitting in the Hilton bar in Addis, rewriting government press releases.'

Mercado replied, 'We are certainly not that.' He added, 'We're *here*.'

Purcell asked rhetorically, 'So have we talked ourselves into this? Are we willing to risk our lives to look for the Holy Grail that probably says "Made in Japan" when you turn it over?'

Mercado forced a smile, then said, 'I think the story is good enough to pursue to the end.'

Purcell reminded him, 'So did Father Armano.'

No one spoke for a while, each lost in thought. Finally, Vivian said, 'If we don't do this, we'll regret it all our lives.'

'Which might be very short if we do,' Purcell pointed out.

Mercado said, 'Or even shorter if we can't get out of here.' He reminded his companions, 'Our immediate problem is that we are in dangerous territory. I don't suggest we try to drive back to Addis. I have a safe-conduct pass from the Provisional government, so we need to join up with the Ethiopian army, which is less than an hour from here. Or if that's not possible, we'll join up with the Royalist forces. What we don't want to do is run into the Gallas.'

'That's not a good story,' Purcell agreed. He suggested, 'We'll spend a few days with the army, reporting on their victory, then we will offer them our Jeep in return for a helicopter ride back to Addis. Then when we come to our senses, we can decide over a drink if we want to come back here and look for the black monastery.'

Vivian said, 'I've already decided.'

'Don't be impulsive,' Purcell advised.

Mercado said, 'We can't be sure this monastery still exists after forty years – or if it ever existed. We'll need to do some research at the Italian Library in Addis, and we'll need terrain maps and all that, and some better equipment—'

'Right,' Purcell interrupted, 'but let's first get away from this spa before the Gallas arrive for a bath.'

Mercado and Vivian stood, and they made their way across the courtyard, then walked through the colonnade, back toward their Jeep.

Vivian asked, 'How do we find the army headquarters?'

Mercado replied, 'Probably by accident. We just need to drive into the hills and with luck we'll come across an army unit or an outpost.' He suggested, 'Practice waving your press credentials.'

They got back to the lobby of the spa hotel and jumped into the Jeep. Purcell started it up and they drove across the lobby, out to the portico, then down the steps they'd ascended the night before. Purcell continued across the grass field and onto the narrow jungle road, then turned toward the hills and accelerated.

They were aware that they were in a battle zone and that anything was possible, especially bad things. The Provisional Army forces were supposed to honor their safe-conduct pass, issued by the Provisional government. The Royalist forces, who'd probably been beaten last night, might not be in a good mood. But their imprisoned emperor, Haile Selassie, had an affinity for the West, and Purcell thought that the Royalists, all Christians, would treat them well if they ran into them first. But as with all armies, you never knew for sure. What Purcell did know for sure was that the Gallas would butcher them without a thought about their status as accredited journalists.

Purcell tried to focus on the bad road and on the problem of avoiding the Gallas. But his thoughts kept returning to the priest and his story. Father Armano had found the black monastery that the Vatican knew existed. Purcell was sure of that part of the story. After that ... well, as Henry Mercado said, it was all medieval myth. The search for the Holy Grail had been going on for about a thousand years, and the reason it was never found was because it never existed. Or it did exist for a brief hour or two at the Last Supper – but it had been cleared with the dishes and it was lost forever. More importantly, it had no special powers; that was a tale spun by storytellers, not historians or theologians. That fact, however, had never stopped anyone from looking for it.

Purcell wondered how many people had spent their lives or lost their lives in a quest to find this thing that didn't exist. He didn't know, but he did know that there might soon be three more idiots to add to that list.

CHAPTER 6

Purcell saw that the narrow mountain road hadn't been repaired since the rainy season ended. As they climbed, the jungle thinned, and behind them, through the dust, they could see the ruins of the white spa in the valley. Ahead, red rock formations jutted out from the red earth. There were no signs of the night's battle, noted Purcell, but he caught the faint odor of cordite and ripe flesh drifting down the hills with the mountain winds.

Vivian asked, 'Why are we not seeing anyone?'

Purcell glanced at her in the rearview mirror. They had taken the canvas top off the Jeep so they could be identified more easily as Westerners. The wind had sifted dust through Vivian's raven black hair and deposited a fine red powder on her high cheeks. She wore a floppy bush hat to keep the sun off her stark white skin. He said to her, 'They will see our dust before we see them.'

Mercado stared absently at the winding road. His mind was elsewhere. Since his release from the Russian Gulag, he had made a career of seeking out religious experiences. In his travels as a journalist, he had spoken with Pope John XXIII, the Dalai Lama, Hindu mystics, Buddhist monks, and people who claimed they were God, or good friends of God. His life and his writing, up to the time of his arrest, had been anti-Fascist and pro-Socialist. But with the collapse of the former system and his imprisonment by a government of the latter, his life and his writings had also collapsed. Both became stale. Empty.

People had urged him to write about his years in the Soviet Gulag, but he had no words to describe his experience. Or, he admitted, he could not find the courage to find the words.

It was his search for God that had revived his flair for the written word and his ability to tell a good story.

He had written a *New York Times* piece on the Dalai Lama fleeing the Red Chinese and living in exile in India, which gained him new postwar fame as a journalist. In 1962, he had gone boldly back to Russia and done articles on religious persecution. He narrowly escaped re-imprisonment and was expelled. There had been some good pieces since, but lately the writing had become stale again.

Mercado was as worried about his career as he was about his flagging religious fervor. The two were related. He needed something burning in his gut — like the priest's mortal wound — to make him write well. His current assignment for UPI was to do a series of articles on how the ancient Coptic Church was faring in the civil war. He also had contacts with the Vatican newspaper, *L'Osservatore Romano*, and they bought much of his output. But there was no fire in his words anymore and his editors knew it. He had almost given up. Until now. Now his brain burned secretly with the experience of the previous night. He felt that he had been chosen by God to tell the priest's story. There was no other explanation for the string of coincidences that had made him privy to this secret. He remained calm on the outside, but his soul was on fire with the anticipation of the quest for the Grail. But that was *his* secret.

Purcell glanced at him in the passenger seat. 'Are you all right?'

Mercado came out of his reverie. 'I'm fine.'

Purcell thought of Henry Mercado as his danger barometer. Henry had seen it all, and if Henry was apprehensive, then a shit-storm was coming.

Purcell, too, was no stranger to war, and both of them had probably seen more combat and death than the average infantry soldier. But Mercado was a seasoned pro, and Purcell had been impressed with the older man's instinct for survival during the three-day ride through the chaos and violence of this war-torn country. Henry Mercado knew when to bluff and bluster, when to bribe, when to be polite and respectful, and when to run like hell.

Purcell thought that despite their imprisonments, both he and Mercado had been mostly lucky as war correspondents, or at least smart enough to stay alive. But Mercado had stayed alive far longer than Frank Purcell. So when Henry Mercado and Vivian had approached him in the Hilton bar, armed with a safe-conduct pass from the Provisional government, and asked him if he'd like to accompany them to the current hot spot, he'd agreed without too much hesitation.

But now ... well, what sounded good in Addis did not look good three days out. Purcell had been in worse places and much tighter situations, but after a year in a Khmer Rouge prison, facing death every day from starvation and disease, and seeing men and women executed for no apparent reason, he felt that he'd used up his quota of luck. Unfortunately, he hadn't come to that realization until he was a day out of Addis Ababa. And now they had reached that point of no return. *Avanti.*

Purcell lit a cigarette as he kept the wheel steady with one hand. He said, 'I'm hoping we hook up with the army. I'm sure they beat the hell out of Prince Joshua last night, and I'd rather travel with the winner. The Gallas travel with the losers.'

Mercado scanned the high terrain with his field glasses as he replied, 'Yes, but I think the better story is with Prince Joshua.' He added, 'Lost causes and crumbling empires are always a good story.'

Vivian said, 'Can we stop speaking about the Gallas?'

Mercado lowered his field glasses and told her, 'Better to speak *of* them than *to* them.'

They continued on, and Mercado sat back in his seat. He said, 'The dangerous thing about a civil war is that the battle lines change like spaghetti bouncing in a colander.'

Purcell inquired, 'Can I quote you on that?'

Mercado ignored him and continued. 'I covered the Spanish Civil War. As long as you travel with one side or the other, you are part of their baggage train. But if you get caught in between or out on the fringes and try to get back in, you become arrestable. You know, Frank, if you had been traveling with the Khmer Rouge, you probably wouldn't have been arrested. I suppose it all has something to do with spy-phobia. They don't like people who run between armies. The trick is to get inside the battle lines without getting shot. If you're challenged by a sentry, you must be bold and wave around your press cards and cameras, as if you had been specially invited to the war. Once you get inside, you'll usually find the top dogs are courteous. But you must never appear to be arrestable. The business of armies, besides fighting, is arrest and execution. They can't help it. They are programmed for it. You must not look arrestable or executable.' He asked Purcell, 'Do you understand?'

'Why don't *you* drive, Henry, and I'll pontificate?'

Mercado laughed. 'Did I hit a sore spot, Frank? Don't fret. I'm speaking from personal experience.'

Purcell thought he was speaking to impress Vivian.

Mercado continued, 'There was one moment there in East Berlin when I could have blustered my way out of arrest. But I started to act frightened. And then they became more sure of themselves. From there on, it was all just mechanics. From a street corner in East Berlin, less than a thousand yards from Checkpoint Charlie, to a work camp in the Urals, a thousand frozen miles away. But there was that one moment when I could have brazened my way out of the situation. That's what happens when you deal with societies where the rule is by men and not by law. I had a friend shot by the Franco forces in Spain because he was wearing the red-and-black bandanna of the Anarchists. Only he didn't know it was an Anarchist bandanna. He was just wearing something for the sweat. A handkerchief he had brought from England, actually. They stood him against a wall and shot him by the lights of a truck. Poor beggar didn't even speak Spanish. Never knew why he was being executed. Had he made the appropriate gestures when he realized that it was the bandanna that was offending them, had he whipped it off and spat on it or something, he'd be alive today.'

'He'd have screwed up someplace else and gotten shot.'

'Perhaps. But never look arrestable, Frank.'

Purcell grunted. There had been one moment there, back in Cambodia ... a French-speaking Khmer Rouge officer. There were things he could have said to the officer. Being an American was not necessarily grounds for arrest. There were Americans with Communist forces all over Indochina. There were American newsmen with the Khmer Rouge. Yet he had blown it. Yes, Mercado had hit a sore spot.

Purcell came around a curve in the road and said, 'Well, you have a chance to prove your point, Henry. There's a man up ahead pointing a rifle at us.'

Vivian sat up quickly and looked. 'Where?'

Mercado shouted, 'Stop!'

Purcell kept driving and pointed. 'You see him?'

Before Mercado or Vivian could reply, the man fired his automatic weapon and red tracers streaked high over their heads.

Purcell knew the man's aim couldn't be that bad, so it was a warning shot. But Mercado dove out of the Jeep and rolled into the ditch on the side of the road.

Purcell stopped the Jeep and shouted to him, 'You look arrestable, Henry!' He stood on his seat and waved with both arms. He shouted, 'Haile Selassie! Haile Selassie!' He added, 'Ras Joshua!'

The soldier in the dirty gray *shamma* lowered his rifle and motioned them to approach.

Vivian peeked between the seats. 'Frank, how did you know he was a Royalist?'

Purcell slid back in the seat and put the Jeep in gear. 'I didn't.'

Mercado climbed out of the ditch and crawled into the passenger seat. 'That was a bloody stupid chance you took.'

'But you weren't taking any chances at all.' Purcell moved the Jeep slowly up the road.

Mercado, trying to explain his dive into the ditch, said, 'I thought he was a Galla.'

'I could see that he wasn't.'

'Do you even know what a Galla looks like?'

'Actually, no.'

They drove closer to the man, who they could now see was wearing a sash of green, yellow, and red – the colors of Ethiopia and of the emperor.

Purcell said, 'Well, we're now in the Royal Army.'

Mercado replied, 'Good. This is where the story is.'

Purcell reminded him, 'The Provisional government forces could have gotten us back to Addis. Prince Joshua probably can't even get himself out of here.'

'We don't know what the situation is.'

'Right. But I know that your safe-conduct pass from the Provisional government won't do us much good with the prince.'

Mercado didn't reply for a moment, then said, 'I've actually met Haile Selassie here in '36, then again when he was in exile in London.' He assured Purcell and Vivian, 'I will tell that to Prince Joshua.'

Vivian, who knew Henry Mercado better than Purcell did, asked, 'Is that true, Henry?'

'No. But it will get us royal treatment.'

Vivian said, 'That's why I love you, Henry.'

Purcell advised, 'Don't look arrestable.'

They were within twenty meters of the soldier and they waved to him. He didn't return the greeting, but he pointed to the right.

Mercado said, 'He wants us to take that small path.'

'I see it.' Purcell swung the Jeep to the right and gave a parting wave to the tattered soldier on the rock. The smell of the dead began to permeate the air, although they saw no bodies yet. Purcell navigated the Jeep up the narrow path that looked like a goat track.

Mercado pointed to a flat area ahead. About a dozen bodies lay ripening under the sun. A soldier with an old bolt-action rifle walked toward them. Purcell wove around the dead bodies and drove the Jeep toward the man, who was looking at them curiously.

Mercado stood up and yelled a few Amharic words of greeting. '*Tena yastalann!*'

'That's the stuff, Henry,' said Vivian. 'Ask him how his kids are doing at Yale.'

'I did.'

The man approached the Jeep and Purcell stopped. Mercado waved his press card and said, 'Gazetanna,' as Purcell held out a packet of Egyptian cigarettes.

The soldier wore a shredded *shamma* and bits and pieces of web gear. He smiled and took the cigarettes. Purcell lit one for him. 'Ras Joshua.'

The man nodded and pointed.

Purcell moved the Jeep farther up the hill through grass that came up to the windshield. There was little evidence of military activity and few physical signs of the night's artillery barrage. As in most third world armies, Purcell knew, the weapons of modern war were more for the sound and the fury than anything else. The artillery barrages were small compared to modern armies, and most of the ordnance went wide of the mark. The real killing was done in a manner that hadn't changed much in two thousand years – the knife, the spear, the scimitar, and sometimes the bayonet of the rifles without ammunition.

They continued on and Purcell realized he was in the middle of the prince's headquarters. Low tents, much too colorful for tactical use, sprang up out of the high grass and bush. Ahead, down a small path, Purcell could make out the green, yellow, and red flag of Ethiopia emblazoned with the Lion of Judah. As he drove toward it, the bush around him came alive with soldiers. No one spoke.

'Wave, Henry,' said Vivian. 'Invite them all to your country place in Surrey. That's a good chap.'

'Vivian, keep still and sit down.'

Purcell stopped the Jeep a respectable distance from the tent with the imperial flag. They all climbed out, waved friendly greetings, and smiled. Some of the soldiers smiled back. A few, however, looked gruff and mean, Purcell noticed, like infantry soldiers all over the world fresh out of battle. They didn't like relatively clean and crisp-looking outsiders walking around. Especially if the army had been beaten. A beaten army was a dangerous thing, Purcell understood, much more dangerous than a victorious one. Morale is bad, respect for superiors is bad, and tempers are rotten. Purcell had seen this with the South Vietnamese Army as the war was being lost. Mercado had seen it all over the world. The embarrassment of defeat. It leads to rape, pillage, and random murder. It's a sort of catharsis for the soldiers who can't beat the other soldiers.

They walked quickly toward the prince's tent, as though they were late for a meeting. Purcell worried about the equipment, but any attempt to carry it with them or to make prohibitory gestures toward the Jeep would have invited trouble. The best thing was to walk away from your expensive possessions as though you expected that they would all be there when you returned. Vivian, however, took one of her cameras.

The prince came toward them. There was no mistaking him. He was young, about forty, and very tall. He wore a European-style crown of gold and precious stones, but he was clad in a lionskin *shamma* with a cummerbund of leopard. He also carried a spear. His aides, who walked behind him, were dressed in modern battle fatigues, but wore lions' manes around their necks. They had obviously put on all the trappings for the Europeans. Mercado knew this was a good sign.

The prince and his entourage stopped. The beaten-down track through the high grass was lined with curious soldiers.

Mercado stepped up his pace and walked directly to the prince and bowed. 'Ras Joshua.' He spoke in halting Amharic. 'Forgive us not announcing our coming. We have traveled a long distance to be with your army—'

'I speak English,' the prince responded in a British accent.

'Good. My name is Henry Mercado. This is Frank Purcell, an American journalist. And our photographer, Vivian Smith.' He bent at the waist again as he took a step to the side.

Vivian came up beside Mercado, who whispered, 'Curtsy.' She

curtsied and said, 'I am pleased to meet you.' Purcell nodded his head in greeting and said, 'Thank you for receiving us.'

'Come,' said Prince Joshua.

They followed him to his tent and entered. The red-and-white-striped pavilion was sweltering and the air smelled sour. The prince motioned them to sit on cushions around a low wood-inlaid table that looked like a European antique with the legs cut down. This, thought Purcell, was as incongruous as everything else in the country.

Ethiopia, he had discovered, was a blend of dignity, pageantry, and absurdity. The antique table with the shortened legs said it all. The battle fatigues with lions' manes maybe said it better. The country was not a mixture of Stone Age, Bronze Age, and modern, like most of Africa below the Sahara; it was an ancient, isolated civilization that had reached towering heights on its own, long before the Italians arrived. But now, as Purcell could see, the unique flavor of the old civilization was dying along with the old emperor.

Mercado asked, 'Would you like to see our press credentials?'

'For what purpose?'

'To establish—'

'Who else could you be?'

Mercado nodded.

Prince Joshua inquired, 'How did you get here?'

Purcell answered, 'By Jeep, from Addis Ababa.'

'Yes? I'm surprised you got this far.'

'So are we,' admitted Purcell.

The prince's servants brought bronze goblets to the table and poured from a bottle of Johnnie Walker Black Label. Mercado and Purcell pretended not to be surprised by the good choice of refreshment, but Vivian made a thing of it, as though she had expected fermented sheep dip. 'Well, what have we here?' She leaned across the table and raised her camera, saying to the prince, 'Do you mind?' and shot a picture of the bottle with Prince Joshua in the background. 'Great shot.'

Mercado was mortified. Bad manners were one thing he could not accept from the very young. It was cute in New York and London, but it was dangerous in countries like this. The prince seemed a charming enough fellow, but you never knew what would set these people off. He smiled at Prince Joshua and said, 'Wattatacc,' the Amharic word for 'youth.'

The prince smiled in return and nodded. 'No soda, I'm afraid. And no ice for the American.' He smiled at Purcell. But Mercado knew it was a strain to be polite when a three-thousand-year-old dynasty was coming to an ignominious end, your emperor was under arrest, and about a hundred members of the royal family had already been executed.

Prince Joshua looked at his guests and asked, 'So, you have come into the lions' den? Why?'

Mercado was keenly aware that this was an Old Testament country, and important things were always said with biblical allusions. He replied, 'So the Lord was with Joshua; and his fame was noised throughout all the country.'

The prince smiled again.

Vivian said, 'Can the Ethiopian change his skin, or the leopard his spots?' She, too, smiled.

Mercado looked at the prince, then at Vivian. 'Vivian.'

'Book of Jeremiah, Henry.' She looked around. 'Bad choice?'

The prince stared at her, then said, 'I am black but comely; thy two breasts are like two young roes that are twins, which feed among the lilies. Song of Solomon.' He eyed her for a long second.

Vivian smiled. 'I like that.'

The prince raised his goblet and said, 'Welcome.'

They all raised their goblets and Mercado said, 'To the emperor.'

Everyone drank, but the prince said nothing further.

Mercado took the lead and began conversationally, 'I was here in 1935 when the Italians invaded your country. I had the honor, then, of meeting his royal highness. And then again in England, when the emperor was in exile, I had the honor of writing a news story on him.'

Prince Joshua looked at Henry Mercado with some interest, then said, 'You don't look old enough for that, Mr Mercado.'

'Well ... thank you. But I assure you I'm that old.'

The prince asked, 'So what can I do for you?'

'Well,' Mercado replied, 'we have come from Addis Ababa to find you and your army. But we have had many mishaps along the way. The Gallas roam the countryside and the fighting is confused. So we ask you to give us safe-conduct passes – perhaps provide us with soldiers so we may return safely to the capital and report—'

'Mr Mercado. Please. I am no fool. You are here because you couldn't find the Provisional government army forces. I cannot give a safe-conduct pass anywhere. I am in control of nothing more than this hill. My forces are badly beaten and at any moment the army will ask for my surrender or they will attack again. Unless, of course, the Gallas attack first. My men are deserting by the hundreds. We are living on borrowed time here.'

Mercado glanced at his companions, then said to the prince, 'I see ... but ... that puts us in a rather tight situation ...'

'Well, I am sorry for that, Mr Mercado.'

Purcell said, 'We certainly understand that your situation is worse than ours. But we would like to be able to tell your story and tell of the bravery of the Royal forces. So if you could spare a few armed men—'

The prince interrupted, 'I will see what I can do to get you into the army forces. From there, perhaps, you can get a helicopter or a resupply convoy to the capital. I have no wish to see you die here with me.' He spoke the words simply, but they were strained. He asked, 'Any news of the emperor?'

Mercado replied, 'He is still well. The army moves him from one palace to another in and near the capital, but he is reported in good health. A fellow journalist saw him last week.'

'Good.' He sipped his scotch. 'I have here another Englishman. A Colonel Sir Edmund Gann. Do you know him?'

Mercado nodded. 'Heard of him, yes.'

'He is my military advisor. He is out inspecting the positions. I told him there were no positions left to inspect, but he insisted.' The prince shook his head at the lunacy. 'The English are sometimes strange.'

Purcell lifted his glass. 'I'll drink to that.'

'He is overdue now. But when he comes, I will try to make plans to get you all to safety if I can.'

'Thank you, Ras.' Mercado felt the old sadness return. It was the Spanish Civil War again; Mount Aradam, 1936; the trapped men at Dunkirk; fleeing Tibet with the Dalai Lama. All the losing causes met here on this hilltop. And always, he, Henry Mercado, had slipped away at the last moment while brave and doomed men waved at him and wished him bon voyage. But he had gotten his. Berlin, 1946. With a lousy US Army surplus Kodak camera. He no longer felt any guilt at slipping away. He felt relief. 'Yes. That would be fine.'

'And if you should get away from here, write a good story about the emperor and his army – as you did when the Italians invaded.'

'I will do that.'

'Good.' The prince rose. 'I must see to my duty.'

Purcell, Mercado, and Vivian stood and bowed. As the prince was turning to leave, Vivian called to him, 'Prince Joshua?'

'Yes?'

'You must know of a Prince Theodore. He fought the Italians when they invaded and he had a fortress in the jungle a few days' march from here.'

The prince nodded. 'Theodore was my uncle. He was killed fighting the Italians with a band of partisans in 1937. My cousin, also Theodore, still keeps the garrison in the jungle. It is a fine fortress. Cement and stone. Why do you ask?'

'I heard there was fighting there. I just wondered if you knew of it.'

'No. I have heard nothing. I would not even know which side controlled the fortress or who attacked it. Why are you asking?'

'Oh, I just thought that if perhaps the fighting were over, we could find sanctuary there.'

'I think not. Excuse me.'

'Prince Joshua?'

The prince turned and breathed a sigh of impatience. 'Yes, madam?'

'There is also a monastery in the area. We thought, perhaps, we could reach that. A monastery of black stone, I think.'

'There is no such place. You will be joined by Sir Edmund shortly and you can ask him your questions. Excuse me.' He turned and left.

Purcell wiped the sweat from his neck. 'You are a pushy bitch, Vivian. But good questions.'

Mercado sat down on a cushion and said to Vivian, 'The man is contemplating a Galla massacre or an army firing squad and you have to annoy him. Really, you are insensitive.'

Vivian sat also and poured another scotch. 'We aren't exactly at the Hilton in Addis, you know, Henry. His fate could very well be ours.'

'Yes. You're right, of course. But *we* have a chance.'

Purcell sat on the low table and helped himself to the scotch. He said, 'Well, at least we know that the garrison in the jungle is real.'

They could hear excited noises outside the tent and the unmistakable sounds of military deterioration. Arguments broke out, and at least one disagreement was settled with a gun. Tents around them were being plundered by the fleeing soldiers, but the flag of the Lion of Judah kept their tent inviolate for the time being, though they felt their perimeter of safety shrinking as they sat sipping scotch in the hot, fetid enclosure.

Purcell said to Mercado, 'You were right, Henry. This is where the story is. And I think we're about to be part of it.'

Mercado did not reply.

Vivian said, 'I'd like to get some photographs.'

Purcell motioned toward a row of ceremonial shields and spears leaning against the tent wall. 'Henry, dress up a bit.'

Again, Mercado did not reply, but he said to Vivian, 'You will not leave this tent.'

Purcell suggested they look around to see if there were any other weapons in the tent aside from the spears.

Mercado said firmly, 'We cannot be found carrying a firearm. We are journalists.'

'Everyone else has one.'

'That's the point, Frank. We can't shoot our way out of here.' He added, 'This is not an American cowboys and Indians movie.'

Purcell stayed silent for a moment, then said, 'I was thinking more along the lines of avoiding a fate worse than death.'

No one replied, then Mercado said, 'You're being a bit fatalistic, Frank.' He asked, 'What would you like to do?'

Purcell thought a moment, then replied, 'There's only one option left.'

'What is that?'

'Another round.' He emptied the remaining scotch into the three bronze goblets and said, 'I hope those lances can drip more scotch into our cups.'

'Don't be blasphemous.'

Purcell took one of the spears and stuck it in the ground next to the table. They all sat on the tabletop, facing the closed tent flap.

Purcell had no idea who would come through that flap – mutinous soldiers, Colonel Gann, the prince, or Gallas. With luck, the cavalry in the form of the government soldiers would arrive and Henry would wave his press credentials and safe-conduct pass and remember how to say in Amharic, 'Thank you for rescuing us from the prince.'

Meanwhile, the sounds of desertion and disintegration outside the tent were growing quieter. In fact, ominously quiet.

Vivian said, 'I think we're alone.'

The tent flap opened and Purcell said, 'Not anymore.' He reached for the spear.

CHAPTER 7

A tall, thin man wearing a sweat-stained khaki uniform stooped and entered. He glanced at the spear in Purcell's hands, then said in a British accent, 'Hello. I think we've lost the war.'

Purcell noted that Colonel Sir Edmund Gann wore a reddish mustache and carried a riding crop. He was hatless, but there was a tan line on his forehead, so he'd lost his hat somewhere, though not his service revolver, which he wore on his hip. He also had a pair of field glasses hanging around his neck. Purcell stuck the spear back in the ground and stood.

Mercado introduced himself, and Colonel Gann said, 'Yes, I've read your stuff.'

'Thank you.' Mercado introduced his companions, and Vivian said to Colonel Gann, 'If you've read Henry's stuff, I like you already.'

Colonel Gann forced a smile and told them, 'We have to move quickly.' He informed everyone, 'There are several hundred nasty-looking Gallas less than a thousand yards from here.'

No one replied, but Purcell saw that Mercado had gone pale.

Colonel Gann added, 'But they are dismounted and moving

slowly.' He explained, 'Stripping corpses, finishing off the wounded, and looking for booty.'

And, Purcell knew, mutilating the dead and wounded, and that takes awhile.

Purcell exited the tent and looked around. The entire camp was deserted, and he noticed that the prince's flag was gone. More importantly, their Jeep was also gone.

Mercado, Gann, and Vivian came out into the bright sunlight, and Purcell asked Gann, 'Do you have horses to go with that riding crop?'

'I'm afraid not.'

Vivian asked, 'Where's our Jeep?'

Gann replied, 'Last I saw it, there were a dozen Royalist soldiers in it, headed south toward the jungle valley.'

Vivian said, 'Everything we own was in that Jeep.'

Mercado added, 'Including our chance to get out of here.' He asked Gann, 'Where is Prince Joshua?'

'Last I saw of him, he and six of his staff were on horseback, also heading south.'

Purcell remarked, 'I hope he remembered to take his crown.'

Vivian said, 'This is not funny, Frank.'

'Look at the bright side, Vivian.'

'And what is that?'

'The Gallas can't castrate you.'

Colonel Gann interjected, 'The Provisional government forces are to the north. I would advise you to try to reach their lines and show your press credentials. However, they apparently have allowed the Gallas to have some fun before the army advances. So that puts the Gallas between you and the government army.'

No one replied, and Colonel Gann continued, 'But you can give it a go if you'd like.'

Vivian asked, 'And will you come with us?'

'No. I'm a known advisor to the Royal Army. The government forces would probably shoot me.'

Purcell said, 'So let's all head south and catch up with the retreating Royalists.'

Colonel Gann informed them, 'I'm afraid they don't fancy me much.' He explained, 'I was a strict disciplinarian. You understand?'

Purcell observed, 'It seems no one likes you, Colonel.'

'I'm not here to be liked.'

Vivian said, 'Well, I like you. So come with us.'

Mercado inquired, 'Where are we going?'

Colonel Gann suggested, 'We can follow the rear guard of the Royal Army, keeping our distance from them, and staying a few steps ahead of the advancing Gallas.'

'Between a rock and a hard place,' said Purcell.

Colonel Gann also suggested, 'You three can probably join up with the Royalist rear guard … though I'm not sure they'd treat you well.' He explained, 'The prince is on the run and discipline has broken down.'

'And,' Purcell reminded him, 'you're no longer in a position to enforce good order and discipline.'

'Correct.'

'Well …'

In the distance, to the north, they could hear a man scream.

Colonel Gann said, 'The Gallas have arrived.'

Mercado, without a word, began moving quickly downhill toward the goat trail.

Vivian snapped a few quick pictures of the prince's tent and the deserted camp, then she and Gann started to follow, but Purcell said, 'I'll look for water in the tent and catch up.'

Gann informed him, 'We looked. There is no water.' He added, 'Whiskey's gone, too, I'm afraid.'

They caught up to Mercado and headed south, retracing the route they'd taken from the spa to Prince Joshua's headquarters. They passed the open area where the bloated bodies lay and found the small, ravine-like goat path, then took it downhill, continuing south toward the jungle valley. Purcell noted that their tire marks had been completely obliterated by the sandal prints and bare feet of Royalist soldiers fleeing toward the jungle.

The sun was hot and bright, and the rocks radiated an intense heat. Behind them, they could hear the war cries of the Gallas, and Purcell guessed that they had reached the prince's deserted camp.

Mercado was having difficulty breathing so they stopped to rest. Colonel Gann pulled an old Italian survey map from his pocket and studied it. Purcell lit a cigarette and studied Henry Mercado. Mercado had seemed to be in good physical shape, but his age was showing now.

Vivian was patting Mercado's face with a handkerchief, and she said, 'We need some water.'

Gann looked up from his map and replied, 'There are a few mountain streams close by, but probably dry now.'

Purcell noticed that Vivian had left her bush hat in the Jeep and her cheeks were bright red.

Colonel Gann climbed out of the ravine and surveyed the terrain through his field glasses. He called softly down to his companions, 'Some of the Gallas on horseback have actually gotten in front of us – between us and the rear guard of the Royal Army. In fact, they are all around us.'

Purcell climbed out of the ravine and took a look through Gann's field glasses. Down the hill, on both sides of the ravine, he saw the mounted men picking their way carefully but skillfully down the rock-strewn slopes.

Farther up the slope, coming toward them, were more horsemen, dressed in black robes, their heads and faces swathed in black scarves. They carried scimitars, and they looked to Purcell like Death.

At the top of the hill where they'd come from, Purcell could see dust clouds that meant more horsemen.

He looked across the ravine to the west. A high, razorback ridge of rock ran up to a neighboring peak.

Purcell lowered the field glasses and pointed to the ridgeline.

Gann nodded and said, 'Yes, almost impassable for horses ...' He consulted his map and said, 'If we can get onto that ridge, it will take us up to that peak.' He showed Purcell the map and pointed. 'A descending ridge will take us to this plateau below the highlands where the government forces are dug in.' He asked Purcell, 'Can you read a terrain map?'

'A little. And I can climb mountains.'

'Good. If we should become separated, just follow the ridgelines – west, then north.'

Purcell and Gann scrambled back into the ravine, and Purcell said, 'Okay, there seems to be a route out of here, but it's a lot of uphill.' He looked at Mercado and asked, 'Can you make it, Henry?'

Mercado nodded, but Purcell noticed he wasn't springing to his feet. Purcell gave him a hand and pulled him up.

Vivian asked Mercado, 'Are you all right?'

'Yes ... can't wait here for the Gallas.'

Gann took the field glasses from Purcell and climbed up the west side of the ravine. He scanned the area, then waved everyone up.

Purcell and Vivian helped Mercado out of the ravine, and they all crouched around the jagged boulders, looking for signs of Gallas between them and the base of the ridgeline about three hundred yards across a rock-strewn slope that was covered with chest-high brown brush.

There were dust clouds upslope and downslope, but no visible horsemen.

Gann led the way, followed by Vivian and Mercado, and Purcell brought up the rear, urging Mercado on. They dashed in a crouch, keeping below the brush, from boulder to boulder.

Now and then, Purcell caught a glimpse of the Gallas and saw that some were dismounted, leading their horses, while others remained mounted. They were proceeding at a leisurely pace, like the scavengers they were, he thought, more interested in fallen men and abandoned equipment than engaging the rear guard of the prince's army.

Gann called for a rest among high, jagged rocks, and commented, 'When the Gallas have picked the field clean, they will regroup, then decide if they are strong enough to attack the Royal Army.' He added, 'They would very much like to get the prince's crown and his head with it.'

'Not to mention the prince's family jewels,' said Purcell.

On that note, Mercado rallied a bit and said, 'Let's get moving.' They covered the remainder of the three hundred yards in a few minutes and stopped at the base of the ridgeline.

Purcell looked up the narrow ridge. It was a steep rise, comprised of large jagged red rocks, and between the rocks was more brown scrub brush.

Gann said, 'Good cover and concealment, not passable on horseback.' He asked, 'Are we ready?'

Purcell looked at Mercado, who nodded without enthusiasm.

They began the climb, picking their way up the ridge between the large rocks. Now and then they had to squeeze sideways between close rock formations, which assured them that Gallas on horseback could not follow – though Gallas on foot could.

About halfway up the ridge, they stopped for a rest and sat in the shade of a large rock formation.

Gann, noticed Purcell, seemed okay, though he wasn't a young man. But he had been hardened by a few wars and he'd probably pushed himself harder than this the night before, trying to rally the prince's army.

Purcell looked at Mercado. He, too, had experienced hardships, but those hardships had taken their toll.

Vivian was wiping Mercado's face again, but Purcell noticed that Mercado was barely sweating, which was not a good sign.

Vivian herself seemed in decent shape, but her arms and face were burning red from the sun. Purcell took off his bush jacket, leaving him in a sweat-soaked T-shirt. He pitched the bush jacket toward her and said, 'Drape that over your head.'

She hesitated, then picked up the khaki jacket and threw it back to him.

Colonel Gann had climbed onto a tall rock and was scouting the terrain through his field glasses. He said, 'The Gallas are coming together … perhaps two or three hundred of them … heading down into the valley. They'll harass the remnants of the Royal Army … and if they think the army is very weakened, they'll go in for the kill.'

No one had anything to say about that, but everyone felt relieved that the Gallas had shifted their attention to the retreating army.

Purcell was hoping he'd see some signs of the Provisional Revolutionary government army in pursuit of the Royalists. That would save them a long hike. He asked Gann, 'Do you see any signs of the army?'

Gann kept scanning as he replied, 'No. They're letting the Gallas do the work. Lazy buggers.' He added, 'Bunch of damned Marxists.'

Vivian said to Gann, 'If we reach the Provisional Army, we can pass you off as a journalist.'

Purcell added, 'But you need to take off your royal insignia, and get rid of that gun and lose the riding crop.'

Gann replied, 'I appreciate the offer. But my presence will endanger you.' He added, 'They'll know who I am, even without the royal insignia on my uniform, and then they can shoot me as a spy instead of as a Royalist.' He informed them, 'I'd rather be shot as a soldier.'

Purcell didn't see what difference it made, but Colonel Gann did, and he made a good point – about him endangering them all. Also, their safe-conduct pass from the Provisional government in Addis had only three names on it, and one of those names wasn't Colonel Sir Edmund Gann.

Purcell looked at Mercado, who hadn't said anything on the subject. 'What do you think, Henry?'

Mercado replied, 'We should cross that bridge when we come to it. We're still in a bad situation.'

Gann agreed, and said, 'I'll try to get you as close as I can to the army lines, then I'll scoot off.'

Vivian asked him, 'To where?'

He informed them, 'Most of the Amharic peasants around here are loyal to the emperor, and I'll look for a friendly village.'

No one replied, but Purcell didn't think much of Colonel Gann's plan. In fact, Purcell thought, Colonel Gann probably didn't think much of it either. Most likely he would die of thirst, hunger, or disease in the hills or in the jungle. But the Gallas would not get him. Not as long as Colonel Gann had his service revolver and one bullet left. Purcell said to Gann and to Mercado and Vivian, 'I think we should stay together. Maybe we can find this Prince Theodore, or some other ras.'

Gann said, 'Nonsense. You have press credentials and a safe-conduct pass. Your best bet is the Provisional government forces, and they are close by.'

Again, no one replied, but then Purcell said, 'Let's play it by ear. Ready?'

Everyone stood and they continued up the ridge. Within half an hour, they reached the summit, which gave them a clear view of the surrounding terrain.

The sun was almost overhead now, and there wasn't much shade, but Mercado lay down in a sliver of shadow at the base of a tall rock. Vivian knelt beside him and put her damp, sweaty handkerchief over his face.

Gann was scanning the terrain with his field glasses, and he said, 'I can see soldiers dug in on the ridgelines.' He passed the glasses to Purcell.

Below was a grassy plateau, like an alpine meadow, between them and the hills to the north, and rocky ridges ran from the hills to the plateau.

Purcell focused on the closest ridge, less than a kilometer away, and saw a group of uniformed men. They'd piled up some rocks to construct a safe firing position, and he thought he saw the long firing tube of a mortar protruding above the rock. He looked farther up the ridge at the next summit and saw more gun positions.

Gann said, 'The bulk of the Provisional Army are in those hills.' He told them, 'They attacked us in force last night, right there on that plateau, and we inflicted a good number of casualties on them. Unfortunately, they had heavy mortars and they pounded us through the night.'

Purcell nodded. That's what they'd seen from the spa.

Gann went on, 'At daybreak we expected another attack, and I was preparing for it, but panic had set in, and the troops started deserting. And once that starts, it's impossible to stop.'

Purcell asked Gann, 'Was the prince paying you enough for this?'

Gann thought about that, then replied, 'A soldier's pay is never enough. You must also believe in the cause.'

Purcell reminded him, 'You're a mercenary.' He added, 'An honorable profession, I'm sure. But not one that believes in causes.'

Gann informed everyone, 'I was here in 1941 with the British Expeditionary Force that drove out the Italians.' He added, 'I developed a fondness for Ethiopia and the people. And the monarchy. The emperor. He's a remarkable man ... the last in a three-thousand-year-old line of succession.'

'Right,' said Purcell. 'The last.'

Gann turned the question around and asked, 'Why are *you* here?'

Purcell replied, 'To cover the war.'

'Are they paying you enough for this?'

'No.' He suggested, 'Let's get moving.' He looked at Vivian, who was kneeling beside Mercado and blocking the sun from him. 'Is he all right?'

'No.'

Purcell said, 'Try to wake him, Vivian.'

'No. He needs sleep.'

'It's all downhill to the plateau.'

Gann suggested, 'Look, I'm not going with you into the army lines, so I'll stay here with him and you two make contact with the government forces, then come back for him with an army medic and a few men to carry him.' He added, 'I'll scoot off before you get up here.'

Purcell thought that was a good idea, but Vivian said, 'I'm not leaving him.'

Gann explained, 'You're not leaving him. You're going for help.'

Purcell said to her, 'You can stay here, too. I don't need company.'

Mercado was awake now and he sat up with his back against the rock. He'd heard the discussion and said to Vivian in a weak voice, 'Go with Frank.'

'No. I'm staying with you.' She knelt beside him and put her hand on his forehead. 'You're burning ...'

Purcell looked at Gann and they both knew that Mercado was close to heatstroke.

Gann said to Purcell, 'You'd better start off now.'

Mercado pulled a plastic wrapped paper from his pocket and gave it to Vivian, saying, 'The safe-conduct pass ... go with Frank.'

She took the pass and handed it to Purcell, but remained kneeling beside Mercado. Purcell put the pass in his pocket and said to Gann, 'I won't be seeing you later. Thanks for your help.'

They shook and Gann said, 'Well, good luck.' He added, 'The commander of the Provisional government forces is a chap named Getachu. Nasty fellow. Red through and through. Likes to shoot Royalists. Doesn't think much of Westerners either. Your pass from the Provisional government should be all right, but be careful with him.'

Purcell replied, 'I know who he is.' He said to Vivian and Mercado, 'See you later.'

Purcell moved toward the descending ridge, then turned and asked Gann, 'Have you ever heard of a black monastery in this area?'

Colonel Gann didn't reply immediately, then said, 'Yes. But not worth the side trip.' He added, 'Maybe after the war is over.'

Purcell nodded, then started to pick his way down the rocky ridge.

CHAPTER 8

Below, the grassy plateau looked inviting, and Purcell thought there could be water there. Or Gallas.

Across the plateau was the base of the rocky hills, and in those hills was the victorious army of the Provisional government. But even if he made it to an army outpost, he wasn't sure what kind of reception he'd get. Theoretically, his American passport and press credentials and the safe-conduct pass from the Provisional Revolutionary government would ensure a good reception – which was why he and his traveling companions were trying to reach the army forces to begin with. But theory, when it butts up against reality, sometimes produces unexpected results. Especially if he had to deal with General Getachu, who was notoriously cruel, and probably insane; the perfect subject for a press interview – if he didn't kill the reporter.

Purcell heard something behind him, and he froze, then squeezed himself into a rock cleft. He listened and heard it again. Someone was coming down the ridge.

He waited, then saw her sliding on her butt down a long flat rock, holding on to her camera that was hanging from her neck. She jumped off the rock and he let her get a little ahead of him, then fell in behind her as she was scrambling over another large rock.

'Change your mind?'

She made a startled sound, then turned toward him. 'God … Frank … you scared the hell—'

'Me too. Where you going?'

'To find you …' She took a deep breath, then said, 'Henry gave you … he didn't give you the pass.'

'Really?' Purcell took the plastic-wrapped sheet from his pocket and opened it. He smiled and said, 'Looks like his bar bill from the Hilton.'

She didn't reply to that but said, 'I have the pass.'

'Good. I'll take it.'

She gave it to him.

He looked at it, put it in his pocket, and said, 'Thanks. See you later.'

She glanced up at the ridge.

He said, 'Right. The climb up will kill you. Stay here.'

'I'm coming with you.'

He didn't respond to that and asked, 'How's Henry?'

'A little better.'

'Good. And how are you?'

'Dizzy.'

He put his hand on her blistered forehead and asked her, 'Tongue swollen?'

'A little …'

He took off his bush jacket and draped it over her head. 'Okay. Let's go.'

She followed him as he moved down the ridge.

She said to him, 'Colonel Gann saw three Gallas on horseback riding through the tall grass ahead.'

'News I can use.'

They continued on and she said, 'I wouldn't have left him ... but he tricked me. Tricked you.'

Purcell didn't reply.

She said, 'He and Colonel Gann thought you'd have a better chance if I were along.'

'You have not increased my chances.'

'In case you got hurt. Or ... whatever. Better to send two people on a rescue mission.'

'True.' Unless one of them was an attractive woman.

The ridge flattened and they stopped a hundred feet from the high grass of the plateau. Purcell said to her, 'You stay here. If all goes well, I'll be back with a medic and some soldiers to collect you and get Henry. If I'm not back in, say, two hours—'

'I am not staying here.'

'You will do what I tell you—'

'Frank, if something happens to you, I'm as good as dead here. And so is Henry.'

'Vivian—'

'I can't get back up that hill, and I will not sit here waiting for the Gallas – or dying of fucking thirst.' She moved toward him and gave him a push on the chest. 'Let's go.'

They continued on and entered the tall grass. Purcell said, 'Keep a separation of twenty feet, and if you hear hoofbeats, drop and freeze.'

They walked silently through the elephant grass, which was taller than they were. Purcell could see evidence of the battle that had been fought here during the night – naked bloated bodies lay strewn in the high grass, covered with big green flies. There was no mutilation, and Purcell guessed that it was not the Gallas but the victorious government forces that had carried off the pitiful war spoils from the slain soldiers of Prince Joshua. Fresh graves marked the spots where the government forces had buried their own dead. If he'd hoped to find a canteen of water among the carnage, that hope quickly faded.

They continued on and the nauseating stench of death hung in the hot air. Vultures circled overhead, and one swooped down and landed near a naked body, then bent its long neck and plucked out an eyeball. Vivian, who had come up behind him, let out a stifled cry of disgust.

Purcell rushed toward the vulture and it flew off. They continued on.

The tall grass was beaten down where horses had passed through, and where men had fought and fallen. He saw craters made by impacting mortar rounds that had set the grass on fire, and in the ash he saw jagged shrapnel and burned body parts. Brass shell casings littered the ground.

Purcell tried to imagine what had gone on here during the night, but despite his years of war reporting he could not conjure up the images of men joined in close combat. But he could imagine how Colonel Gann had felt when he realized the battle was lost.

The plateau began to rise toward the base of the high hills and the ground became rocky and the grass began to thin as they continued up the slope.

Somewhere to the west he could hear hoofbeats, and he hoped Vivian also heard them. Ignoring his own advice to freeze and drop, he doubled back and saw her walking toward him. The hoofbeats got louder and she heard them at the same time as she saw him. They both dove to the ground in the thin grass and remained motionless, staring at each other across a patch of open space.

The hoofbeats were close now, and Purcell guessed there were three or four horses, about twenty or thirty yards' distance. The hoofbeats stopped, and he could hear the rustle of grass as the riders moved slowly, looking for anything of value, and for anyone unfortunate enough to still be alive.

Purcell made eye contact with Vivian and he could see she was terrified, but she remained motionless and resisted the instinct to run.

The Gallas were so close now that he could hear them speaking. One of them laughed. A horse snorted.

After what seemed like an eternity, he heard them ride off.

He motioned for Vivian to remain still, tapped his watch, and flashed five fingers twice. She nodded.

They waited the full ten minutes, then Purcell stood and Vivian moved quickly toward him. He glanced at the rising ridge about three hundred yards away and said, 'We're going to make a run for that. Ready?'

She nodded, but he could see she was close to collapse.

He took her arm and they began moving at a half run toward the rising ridge of red rock, which he could see was impassable for mounted riders.

They had to stop every few minutes and rest, and Vivian scanned the ground for water. At one rest stop she announced she saw a pool of water that turned out to be a flat rock. Purcell recognized the signs of severe dehydration, which were confusion and hallucination. Water, water everywhere. He thought of all those bloated bodies – ninety-eight percent water ... but he wasn't that desperate yet.

They reached the base of the ridge and continued up the exposed slope of sun-baked rock. Vivian suddenly scrambled away from him and he caught her by the ankle, but she kicked free and continued off to her left.

Purcell followed and saw what she'd seen; a clump of what looked like spiky cactus, nestled between two flat rocks.

She grabbed at the vegetation and brought it directly to her mouth. Purcell did the same and guessed, by the soft viscous flesh of the plant, that it was some sort of aloe. He squeezed some pulp into his hand and rubbed it across his burning face, then did the same for Vivian as she continued to chew on the plant.

Within a minute or two, the aloe plants were eaten and Purcell dug out the shallow roots with his penknife and they ate those as well.

Neither of them spoke for a while, then Vivian said, 'Thank God . . .'

Purcell retrieved his bush jacket, which she'd let fall off her head, and covered both their heads with it as they sat and looked down onto the plateau below. He treated himself to a cigarette.

A few hundred yards away, he could see four Gallas on horseback, riding slowly through the elephant grass, heads down, still looking for the living and the dead.

Vivian followed his gaze and said softly, 'Ghouls.'

Purcell looked across the plateau at the mountain they had descended, and where Henry and Colonel Gann were hopefully still alive. Possibly Gann was able to follow their progress through his field glasses, so Purcell waved his arms.

Vivian, too, was waving, and Purcell heard her murmur, 'Hang on, Henry.'

Purcell didn't want to attract the attention of the Gallas, who, if they spotted them, would start taking potshots at them – or they'd dismount and start climbing up the ridge. Assuming the Gallas were in better shape than he or Vivian, they would catch up with them before he and Vivian reached the army lines.

He glanced at Vivian. Her lips were cracked and her face was a mess, but her eyes looked more alert now. Her torn khakis were crusted with sweat salt, but not damp with new sweat. He guessed she had been very near heatstroke, but she should be able to finish the climb. He, himself, felt better. He'd had worse days in the Khmer Rouge prison camp, sick with dysentery and fever ... Another interned reporter, a Frenchman, had saved his life, then died a few weeks later.

He asked Vivian, 'How are you doing?'

She stood and moved up the ridge and Purcell followed.

They continued the climb, rock by rock. It would have been an easy climb if they'd had something in their stomachs aside from a few aloe plants. Also, their goal – the government forces – might not be a touchdown if Getachu was playing by his own rules.

Purcell stood on a flat rock, shielded his eyes with his hand, and scanned the jagged slope ahead. Less than two hundred yards up the ridgeline he spotted what looked like a revetment of stones. Then he saw a figure moving among the rocks. He said to Vivian, 'I think I see an army outpost.'

They continued up the ridge. As they got closer to the piled stone, Purcell could see at least five men in camouflage uniforms sitting beneath a green tarp that had been strung between tent poles. The men seemed engaged in conversation and didn't notice that anyone was approaching.

This was the critical moment, Purcell knew, the two or three seconds when the guys with the guns had to decide if you were friend or foe, or something else.

He motioned for Vivian to lie flat behind a rock, then he took his white handkerchief from his pocket and shouted one of the few Amharic phrases he knew. 'Tena yastalann!' Hello.

A shot rang out and Purcell threw himself on the ground. More shots rang out and Purcell realized the shooting was coming from behind him – the Gallas – then return fire started coming from the soldiers. He put his hand on Vivian's back and pressed hard to keep her from moving.

The exchange of gunfire lasted a few minutes, then abruptly stopped.

Purcell whispered to Vivian, 'Don't move.'

She nodded.

He raised his body slightly and craned his head around the rock to see if the Gallas were behind them. He didn't see any movement below and he turned his head toward the army out-post. An arm's length from his face were two dark feet in leather sandals. He looked up into the muzzle of an AK-47.

The soldier motioned with the barrel of his gun for him to stand.

Purcell got slowly to his feet. Keeping his hands up, he smiled and said to the man dressed in camouflage fatigues, 'Amerikawi. Gazetanna.'

Vivian was also standing now and she asked, 'Capisce Italiano?'

The soldier understood the question, but shook his head. He

kept his automatic rifle pointed at them, but glanced down the ridge to see if the Gallas were still coming.

Purcell motioned up the ridge and said in English, 'Okay, buddy, we're here to see General Getachu.'

Vivian added, 'Giornalista. Gazetanna.' She tapped her camera. 'General Getachu.'

The soldier stared at her.

Two more soldiers in cammies came down from the gun emplacement carrying their Soviet-made AK-47s. The three men began conversing in what sounded like Amharic. As they spoke, they kept glancing at Vivian, who Purcell thought looked awful, but maybe not to the soldiers.

Vivian tapped her pants pocket to indicate she had something for them, then slid out her passport and press credentials.

One of the soldiers snatched the items from her hand and stared at the press credentials, which were written in several languages, including Amharic. He then opened Vivian's passport, which Purcell knew was Swiss – a good passport to have – and flipped through it.

Purcell drew his American passport and press credentials from his pocket along with the safe-conduct pass wrapped in plastic. One of the soldiers took the documents from him and all of them gave a look, though it appeared that none of them could read even Amharic.

Purcell pointed to the safe-conduct pass and said, 'Signed by General Andom.' He added, 'Brezhnev is numero uno. Power to the people. Avanti.'

One of the soldiers looked at him, then motioned for him and Vivian to walk up the ridge. The soldiers followed.

On the way up, Vivian asked, 'Are we going to get a bullet in the back?'

Purcell remembered the executions he'd seen in Cambodia; the victims were almost always naked so that their clothes wouldn't he ruined. Also, the women were usually raped first. He suspected it was the same here. 'No,' he replied. 'Reporters can be shot only by the general.'

They reached the gun emplacement and Purcell could see an 81-millimeter mortar surrounded by piled stone. A fire pit held the charred wooden remains of ammunition crates and the blackened bones of small animals.

They stopped and Purcell said, in Amharic, 'Weha.'

One of the soldiers indicated a five-gallon jerry can, which Purcell lifted and poured over Vivian's head and clothes to bring down her body temperature. She took the can and did the same for him, saying, 'Spa, Ethiopian style.' A soldier handed them a canteen and they drank.

Vivian smiled at the soldiers and thanked them in Amharic: 'Agzer yastalann.'

Purcell gave the soldiers his last pack of Egyptian cigarettes and they all lit up. So far, so good, he thought, though Vivian's gender was a complication.

One of the soldiers was talking on a field radio, then he said something to his companions. The soldier who seemed to be in charge handed them their documents and motioned them up the ridge.

Before anyone changed their minds, Purcell took Vivian's arm and they continued unescorted up the mountain.

Vivian said, 'I think we're all right.'

'I think I could have done this on my own.'

'Me too.'

He didn't reply and they continued on in silence.

Finally, she said, apropos of something she was thinking, 'Go to hell.'

'Already here.'

She asked him, 'Are you married? Girlfriend?'

'No.'

'I can't imagine why not.'

'Can we save this for the Hilton bar?'

'I don't ever want to see you again after this.'

'Sorry you feel that way.'

'And we don't need you to look for the black monastery.'

He didn't reply and they continued on toward the top of the mountain.

Purcell thought about Father Armano, the black monastery, and the so-called Holy Grail. There was no Holy Grail, but sometimes his editors or other war correspondents described a story as the Holy Grail of stories – the story that would win a Pulitzer, or a National Journalism Award, or at least the admiration of their colleagues and a few drinks in a good bar.

He glanced at Vivian, and thought of Henry Mercado. Could he let them go without him? What if they died? What if they didn't and they found something? He wished he had something better to do with his life.

CHAPTER 9

Purcell and Vivian sat side by side on a cot inside the medical aid tent. Vivian's face was covered with white ointment and she wore a reasonably clean gray shamma, as did Purcell.

The army doctor sat in a camp chair and smoked a cigarette. Purcell also smoked one of the doctor's cigarettes, while Vivian finished the bowl of cooked wheat that Dr Mato had brought.

Vivian said in Italian, 'Thank you, Doctor. You have been very kind.'

The big Ethiopian smiled. 'It was nothing. You are both fine. Continue to rehydrate.' He added, 'You may keep the ointment.'

Vivian translated for Purcell, then she asked the doctor, 'Any word on our colleague?'

Doctor Mato replied, 'As I said, we have sent ten armed men and a mule. I'm sure your colleague will be joining you shortly.'

Vivian nodded, and again translated for Purcell.

The doctor stood. 'I have many sick and wounded. Excuse me.' He left.

Purcell said, 'I'm sure Henry is enjoying the mule ride.'

She nodded absently, then said, 'I hope they reach him in time.'

He didn't reply.

She continued, 'I worry about the Gallas.'

'The Gallas,' said Purcell, 'attack the weak and the dying. Not ten armed soldiers.'

She looked at him, forced a smile, and said, 'You do know how to con a worried lady.'

He smiled in return, though he found himself for some reason annoyed at her worry about Mercado, justified as it might be. He stood and looked around the aid tent. His and Vivian's personal possessions were in neat piles at the foot of their cots, but their clothes and boots were gone, and he didn't see any native sandals for either of them. He said, 'I'm going to take a look around.'

She stood. 'I'll go with you.'

'Be here when they bring Henry in.'

She hesitated, then nodded, and said, 'Find a toothbrush.'

As he began walking, he could see soldiers lounging under jerry-rigged tarps, eating, talking, and smoking, which was what soldiers did when they weren't killing other soldiers. In any case, they didn't seem that interested in the white guy walking around bare-foot in a gray *shamma* — though a few did point to him. If Vivian had been with him, the soldiers may have shown more interest.

He passed a long open-sided tent marked with a white medical cross, and inside the tent he could see men lying close together on the dirt floor, mostly naked and bandaged. An over-powering stench came from the tent, and he could hear the moaning and crying of men in pain. Human misery. War, pestilence, famine, and civil strife. Ethiopia had it all.

In the distance, on a low hill, he noticed a big pavilion-style tent that flew the revolutionary red-starred flag of the new Ethiopia. That must be the headquarters, and when — or if — Henry arrived, they'd all go over there and see if General Getachu was in a good enough mood to offer them a helicopter ride to Addis — after they interviewed the victorious general, of course. There wasn't much frontline reporting in this war, and based on the events of the last forty-eight hours, he could see why.

Near the hill, he saw a windsock, indicating a helipad, though there was no helicopter there. He pictured himself in Getachu's helicopter, with Mercado and Vivian, high above the heat and stench of this place. The helicopter was the magic carpet of modern war, and if they left here by noon tomorrow, they could be in the Hilton bar tomorrow night, answering questions from their colleagues about their excursion into the interior of this benighted country. The etiquette was to modestly downplay the big dangerous adventure, but make it interesting enough to keep everyone's attention, and keep the drinks flowing. He thought about how to mention finding the dying priest without giving away the whole story.

He thought, too, about Colonel Gann. He'd taken a liking to the man and had acquired a respect for him after seeing that battlefield. Purcell hoped the colonel could find a village of friendly natives and eventually make his way out of Ethiopia. But the chances for that were not good, and Purcell thought about writing a posthumous story, titled 'Knight Errant.' Also a trip to England to find Edmund Gann's family.

The sun was going down and deep purple shadows filled the gullies and gorges that ran through the camp, and which held the human excrement of thousands of soldiers. A few military vehicles were parked haphazardly, but the main form of transportation seemed to be the mules and horses that were tethered to tent poles.

Purcell had seen a hundred army field camps in the course of his career, and every one of them — whether they were filthy like this place or spotless like the American camps — had the same feeling of life on hold, and death on the way.

Purcell felt he had seen enough of Getachu's camp, and he decided that he would go see General Getachu himself, without informing his photographer, who would insist that they wait for the missing Mercado. In any case, he felt that he should at least register their presence, which was the protocol.

As he made his way toward the headquarters tent, Purcell recalled what he'd read about General Getachu in the English-language newspaper in Addis. According to this government-censored and self-censored puff piece, the general was quite a remarkable man — loyal to the revolution, a competent military commander, and a man of the people, born into a poor peasant family. His parents had put themselves on starvation rations to have enough money to send their young son to the British missionary school in Gondar. Mikael Getachu had proven himself a brilliant student, of course, and he had learned English before he was seven. Also, he'd rejected most of his bourgeois teaching and secretly embraced Marxism at an early age. He never attended university, but had returned to his village and organized the oppressed peasants in their struggle against the local *rasses*, whom Purcell thought must have included *Ras* Joshua.

The flattering article went on to say that Mikael Getachu joined the Royal Army to infiltrate its ranks, and was stationed in Addis Ababa. And when the military seized power and overthrew the emperor, young Captain Getachu was in the right place at the right time, and he was now a general, and the commander of the army in his former province. Local boy makes good and comes home to bring peace and justice to his people.

According to the word in the bars and embassies in Addis, however, Getachu was a psychopath, and was rumored to have strangled a dozen members of the royal family in their palaces, including women and children. Even the revolutionary council — the Derg — feared him, and they'd made him commander of the Northern Army to keep him out of the capital.

As Purcell walked up the hill toward the large headquarters pavilion, he noticed something on the far side that he hadn't seen before. He couldn't quite make it out in the fading light, but as he got closer he realized that what he was seeing was a pole suspended between two upright poles — and hanging from the horizontal pole were about a dozen men. As he got closer he saw they were dressed in the uniforms of the Royal Army.

He stopped about ten feet from the scene and could see that the men had been hanged by their necks with what looked like commo wire, to ensure a slow, painful strangulation. Their hands were not tied so that they could grip the wire around their necks and try to ease the stranglehold, but in the end they'd become exhausted and lost the battle with gravity and with death.

Purcell took a deep breath and stood there, staring at the contorted faces, the bloody fingers and bloody necks. He counted thirteen men hanging motionless in the still air. He wondered how many more Royalists had been shot where they were captured. Taking prisoners was not a well-understood concept in this country and in this war.

Purcell noticed that a few of the sentries posted near the

headquarters tent were watching him, and he rethought his visit to General Getachu.

He turned and made his way back toward the medical tent. Vivian was not there, and the sole orderly in the tent was not helpful in answering his pantomimed questions.

The standard procedure in situations like this was to stay put in a known location and wait for the missing colleague. If he went looking for her, they'd probably miss and keep coming back to the tent to see if the other was there, sort of like a Marx Brothers routine. He looked to see if she'd left him a note. She hadn't, but he saw that her camera, passport, and press credentials were gone, which meant she'd taken them. But then he noticed that his passport was also gone, and so was his wallet, his press credentials, and the safe-conduct pass. 'Shit.'

He walked out of the tent, looking for any sign of her in the darkening dusk. Maybe she'd gone to find a latrine, which didn't exist here, so that could take some time. He decided to give it ten minutes, then he'd go straight to the headquarters tent and demand to see Getachu. Or Getachu would send for him. In fact, he thought, that's what might have happened to Vivian.

He waited, but he wasn't the waiting type. After about five minutes, he headed toward Getachu's headquarters.

He saw a figure running toward him in the darkness. It was Vivian and she spotted him and called out, 'Frank! They've got Henry!'

'Good.'

She stopped a few feet from him, breathless, and said, 'They've got Colonel Gann, too.'

Not good.

She explained quickly, 'Colonel Gann had passed out on the mountain. Henry, too. The soldiers found them both—'

'Hold on. Who told you this?'

'Doctor Mato. They're in the hospital tent. Under arrest. Doctor Mato says they'll be all right, but—'

'Okay, let's go see them.'

'They won't let me in the tent.'

Which, he thought, was just as well. 'Okay, let's see the general.'

'I tried, but—'

'Let's go.'

They moved quickly up the hill to where the headquarters tent sat. A few of the side flaps were open and they could see light inside.

He'd noticed she didn't have her camera, and there was no place in her *shamma* where she could have put their papers, but she may have hidden everything, so he asked, 'Do you know where our passports and papers are?'

'No ... when Doctor Mato came to get me, I ran out—'

'Well, everything is gone, including your camera.'

'Damn it ...'

'That's all right. Getachu has it all.'

'That bastard. That's *my* camera, with thirty pictures—'

'Vivian, that is the least of our problems.'

He could see that she was distraught over Mercado's arrest, and now was becoming indignant over the confiscation of her property. This was all understandable and would have been appropriate in Addis, but not here at the front.

She needed a reality check before they saw Getachu, so Purcell steered her around to the far side of the headquarters tent and said, 'That is what General Getachu does to Royalists. We don't know what he does to Western reporters who annoy him.'

She stared at the hanging men. 'Oh ... my God ...'

'Ready?'

She turned away and nodded.

They approached the guarded entrance of the headquarters tent. Two soldiers carrying AK-47s became alert and eyed them curiously. They'd already sent the woman away, and they wondered why she'd returned. One of the men made a threatening gesture with his rifle, and the other motioned for them to go away.

Purcell said to them in the Amharic word that all reporters in Ethiopia knew, 'Gazetanna.' He added, 'General Getachu.' He tapped his left wrist where his missing watch should be, hoping they thought he had an appointment.

The two soldiers conversed for a second, then one of them disappeared inside the tent. The remaining soldier eyed Vivian's ointment-splotched face, then her legs beneath the *shamma*.

Vivian said softly, 'I'm frightened. Are you?'

'Check with me later.'

The soldier returned and motioned for them to follow.

They entered the pavilion, which Purcell noticed was much larger than Prince Joshua's. He noticed, too, that there were no ceremonial spears or shields in this sparse tent — only field equipment, including two radios on a camp table. Coleman-type lamps barely lit the large space.

The tent was divided by a curtain, and the soldier motioned for them to pass through a slit. It was darker in this half of the tent, and it took them a few seconds to make out a man sitting behind a field desk. The man did not stand, but he motioned toward two canvas chairs in front of his desk and said in English, 'Sit.'

They sat.

General Getachu lit a cigarette and stared at them through his smoke. A propane lamp hung above the desk illuminating his hands, but not his face.

As Purcell's eyes adjusted to the dim light he could see that Getachu wore a scruffy beard, and his head was bald or shaven. A tan line ran across his forehead where his hat had sat, and his skin was naturally dark, but further darkened by the sun.

Purcell had seen a photograph of General Getachu in an Ethiopian newspaper, and he'd noted that Getachu had the broader features of the Hamitic people and not the Semitic features of the aristocracy or the Arabic population. In fact, that was partly what this war was about – ancestry and racial differences so subtle that the average Westerner couldn't see them, but which the Ethiopians equated with ruler and ruled. Indeed, he thought, the Getachus of this country were getting their revenge after three thousand years. He couldn't blame them, but he thought they could go about it in a less brutal way.

He had dealt with the newly empowered revolutionaries in many countries, and what they all had in common was xenophobic paranoia, extravagant anger, and dangerously irrational thinking. And now he was about to find out how psychotic this guy was.

Getachu seemed content to let them sit there in his office while he perused the papers on his desk. Also on Getachu's desk was Vivian's camera, his wallet and watch, their passports, and their press credentials, but he couldn't see what would have been their safe-conduct pass, issued by the Provisional Revolutionary government. It occurred to Purcell that Getachu had chosen to deal with that inconvenient document by destroying it.

Getachu lit another cigarette and took a drink from a canteen cup. He looked at them and asked with a slight British accent, 'Why are you here?'

Purcell replied, 'To report on the war.'

'To spy for the Royalists.'

'To report on the war.'

'Spies are shot. If they are lucky.'

'We are reporters, certified by the Provisional Revolutionary government, and we have a safe-conduct pass issued by the Derg and signed by General—'

'You have no such thing.'

Vivian said, 'We do.' She asked, 'Why have you arrested our colleague?'

He looked at her and said, 'Shut up.'

Again, Getachu let the silence go on, then he said, 'You two and your colleague were in the Royalist camp.'

Purcell replied, 'We got lost. On our way here.'

'You met your colleague Colonel Gann.'

'He is not our colleague.'

'You fled with him to escape the Revolutionary Army that you say you were trying to find.'

'We fled to escape the Gallas.' Purcell also pointed out, 'We climbed this mountain to find you.'

Getachu did not reply.

Purcell didn't think he should bother to explain the actual

circumstances of what had happened. General Getachu had drawn his own conclusions, and though he probably knew they were not completely accurate conclusions, they suited his paranoia.

Purcell said, 'We are here to report on the war. We take no sides—'

'You have a romantic notion of the emperor and his family, and of the rasses and the ruling class.'

Purcell thought that might be true of Mercado and maybe Vivian, and certainly of Colonel Gann, but not of him. He said, 'I'm an American. We don't like royalty.'

'So do you like Marxists?'

'No.'

Getachu stared at him, then nodded. He said, 'Colonel Gann has caused the death of many of my men. He has been condemned to death.'

Purcell already guessed that, but he said, 'If you spare his life and expel him, I and my colleagues promise we will write—'

'You will write nothing. You are all guilty by association. And you are spies for the Royalists. And you will be court-martialed in the morning.'

Purcell saw that coming, and apparently so did Vivian, because she said in a firm, even voice, 'My colleague, Mr Mercado, is an internationally known journalist who has met frequently with members of the Derg and who has interviewed General Andom who is your superior. It was General Andom who signed the safe-conduct pass—'

'General Andom did not give Mercado – or you – permission to spy for the counterrevolutionaries.'

Purcell tried another tack. 'Look, General, you won the battle, and you've probably won the war. The Provisional government has invited journalists to—'

'I have not invited you.'

'Then we'll leave.'

Getachu did not reply, and Purcell had the feeling that he might be wavering. Getachu had to weigh his desire and his instinct to kill anyone he wanted to kill against the possibility that the new government did not want him to kill the three Western reporters. In any case, Colonel Gann was as good as dead.

Purcell had found himself in similar situations, each with a happy ending, or he wouldn't be here in *this* situation. He recalled Mercado's advice not to look arrestable, but he was far beyond that tipping point. He wasn't quite sure what to say or do next, so he asked, 'May I have a cigarette?'

Getachu seemed a bit taken aback, but then he slid his pack of Egyptian cigarettes toward Purcell along with a box of matches.

Purcell lit up, then said, 'If you allow me access to a typewriter, I will write an article for the *International Herald Tribune* and the English-language newspaper in Addis, describing your victory over Prince Joshua and the Royalist forces. You may, of course, read the article, and have it delivered to my press office in Addis Ababa along with a personal note from me saying that I am traveling with General Getachu's army at the front.'

Getachu looked at him for a long time, then looked at Vivian, then at her camera. He asked her, 'And if I have this film developed in Addis, what will I see?'

Vivian replied, 'Mostly our journey from the capital to an old Italian spa … then a few photos of Prince Joshua's camp.'

'Those photographs will be good to show at your court-martial, Miss' – he glanced inside her Swiss passport – 'Miss Smith.'

Vivian replied, 'I am a photojournalist. I photograph—'

'Shut up.' He leaned forward and stared at her, then said, 'On the far side of this camp is a tent. In this tent are ten, perhaps twelve women – those with Royalist sympathies, including a princess – and they are there for the entertainment of my soldiers.' He pushed Vivian's camera across the desk. 'Would you like to photograph what goes on inside that tent?'

Purcell stood. 'General, your conduct—'

Getachu pulled his pistol and aimed it at Purcell. 'Sit down.'

Purcell sat.

Getachu holstered his pistol and said, as if nothing had happened, 'And you, Miss Smith, can also photograph the Royalists that you saw hanging. And also photograph Colonel Gann's execution. And your friend Mr Mercado's execution as well. Would you like that?'

Vivian did not reply.

Getachu stared at her, then turned his attention to Purcell and said, 'Or perhaps, as Mr Purcell suggested, he can write very good articles about the people's struggle against their historic oppressors. And then, perhaps, there will be no court-martial and no executions.'

Neither Purcell nor Vivian replied.

Getachu continued, 'The enemies of the people must either be liquidated or made to serve the revolution.' He added, 'You could be more useful alive.'

Vivian asked, 'And Mr Mercado?'

'He was once a friend of the oppressed people, but he has strayed. He needs to be reeducated.'

Purcell asked, 'And Colonel Gann?'

'A difficult case. But I respect him as a soldier. And I have a certain fondness for the British.' He explained, 'I attended a British missionary school.'

And apparently missed the class on good sportsmanship and fair play, Purcell thought.

Getachu added, 'The headmaster was fond of the switch, but perhaps I deserved it.'

No doubt.

Getachu said, 'Perhaps Colonel Gann can be persuaded to share his military knowledge with my colonels.'

Purcell said, 'I will speak to him.'

Getachu ignored this and said, 'Shooting a man – or a woman – is easy. I would rather see men broken.'

Purcell had no doubt that Getachu was sincere.

Getachu said, 'You may go.'

Vivian said, 'We want to see Mr Mercado. And Colonel Gann.'

'You will find them in the hospital tent.'

Purcell took Vivian's arm and turned to leave, but Getachu said, 'Before you go, something that may interest you.'

They looked at him and saw he was retrieving something from the shadow beside his chair. Getachu held up a gold crown, encrusted with jewels. Purcell and Vivian recognized it as the crown of Prince Joshua.

Getachu said, 'I allowed the Gallas free rein to hunt down the Royalists. All I asked in return was that they bring me the prince, dead or alive, along with his crown. And here is his crown.'

Again, Purcell and Vivian said nothing.

Getachu examined the crown under the hanging lantern as though he were considering buying it. He set it down on his desk, then said, 'Let me show you something else.' He moved to the far side of the tent, and a soldier in the shadows lit a Coleman lamp.

Lying facedown on the dirt floor of the tent were three men, each naked. Getachu motioned for Purcell and Vivian to come near and they took a few steps toward the circle of light. They could see that the men's backs and buttocks were streaked with blood as though they'd been whipped.

Getachu barked something in Amharic and the men rose to their knees.

Each man had a collar around his neck – like a dog collar – with a chain attached to it. In the lamplight, Purcell could make out three battered faces, one of which was that of Prince Joshua. His long aristocratic nose was broken, and his eyes were swollen almost shut, but the prince was looking at him and Vivian.

Getachu said, 'You see, I did not shoot them or hang them as I thought I would. But if you look closely, you will see that the Gallas have castrated them.'

Purcell kept looking at the prince's face, but Vivian turned away.

Getachu reached into the pocket of his fatigues and extracted a piece of bread, which he held to the prince's swollen lips, and said, in English, 'Eat.'

The prince bit into the bread. Getachu did the same with the other two men, who Purcell thought must be what was left of the prince's staff.

Getachu dropped the bread to the ground and said, 'The Revolutionary government has executed nearly all of the royal family and many rasses, so they are becoming more rare. It is my idea to put them to some use.' He further explained, 'These men are now my servants, and they attend to my personal needs. When I am sick of looking at them – which will be soon – they will become the eunuchs assigned to the tent of the women who are their loyal subjects.' He added, 'These men will also give pleasure to my soldiers who enjoy something different.'

Vivian had turned her back to the scene, but Purcell continued to look at Prince Joshua, whose head was now bowed.

Getachu said to the prince, 'Is this not better than death?'

The prince nodded his head.

Getachu again barked something in Amharic and the three men dropped to their hands and knees. Getachu produced a riding crop from the deep cargo pocket of his pants and moved behind the men. He said, 'Colonel Gann's riding crop.' He swung the leather crop across the prince's buttocks and the man yelled out in pain. The soldier holding the lamp laughed.

Getachu delivered a blow to each of the other two men, who also cried out, causing the soldier to laugh louder.

Getachu put the crop away and said, 'Much better than hanging or shooting. Better for me.' He came around to the front of the men and made an exaggerated bow, saying to Prince Joshua, 'Forgive me, Ras. I am just a simple peasant who does not know how to show proper respect to my master.'

The soldier again laughed.

Getachu turned to Purcell and Vivian. 'That will be all.'

Purcell took Vivian's arm and they passed through the curtain and out of the tent. Vivian was shaking and Purcell put his arm around her.

As they walked toward the hospital tent, she said in a breaking voice, 'Those poor men ... Frank ... promise me ...'

'That will not happen to us.'

'He's insane ... sadistic ...'

'Yes.' And he was history, getting its revenge. Purcell said, 'But he's not stupid. He knows what he can get away with and what he can't get away with.'

Neither of them believed that, but it was all they had at the moment. Purcell thought about their ill-advised decision to leave the relative safety of the capital to find General Getachu. Henry Mercado had miscalculated the situation, and ironically Mercado had half believed the good press that General Getachu was getting in the English- and Italian-language newspapers in Addis. Purcell was angry at Mercado, and angry at himself, but anger wasn't going to get them out of here. They needed to work on Getachu. A little flattery, a little bluster, and a lot of luck.

Vivian, however, had another thought and she said in a barely audible voice, 'We will get out of here because we are supposed to find the black monastery and the Grail.' She asked him, 'Do you believe that?'

'No. But you do. And I'm sure Henry does.'

'The signs are all there, Frank.'

'Right.' The signs all said Dead End. But he recalled that Henry had said that faith had kept him alive in the Gulag, so he said to Vivian, to keep her spirits up, 'You may be right.'

She took his arm and they moved quickly toward the hospital tent.

CHAPTER 10

Purcell and Vivian entered the long hospital tent, which was badly lit by candles and oil lamps. The air was filled with the stench of blood and excrement, and with the moans and cries of the sick and wounded. A bright Coleman lamp hung in the rear, and Purcell could see three men with surgical masks standing around a table, attending to a patient.

Purcell took Vivian's arm and they picked their way between the rows of bandaged men who lay naked on dark blankets. Huge flies landed on their faces and Vivian covered her mouth and nose with her hand as she walked, her head and eyes darting around the darkness, looking for Mercado and Gann.

Doctor Mato spotted them and pulled off his surgical mask, and he and Vivian exchanged a few sentences in Italian, then Dr Mato returned to his patient.

Vivian said to Purcell, 'Henry and Colonel Gann were taken away as soon as Doctor Mato pronounced them well enough to be moved. They are under arrest.'

'We know that. Where were they taken?'

'He says there is a campo ... parata militare – a parade ground where prisoners are kept. Due east about five hundred meters.'

Purcell took her arm and led her quickly out of the tent.

A nearly full moon was rising over the eastern hills, and the quiet camp was bathed in an eerie silver glow. Red sparks rose from a hundred campfires, and the air was heavy with the smell of burning straw and dried dung.

They headed east, avoiding the clusters of men around the fires, and avoiding the scattered tents as they tried to maintain their heading across the sprawling camp. In the dark, in their *shammas*, they attracted no attention.

No military camp, thought Purcell, was complete without a stockade where an army's misfits and criminals were held to await trial and punishment, and he scanned the moonlit camp for a structure in a field that could serve as a stockade, but he didn't see anything more substantial than canvas tents.

They continued on, and Purcell spotted the other thing that was a necessity in many military camps; the thing that Getachu had mentioned to Vivian. A long line of soldiers stood smoking and joking in front of a large tent, waiting their turn.

Vivian asked, 'What's going on there?'

Purcell did not reply, and Vivian said, 'Oh . . .'

They moved on.

Vivian was becoming concerned, and she said, 'I think we missed it. Let's ask—'

'Let's not.'

They continued on and ahead was a large sunken field, which formed a natural amphitheater. At the end of the field, Purcell saw a raised wooden platform, and he realized that this was the parade ground and the muster area where General Getachu and his officers could address their troops.

In front of the platform Purcell also saw a line of poles driven into the ground, which he recognized from too many other third world military camps as whipping posts, or tethering posts where soldiers were chained for punishment and humiliation in front of their comrades. He saw a movement near one of the posts and said, 'There.'

They ran toward the posts, and as they got closer they could see three men with their arms over their heads, hanging by their wrists.

Purcell saw that Mercado and Gann were still wearing the clothes he'd last seen them in, but they were barefoot. The third man, a naked and unconscious Ethiopian, hung between Gann and Mercado.

Vivian ran up to Mercado and threw her arms around his chest. He, too, seemed unconscious – or dead – but then Purcell saw his chest heave. Vivian sobbed, 'Henry ... wake up ...' She shouted, 'Henry!'

He opened his eyes and looked at her. She stood on her toes and kissed his cheeks.

Purcell saw that the three men wore wrist shackles connected to chains that hung from iron rings embedded in the posts. Their feet touched the ground so they could stand until their knees buckled from fatigue or unconsciousness.

Purcell looked at the Ethiopian in the bright moonlight and saw that the man's face was puffy and blistered, and his dark skin showed the result of a whipping.

Mercado was fully awake now and standing straight up as Vivian put her face into his chest and sobbed as she squeezed him in her arms.

Purcell moved over to Gann, who was awake and alert, and

Gann said to him, 'I'm very glad to see you and to see that you and Miss Smith are well and free.'

Purcell found he was slightly embarrassed by their relative fortunes. But that could change quickly. He did not want to give false hope to a man hanging by chains who was condemned to death, but he said, 'I've spoken to Getachu and there is a chance—'

'Getachu plays with his intended victims. Save your breath.'

Purcell changed the subject and asked, 'Is there anything I can get you?'

'We were fed by Doctor Mato and made well enough to hang here until dawn.' He added, 'I will be able to walk to my own execution.'

Purcell didn't respond.

Colonel Gann continued, 'Just see if you can convince Getachu to make it quick and clean with a firing squad.'

'He said he respects you as a soldier.'

'I can't say the same for him. But I'll take him at his word and expect a proper firing squad.'

Purcell did not reply, but he nodded, then said, 'We'll stay with you through the night.'

'Good. Plenty of empty poles, old boy.'

Purcell smiled at the gallows humor despite the circumstances. He looked up at the shackles and saw they were held by a padlock, as were the chains on the iron ring. If he could find something to cut the locks or the chains, he could free Gann and Mercado and they could all make a run for it.

Gann saw what Purcell was looking at and said, 'There hasn't been a single guard by here, but if you look to your right, you'll see a watchtower a few hundred meters' distance.'

'Okay ... maybe after the moon sets.' Purcell considered telling Colonel Gann that his old boss, Prince Joshua, had been captured and was no longer a prince or a man. But that wasn't news that Colonel Gann would find helpful or hopeful. He said to Gann, 'I'll be right back.'

'I'll be here.'

Purcell walked past the Ethiopian, who was still unconscious, and came up beside Vivian, who was murmuring to Mercado and caressing his chest and hair.

He stared at Mercado and they made eye contact. Finally Mercado took a deep breath and said, 'Sorry about all this.'

'It's been interesting, Henry.'

'Good story if you can file it.'

'Right.'

Mercado said to Vivian, 'Go see Colonel Gann. He's feeling left out.'

She hesitated, then moved past the Ethiopian, but then came back and looked at him. She put her hand on his face and his chest and said, 'He's dying.'

Purcell looked at the three men hanging from the posts. In the morning, Getachu would muster his troops so they could see what happens to people who annoy the general. If he was insane, which he was, he would harangue the troops and threaten them with the same punishment if they stepped out of line. But if he was an accomplished sadist, he would speak to them about their victory, or some other matter, without explaining the three men hanging there. The soldiers could draw their own conclusions.

It also occurred to Purcell that he and Vivian might be paraded out at first muster and also chained to the poles. Or ... Vivian could be taken to the tent. Recalling the prince's fate, he also knew that he, Mercado, and Gann could be serving time in that tent.

It was not a good thing to be at the mercy of an omnipotent psychopath who was probably also a sexual sadist. He realized he had to do something while he could. But what? Escape was still possible. But could he leave Henry and Colonel Gann? And should he take Vivian?

Mercado said, 'My fault, really. Shouldn't have left Addis.'

'Seemed like a good idea at the time.'

'Shouldn't have gone to sleep. Gann asked if I could stay awake while he caught a few winks ... I said, "Get some rest, old man," and next thing I know, we're surrounded by soldiers and a donkey.'

'Mule.'

'Whatever. And now we're all guilty by association.'

'Henry, we are guilty of nothing except being stupid enough to come here expecting to be treated as accredited journalists.'

'Well ... it may have gone better if we hadn't teamed up with Colonel Gann.'

Purcell thought that Colonel Gann had probably saved them all from the Gallas, but Henry needed to share the blame.

Mercado sensed that Purcell was not sympathetic to his interpretation of their predicament, so he said, 'Fate. Fate is what brought us here. There is a reason for this ...'

'Let me know when you find out.'

Mercado continued, 'When Doctor Mato told me that you and Vivian were here and well, I knew that there was a higher power watching over us.'

'That thought never once crossed my mind, Henry.'

'You need to have faith, Frank. Faith will see us through this.'

Purcell was tempted to point out that he of little faith was not hanging from the pole, but instead he said, 'Vivian and I saw Getachu.'

Mercado did not respond.

Purcell continued, 'He's basically held a court-martial in his head and condemned Gann to death.'

Again, Mercado didn't respond, and Purcell looked at him to see if he was conscious. He was, and he was staring at Purcell waiting for news of his own fate. Purcell said, 'You, I, and Vivian are to be court-martialed in the morning.' He added, to ease Mercado's anxiety, 'But maybe not.'

Mercado had no response, so Purcell related his and Vivian's meeting with Getachu, trying to sound optimistic, but also realistic, though he didn't mention Getachu's thinly veiled threat to put Vivian in the camp bordello. Henry had enough on his mind. Purcell concluded, 'Getachu may be waiting to hear from his bosses. Or he may have something else in mind for us that he's not saying.'

Mercado did not respond immediately, then said, 'We're more useful to him alive than dead.'

'Unfortunately, that may be true.'

'Or the Provisional government will just order him to release us. In fact, I'm sure they will.' He added, 'General Andom and I have a good relationship.'

'Good. I hope General Andom and General Getachu have as good a relationship.'

Mercado did not reply.

Purcell asked, 'Did Vivian tell you that the Gallas captured Prince Joshua and two of his staff and turned them over to Getachu?'

'No . . . God take pity on them.'

'God is on holiday this week, Henry. In the meantime, I'll do what I can for all of us as long as I'm not hanging on the next pole.'

'I know you will, Frank. If you can keep talking to Getachu—'

'But I have to tell you, Henry, I may decide to bust out of here. Without Vivian. If I can get to Gondar, I may be able to get a flight to Addis and get to the American, Swiss, or British embassy, and get you all sprung.' He looked at Mercado and asked, 'Are you all right with that?'

Mercado seemed to be thinking, then replied, 'You'll never make it, Frank.'

'Worth a try.'

'You have no money, no credentials, no . . . no shoes for God's sake.'

'I'll try to do what Gann was going to do – find some friendly Royalists.'

'They can't even help themselves. They're finished. Hunted down like dogs.' He said, 'You need to stay here. To help us all here.'

'I'll leave you here in God's hands.'

Vivian returned and embraced Mercado, saying to Purcell, 'We need to get them some water, Frank.'

'All right. Stay here.'

He headed up the slope of the amphitheater, got his bearings, and walked west toward the hospital tent – the only oasis of humanity in this desert of death. Though to be less cynical, probably any man here would offer water, as the soldiers did at the outpost. These were not bad people, but war, as he'd seen too many times, in too many places, changes people.

Whenever he started to believe in humanity, he thought of the Khmer Rouge who murdered millions of their own people. And now he'd made the acquaintance of the Gallas, who were a barbaric throwback to the dark side of humanity. In fact, he admitted, his chances of making it to Gondar and Addis were nil.

Faith, said Henry Mercado. *A higher power is watching over us. There is a reason for all this.* Well, he thought, it better be a very good reason. And, he supposed, Henry, and also Vivian, thought the reason had to do with them coming upon Father Armano, which Purcell thought was pure chance, but which Henry and Vivian believed was divinely ordained. In any case, they'd see in the morning who was right.

He reached the hospital tent and helped himself to two canteens of water that he found among what was called the muddied and bloodied – the discarded uniforms and field gear of the dead and wounded.

He looked, too, for a knife or bayonet, or anything else that could be useful, but the pile had been picked over.

Purcell wrapped the canteens in a fatigue shirt and made his way back.

He wasn't quite sure why Getachu had allowed him and Vivian to wander around freely, but his experience with sadistic despots had always had an element of inconsistency – random acts of cruelty, tempered with expansive acts of kindness. The despot wants to be feared, but also loved for his mercy. The despot wants to be like God.

Purcell got back to the parade ground and handed a canteen to Vivian, who held it to Mercado's lips.

Purcell moved to the Ethiopian, but it appeared that the man was dead. Purcell put his hand on the man's chest, then put his ear to his still heart.

Gann, on the next pole, called out, 'Saw him go through his death throes.'

Purcell moved to Gann and held the canteen to his lips while he drank.

Gann said, 'Save some of that.'

Purcell assured him, 'This will all be over in the morning.'

'Indeed.'

There wasn't much else to say, so Purcell moved toward Vivian, who was washing Mercado's face with the water.

Purcell stood there, watching this display of womanly compassion and grief. *Pietà.* Which he knew in Italian meant both pity and piety. The dying son or husband, the warrior or father, comforted in the hour of death by the mother or wife, the pious woman, filled with love and pity. We should all be so fortunate, Purcell thought, to die like that.

He said to Vivian and to Mercado, 'I'm going to go up on that platform and get some sleep.' He assured Mercado, 'I'm here if you need anything.' He gave Gann the same assurance, then climbed the three steps onto the crudely built platform. The moon was overhead now and illuminated the large, empty field.

He counted ten poles running in front of the platform. Gann was to his left, standing straight, and the Ethiopian was also to his left, hanging dead by his wrists. He wondered what the man had done to suffer a death like that. Probably not much. To his immediate front was Henry Mercado, barely ten feet away, and he could hear Vivian speaking softly to him as she stroked his face. Mercado said something now and then, but Purcell couldn't hear the words, and in any case he didn't want to eavesdrop on their private moment – if one could call this place of public punishment and death private. He did hope, however, that Mercado was man enough, like Gann, to suffer in dignity, and that his words to his lover were as comforting as hers to him.

Purcell spread the shirt from the hospital on the logs that made up the floor of the platform and lay down. He was fatigued beyond sleep and found he couldn't put his mind to rest.

At some point, maybe fifteen minutes later, Vivian joined him and without a word lay down beside him, though the platform was large.

He shifted to his left and said to her, 'Lie on this shirt.'

She moved onto the shirt and lay on her back, staring at the sky.

A wind came down from the surrounding mountains, and she said, 'I'm cold. Move closer to me.'

He moved closer to her, and she rolled on her side, facing him, and he did the same, and they wrapped their bare legs and arms around each other and drew closer for warmth.

He could feel her heart beating, and her breathing, and her breasts pressing against him. Their *shammas* had ridden up to their thighs, and she rubbed her legs and feet over his, then rolled on her back with him on top.

He hesitated, then kissed her, and she threw her arms around his neck and held her lips against his.

He pulled both their *shammas* up to their waists and entered her without resistance. She raised her legs, then crossed them over his buttocks and pulled him down farther as he thrust deeper into her.

Her body began to tremble, then stiffened, and suddenly went loose as she let out a long moan. He came inside her and they lay still, breathing heavily into the cool night air.

'My God . . .' Tears ran down her cheeks.

They lay on their backs, side by side, holding hands, staring up at the starry sky.

They hadn't spoken a word, and Purcell thought there was nothing to say, but finally he said, 'Try to get some sleep.'

'I need to check on Henry. And Colonel Gann.'

He sat up. 'I can do that.'

She stood, took the canteen, and said, 'Be right back.'

Purcell stood as she descended the steps, and he watched her as she moved first toward Gann.

The moon was in the west now and it cast moonshadows down the line of poles. Purcell realized that Mercado had walked himself around his pole and was now facing the platform.

Vivian checked on Gann, then moved slowly toward Mercado, who was not looking at her but looking up at him.

Was it possible, he wondered, that Mercado had seen – or heard – what happened?

Vivian approached Mercado and he seemed to notice her for the first time.

As she lifted the canteen to his lips and touched his face, he said in a surprisingly strong voice, 'Get away from me.'

She spoke to him softly, but he shook his head and wouldn't drink from the canteen. She tried again, but again he said, 'Get *away* from me.'

Finally, she turned and moved back to the platform, and

Purcell noticed that she was walking slowly, with her head down.

He glanced at Mercado, who was looking at him again, and they made eye contact in the bright moonlight.

Purcell turned and watched Vivian come up the steps. She threw the canteen on the floor, then lay down on the shirt and stared up at the sky.

Purcell knelt a few feet from her and said, 'Sorry.'

She didn't reply.

He put ten feet between them and lay on his back.

He heard her say, 'Not your fault.'

No, he thought, it certainly was not. He said, 'Get some sleep. We're going to have a long day.'

'We'll all be dead tomorrow. Then none of this matters.'

'We will be in Addis tomorrow.'

'I think not.' She asked him, 'Will you make love to me again?'

'No ... not here. In Addis.'

'If we get out of here, this won't happen again.'

He asked, 'Will you be with Henry?'

'Maybe ... he'll get over it.'

'Good. We'll all get over it.'

'We will.' She said, 'Good night.'

'Night.'

He looked up at the starry African sky. Beautiful, he thought. So very beautiful up there.

He closed his eyes, and as he was drifting into sleep he heard her sobbing silently. He wanted to comfort her, but he couldn't, and he fell into a deep sleep, and dreamt of Vivian naked in the water, and of Mercado shouting her name.

CHAPTER 11

At dawn, Purcell watched as a squad of soldiers marched through the ground mist toward the three men hanging from the posts.

It was too early for a firing squad, he thought – the troops had not yet arrived to witness the execution.

Purcell let Vivian sleep and he came down from the platform.

The ten soldiers didn't seem bothered by his appearance – they had no orders regarding him, and they didn't know if he was the general's guest or his next victim, so they ignored him.

Purcell saw that Mercado was half awake, watching the soldiers approach. Purcell asked him, 'How are you doing?'

He looked at Purcell but did not reply.

Purcell held the canteen to Mercado's lips, and he drank, but then spit the water at Purcell.

Purcell said to him, 'You were delirious last night.'

'Get out of my sight.'

In fact, Purcell thought, Henry was having a recurring nightmare about Vivian that had come true.

The soldiers were now unshackling Gann, who was able to stand on his own, then they moved to Mercado, leaving the dead Ethiopian hanging for the troops to see at the morning muster.

Purcell went over to Gann, who was rubbing his raw wrists, and handed him the canteen. Gann finished the last few ounces, then asked, 'How is Mercado?'

'Seems okay.'

'He had a bad night.'

Purcell reminded Gann, 'Neither of you would be hanging here if he'd stayed awake on the mountain.'

'Don't blame him. I should have stayed awake.'

Purcell didn't reply, and Gann said, 'He was shouting at God all night.'

Again, Purcell did not reply, but he'd heard Henry shouting at God, and also cursing him and Vivian, and Gann had heard that too, and probably surmised what and who Henry was angry at. But that was the least of their problems.

Gann asked, 'Where is Miss Smith?'

'Sleeping.' He asked Gann, 'What's happening?'

'Don't know, old boy. But it's either something very good, or very bad.'

'I'll settle for anything in between.'

'That doesn't happen here.' He asked Purcell, 'Why didn't you make a run for it last night?'

'I fell asleep.'

Purcell noticed now in the dawn light that the post from which Gann had hung was splintered and pocked with holes that could only have been made by bullets.

Gann, too, noticed and said, 'Well, the good news is that they do execute people by firing squad.' He nodded toward the dead Ethiopian. 'Not like that poor bugger.'

Purcell didn't want to get into that conversation, so he returned to Gann's other subject and said, 'If I did make a run for it, where would I go?'

Gann replied, 'Well, first, I'd advise you to go alone. You don't need a photographer.'

Purcell did not reply, but he didn't want to leave Vivian here.

He continued, 'About ten kilometers south and east of the Italian spa is a Falasha village. Ethiopian Jews. They'll take you in and you'll be safe there.'

'How do you know?'

'I know Ethiopia, old boy. That's where I was going to head. They're Royalists.'

Recalling what Mercado had said, Purcell pointed out, 'The Royalists are being hunted down.'

'The Falashas are immune for the moment.'

'Why?'

'It's rather complex. The Falashas trace their ancestry to the time of Solomon and Sheba, and they are revered by some as a link to the Solomonic past, as is the emperor.'

'And we know what happened to him.'

'Yes, but the Ethiopians are a superstitious lot, and they believe if you harm a Falasha you have angered God – the common God of Christians, Jews, and Muslims.'

'Works for the Falashas.'

'For now. The name of this village is Shoan.' He suggested, 'If you're not being shot or chained up today, you should give it a try tonight.'

'I was hoping for a helicopter ride to Addis this morning.'

'And I hope you are having a whiskey for me tonight in Addis. But you should have an alternate plan.'

'Right.'

'And if you should ever find yourself in Shoan, tonight or some other time, they will know a thing or two about the black monastery.' He looked at Purcell. 'If you are still interested in that.'

Purcell had the feeling he'd stepped into Tolkien's Middle-Earth. The mysterious dying priest, the surreal Roman ruin, the fortress city of Gondar, the good Prince Joshua, the evil General Getachu, Sir Edmund Gann, and the black monastery. And the Holy Grail, of course. And now the village of the Falashas. None of this seemed possible or real – but it was. Except for the Grail.

Purcell looked at Gann. 'Thanks.' He felt he needed to tell Gann about his former employer, Prince Joshua, so he did, sparing no detail.

Gann listened without comment, and Purcell could see he was more angry than he was frightened that this could also be his fate. When Purcell had finished, Gann said, 'Bloody bastard.'

'He's insane.'

'Yes, but I'm sure you can convince him that a British soldier rates a firing squad, or at least a quick bullet in the head.'

'I'll try to do better than that.' He reminded Gann, and himself, 'I'm not sure what Getachu has planned for any of us.'

'He's treading lightly with you and Miss Smith, or you'd be hanging on these posts.'

'Good thought.'

'Getachu may be insane, but he's not reckless enough to endanger his own position with the Derg.' He explained, 'They'd like nothing better than to find an excuse to summon him to Addis, and General Andom would be glad to arrest his rival and have him shot.'

'That's good.'

'Or strangled.'

'Even better.'

'The Revolution,' said Colonel Gann, 'eats its own.'

'It always does.'

'I predict that Getachu will put you and Miss Smith on a helicopter to Addis.'

'And Mercado?'

'Getachu will send him off to Addis to be dealt with at a higher level. Probably get expelled.' He added, 'They're not shooting Western reporters yet.'

'Good. Well, you seem to know these people.' He informed Colonel Gann, 'Getachu hinted that he may want you to train and advise his officers.'

'That will not happen.'

'Don't turn down that job.'

Gann did not reply, and Purcell pointed out, 'The war is almost over. You won't be helping him much.'

'I won't be helping him at all.'

'Don't be stupid.'

'I've asked a favor of you. Please do it.'

'Do it yourself.' He made eye contact with Gann and said, 'Look, Colonel, I'm trying to save your life, and you're not helping. Don't take the knight thing too seriously.'

Gann didn't reply, but he looked past Purcell and said, 'I think it's time to go.'

Purcell turned around and saw that Mercado was on his feet without help from the soldiers, and Vivian had awoken and was trying to minister to her lover, who was having none of it – which seemed to confuse the soldiers who'd missed the reason for Mercado's bad behavior toward the lady.

Purcell looked up at the dead Ethiopian, who seemed almost Christlike hanging there with his flesh torn. It occurred to Purcell that the new Ethiopia didn't look much different than the old Ethiopia.

Purcell turned to the rising sun above the eastern mountains, then to the large open field shrouded in morning mist. God did a good job with the heaven and the earth. Not so good with the people.

The squad leader formed everyone up in a line of march and barked something in Amharic, then shouted, '*Avanti!*'

Forward.

CHAPTER 12

General Getachu sat at his camp desk in his headquarters tent, speaking to an aide in Amharic and ignoring his four guests who were sitting facing him.

Mercado sat on the far right, and Vivian had taken the chair next to him, though Mercado was pointedly ignoring her. Gann had sat himself between Vivian and Purcell, and behind them was a soldier armed with an AK-47 automatic rifle.

Purcell was surprised that Getachu had included Gann in this meeting, but possibly this was a summary court-martial, with the general acting as judge and jury, and the soldier as instant executioner.

The tent was not as dark as it had been at night, and the morning sun shone through mosquito net windows, revealing a dirt floor strewn with cigarette butts. Getachu took a call on his field phone, and spoke as he signed papers for his aide. A busy executive, thought Purcell, but there's always time for fun and sport.

On that subject, Purcell saw that neither Prince Joshua nor his two officers were present, and Purcell wondered if Getachu had sent his royal highness to the women's tent.

The aide left and Getachu looked at Gann and asked, 'Do you know that your prince is here?'

Gann did not reply, and Getachu seemed angry at the insolence.

Purcell volunteered, 'I informed him.'

'Do not speak unless spoken to.' Getachu looked at Gann again, smiled, and said, 'That is what I learned in the English missionary school.' He also informed Colonel Gann, 'The prince has confessed that you and he have engaged in war crimes.'

Gann had no response.

Getachu saw that this was not productive, so he looked at Purcell and asked, 'Who gave you permission to leave the medical tent and walk through my camp?'

'We had no indication that we were under confinement.'

'This is a secure military facility.'

'As you know, we were looking for our colleagues.'

'Yes? And is Colonel Gann your colleague?'

'According to you he is.'

'Then you are all guilty by association.'

'According to you.'

Getachu was sipping water from a canteen cup and Purcell said, 'We need something to eat and drink.'

'Why should I waste food and water on people who are to be executed? But I promise you a cigarette before you are shot.' Getachu thought that was funny and he translated for the soldier, who laughed.

Getachu tapped Vivian's camera, then held up three notepads and said, 'There is enough evidence here to condemn you, Mr Purcell, and you, Miss Smith, and you, Mr Mercado, to death by firing squad.'

Purcell didn't think so, but he also knew that Getachu didn't need any evidence, except maybe to justify an execution to his superiors in Addis.

Purcell said, 'I must ask you, General, to return our personal property, including our credentials and passports, and to provide us transportation to the capital.' He reminded Getachu, 'We came here expecting to be treated as journalists, not as criminals.'

Getachu pointed out, 'I think we have had this conversation.'

'I think we need to have it again.'

General Getachu looked at Colonel Gann, then said to his other guests, 'Before we discuss your status, do you agree that this man deserves what he is to suffer?'

Purcell replied, 'No, we do not. Colonel Gann was captured in uniform and he is to be treated as a prisoner of war under the Geneva Convention, which Ethiopia has signed.'

'That was the previous government.'

Gann said to Purcell, 'Save your breath.'

'Excellent advice,' agreed Getachu.

Mercado cleared his throat and said, 'General ... if you agree to release us, we will write and sign statements of any wrongdoing that we may have engaged in. We will also write a press story praising your victory and your qualities as a leader. We also agree to have our passports held by your foreign office and to stay in Addis writing articles for the duration of this war.'

Getachu looked at Mercado. 'Well, you are offering less than Mr Purcell and Miss Smith have already offered.' He informed Mercado, 'They offered to stay here with me for the duration of the war. I was looking forward to their company.'

Vivian took a deep breath, hesitated, then said, 'General, if this is supposed to be an inquiry or a trial, it's actually a farce.' She concluded, 'You are keeping us here unlawfully and against our will, and our press offices and our embassies know where we are, and they will be making inquiries, if they haven't already. Please provide us with transportation to the capital and please return our belongings.'

Getachu stared at her for a long time, then said, 'But you look very good in the shamma.'

Vivian did not reply, but she held Getachu's stare.

Finally, he said, 'The Revolutionary Army came into possession of some interesting equipment which the Americans provided to the Royal Army. One such item was a device called a starlight scope. You know of this? A telescopic sight that allows one to see in the dark, which my sentries use in the watchtower to look for the enemy, outside and inside the camp.'

No one responded, and Getachu continued, 'So it appeared – to my sentry at least – that you, Miss Smith, and you, Mr Purcell, engaged in a behavior that did not please Mr Mercado.' He asked, 'Or did my sentry misunderstand what he saw?'

Again no one replied, and if anyone thought that Getachu had brought this up solely to amuse himself, Purcell knew otherwise.

Getachu said to Mercado, 'So perhaps you will write in your confession that you discovered that Mr Purcell and Miss Smith were spying for the Royalists.' He assured Mercado, 'You need not write that about yourself. That would condemn you to death.'

Purcell glanced at Mercado, expecting that Mercado understood that he needed to reply with a firm fuck you, but Mercado did not reply.

'Mr Mercado?'

'I ... don't know what you're talking about, General.'

'You do. And you should consider my offer.'

Again, Mercado made no reply.

Getachu glanced at his watch as though this was all taking more time than he'd allowed for it. He said, 'To my mind, you are all guilty, but as I said to Mr Purcell and Miss Smith last night, it is possible to make your punishment less severe.' He looked at Gann. 'Even you, Colonel, could be spared from death.'

'As you spared Prince Joshua?'

'I'm glad to see that Mr Purcell has told you everything, and I'm glad to see that you speak.'

'Go to hell.'

'There is no hell. And no heaven. There is no more than what you see here.'

Gann did not reply, and Getachu continued, 'They taught me otherwise in the missionary school, but I did not believe them then or now. But I do believe in the use of earthly pain to punish bad behavior, or to make a person confess to his sins.' He pulled Gann's riding crop from his pocket and said, 'Or simply to give me pleasure.' He flexed the crop.

Gann stared at Getachu and they made eye contact.

Getachu stood and said to Gann, 'So, the good headmaster beat me in that English school, and he taught me something. But not the lesson he thought. He taught me that some men can be broken with the whip, and some cannot. My spirit was not broken.'

Purcell thought Getachu's mind was broken, and he saw what was coming, so he said, 'General, we will not sit here and witness—'

Getachu slapped the crop on his desk. 'Shut up!' He said to

Gann, 'I will spare your life if you drop your pants, as I did many times, and allow me to deliver thirty blows to your bare buttocks.' He added, 'Here and now, leaning over this desk, in front of your friends.'

'I think it's you, Mikael, who needs another good beating.'

Getachu literally shook with rage, then pulled his pistol, aimed it at Gann, and shouted, 'I give you five seconds to do what I say!'

'You can give me five years and I will tell you to go to hell.'

'One—'

Purcell stood. 'Stop this.'

The soldier behind Purcell pushed him down into his chair.

'Two.'

Vivian said, 'Colonel, please. Just do what he wants … please …'

'Three.'

Mercado closed his eyes and lowered his head.

'Four.'

Gann stood and Getachu smiled. Gann turned, dropped his pants, and said, 'Kiss my arse.'

Purcell thought he'd hear the loud explosion of the gun, but there was complete silence in the room.

Finally, Getachu let out a forced laugh, then said, 'Very good, Colonel, you may sit.'

Gann pulled up his pants, but did not sit and kept his back to Getachu.

Getachu saw that Gann was not going to turn around, and he said, 'You will not provoke me into giving you an easy death.'

Gann remained standing with his back to the general, and Getachu said something to the soldier, who came around and drove the butt of his rifle into Gann's groin. Gann doubled over, and the soldier pushed him into his chair.

Getachu holstered his gun and put down the riding crop, but remained standing. 'You all understand, I hope, that I can have each of you shot as spies.'

Vivian surprised everyone, and herself, by saying, 'If that were true, you would have done it.'

Getachu looked at her and said, 'It *is* true, Miss Smith, but as we discussed, there are some men – and women – who I would rather see broken than dead.' He reminded everyone, 'And those who agree to serve the people's revolution may also be spared.'

Mercado spoke up. 'I did serve the revolution for many years, and I would be willing to serve it again with my written words—'

'Your written words are like adding your shit to a fire.'

Mercado seemed to shrink in his chair.

Getachu looked at Gann, who was obviously in extreme pain, and said, 'Colonel, if you agree to become an advisor to my army – as you did for the former prince's army – I will spare your life.'

Gann shook his head.

Getachu seemed frustrated with the man's stubbornness and said, 'I will take you to see your former employer and also his aides, who I am sure you know, and then you can decide if you wish to help the revolution or if you wish to assist the prince in his new duties.'

Gann did not reply, and Getachu said, 'Or perhaps I will turn you over to the Gallas, and wash my hands of you.'

Purcell leaned toward Gann and said softly, 'Just *say* you'll do it.'

Gann shook his head, and Purcell wondered if Getachu really wanted or needed Colonel Gann's military skills, or if he just wanted the satisfaction of seeing the Englishman — the knight — crawling to him before he killed him. Getachu had tried the carrot and the stick, and neither was working on Gann, who Purcell suspected knew Getachu's game better than anyone.

Getachu's field phone rang, he answered it, spoke briefly, then hung up and said, 'My helicopter has arrived from Gondar.' He asked, 'Would you all enjoy a ride to the capital?'

Purcell assumed there was a small catch, but the carrot sounded good. He said, 'We're ready to go.'

'So you said. But first I need some information from all of you. If you give me this information, you will be put on my helicopter and flown to the capital. If you do not give me what I am looking for, then a fate worse than death awaits you here.' He looked at Vivian and said, 'Unless, of course, you enjoy the attention of thirty or forty men a day.'

Purcell knew these were not empty threats, but everyone seemed to have become numb to Getachu's words, and Getachu sensed this as well, so he sat and lit a cigarette, then remembered to offer the pack to Purcell, who declined.

Getachu seemed deep in thought, then began, 'A company of my soldiers occupied the Italian spa, where they found empty cans of food and tire tracks.' He looked at Purcell. 'You were there?'

Purcell replied, 'We said we were.'

'Correct.' He continued, 'My men also found fresh earth which they took to be a grave, and which they dug up.' He asked his guests, 'Did you dig that grave?'

The easy answer, Purcell thought, was, *Yes, so what?* But Getachu was not asking out of idle curiosity, and a better answer might be no. Vivian, however, had taken a photograph of the grave, and her camera was sitting on Getachu's desk. Still, they could deny digging the grave, and he would have done so if it was only he and Vivian answering this psychopath's questions; but Henry, he realized, was ready to say or do anything to save himself from death or torture. Some men, like Gann, could hang from a pole all night and say, 'Kiss my arse.' Others, like Henry, cracked easy and early. But Purcell couldn't judge Mercado unless he himself had been hanging from the next pole.

'Did you dig that grave?'

Purcell replied, 'We did.'

'Who did you bury?'

'We buried who you dug up.'

'My men dug up the body of an old man, Mr Purcell. I am asking you who it was.'

'A man we found dying in the spa.'

'Why was he dying?'

'He had a stomach wound.'

'How did he get this wound?'

'I have no idea.'

'Did you not speak to him?'

Purcell thought it was time to turn this over to Henry to see what, if anything, he had to say about this, so he replied, 'The man spoke Italian and I do not.'

Getachu looked at Mercado. 'Doctor Mato informs me that you speak Italian.'

Mercado nodded.

'Did you speak to this dying man?'

'I ... I did ... but, he died before I could ... find out much about him.'

Purcell was not completely surprised that Mercado was keeping a secret from Getachu, because to Mercado it was a secret worth keeping.

Getachu looked long at Mercado. 'If you are lying to me, I will find out and then we have no agreement, Mr Mercado. And then ... well, you have sealed your fate.'

Mercado kept eye contact with Getachu. 'The man died without telling us who he was.'

Getachu kept staring at him, then shifted his attention to Vivian. 'And Doctor Mato informs me that you speak Italian.'

'I do.'

'And what did this dying man say to you?'

Purcell wondered if Vivian would take this opportunity to repay Mercado for not firmly defending her against Getachu's charges of spying. But women, Purcell had learned, are loyal to men who don't deserve loyalty. On the other hand, it was Vivian who'd been disloyal first, and probably she was feeling as guilty as Henry was feeling angry. Sex has consequences beyond the act.

'Miss Smith?'

Vivian replied, 'The man said nothing more to me than he said to Mr Mercado.'

'How convenient. Well, let me tell you who I think this old man was. It could only have been Father Armano.' He looked at his guests. 'As I'm sure he told you.'

No one replied, and Getachu continued, 'Two nights ago, one of my artillery batteries bombarded the nearby fortress of Ras Theodore, who is of the family of my present guest, Joshua.

Within this fortress was this Father Armano, who had been imprisoned there since the days of the Italian war.' He asked his guests, 'Do you know this story?'

Vivian and Mercado shook their heads.

Getachu went on, 'The bombardment attracted the attention of the Gallas, as it always does, and they descended on the fortress and massacred the Royalist survivors, though some managed to flee into the jungle. But my infantry company captured some of these men and brought them here. In fact, you may have seen these soldiers of Ras Theodore hanging outside this tent alongside the soldiers of Ras Joshua.'

Getachu lit another cigarette, sipped some water, then continued. 'But before they were brought here, they were brought back to their fortress. Why? To assist my men in determining the fate of Father Armano – and as they discovered, the prison cell of this priest was empty, and the captured soldiers could not identify a body as that of the priest. But they did find a Bible, in Italian, on the floor of his cell, with a hole in it – perhaps a bullet hole. So it is my assumption that the wounded man you discovered was Father Armano.' He looked at his guests closely, then asked Mercado directly, 'Why do you think this priest who you came upon was so important?'

Mercado replied, 'I don't know.'

'Then I will tell you. Well, perhaps I won't. You seem to have no information about this man or this matter, so we have nothing to discuss, and you have nothing to trade for your freedom or your lives.'

Purcell said, 'I hope you had the decency to rebury the old man.'

154

'I have no idea if he was reburied, and I don't care if the jackals eat his body. But it is interesting that you took the time and effort to give an unknown man a burial.'

'Interesting to you. Common decency to us.'

'I don't like your attitude of moral superiority, Mr Purcell. I had enough of that in school.'

'Apparently not.'

'Don't provoke me.'

'We have no information for you, General. May we leave?'

Getachu seemed not to hear him, and he sat back in his chair and said, 'I will be open with you, and perhaps you will do the same for me.' He looked at each of them, then said, 'The black monastery. You know of this place. What is in it, I do not know, nor do I know its exact location. But Father Armano knew its location and he may have told you something of this.' He looked at Purcell, then Vivian, then Mercado, and said, 'I hope for your sake that he did.'

Mercado said, 'He did not.'

'I will ask you again later. But for now, I will explain to you my interest in the black monastery.' He leaned forward and said, 'The Provisional Revolutionary government is interested in selling precious objects to museums and churches outside the country. The government is selling most of the emperor's trinkets now. We need the money for food and medicine for the people. But when a very old regime ends, some people become upset. Nostalgic. Some people are fond of kings and emperors and aristocrats on horses — as long as it's not in their own country. You understand? The end of the empire is a historical necessity. And gold and jewels are worthless in a modern state. We need capital. And we are acquiring it in the only way we can. The traditional way of revolutionary governments. We rob the rich of their baubles. A few suffer. Many gain. The churches, especially, are better off without their gold. They can concentrate more on God and saving souls without the worry of keeping their property intact. Everyone benefits. So in exchange for any information you might have on the location of this monastery – and what is in it – I will allow you all to return to the capital, including Colonel Gann, who will be dealt with at a higher level, and therefore dealt with less severely than I would here at the front.' He added, 'You all have my word on that.'

Purcell wondered if Getachu knew specifically about the so-called Holy Grail, or if he was just interested in looting another Coptic monastery. It made no difference to Purcell, but it did to Henry Mercado. Henry wanted to get out of here and go look for the monastery and the Grail; Henry wanted to have his cake and eat it too. But he couldn't.

Getachu suggested, 'Perhaps you would like a private moment to discuss this.'

Purcell knew, and he hoped Henry and Vivian also knew that even if they could take Getachu at his word, what little they knew was not enough to get them out of here. But it *was* enough to keep them as Getachu's guests for a long time – just as Father Armano had been a guest of Ethiopia for a very long time. Or Getachu would just do away with them if Henry decided to clarify his lie.

'Mr Mercado?'

Mercado said, 'We told you all we know about this man. He was dying, and in pain, and he said almost nothing except to ask for water.'

'I know you are lying.'

Purcell didn't think that Mercado was doing a good job of putting this to rest, so he pointed out, 'Why would we lie about something that has no meaning to us?'

'I told you. Some people are fond of the old regime and the old church, which are one.'

'I don't care about either.' Purcell added, 'And if this old man did speak to us, and if he was Father Armano, what do you think he would tell us? The location of the monastery? I don't understand how he would know that. You said he was in this fortress for almost forty years. I'm not understanding what you think we should know.'

Getachu seemed to have a lucid moment, and he nodded. 'You make a good point. In fact, you have nothing to give me.' He added, 'And I have nothing to give you.'

'Except,' Purcell suggested, 'our belongings, and a ride to Addis.' He added, 'Our embassies and our offices are awaiting word from us.'

'Then they will have a long wait.' Getachu informed everyone, 'This proceeding is finished. I will consider my judgment. You remain under arrest.' He said something to the soldier, who escorted them out into the bright sunlight where a squad of soldiers waited with leg shackles.

CHAPTER 13

They were marched to a deep ravine, and Purcell saw that there was fresh earth at the bottom, and shovels, and it was obvious that this was a mass grave, and perhaps a place of execution. They were ordered to climb into the ravine, and it seemed to Purcell that Getachu's judgment had traveled faster than they had. But to be more optimistic, he didn't think that Getachu was through with them yet.

At the bottom of the ravine, they could smell the buried corpses. Purcell and Gann looked up at the soldiers, to see if these men were their executioners, but the soldiers were sitting at the edge of the ravine smoking and talking.

Gann said to Purcell, 'Sloppy discipline.'

'You should have taken the job.'

'They're a hopeless lot.'

'Right.' But they won.

No one had anything else to say, and Purcell was sure that each of them was thinking about what had transpired in Getachu's office. It had been a very unpleasant experience, he thought, but it could have gone worse, though not better. In any case, everyone seemed relieved that it was over, even if it wasn't.

Finally, Gann said, 'The man's a bloody lunatic.'

No one argued with that, and Gann added, 'Ungrateful bastard. Got a decent education from the good Church of England missionaries, and he complains about a few strokes on his arse. Did him more good than harm, I'm sure.'

Purcell smiled despite the fact that little Mikael had grown up fucked up and was looking for payback. And he didn't have to look too far.

Vivian admitted, 'I was very frightened.'

Purcell wanted to tell her she did fine, but that was Henry's job, though Henry wasn't speaking to her. Mercado, in fact, was glancing nervously up at the soldiers with the automatic rifles.

Gann noticed Mercado's anxiety and assured him, 'We're not getting off that easily, Mr Mercado.'

Mercado did not reply.

Vivian looked at Purcell and said, 'You gave me courage, Frank.'

He didn't reply.

Vivian said to Gann, 'You're very brave.'

'Thank you, but you were seeing more anger than bravery.' He added, 'Men like that are taking over the world.'

That might be true, Purcell thought. He'd seen the Getachus of Southeast Asia, and they seemed to be springing up everywhere. Or maybe they'd been around since the beginning of time. He'd written about these men and about their so-called ideologies without comment or judgment. He reported. Maybe, he thought, if he got out of here, he should start being more judgmental. But then he'd sound like Henry Mercado.

Purcell looked at Mercado, who was sitting on a pile of fresh earth, staring off into space, unaware that there was probably a rotting corpse under his ass. No one had told Henry how brave

159

he'd been. Maybe because he hadn't been. But he *had* lied, boldly and recklessly, to Getachu about Father Armano. And Vivian had loyally backed him up on that lie. It was a good lie and the right lie, but Purcell knew that Mercado had lied for the wrong reason. So, this being the private moment that Getachu had offered them, he said to Mercado, 'You put us in some jeopardy, Henry, by lying about the priest.'

Clearly, Henry Mercado had nothing to say to Frank Purcell, but he replied for everyone's benefit, 'Getachu has no way to discover the truth.'

'Well, he does if he hangs us all from a post for a few days.'

Mercado said impatiently, 'It may have occurred to you that even if I told him what little we knew, he wouldn't have released us.'

'Right. In fact we'd be here forever. But you're not answering my question, Henry. *Why* did you risk lying to him about Father Armano and the black monastery?'

Mercado replied sharply, 'You know damned well why.'

'I do, but if we do get out of here, none of us should be coming back to find the black monastery.'

Mercado glanced at Gann and said to Purcell, 'I don't know if we're getting out of here or if I'm ever coming back, but I don't want *them* to find it.'

Henry Mercado, Purcell knew, was comforted by thinking he was protecting the Holy Grail from the Antichrist, or whatever, and he could go to his martyrdom happy in the knowledge that when he met Jesus he could say, 'I saved your cup.'

Colonel Gann could feel the tension between the two men, and he knew the cause of it, which was a very old story; one chap had cuckolded the other, and to make matters worse, the lady in question was not declaring herself for one or the other. Awkward, he thought, and though he was sure he had far greater issues to worry about, it made him uncomfortable nonetheless.

To clear the air on at least one thing, however, Gann said, 'As I've acknowledged to Mr Purcell, I know about the black monastery, and though it's well hidden in the jungle, Getachu will eventually find it. You can be sure of that.'

No one responded, and Gann continued, 'As you may also have heard, perhaps from this Father Armano, there is a legend that this monastery is the resting place of the Holy Grail.'

Again, no one responded, and Gann went on, 'Can't say I believe in all that, but I can assure you that whenever the revolutionary bastards here show up at a church or monastery, the priests and monks make off with their earthly treasures.'

Purcell figured as much. There were two things the churches were good at: acquiring gold and keeping gold. Half the world's priceless religious objects had been on the lam at one time or another. And there was no reason to think that this would be any different when the Ethiopian revolutionaries got close to the black monastery. Same if Henry Mercado or Vivian got close. Poof! The Grail disappears again.

Purcell said to Mercado, 'We *are* getting out of here, and I can guarantee you I'm never coming back. My advice to you and to Vivian is to forget you ever met Father Armano or ever heard of the black monastery. This is not a good thing to know about.'

Mercado did not reply.

Purcell added, 'God is not telling you to find the Holy Grail, Henry. He is telling you to go home.'

'And I'm telling you to mind your own business.'

Purcell changed the subject to something more immediate and asked Gann, 'Do you think Getachu is at all concerned about overstepping his authority?'

'That's the question, isn't it? Well, I can tell you that he can't overstep his power, which is absolute here, as you see. But he *can* overstep his authority and get on the wrong side of the Derg and his rival, General Andom. Not that those two care about us, or about international law, but Andom has to decide if it would be good for him or bad for him if Getachu kills us.'

Vivian asked, 'Do we think anyone outside of the Revolutionary government even knows we're here?'

Mercado reminded everyone, 'Our press offices know we were heading this way, and we mentioned to some of our colleagues that we had a safe-conduct pass to make contact with General Getachu.'

Which, Purcell thought, meant very little. Basically, they were all freelancers, which worked well except when they got in trouble or went missing. Possibly, if they didn't show up in the Hilton bar in a week or so, someone might think to contact their respective embassies if they could remember their drinking buddies' nationalities.

As for himself, Purcell was aware that the American embassy in Addis was barely open, and not on good terms with the new government. If he wasn't wearing leg shackles, he'd have kicked himself in the ass for making this trip.

And as for Mercado with his UK passport, and Vivian with her Swiss passport, any requests for information made by their respective embassies to the Ethiopian government would be met by indifference on a good day, and hostility and lies on most days.

Bottom line here, Purcell thought, there was no outside help on the way. Mercado should know that, but maybe Vivian should not.

The sun was higher and hotter now, and the temperature at the bottom of the ravine had to be over a hundred degrees. Purcell noticed that most of Vivian's white ointment was gone, and her face and arms were getting redder. He called up to the soldiers at the top of the ravine, '*Weha!*'

They looked down at him, then one of them unhooked a canteen from his belt and threw it to him.

He gave the canteen to Vivian, and she drank, but then seemed uncertain who to pass it to. Old lover? New lover? She gave it to Gann. He drank and passed it to Mercado, who drank and held it out for Purcell to take.

Purcell finished the last few ounces, then suggested to Mercado, 'Give Vivian your shirt for her head.'

Mercado seemed angry at being told by Purcell to be a gentleman, and he snapped, 'Give her your own shirt.'

Purcell would have, if he'd had a shirt, but he had a *shamma*, and no underwear, and he didn't want to bring that up. He stared at Mercado, who started to unbutton his khaki shirt.

But Gann had already taken off his uniform shirt and handed it to Vivian, who said, 'Thank you,' and draped it over her head.

Purcell understood Mercado's anger, but it amazed him that the man could hold on to it while he was contemplating a firing squad or worse. But on second thought, men are men. He thought, too, that if he had a chance to do last night over, he'd do the same thing, but twice. No regrets. He wondered if he could convince Mercado that what happened last night was God's will.

He looked at Vivian sitting at the side of the ravine, closer to Mercado than to him. They made eye contact, and she held it, then looked away.

He wondered what she was thinking or feeling. Probably he'd never know, and that was just as well.

Another group of soldiers appeared at the top of the ravine, and it was obvious that something was going to happen, and probably not anything good.

Vivian suddenly moved closer to Mercado and grabbed his arm. 'Henry ...'

Mercado appeared more aware of the soldiers, thought Purcell, than of Vivian's hold on him. Purcell could hear her say softly, 'I love you ... please forgive me.'

Mercado seemed to notice her for the first time, and he hesitated, then asked, 'Are you truly sorry?'

'I am.'

'Then I will forgive you.'

She put her arms around him and buried her face in his chest.

Purcell assumed that Mercado's absolution didn't include him, even if he asked for it, but he didn't think he needed forgiveness, so he didn't ask. He did, however, want to say something to Vivian, in case this was the last time they'd see each other. But what he wanted to say, he couldn't say, so he turned away and looked at the soldiers, who were speaking rapidly and glancing down at the prisoners at the bottom of the ravine.

Mercado spoke some Amharic, but he seemed preoccupied, so Purcell asked Gann, 'Can you understand what they're saying?'

'A bit … I think you three are going to be taken somewhere else.'

'Why do you think that?'

'The leg shackles are for traveling, old boy. When they tie your hands behind your back, you know you're not going far.'

Purcell knew this made sense, but he pointed out, 'Your legs are also shackled, Colonel.'

'Yes, I noticed. Can't say why, though.'

Henry and Vivian seemed oblivious to what was going on, but then one of the soldiers shouted to them, 'Come! Come!' He motioned for all of them to climb out of the ravine.

They all looked at one another, then stood and began climbing up the slope, dragging their chains with them as the soldier kept shouting, 'Come! Come!'

They reached the top of the ravine and stood among the soldiers, who seemed indifferent to them. Purcell noticed that in the distance, where he'd spotted the helipad, an American-made Huey sat with its rotor spinning.

The soldier in charge pointed to the helicopter and shouted, 'Go! Go!'

Purcell looked at Gann, expecting that he'd be pulled aside, but one of the soldiers gave Gann a push and shouted, 'Go!'

Vivian and Mercado joined hands and began running as fast as their chains allowed. Purcell and Gann followed. Four soldiers accompanied them, urging them to move faster. Vivian stumbled and Mercado helped her up, and they continued toward the helicopter.

Vivian and Mercado reached the open door of the aircraft and were pulled aboard. As Purcell got closer, he could see a large red

165

star painted on the olive drab fuselage – the red star of the revolution, which he knew covered the old emblem of the Lion of Judah.

Gann scrambled aboard without help, and Purcell followed.

Vivian called out over the noise of the engine and rotors, 'Pilot says we're going to Addis!' She flashed a big smile and shouted, '*Avanti!*'

The helicopter lifted, pivoted, and headed south toward Addis Ababa.

— PART II —

Rome, December 1974

Tutte le strade conducono a Roma.
All roads lead to Rome.

CHAPTER 14

'Hello, Henry.'

Henry Mercado didn't turn toward the voice behind him, but he did glance into the bar mirror.

Frank Purcell took the empty stool beside Mercado and ordered a Jack Daniel's on the rocks. He said, 'You look well.'

'Is this an accident?'

'I heard you were in Rome.'

Mercado did not reply.

'Can I buy you a drink?'

'I was just leaving.'

The bartender poured Purcell's drink and he raised his glass. 'Centanni.'

Mercado called for his tab.

Purcell stirred his drink and said, 'I left you a note at the Addis Hilton.'

'I was taken directly from the prison to the airport.'

'Vivian left you a note, too.'

He didn't reply.

Mercado's bill came and he put a twenty-thousand-lire note on the bar, which Purcell reckoned was about three drinks at Harry's Bar prices.

It was four in the afternoon, and the quiet, elegant bar was not yet in full swing. A few perfunctory but tasteful Christmas decorations were placed here and there.

Outside, the Via Veneto was crowded with cars and people as always, but maybe more so, thought Purcell, because of the Christmas season. The sky was low and gray, and the air was damp, so he wore a trench coat, but he noticed that Mercado was wearing only a tweed sports jacket, which seemed too big for him. In fact, Henry did not look well and there was a lot of space between his neck and his collar and tie. They'd both lost their Ethiopian tans, and Mercado's skin looked as gray as the winter sky.

Mercado slid off his stool and said, 'I'm living at the Excelsior, and usually at the bar there.'

'I know.'

'Then you also know not to run into me there.'

Purcell nodded and said, 'Merry Christmas, Henry.'

Mercado turned toward the door, then turned back and said, 'All right, I will ask you. How is she?'

'*Where* is she might be a better question.'

'All right, *where* is she?'

'Don't know. She left me in Cairo, end of October. Said she had business in Geneva, and she'd be back in two weeks. What's today?'

Mercado stood there awhile, then asked, 'How long have you been here?'

'Two days. Let me buy you a drink. I came to Rome to see you.'

'Why?'

Purcell slid off his stool and took Mercado by the arm. 'I need ten minutes of your time. I have some good news about Colonel Gann.'

Mercado hesitated, then let Purcell steer him to a table by the window. Purcell called out to the bartender, 'Another round, please.'

They sat across from each other, and Mercado glanced at his watch. 'I'm meeting someone at five.'

'Okay. Well, I just heard from a guy named Willis at the AP office in Addis. You know him? He says that Gann has been released from jail and will be flying to London in time for Christmas.'

Mercado nodded. 'I'm glad to hear that.'

'Me, too. Only in a place like Ethiopia can you be condemned to death, then released on bail and allowed to leave the country.'

'I'm sure the British government paid dearly for their knight errant.'

'Right. Money talks, and the Revolutionary government needs money, so they sold Gann. Works for everyone.' He also informed Mercado, 'The bad news is that Gann has to return to Addis after the holidays for a hearing on his appeal or he forfeits his bail.' He smiled. 'I don't think he'll be making that trip.'

Mercado smiled in return. 'If he does, he *deserves* a firing squad.'

'*Two* firing squads.'

Mercado said, 'It's important for these people to save face. Before they kicked me out, I got handed a five-year sentence for my association with counterrevolutionaries.'

'Only five? When are you supposed to report back?'

'I'm not clear about that.' He asked Purcell, 'How about you?'

'I just did that week in the slammer.'

'Then a week of house arrest in the Hilton.'

'Correct.'

'With Vivian.'

'Correct.'

'You both got off easy.'

'Right.' He reminded Mercado, 'You're the one who got caught sleeping with Gann. Vivian and I didn't do anything wrong.'

'Well, I'm sure you did in the Hilton.'

Purcell changed the subject. 'We should go see Gann in London.'

Mercado kept to the subject, 'I didn't do anything wrong and I spent a month in the foulest prison I've ever seen, while you and Vivian—'

'Was it that long? Well, we've both been in worse places.'

'Where did you go after you left Addis?'

'I went to Cairo.'

'Alone?'

'No.' Purcell explained, 'It wasn't our choice to go there ... or to go together,' which was partly a lie. He said, 'Cairo seems to be the dumping ground for people expelled from Ethiopia.' He asked, 'Where did they send you?'

'Cairo.'

'I wish I'd known you were there.'

'I was there two hours and took the first flight to London.' Mercado asked, 'Why did you stay?'

'I needed a job. So I contacted the AP office, and the bureau chief, Gibson, was looking for a freelancer.' He added, 'He's expecting another war with Israel, and I am a very good war correspondent.'

Mercado didn't respond to that, nor did he ask why Vivian stayed in Cairo. In fact, she had told Purcell she was excited about photographing the pyramids and all that, plus she wanted to be his photographer if another war broke out. Also, they were in love.

The waiter brought their drinks and Purcell saw that Henry was still drinking gin and Schweppes. Purcell raised his glass and Mercado hesitated, then did the same. Purcell said, 'To freedom.'

'And life.'

They touched glasses and sat back in their chairs and watched Rome go by.

Rome, Purcell had noticed, wasn't as garishly decorated for Christmas as, say, London or New York. He'd like to be in one city or another for the holiday, and he had thought he'd be with Vivian, but that didn't look likely. Christmas in Cairo would not be festive.

He thought back to Addis. The whole two weeks had a surreal feeling. They'd all been taken from the helicopter in separate vehicles, still in chains, to the grim central prison and kept in separate cells, unable to communicate. Some prosecutor with a loose grasp of English had interrogated him every day and told him that his friends had all confessed to their crimes, whatever they were, and had implicated him.

The prison had an enclosed courtyard, with a gallows, and one or two men were hanged each day. He asked Mercado, 'Did you have a room with a view of the hangings?'

'I did. Hoped I'd see you.'

They both smiled.

Purcell lit a cigarette and stirred his drink.

After a week in prison, with no bath or shower, rancid food, and putrid water, a nice lady from the American embassy arrived and escorted him, still barefoot and wearing his *shamma*, to a waiting car and took him to the Hilton a few blocks away.

The lady, Anne, had instructed him to stay in his room, which the hotel had held for him and were billing him for. She didn't suggest a bath, but she did suggest he call a doctor to his room for a checkup. In answer to his questions about Vivian, Gann, and Henry Mercado, she replied, 'Miss Smith is here. The others remain in custody.'

She offered to walk him to the front desk, but he declined, and she handed him his passport and wished him luck.

He walked barefoot in his *shamma* to the front desk, where the clerk said, 'Welcome back, Mr Purcell,' and gave him his key.

His room had been searched and most of his possessions had been taken, including his notebooks, but that was the least of his problems.

He had waited a full day before calling Vivian, and they met in her room for drinks because they were both confined to quarters, and in any case neither of them wanted to run into their colleagues in the bar, or the security police in the lobby.

Vivian, too, had had her room ransacked and all her film had been taken, which made her angry, but she, too, understood that their real problem was getting out of Ethiopia.

As he'd finished his drink, she'd reminded him, 'As I said, nothing is going to happen between us here.'

'I understand.'

Later, in bed, she told him, 'When they release Henry ...'

'I understand.'

'Sorry.'

'Me too.'

But they didn't release Henry, and a week later Purcell and Vivian were officially expelled from Ethiopia and found themselves on an EgyptAir flight to Cairo.

Purcell said to Mercado now, 'Vivian and I made daily inquiries to the British embassy about you and Gann, and they assured us you were both well, and they were working on your release.' He added, 'We were worried about you.'

'And you didn't want me showing up unexpectedly.'

Which was true, but Purcell stuck to the subject and said, 'I was sure they were going to shoot Gann. Or hang him.'

'All's well that ends well.'

'Right.' Purcell looked out at the Roman wall that surrounded the city. He realized that the bricks of the ancient city wall looked exactly like the bricks of the Italian-built prison in Addis. He pointed this out to Mercado and said, 'The Italians know how to build.'

Mercado did not respond.

'Those mineral baths were impressive.'

'Don't get nostalgic on me, Frank.'

'Henry ... have you thought about going back?'

Mercado stayed silent for a moment, then replied, 'I have, actually. But it's obviously too risky.'

'Well, if you decide to go back, let me know.'

'You'll be the last to know.'

The waiter came by and Purcell ordered two more. He asked Mercado, 'Did you hear the news out of Ethiopia today?'

'I did not.'

'Well, a guy named General Banti took over the military council and announced a new government. Same group of thugs in the Derg, but with different leaders, and I'm thinking it may be possible now to go back if these new guys are not as crazy as the last bunch.'

'Speaking of crazy.'

'Just a thought.' He informed Mercado, 'The big story is the Mideast. The canal is still closed and Sadat is saying things like, "Mideast time bomb." He's pissed off at all the Russian Jews immigrating to Israel. It really looks like there could be another war.'

'If there is, cover this one from Cairo.'

'Right. Those safe-conduct passes to the front don't work that well.' He smiled, then said, 'I hear you're working for *L'Osservatore Romano*.'

'Yes. I'm doing some English-language stuff for them on the coming Holy Year. Mostly press releases.'

'Bored?'

'I like Rome.'

'Cairo sucks.' He asked, 'Are you working on anything else?'

'You mean like our Ethiopian adventure?'

'That's what I mean.'

'No, I'm not. But I expected to see something from you about that.'

'I'm holding off,' Purcell replied. 'I wanted to speak to you first.'

'You don't need my permission or my collaboration.'

'I thought we'd do something together.'

'I'm not interested.'

'Really?'

Mercado thought a moment, then said, 'If you — we — wrote about this, then not only Getachu but a lot of other bastards and idiots would be smashing through the jungle looking for the black monastery.'

Purcell nodded. He'd certainly thought about that. He said to Mercado, 'Getachu may have already found it.'

'Perhaps. But if he did, I think we'd have heard that an important religious object was for sale.'

'A lot of that stuff is sold privately,' Purcell reminded him.

'True. And this one goes to the Vatican.' He added, 'Or perhaps the monks have spirited it away.'

'Well, we could go check.'

'Not interested.'

'All right.' He asked Mercado, 'Did you report Father Armano's death to the Vatican?'

'No.'

'Why not?'

'I . . . there doesn't seem to be any urgency. I'll get around to it.'

'Your offices are in Vatican City, Henry.'

'I'll get around to it.'

'Good. Maybe we should go to Berini and look up his family.'

'Why?'

'He asked us to do that. He also asked us to tell his story to someone in the Vatican. Or you can tell your people at *L'Osservatore Romano*.'

'All right. I'll do that.'

'I'm not quite understanding, Henry, why you're sitting on this.'

'Why have *you* sat on it?'

'I told you. I wanted to speak to you first.' He reminded Mercado, 'We made sort of a pact.'

Mercado asked, 'What does Vivian think?'

'She wants to go back and find the Holy Grail. That's what she thinks.'

'Insane.'

'I'm sorry you've lost your enthusiasm for this, Henry.'

'I'm sorry you've found it.'

'I've been thinking.'

'Try not to do that.'

'It's a great story, Henry.'

'It seemed so at the time.'

Purcell looked at him and asked, 'Have you been snooping around the Vatican archives? Like, on your lunch hour?'

'Yes … to satisfy my curiosity about a few things.'

'Find anything?'

'I'll get you a pass and you can do your own research.'

'May be a language problem.'

'You can hire translators there.'

'I need to get back to Cairo in a few days.'

'Forgive my curiosity, Frank, but I don't understand why you're not going to Geneva.'

Purcell ordered another round, and Mercado did not object.

Neither man spoke for a while, then Purcell said, 'I received one letter from Geneva telling me … well, telling me that she felt awful about leaving you in Addis, and that she was feeling guilty because of what happened and how it happened.'

'And well she should.'

'Right. Me too.'

Mercado stared into his drink, then said, 'I've gotten over this, Frank. Except for the anger. You both behaved badly.'

'We know that.'

'And I did too ... that moment in Getachu's tent ... when he asked me—'

'You are forgiven.'

Mercado looked at him. 'Thank you for that.'

'Vivian never once mentioned it.'

'I'm sure she thought about it.'

'We all need to move on.' He smiled and said, 'Avanti.'

'I need to go.'

'Some news, too, about Prince Joshua. They executed him in Addis.'

'That was a mercy.'

'It was.' He asked Mercado, 'Did you read about the mass executions at the end of November?'

'I'm not really following Ethiopia.'

'You should.'

Mercado asked, 'What happened?'

'Well, they shot another bunch of guys from the old regime. The former premier, Makonnen, a general named Aman who was former chief of staff or something, another former premier named Wolde, and Rear Admiral Alexander Desta, a grandson of the emperor.'

Mercado nodded and observed, 'The revolution lives on blood.'

'Right. And they shot fifty-six other guys, including Prince Joshua.'

'Let me know when they shoot Getachu and Andom.'

'I'll keep an eye on the wire.'

Mercado stood and walked unsteadily to the *bagno*.

Purcell lit another cigarette and watched the Romans. It was almost dark now, and the cafés along the Via Veneto would be getting full.

Inside Harry's, the bar and the tables were filling up with what looked like mostly American tourists who needed to have a drink with the ghost of Ernest Hemingway, or to experience a little of *la dolce vita*.

Purcell had not expected to find Henry Mercado in a place like Harry's, but the bartender at the Excelsior said he might be here, and here he was, drinking with the tourists. But, Purcell thought, Henry was a pre-war character and he'd probably started coming here when it was the thing to do, and when it was a hangout for journalists and expat writers. Henry didn't seem to notice that the world was changing, and Purcell pictured himself at Henry's age — if he lived that long — staying at the wrong hotels, eating in the wrong restaurants, and getting drunk in the wrong bars with the wrong people.

He half understood Vivian's attraction to Henry Mercado in Ethiopia, but he didn't understand why she remained emotionally attached to him in absentia. Or why she hadn't tried to find him. It occurred to him, though, that she wanted Frank Purcell to find Henry Mercado. In fact, her letter hinted at that. She wanted the three of them to go back to Ethiopia to find the black monastery and the Holy Grail. Well, that sounded like a trip to hell on several levels. And yet ... it made him think about it. And maybe that's why he had asked around about Henry Mercado.

Mercado returned but did not sit, and said, 'I have to go. Let's split the bill.'

Purcell stood. 'You buy tomorrow night.'

'I think we've said what we had to say.'

'I'm staying at the Forum. Rooftop bar. Six P.M.' He put out his hand, and Mercado hesitated, then took it. Purcell said, 'I'm sorry about what happened.'

'If you're looking for forgiveness, there are nine hundred churches in Rome.'

'Let's be happy we're alive. We survived the camps and we survived Ethiopia. We'll survive cocktails. See you tomorrow night.'

Mercado turned and walked out into the cold night.

Purcell watched him disappear into the crowd, then sat and finished his drink. He understood, as did Vivian, that they were not all through with each other yet. And Henry understood that, too.

CHAPTER 15

Frank Purcell sat at the bar of the glass-enclosed Hotel Forum restaurant. The real Forum lay five stories below, its marble ruins bathed in floodlights. A crescent moon hung above the Colosseum, and three thousand years of history hung over the city.

He'd spent the morning writing in his room — a piece about Egyptian president Anwar Sadat, whom he'd characterized as a Jew-hater with a pro-Nazi past, and not the moderate peacemaker and reformer that the rest of the news media were making him out to be.

His editors in the States would cut that, of course, or kill the whole story, and the Cairo bureau chief would remind him that he wasn't hired to write an opinion column. But he'd written it because he — and thus his writing — had been transformed.

In the afternoon, he'd taken a long walk, first to the Piazza Venezia where Mussolini used to stand on the balcony of the Palazzo, making a fool of himself *Urbi et Orbi* — to the city and the world. But the city and the world should have taken him more seriously, as Father Armano had at the blessing of the guns.

Next, he walked through the baths of Caracalla, the mother of all Roman spas, then over to the Fascist-built Foreign Ministry where the looted stone steles from Axum sat out front, a monument to European imperialism and good taste in stolen art. Rome, in fact, was filled with looted treasures going back over two thousand years, and, he admitted, they all looked good in their extrinsic settings. And in return for what they'd taken, the Romans had built roads and bridges all over their empire, amphitheaters and baths, temples and forums. So what Mussolini had done in Ethiopia was just a continuation of a long and venerable tradition of imperial stealing and giving. The Vatican, however, had planned a snatch of the Holy Grail without so much as an IOU.

The point of his walk, aside from physical exercise, was to get his head into the right mindset regarding the story – which was turning into a book – that he was writing about Father Armano, the black monastery, and the Holy Grail.

That story, however, would never see the light of day unless or until he went back to Ethiopia to discover the ending. Or, he supposed, it could be published posthumously, with an editor's epilogue regarding the fate of the author.

Now, Jean, the attractive lady next to him at the bar, was looking through her guidebook and said, 'It says here that the Piazza Navona is all decorated for Christmas.'

'I actually walked through there last night. Worth seeing.'

'All right. Campo de' Fiori?'

'Produce market by day, meat market by night.'

'All right …' She went back to her Roman guidebook, and Purcell went back to his Ethiopian book. The questions raised in his story, and in his mind, were: Who owns a two-thousand-year-old relic? Obviously, whoever has it owns it. But how did the present owner get the object? And does the object, if it is priceless, actually belong to the world?

The other question, of course, had to do with the authenticity of the object. Purcell had no doubt that whatever it was that now sat in the black monastery had no mystical powers, despite Father Armano's claim that it healed his wound and his soul, whatever that was. But the cup could be authentic in the sense that it was the actual chalice used by Christ at the Last Supper. Or it could be an object of faith, like most religious relics he'd seen in Rome and elsewhere.

He recalled what he'd once seen in the small chapel of Quo Vadis on the Appian Way, outside the gate of the city wall: a piece of black basalt paving stone, in which was a footprint. Specifically, the footprint of Jesus Christ who had appeared to Peter on the Appian road as the saint was fleeing for his life from Rome. Peter, stunned at seeing his risen Lord, blurted, '*Domine, quo vadis?*' Where are you going, Lord? And Christ had replied, 'To Rome, Peter, to be crucified for a second time.' And Peter, feeling guilt at fleeing, and understanding what Christ was saying to him, returned to Rome to meet his fate and was crucified.

The story, Purcell understood, was apocryphal, and the outline of a foot in the paving stone was not actually made by Jesus's size nine sandal. But an Italian friend once said to him about the stone of Quo Vadis, 'What is real? What is true? What do you believe?' *Quo Vadis?*

Well, he thought, maybe he was going back to Ethiopia to be crucified a second time. And that depended on Henry Mercado, who was half an hour late for his date with destiny. Purcell knew he was coming; Mercado had no choice, just as Peter had no choice.

Purcell ordered another Jack Daniel's and another red wine for the lady. The bar was full – best view in Rome – but the dining tables were almost empty – not the best food in Rome.

Jean, aged about forty, was a blonde Brit, and looked nothing like Vivian, but she made him think of Vivian because she was a woman. She was interesting and interested, and they were both staying at the Forum, alone, and what the hell, it was Christmas in Rome. Coffee and *cornetti* in bed. A wonderful memory.

She observed, 'Your friend is late.'

'He's always late.'

'He must be Italian.'

'No. But when in Rome.'

She laughed, then informed him, 'Did you know that this hotel was once a convent?'

'I'm checking out tomorrow.'

She laughed again and returned to her guidebook.

His mind went back to Addis Ababa. The week at the Hilton after their release from prison had been intense and tense as they waited for news of Henry and Gann, and also waited for a midnight knock on their door, or a call or visit from their respective embassies telling them they were free to leave Ethiopia. That was the tense part. The intense part was their lovemaking, knowing or believing that this was all coming to an end, one way or the other.

He thought that if they'd left it there – if they'd separated at the airport in Cairo, as they said they would – then that would have been the end of it. She'd be with Mercado now, and they'd all be going to London to see Gann. But they had decided to spend a last night together in Cairo at the Grand Nile. Then they found a furnished sublet together.

Cairo, as he knew from previous experience, was not Paris, or London, or Rome; Cairo was a challenge, and whatever romance it had in its streets and its stones was overshadowed by its repressive atmosphere.

Despite that, and despite the rumors of war, and the unpleasant memories of Ethiopia, he and Vivian had had a very good month in Cairo before she announced her departure for Geneva, where she had, she said, business and family.

In retrospect, he should have asked her to be more specific about her plans to return to Cairo, but it never occurred to him that she wasn't coming back. He had no phone number for her, and the return address on her single letter was a post office box. His reply letter, as he recalled, had been short and not filled with love or longing, or understanding. In fact, he was angry, though that didn't come through either. This was not the kind of writing he was good at, and his note may have sounded terse and distant. And that was the end of the letters, and presumably the end of the affair. And that was what he'd implied to Mercado, and that was the truth – or the truth as it stood at this time.

Also, in retrospect, he realized that the good news they'd gotten from the British embassy in Cairo – that Henry Mercado was about to be released – had something to do with her departure. He'd had a brief thought that she had left to find Henry, but if that were the case, she'd have told him to his face in Cairo. Vivian was forthright and honest, and brave enough to say, 'It's over. I'm going back to Henry.'

But Vivian knew that despite Henry's forgiving her for her one-night indiscretion when they thought they were about to be shot, he would not forgive her for her week with Frank Purcell in Addis or for their month together in Cairo. Yet for some reason, she couldn't stay in Cairo with him after Henry was free. He sort of understood that, but he also understood that she wanted the three of them to be together again, in some fashion or another, and to go back to Ethiopia together.

Jean asked, 'Is that your dinner date?'

He looked at the entrance, where Mercado was standing, scanning the bar. Purcell caught his attention, and Mercado headed toward him. Henry still didn't have a topcoat, and he was wearing what he'd worn last evening, except he'd added a scarf.

They didn't shake, and Purcell introduced him to Jean, whose last name Purcell didn't know, along with not knowing her room number. They made small talk for a minute, and Purcell noted that Henry seemed to be in a better mood, and also that Henry could be charming to an attractive lady. He pictured him in the Addis Hilton bar, chatting up Vivian for the first time.

Under normal circumstance Purcell might have asked Jean to join them for dinner, but tonight he needed Henry to himself, without Jean, and without the absent presence of Vivian. He said to Jean, 'Try the Piazza Navona tonight.'

Henry suggested, 'Trastevere would be better.' He gave her the name of a restaurant.

Jean thanked them and went back to her guidebook.

Purcell led Mercado to a reserved table near the window and they sat.

Mercado said, 'I'm not actually staying for dinner. But let's have a bottle of good wine.'

'Whatever is your pleasure.'

Mercado scanned the wine list, summoned a waiter, and they discussed vino in Italian.

Purcell lit a cigarette and looked out at the city. He never quite understood why Peter, and then Paul, had traveled all the way from their world to Rome, the belly of the beast. Surely they knew that was suicidal.

Mercado said, 'You got off easy with a 150,000-lire bottle of amarone.'

'I thought you were buying tonight.'

'Let's first see what you're selling.'

'Right.' Purcell pointed to the Forum. 'What's that building?'

'That's where the Roman senate sat and debated the affairs of the empire.'

'Amazing.'

'Truly the Eternal City. I think this is where I will end my days.'

'Could do worse. Which is what I want to talk to you about.'

'I am not going to Ethiopia.'

'Okay. But hypothetically ... if we could get back in, legally, as accredited reporters, would you consider it?'

'No.'

'Let's say you said yes. Would you feel comfortable with the three of us going?'

'I do not want to see her – or you – again.'

'We're making progress.'

'Frank, none of us will ever be allowed back. So even if I said yes, it's moot.'

'Right. But if we could swing it—'

'I'm facing a five-year prison sentence the moment I set foot on Ethiopian soil.'

'Okay. Maybe we should sneak in.'

'Maybe you should just step out into Roman traffic and save yourself some time and effort.'

The waiter brought the wine, Mercado tasted it and pronounced it *meraviglioso*, and the waiter poured.

Purcell held up his glass and said, 'To Father Armano, and to God's plan, whatever it is.'

'I'm sure you're going to tell me what it is.'

'It's coming to me.' Purcell informed him, 'I actually have a private pilot's license. Single-engine. Did I ever mention that?'

Mercado swirled his wine.

'If we could rent a bush plane in Sudan—'

'You're not making God's plan sound attractive.' He asked, 'What do you think of the wine?'

'Great. So let's think about false IDs. I have several sources in Cairo.'

Mercado pointed out, 'You don't actually need me along. It would be easier for you to just apply for a visa and see what happens. The new regime may let you in.'

'I want you with us.'

'By *us*, I assume you mean Vivian as well.'

'Right.'

'But she's left you. Or at least that's what you seemed to have told me last night.'

'Right. But I also told you she wants us to go back to look for the black monastery.'

Mercado mulled that over, then said, with good insight, 'There are easier ways for you to regain her affection.'

Purcell did not reply.

'If you, Mr Purcell, want to go back, you need to go for the right reason. Your reason is not the right reason.'

Purcell thought a moment, then replied, 'I'm not going to tell you that I believe in the Holy Grail. But I do believe there is a hell of a story there.'

'But Vivian, dear boy, believes in the Grail. You need to believe in it as well if you're going to drag her back there – or if she's dragging you back.'

Purcell asked, 'What do you believe?'

'I believe what Father Armano told us.'

'All of it?'

'All of it.'

'Then how can you *not* go back?'

He reminded Purcell, 'Father Armano seemed to think that the Grail should be left where it was in a Coptic monastery – and he's a Catholic priest who was under papal orders to find it and take it for the Vatican.'

'I'm not suggesting we should steal it. Just … look at it. Touch it.'

'That would probably end in life imprisonment. Or death.'

'But if you really believe, Henry, that we're going back to find the actual Holy Grail, what difference does death make?'

Mercado looked closely at Purcell.

'Father Armano risked death by going on that patrol to find the black monastery. Because he believed in the Grail, and he believed in eternal life.'

'I understand that. But . . .'

'The Knights of the Round Table risked their lives to look for the Grail—'

'Myth and legend.'

'Right. But there's a moral to that myth.'

'Which is that the Grail will never be found.'

'Which is that we should never stop looking for what we believe in. Death is not the issue.'

Mercado did not reply.

'Why did Peter come to Rome?'

Mercado smiled. 'To annoy the Romans with his arguments, as you are annoying me with yours.'

'And to bring them the word of God. And why did Peter return to Rome?'

'To die.'

'I rest my case.'

Mercado seemed lost in thought, then said, 'Look, get a good night's sleep' – he nodded toward Jean who was still at the bar but settling her bill – 'and if you're still suicidal in the morning, give me a call.' He put his business card on the table and stood.

Purcell stood and said, 'Henry, this is what we have to do. We think we have a choice, but we don't.'

'I understand that. And I also understand that you're not as cynical as you think you are or pretend to be. You are not going to risk your life for a good story – or for a woman. You're not *that* much of a reporter or that romantic. But if you believe in love, then you believe in God. There may or may not be a Holy Grail at the end of your journey, but the journey and the quest is itself an act of faith and belief. And as we Romans say, "Credo quia impossibile." I believe it because it is impossible.'

Purcell did not reply.

They shook hands and Mercado went to the bar, spoke to Jean, then left.

Jean walked toward his table, smiling tentatively. Purcell stood, and thought: Good old Henry, up to his old tricks again, sticking me with the bill, the lady, and the next move.

CHAPTER 16

Rome was always crowded at Christmas with visiting clergy, pilgrims, and tourists, and even more so this year in anticipation of the pope's Christmas Eve announcement of the coming Holy Year. The taxi driver was swearing at the holiday traffic and at the foreign *idioti* who didn't know how to cross a street.

Purcell had decided to stay in Rome for Christmas and he'd sent a short telex to Charlie Gibson in Cairo telling him that. The return telex, even shorter, had said, YOU'RE FIRED. HAVE A GOOD CHRISTMAS.

He'd hoped that would be Charlie's response, and he dreaded a second telex rescinding the first. But if war broke out, as it might after all the Christian tourists left Jerusalem, Bethlehem, and Nazareth, then the Cairo office would want him back. In the meantime, he was free to pursue other matters. Also, as it turned out, Jean needed to get back to England for Christmas, which further freed him to write, and to think about what he wanted to do about the rest of his life.

He hadn't called Henry the morning after as Henry had suggested, and Henry hadn't called him, nor would he ever. So now, three days later, Purcell had made the call to *L'Osservatore Romano* that morning and he had a 4 P.M. meeting with Signore Mercado. It was 3:45 and the traffic was slower than the pedestrians, so Purcell asked the driver to drop him off at the foot of the Ponte Vittorio Emanuele, and he walked across the Tiber bridge.

It was windy, and the sky was dark and threatening with black clouds scudding across the gray sky, and the Tiber, too, looked black and angry.

Saint Peter's Square was packed with tourists and with the faithful who were praying in large and small groups. In the center of the square stood the three-thousand-year-old Egyptian obelisk, and at the end of the square rose the marble mountain of Saint Peter's Basilica, beneath which, according to belief, lay the bones of the martyred saint, and Purcell wondered if Peter, dying on the cross, had regretted his decision on the Via Appia.

Purcell did not enter the square, but walked along the Vatican City wall to the Porta Santa Rosa where two Swiss Guards with halberds stood guarding the gates of the sovereign city-state. He showed his passport and press credentials to a papal gendarme who was better armed than the Swiss Guards, and said, 'Buona sera. *L'Osservatore Romano*, Signore Mercado.'

The man scanned a sheet of paper on his clipboard, said something in Italian, and waved him through.

He'd been there once before and easily found the press office on a narrow street lined with bare trees. The windows of the buildings cast squares of yellow light on the cold ground.

He was fifteen minutes late, which in Italy meant he was a bit early, but maybe not in Vatican City. The male receptionist asked him to be seated.

The offices of *L'Osservatore Romano* were housed in a building that may have preceded the printing press, but the interior was modern, or had been when the paper was founded a hundred years before. Electricity and telephones had been added, and the result was a modern newspaper that published in six languages and was a mixture of real news and propaganda. And not surprisingly, the pope made every issue.

A lot of articles focused on the persecution of Catholics in various countries, especially Communist Poland. Occasionally the paper covered the plight of non-Catholic Christians, and Purcell recalled that Henry Mercado had been in Ethiopia to write about the state of the Coptic Church in the newly Marxist country, as well as Ethiopia's small Catholic population. Now Henry was writing press releases about the Holy Year. Purcell was sure that Mercado would like to return to Ethiopia to continue his important coverage. And hadn't Henry promised General Getachu a few puff pieces about the general's military prowess?

Mercado came into the waiting room wearing a cardigan over his shirt and tie. They shook hands and Mercado showed Purcell into his windowless office, a small room piled high with books and papers, giving it the look of a storage closet. He could see why Henry was in Harry's Bar at 4 P.M.

Mercado shut off his IBM electric typewriter and said, 'Throw your coat anywhere.' He spun his desk chair around and faced his guest who sat in the only other chair. Purcell asked, 'Mind if I smoke?'

Mercado waved his arm around the paper-strewn room and replied, 'You'll set the whole Vatican on fire.'

But he did have a bottle of Boodles in his desk drawer and he poured into two water glasses.

Mercado held up his glass and said, 'Benvenuto.'

'Cheers.'

They drank and Mercado asked, 'Are you here to tell me you've come to your senses?'

'No.'

'All right.' He informed Purcell, 'Then I've decided to go to Ethiopia.'

Purcell was not completely surprised that Mercado had changed his mind. In fact, he hadn't. Whatever it was that had taken hold of him that night at the mineral spa still had him, and Henry, like Vivian, had been transformed by Father Armano and by that admittedly strange experience that Henry and Vivian took as a sign.

Mercado continued, 'But I can't promise you that I will go any farther than Addis. I am not keen on going back into Getachu territory.'

'I thought you wanted to write a nice piece about him.'

'I do. His obituary.' He tapped a stack of papers on his desk and said, 'I am calling in favors and pulling some strings to get you and Vivian accredited with *L'Osservatore Romano*.'

'Good. I just lost my AP job.'

'How did you do that?'

'Easy.'

'All right, we will be covering the religious beat, of course, and your starting salary is zero, but all expenses are paid to and in Ethiopia.'

'And back.'

'Your optimism amazes me.' He asked, 'Should I finalize this?'

'Where do I sign?'

Mercado finished his gin and contemplated another, then reminded Purcell, 'This will all be moot if we can't get visas.'

'It's a good first step.'

'And *L'Osservatore Romano* will look good on our visa applications.'

'Si.'

Mercado smiled, then asked, 'Are you sure Vivian wants to go?'

'She said so in her letter.'

'Have you heard from her?'

'I have not.'

'Can you contact her?'

'I'll try her last known address. A P.O. box in Geneva.'

Mercado nodded and said, 'Tell her to come to Rome.'

Purcell replied, 'Tutte le strade conducono a Roma.'

'Did you practice that?'

'I did.' Purcell asked, 'Are you all right with this?'

'I told you, I'm over it.'

Purcell didn't think so, and he had issues of his own with Vivian.

Mercado, in fact, asked, 'Are *you* all right with Vivian coming along?'

'No problem.'

'I'm not sure I'm understanding your relationship.'

'That makes two of us. Probably three.'

'All right ... By the way, how did you make out with that lady? Jean?'

'She had to go back to England.' Purcell added, 'She did nothing but talk about you.'

Mercado smiled.

Purcell asked, 'What do you think our chances are of actually getting a visa?'

'I think you were right about the regime change. They seem to want to smooth things over with the West.'

'They're just playing the third world game – flirting with the West while they're in bed with the Russians.'

'Of course. But that could work for us.'

Purcell asked, 'Would you be suspicious if those visas were granted?'

'"Will you walk into my parlor? said the spider to the fly."'

'Precisely.'

'Well, if you want my opinion, this whole idea is insane. But I think we've decided, so save your paranoia for Ethiopia.'

'Right.'

'And have you thought about *why* you are going back into the jaws of death?'

'I already told you.'

'Again, please.'

'To find the Holy Grail, Henry, to heal my troubled soul. Same as you.'

'Well, we should save this discussion for when Vivian joins us.'

Purcell did not reply.

Mercado poured two more gins and said, 'I'm going to ask Colonel Gann to join us in Rome.'

'Why?'

'I think he'd be a good resource before we set out. Also, I'd like to see him and thank him.'

'Me too.'

'I want you to buy him a spectacular dinner at the Hassler.'

'Don't you have an expense account, Henry?'

'Yes, a rather good one, which is why they're putting me up at the Excelsior until I find an appartamento.'

It seemed to Purcell that Henry Mercado had more influence at *L'Osservatore Romano* than his office or his job would indicate. The thought occurred to him that Henry had spoken to someone here about their Ethiopian adventure, including – contrary to what Mercado had told him – the appearance and death of Father Giuseppe Armano. If that were true, then someone here had probably gotten excited about pursuing this story. And maybe Henry had been stringing his bosses along, like the old trickster he was, sucking silver out of the Vatican treasury. And he'd been at it for a few months, and the time had come to put up or get out.

Purcell asked, 'Will you do a piece on Father Armano for your paper?'

'Of course. But not until we get back, obviously. And you?'

'I work here, Henry. Remember?'

'That's right.' He drained his glass. 'We'll do a series of stunning articles together – yours in English and mine in Italian, and they will be translated into every world language, and you will achieve the fame and respect that has always eluded you, and I will add to my global reputation.'

Purcell smiled.

'We'll do the talk show circuit. Who carries the Grail?'

'Vivian.'

'Yes, the pretty girl. And we'll do a slideshow with her photography.'

Neither man spoke, and Purcell thought about what would

actually happen if they *did* find the black monastery and somehow got possession of the Coptic monks' Holy Grail. He said to Mercado, 'Be careful what you wish for.'

Mercado changed the subject. 'It would be very good if Colonel Gann could come along.'

'The Ethiopian government would love to see him.'

'I mean, if he could be pardoned or cleared of all charges.'

'That's not going to happen.'

'Perhaps he could offer his services as a military advisor.'

'That's a long shot, Henry. And I'm sure he's not interested.'

'We'll find out at our reunion. I'll get Gann's contact information in the UK, and call or write him. I'll suggest early January for our reunion.'

'I'll be here.'

'And Vivian, too, I hope.'

'I'll let you know.'

'And we'll go to Sicily where it's warmer, and visit Father Armano's village and find his people.'

'That would be a good first step on our journey.'

'It is the right thing to do,' Mercado agreed. 'Meanwhile, if you are not too busy, I will meet you day after tomorrow at eight A.M., at the Vatican archives, and show you what I've found.'

'It doesn't really matter, Henry. We are going forward on faith.'

'Indeed, we are. But you might find this interesting, and even informative and useful. Good background for your story.'

'Our story.'

'Our story.' He asked Purcell, 'Have you written anything not for immediate publication?'

'I have.'

'Good. Saves us some work. Leave out the illicit sex for *L'Osservatore Romano.*'

Purcell did not smile.

Mercado asked, 'Will you be in Rome for Christmas?'

'I'm undecided.'

'Where is home?'

'A little town in upstate New York.'

'Friends? Family? Old girlfriends?'

'All of the above.'

'Then go home.'

'How about you?'

'Christmas in Rome.'

'Could do worse.'

'If you're around, I'll get us in the back door for Christmas Eve Mass at Saint Peter's. You need a papal blessing.'

'I'll let you know.'

Mercado stood. 'I'll see you day after tomorrow. Your name will be at the library door.'

Purcell stood and put on his trench coat. On their way out, he said, 'It doesn't matter if we never even get into Ethiopia, or if we do, it doesn't matter what happens there. It matters that we try.'

'I've lived my life that way, Frank.' He reminded Purcell, 'This will be my third trip to Ethiopia, and I nearly got killed the first two times.' He added, 'As they say, boats are safe in the harbor, but that's not what boats are made for.'

Purcell left the offices of *L'Osservatore Romano* and walked along the lane lined with bare trees. It was dark now, but the narrow streets were lit, and with no place to go, he walked farther into the papal enclave until he reached the open spaces of fields and gardens behind the basilica.

He found a bench by a fountain – the Fountain of the Eagle – and sat. He lit a cigarette and watched the tumbling water.

The troubling thought came to him that Henry Mercado might be right about Frank Purcell's motives. That somewhere, deep in his mind or his soul, he believed what Henry and Vivian believed. And what Father Armano believed. And he believed it because it was impossible.

CHAPTER 17

Frank Purcell and Henry Mercado sat at a long table in a private reading room within the large Vatican Library. The windowless room was nondescript except for a few obligatory religious portraits hanging on the yellowed plaster walls. Three ornate lamps hung from the high ceiling, and Jesus Christ hung from a wooden cross at the end of the room.

On the long mahogany table, neatly arranged documents were enfolded in green felt, and Mercado informed Purcell, 'I assembled all of this over the last month or so. Some of these parchments and papyri are almost two thousand years old.'

'Can I smoke?'

'The library monks will execute you.'

Purcell took that as a no. Also, it was interesting that Henry had spent so much time here.

Mercado had a briefcase with him that he emptied onto the table, and Purcell could see pages of handwritten notes.

Mercado gave him a notebook to use, then motioned toward the documents and said, 'I employed the services of the library translators – classical Greek and Latin, Church Latin, Hebrew—'

'I get it.'

'We will begin at the Last Supper.'

'Coffee?'

'After the Last Supper.' He explained to Purcell, 'I'm not only trying to prove the existence of the Grail, but also to plot its long journey from Jerusalem to Ethiopia.'

'Why?'

'This will be useful information when we write our series of articles. And perhaps a book. Have you thought about a book?'

'I have.'

He also informed Purcell, 'When we're finished here, we will go to the Ethiopian College, which is here in Vatican City.'

'Why is it here?'

'Good question. The answer is, the Italians and the Vatican have had a long interest in Ethiopia, going back to the arrival in Rome of Ethiopian pilgrims in the fifteenth century. Interest was renewed when the Italians colonized Eritrea in 1869, then tried to conquer neighboring Ethiopia in 1896, then invaded again in 1935.'

'Did you also cover the 1896 war?'

Mercado ignored that and continued, 'The Ethiopian College is also a seminary where the Vatican trains and ordains Catholic priests, and instructs lay people, mostly Ethiopian, to go to Ethiopia and spread the Catholic faith.'

'And maybe to look for the Holy Grail.'

Mercado did not respond to that but informed Purcell, 'The Ethiopian College has a good library and a cartography room with some rare ancient maps of Ethiopia and some hard-to-find modern ones, made in the 1930s by the Italian Army. We can use those maps to narrow down the location of the black monastery, based on what we know from Father Armano.'

'Good idea. Let's go.'

'We need to start at the beginning.' Mercado slid a large English-language Bible toward him and thumbed through the pages. 'Here — Matthew, at the Last Supper.' He read, 'And he took the cup, and gave thanks, and gave it to them, saying, "Drink ye all of it; For this is my blood of the new testament for the remission of sins."'

Mercado looked at Purcell and said, 'Mark and Luke make similar brief references to what has become the central sacrament of Christianity — the Holy Communion, the transubstantiation of the bread into the body of Christ, and the wine into his blood.' He added, 'But John does not mention this at all.'

Purcell had had similar reporting lapses — missing or down-playing something that later turned out to be very important. 'John may have been out of the room.'

Mercado responded, 'The fact that the gospels differ actually give them credibility. These are men recording from memory what they saw and experienced, and the differences show they were not colluding to make up a story.'

'That's what I tell my editors.'

Mercado continued, 'Notice that the cup — the Grail — has no special significance in the telling of this story of the Last Supper. But later, in myth and legend, the cup grows large.'

'It gets magical.'

'Indeed it does. As does the lance of the Roman soldier Longinus, and the robe of Christ, and the thirty pieces of silver that Judas took to betray Christ, and everything else that has to do with the death of Jesus Christ.'

Purcell observed, 'You're making a good case for why Christ's cup at the Last Supper is just a cup.'

'Perhaps ... but of all the artifacts associated with the New Testament, the cup — the Grail — has persisted for two thousand years as a thing of special significance.' He continued, 'And I think one of the reasons is that the chalice is used in the sacrament of Holy Communion. The priest literally — or figuratively — turns the wine into the blood of Christ, and that miracle — or mystery — has taken hold in every Christian who ever went to church on Sunday.'

'I guess ... I never thought much about it.'

'Then you should be taking notes, Mr Purcell. You have a story to write.'

'More importantly, we have a Grail that needs to be found.'

'We are finding it — first in our heads, then in our hearts.' He reminded Purcell, 'This is a spiritual journey before it becomes a physical journey.'

Purcell picked up his pen and said, 'I will make a note of that.'

Mercado continued, 'The chalices used by priests and ministers are often very elaborate. Gold and precious stones. But the cup used by Christ was a simple kiddush cup — probably a bronze goblet used at the Passover. So the kiddush cup, like the story itself, has been embellished over the years, and now looks very different at the altar. It gleams. But that is not what we are looking for. We are looking for a two-thousand-year-old bronze cup — something that would have disappointed many of those who have searched for it, if they'd found it.'

Purcell nodded, trying to recall what, if anything, Father Armano had said about the cup that he claimed he saw.

Mercado went on, 'But there is an essential truth to this story — Jesus saying, in effect, "I have turned this wine into my blood for the remission of your sins."'

'But that has more to do with Jesus than it has to do with the wine or the cup.'

'You make a good point.'

'Also,' Purcell pointed out, 'there is a lot of allegory and symbolism in the Old and New Testaments.'

'That is where some Christians, Jews, atheists, and agnostics disagree.'

'Right.'

'You either believe or you don't believe. Evidence is in short supply. Miracles happen, but not often, and not without other explanations.'

'We should have mentioned that to Father Armano.'

'I completely understand your skepticism, Frank. I have some of my own.'

That wasn't what he'd said on previous occasions, but Purcell left it alone.

Mercado had his Bible open again, and he said, 'We move on from the Last Supper, and through the crucifixion, and we come to Joseph of Arimathea, who plays a central role in subsequent Grail legends.' He looked at the open Bible. 'From Mark 15:42–47.' Mercado read, 'And now when the even was come, because it was the preparation, that is, the day before the Sabbath, Joseph of Arimathea, an honorable counselor, who also waited for the kingdom of God, came, and went in boldly unto Pilate, and craved the body of Jesus. And Pilate marveled if he were already dead: and calling unto him the centurion, he asked him whether he had been any while dead. And when he knew it of the centurion, he gave the body to Joseph. And he bought fine linen, and took him down, and wrapped him in the linen, and laid him in a sepulcher which was hewn out of a rock, and rolled a stone unto the door of the sepulcher.'

Mercado looked up from the Bible and said, 'This is the last we hear of Joseph of Arimathea in the New Testament, but not the last we hear of him from other sources.'

'Are these sources credible, Henry?'

Mercado pulled a notebook toward him and said, 'I've read several accounts of the journey of the Holy Grail. You can call them legends or myths, or quasi-historical accounts. I've had access here to some primary source material, written on parchment and papyrus' – he motioned toward the green felt folders – 'and the earliest date I was able to determine is from a papyrus, written in classical Greek, about forty or fifty years after the death of Christ.' He informed Purcell, 'I've written a summation of all these stories, based on the parts that seem to agree.'

Purcell agreed with Mercado that it would be useful to get some backstory, but he was here mostly to … well, to humor Henry. To bond with him. Or maybe he was here in the musty Vatican Library, on what turned out to be a gloriously sunny morning, because he felt guilty that he'd taken Vivian from Henry. That was it. This was atonement. Punishment, actually. And he deserved it.

Henry was looking at his notebook and said, 'Here's what I've written, combining most of what I've read. It begins as a continuation of the New Testament account of the crucifixion.' He began, 'And Joseph of Arimathea, believing in Christ, wished to possess something belonging to him. He therefore carried off the chalice of the Last Supper—'

'Was he there to clean up?'

Mercado ignored the interruption and continued, 'And having begged Pilate for the Lord's body, Joseph used the chalice to collect the blood flowing from Jesus's wounds. And it came to pass that Joseph of Arimathea was imprisoned for his good deed by Pilate, at the urging of the same angry crowd that had demanded Christ's death. And Joseph lay forty years in a hidden dungeon, but he was sustained by the Holy Grail, which was still in his possession.'

Mercado stopped reading and looked at Purcell.

Purcell nodded. Indeed, this ancient tale had a little of Father Armano's story in it. And Father Armano probably knew the story.

Mercado continued, 'And in the fortieth year of Joseph's imprisonment, the Roman emperor, Vespasian, was cured of his leprosy by the veil of Saint Veronica, and believing now in Christ, the emperor took himself to Jerusalem to avenge the death of Christ, but all who had been responsible for his death were now themselves dead. But through a vision, Vespasian learned that Joseph, who was believed dead, was still imprisoned in the hidden dungeon. Vespasian had himself lowered into the dungeon and freed Joseph. The emperor Vespasian and Joseph of Arimathea were then baptized together by Saint Clement.'

Mercado put his notebook aside and said, 'There are a number of historical inaccuracies – or stretches – in that story. But the story has persisted for two thousand years, and is believed by millions of Catholics and others.'

'And what does the Church of Rome think?'

'The Church of Rome neither confirms nor denies. The Church of Rome likes these stories, but understands, intellectually, that they are a stretch. But stories like this are good press, and they circulate among the faithful and reinforce their beliefs.'

'That's what good propaganda does.'

'So we've heard that Joseph took Christ's cup after the Passover meal, and we've heard that Joseph had it with him in the dungeon, and that the Grail sustained him for forty years.'

Purcell made a note to show he was listening.

Mercado flipped a page in his notebook and read, 'Joseph journeyed with a flock of new Christians through the Holy Land and in time came into Sarras in Egypt. In Sarras, Joseph was instructed by the Lord to set out a table in memory of Christ's Last Supper, and the sacrament of Communion was performed with the Grail for the new converts. After a time, Joseph was instructed by the Lord to journey to Britain, and there the Grail was kept in the Grail Castle, which was located, some say, near Glastonbury. The Grail was kept there by a succession of Grail Keepers, who were all descendants of Joseph of Arimathea, and after four hundred years, the last in the line of the Grail Keepers of the castle lay sick and dying.'

Mercado stopped reading and said, 'So now we have the Grail in Britain, which also seems a stretch, but Britain was a Roman province, part of Joseph's Roman world, so this is possible.'

'Henry, I don't mean to be cynical, but this whole thing is a stretch.'

'If you had read all that I have read here—'

'You started with a belief, and you cherry-picked your facts and gave credence to unconfirmed sources. The worst kind of reporting.' He added, 'You know better than that.' Or maybe, Purcell thought, Henry had been working at *L'Osservatore Romano* too long.

'I'm not the first one to do this scholarship and come up with the same conclusions.'

'There's a guy now writing books based on his scholarship saying that extraterrestrials visited the earth and built the pyramids.'

Mercado did not reply for a few seconds, then said, 'We are all searching for answers to who we are, what our place is in this world and this universe. We hope there is more than we know and see. We hope there is a God.'

'Me too, Henry, but ... okay. The Holy Grail is in Glastonbury.'

Mercado referred to his notes and continued, 'This brings us to the time when the Roman legions withdrew from Britain. The Roman world is disintegrating and Britain has been invaded by various Germanic tribes. The legendary – or historical – Arthur is king of the Britons and we begin the well-known legend of Arthur and the Knights of the Round Table.'

Purcell had seen the movie, but he let Henry continue.

Mercado read from his notebook, 'The magician Merlin told King Arthur of the presence of the Holy Grail in Britain and bid him form the Round Table of virtuous knights to seek out the Holy Grail. The table was formed, with an empty place to represent Judas, in the tradition of the Last Supper and the table of Joseph of Arimathea. After many adventures and dangers during their quest for the Grail, one of Arthur's knights, Sir Perceval, who was unknowingly a descendant of Joseph of Arimathea, discovered the Grail Castle and there found the Holy Grail, and also the lance of the Roman soldier, Longinus, that had pierced the side of Christ on the Cross. The lance hung suspended in thin air and dripped blood into the Grail cup.'

Purcell looked at Mercado, who had stopped reading. It must have occurred to Mercado that this was a story known by all, but believed by virtually no one in the modern world. Except maybe Henry Mercado, Father Armano, maybe Vivian, and a few select others. But Purcell understood that even if the legends were untrue, that didn't mean that the Grail did not exist. The paving stone with Christ's footprint existed in the physical world, as did the Shroud of Turin and a thousand other religious relics. The Grail, however, was always associated with the power to heal. So if they found the black monastery and the Grail, then they would know if it was real. Especially if there was a lance hanging above it in thin air, dripping blood. He'd believe *that* if he saw it.

Mercado continued, 'Sir Perceval was told by the old Grail Keeper of their kinship, and when the Grail Keeper died, Sir Perceval and Sir Gauvain, perceiving that the times had grown evil, knew that the Grail must again be hidden from sinful men. The Lord came to them and told them of a ship anchored nearby the castle, and bid them take the Grail and the Lance back to the Holy Land. The two knights set off in a fog and were never seen or heard from again.'

Mercado closed his notebook.

After a few seconds, Purcell inquired, 'Is that it?'

Mercado replied, 'No. The Grail, and sometimes the Lance, appear again in other references throughout the Dark Ages, Middle Ages, and into modern times.'

Right, Purcell thought. Like a few months ago.

Mercado asked, 'Did you find any of that interesting or useful?'

'Interesting, but not useful.'

'Do you believe any of it?'

'You lost me after Mark.'

'Why even believe in the New Testament?'

'You're asking questions I can't answer, Henry.'

'That's why we're here. To find answers.'

'The answers are not here. Half of the archives in the great Vatican Library are myths and legends. The answer is in Ethiopia.'

'The answer is in our hearts.'

'Let's start with Ethiopia.' Purcell reminded him, 'And we have less than a fifty-fifty chance of being allowed back there.'

'We are going to Ethiopia.'

'You have our visas?'

'No. But I will.' He looked at Purcell. 'You don't understand, Frank. We – you, me, Vivian, and also Colonel Gann – have been chosen to go back to Ethiopia to find the Holy Grail.'

Purcell didn't bother to ask who had chosen them.

Mercado agreed it was time for a coffee break, and they walked out into the sunshine.

Purcell easily understood how early humans believed in the sun as God; it acted in mysterious ways, it rose and set in the heavens, and it gave life and light. The religion of the Jews, Christians, and Muslims, however, was more complex. They asked people to believe in things that could not be seen or felt like the sun on his face. They asked for faith. They asked that you believe it because it was impossible.

And on this basis, he was going back to Ethiopia.

CHAPTER 18

They walked the short distance to the commissary, where they got coffee and biscotti that they took outside to a bench. The barracks of the Swiss Guard was across the lane, and Purcell watched them forming up for some occasion. The Vatican post office, too, was run by the Swiss, and he said to Henry, 'Swiss efficiency and Italian biscotti. Truly a blessed place.'

Mercado responded, 'The Italians are the only people on earth who have monumental egos *and* an inferiority complex.' He added, 'I find it charming.'

'So you're staying here?'

'I will die here or in Ethiopia.'

'Can I ask ... do you have a lady here?'

He hesitated before replying, 'I ... have a lady of my own age whom I see whenever I'm in Rome.'

Purcell didn't pursue that. He lit a cigarette and watched the people.

There were no tourists in this part of Vatican City, and everyone on the streets here was employed by the Vatican in one way or another or they were official visitors like himself. There were, he knew, about a thousand actual residents of this sovereign city-state, mostly clergy, including the pope's staff or retinue, or whatever they were called. The art and the architecture here were without parallel in the world, and he understood, sitting there, why the popes and the cardinals and the hierarchy believed that this was the one true church of Jesus Christ. This was where the bones of Peter, the first pope, were buried somewhere beneath the basilica that bore his name, and Peter had taken the cup from Jesus's hand and drunk his Lord's blood. And so, the argument would go, this was where that same Holy Grail, if it existed, belonged. Case closed.

But even Father Armano had second thoughts about that. And so did Frank Purcell.

Mercado asked, 'Are you thinking about what you've just learned?'

'No. I'm thinking about Father Armano and the black monastery.'

'We will get to the black monastery.'

Purcell didn't know if Henry meant get to it in the next library seminar or get to it in Ethiopia. Hopefully the latter. He said, 'Good coffee.'

'Made from holy water.'

Purcell smiled.

'And Ethiopian coffee beans.'

'Really?'

'The Italians still own and run some coffee plantations in Ethiopia. Though they've probably been seized by the bloody stupid Marxists.'

'Right.'

'There's a chap lives in Addis. Signore Bocaccio. Owns

coffee plantations around the country. Visits them with his air-plane.'

Purcell nodded.

'They may have kicked him out, of course, or put him in jail, but if he's still in Addis, we may want to look him up when we get there.'

'What's he fly?'

'I don't know. Never been up with him, but a few journalists have.'

'Would he rent the plane without him in it?'

'Ask.'

Purcell nodded. His piloting skills were not great, but he thought he could fly nearly any single-engine aircraft if someone gave him an hour or so of dual flying instructions.

Also, he realized that Henry had already thought some of this out. They couldn't just head off into the jungle and expect to run into the black monastery. Few people had been so lucky, and those who had, like Father Armano and his army patrol, had discovered that their luck had run out at the monastery – or before then, when they met the Gallas. And now General Getachu was also interested in the monastery.

So, yes, they should do aerial recon to see if they spotted any-thing that looked like a black monastery – or like something they didn't want to run into on the ground.

Mercado glanced at his watch and said, 'We'll go back to the library, then over to the Ethiopian College.'

'Are you taking the day off?'

'No. I'm working. And so are you.'

'Right. I work here.' Purcell asked, 'When do I get my creds?'

'In a week or two. Or three.' He smiled. 'This is not Switzerland.' He said, 'After you left my office the other night, I sent a telex to the British Foreign Office, who have taken responsibility for the repatriation of Colonel Sir Edmund Gann. I asked them to have Gann call or telex me at my office.'

'Good.'

'Have you written to Vivian?'

In fact, he had after he'd left Mercado's office that night and returned to the Hotel Forum. The letter had said, simply, 'I am in Rome, staying at the Forum. Henry is here, working for *L'Osservatore Romano*, and we have met and spoken. We would like you to join us in Rome, before Christmas if possible. We are discussing the possibility of returning to Ethiopia, and we would like to include you in those discussions if you are still interested. Please telex me at the Forum either way. Hope you are well. Frank.'

He'd felt that the letter, like his last, was a bit distant, and he wanted her to respond, so he'd added a P.S.: 'I have been very lonely without you.'

'Frank?'

'Yes ... I wrote to her. Posted it yesterday morning.'

'Hopefully the Italian postal service is not on strike this week.' He joked, 'Half of Paul's letters to the Romans are still sitting in the Rome post office.'

Purcell smiled. 'I actually sent it from the Swiss post office here.'

'Excellent thinking. It should be in Geneva today.' He stood. 'Ready?'

Purcell stood and they walked back to the library.

*

Mercado informed Purcell, 'There are over half a million printed volumes in this library, and over fifty thousand rare manuscripts, including many in the hand of Cicero, Virgil, and Tacitus.'

'So no coffee allowed.'

Mercado continued, 'It would take a lifetime to read just the handwritten manuscripts, let alone the printed volumes.'

'At least.'

'In any case, after a month of research, I have no documentary evidence of how the Grail, which was bound for the Holy Land, wound up in Ethiopia. But I have a theory.' He said to Purcell, 'If you know your history, you will know that the Council of Chalcedon was called in A.D. 451 to try to resolve some of the theological differences that existed in the early Christian Church.'

'Right.'

Mercado continued, 'The pope, Leo I, and the Christian emperor of the Eastern Roman Empire, Marcian, had a disagreement with the Egyptian and Ethiopian emissaries to this meeting because these emissaries refused to accept the complex doctrine of the Trinity and insisted that Christ was one and that he was wholly divine. These emissaries were expelled, and the dissenting churches came to be called Egyptic, and later Coptic, and this was the beginning of Ethiopia's isolation from the larger Christian world, which persists to this day.'

'I noticed.'

'In any case, the missing piece of the journey of the Grail could be this – Perceval and Gauvain—'

'Who we last saw sailing off in a fog.'

'Reached the Holy Land, which was part of the Eastern Roman Empire, ruled by the emperor in Constantinople.' He continued, 'Perceval and Gauvain would have given the Grail to the Christian bishop in Jerusalem, who was at that time a powerful figure in the church.' He informed Purcell, 'There is some documentary evidence here in the archives that the Grail was circulated among the important Christian churches in Jerusalem over the next few centuries.'

Mercado continued, 'But in A.D. 636, Jerusalem was conquered by the armies of Islam, and many important Christian religious objects were lost or were spirited away to Rome, Constantinople, and Alexandria, Egypt, which was still part of the Eastern Roman Empire.'

'How'd it wind up in Ethiopia, Henry?'

'I'm speculating that the Grail wound up in Alexandria, or someplace else in Egypt, and six years later, in 642, Christian Egypt fell to Islam. I'm further speculating that the Grail, now in the possession of Coptic priests or monks in Egypt, was taken by Nile riverboat to Ethiopia for safekeeping in Axum.' He explained, 'That would make sense, historically, geographically, and in terms of theology – the Egyptians were Copts, and they came into possession of the Grail from Christian refugees from Jerusalem who were fleeing Islam. Six years later, they themselves were conquered by Islam, and they needed to safeguard the Grail, so they took it by a safe route on the Nile to their co-religionists in Ethiopia.'

'That's an exciting story.'

'And based on known historical events. Also, after this time, there are historical references to the Holy Grail in Ethiopia – and no references to it being anywhere else.'

Purcell did not respond.

'I'm not asking you to suspend belief. I'm trying to fill in the blanks between when the Grail left Glastonbury and when it is mentioned in primary source documents as being in Ethiopia.'

A far simpler explanation, Purcell thought, was that the cup used by Christ at the Last Supper had never left Jerusalem. But the Brits liked their story of King Arthur and the Knights of the Round Table and the Holy Grail, and people like Mercado worked it into the legend. In the end, it didn't matter how it got to Ethiopia, assuming it did, and assuming it existed.

Purcell said, 'You understand, Henry, that we are not trying to locate the Holy Grail or even figure out how it got to Ethiopia. We have been told by a credible source – Father Armano – that it's sitting in the black monastery. Now all we have to do is go find this place.'

'And I've explained to you that our journey – spiritual and intellectual – begins here.'

'I'm not arguing with you, Henry. I just want this part of the journey to end before lunch.'

'If we do find the Grail, it would be important if we could establish its provenance, as you would do with any ancient object – to establish its authenticity.'

'If we find the Grail, Henry, we will know it is authentic. Especially if it has a lance dripping blood into it. And even if it doesn't, we will know it when we see it. We will *feel* it. That much I believe. And that's what *you* should believe. So it doesn't matter how it got there, and *we* don't have to prove anything to anyone.' He said, 'Res ipsa loquitur. The thing speaks for itself.'

Mercado looked at him and said, 'I didn't know you spoke Latin.'

'Neither did I.'

Both men stayed silent. Then Mercado asked, 'But did I make my case?'

'You did an excellent job.' He asked Mercado, 'Did you do all this on company time? Or are you doing it *for* the company?'

Mercado did not reply.

Purcell closed his notebook and said, 'Well, I have enough to write the story. Now let's find the black monastery so I can write the end.'

Purcell stood, and Mercado said to him, 'For a writer, a journey of a thousand miles begins in a library and ends at the typewriter.'

'We should be so lucky as to end this journey at a typewriter.'

They left the room and Mercado said something in Italian to a monk, who walked toward the reading room with a large key in his hand.

They walked out into the December sunshine, then headed into the Vatican gardens toward the Ethiopian College, where Purcell hoped they'd find a map with a notation saying, *Black monastery — home of the Holy Grail.*

They should be that lucky. Or not.

CHAPTER 19

Priests and nuns strolled the garden paths, and Purcell thought that wherever they had come from, they had arrived here at the center of their world and their faith. Their spiritual journey would never end, until they were called home, but their physical journey had ended and they seemed at peace with themselves.

He and Henry, on the other hand, had a ways to go to find whatever they were looking for. And Vivian, too, who had seemed happy just to be out of Ethiopia and to be with him, had not gotten Ethiopia, Henry, or Father Armano out of her head. But if everything went right, three troubled souls would come together in Rome and make their peace and begin their journey.

Mercado spoke as they walked. 'The next significant mention of the Grail in Ethiopia is dated 1527.'

'Are we back in the library?'

'Yes. I found a report, written in Latin by a Portuguese Jesuit named Alvarez, written for Pope Clement VII. Father Alvarez says to Pope Clement that he has just returned from Ethiopia and while there he met another Portuguese gentleman, an explorer named Juscelino Alancar, who had reached the Ethiopian emperor's court at Axum with his expedition forty years earlier.

Father Alvarez further states that Alancar had been treated well, but he and his men had been put under house arrest by the Coptic pope for the remainder of their lives.'

'That seems to be a recurring theme in Ethiopia.'

'I also learned that as a result of Alancar's visit to Axum, a number of Ethiopians, most of them Coptic monks, made a pilgrimage to Rome to see the Holy City and were welcomed by Pope Sixtus IV, who granted them the use of the Church of Saint Stephen, near Saint Peter's Basilica, and this was the founding of the Ethiopian College that we are about to visit.'

'Very generous of the pope. What did he want in return?'

'Perhaps some information.' Mercado returned to the story of Father Alvarez. 'Father Alvarez with some other Jesuit priests had been looking for Axum because its name appeared in many ancient writings that were being circulated during the Renaissance. Also, Father Alvarez believed that Axum was the legendary lost Christian kingdom of Prester John.'

'Did he find that?'

'No, what Father Alvarez actually found was the capital of Ethiopia and the seat of the Ethiopian Coptic Church. He also found the last surviving member of the Alancar expedition, who was Alancar himself.' Mercado added, 'Father Alvarez says in this report to Pope Clement VII, that, quote, "Juscelino Alancar told me that he found and saw the cup – the *gradale* – that his Holiness Sixtus had sent him to find."'

'Which got Senhor Alancar life in Ethiopia.'

'Apparently. And because Alancar told Father Alvarez what it was that he had found and seen, Father Alvarez was also kept in Axum under house arrest.'

'But he got out and wrote to the pope.'

'Yes, what happened was that Ethiopia was being attacked by the Turks, so the Ethiopian emperor, Claudius, let Father Alvarez go so he could tell King John III of Portugal about the lost Christian empire of Ethiopia, and to ask the Portuguese king for military aid. Alancar himself was dead by this time, so Father Alvarez and his fellow Jesuits left Axum and made their way back to Portugal. King John actually sent an expeditionary force to Ethiopia, and in 1527 a combined Ethiopian and Portuguese force defeated the Turks, and the Ethiopian emperor Claudius pledged everlasting thanks to King John III and to the Jesuits, who, Father Alvarez says in his report to the pope, are now welcomed back into Ethiopia by the emperor Claudius.'

They continued through the acres of gardens, and Purcell could see a building ahead that Mercado identified as the Ethiopian College.

Mercado slowed his pace and continued his story. 'There is another report from a Jesuit priest named Father Lopes to the next pope, Paul III, which tells of the Jesuit missionary influence in Ethiopia, and of all the good works that they had done in spreading the Catholic faith. But this report also says that the Jesuits are being expelled again because the Ethiopian emperor and the Coptic pope have accused them of excessive prying into the affairs of the Coptic Church and for making inquiries about the monastery of obsidian.' He added, 'This is the first reference to the black monastery and to the Grail possibly being there.'

'Where it remains.'

'Yes. Also, it would seem that a succession of Catholic popes had an interest in Ethiopia, and in the black monastery, and therefore the Grail.' Mercado continued, 'I guess you could make the case that this is a secret passed on from pope to pope, and that's why Father Armano got the sealed envelope from Pius XI. And it also appears, from other oblique references I've read, that the Jesuits, who are the shock troops of the papacy, have been tasked with the mission to find the Holy Grail.'

'If that's true, they haven't done a good job of it.'

'They are patient.' He thought a moment, then said, 'Or, more likely, they and the recent popes have lost interest in this because they no longer believe in the existence of the Holy Grail.'

'It's a hard thing to believe in, Henry.'

'It is. But—'

'You believe it because it is impossible.'

'I do.'

They reached the Ethiopian College, a Romanesque-style structure that Mercado said was built in the 1920s when the college was moved from the five-hundred-year-old monastery of Saint Stephen. Purcell saw a number of black-robed, dark-skinned monks going in and out of the main entrance, and he couldn't help but recall Father Armano's story of the monks in the black monastery who'd greeted him and the Italian soldiers with clubs. 'Is this place safe, Henry?'

Mercado smiled. 'They're good Catholics, not Copts with clubs.'

'Good.'

But he saw that Mercado crossed himself as he entered, so he did the same.

Mercado confessed, 'I haven't been here before, but we have permission and we have an appointment and we are on time.'

They stood in the large antechamber and waited.

A tall, black, and bald monk came toward them and Mercado greeted him in Italian. They exchanged a few words, and Purcell could tell that there seemed to be some problem, notwithstanding their appointment.

Purcell suggested, 'Tell him all we want to do is see the map that shows the black monastery.'

Two more monks appeared from somewhere and the discussion continued. Finally, Mercado turned and said to Purcell, 'They are refusing entry. So I'll need to go through channels again.'

'Try a different channel.'

'All right, let's go. I'll work this out.'

They exited the Ethiopian College and walked down the path through the gardens.

Purcell asked, 'What was that all about?'

'Not sure.'

'When you asked permission, to whom did you speak?'

'I spoke to a papal representative.' He explained, 'The pope is considered the special protector of the college.'

'Doesn't look like that place needs any outside protection.'

Mercado didn't respond.

'So what did you tell this papal representative?'

'The truth, of course.' He added, 'That I had just returned from Ethiopia and I wanted to do some research on a series of articles I was writing for our newspaper about the Coptic and Catholic churches in post-revolutionary Ethiopia.'

'Which is the truth, but not the whole truth.'

Mercado did not reply and they continued to walk back toward the Vatican Library, or, Purcell hoped, the offices of

L'Osservatore Romano, or, better yet, lunch. He said, 'I assume you didn't mention the black monastery.'

'It didn't come up.'

Purcell thought about this. If Henry were actually in league with someone or some group here in the Vatican who wanted him to look for the Holy Grail, then there must be another group here who didn't want him to do that. Or the only people here whom Henry Mercado was working for were his editors at *L'Osservatore Romano*, and he, Purcell, was seeing conspiracies where there were only bureaucratic screwups or miscommunication. He wasn't sure, but at some point, here or in Ethiopia, he'd know what, if anything, Henry was up to.

Mercado said, 'Just as well. When Gann gets here, we'll have this all straightened out, and I'm sure Colonel Gann can read a map far better than you or I.'

'Good point.'

'Would you like to go back to the library? There's more.'

'The monk locked the door.'

'He'll open it.'

'Let me buy you lunch.'

'All right ...'

'The Forum.' Purcell explained his restaurant choice: 'I'm waiting for a telex.'

Mercado looked at him and nodded.

They exited the Vatican through Saint Peter's Square and hailed a taxi on the Borgo Santo Spirito, which took them to the Hotel Forum.

Purcell said, 'Go on up and get us a table by the window, and a good bottle of wine.'

Mercado hesitated, then walked to the elevators.

Purcell went to the front desk and asked for messages. The clerk riffled through a stack of phone messages and telexes and handed him a sealed envelope.

He opened it and read the telex: ARRIVING FIUMICINO TONIGHT. WILL TAXI TO CITY. HOTEL UNDECIDED. WILL MEET YOU AT FORUM BAR, 6 P.M. I MISS YOU, V.

He put the telex in his pocket and walked to the elevator.

Well ... no mention of Henry. Hotel undecided. Don't meet me at the airport. See you at six. I miss you.

And, Purcell thought, I miss you too.

He rode up to the Forum restaurant and found Henry speaking on the maître d's phone. Henry motioned to a table by the window, and Purcell sat.

Mercado joined him and asked, 'Any messages?'

'No.'

Mercado looked at him and said, 'It's all right.'

He wasn't sure what that meant, but he nodded.

'I ordered the same amarone.'

'I thought we drank it all.'

'Do you feel that you are intellectually and spiritually prepared to go on this quest?'

'I do, actually.'

'And do you think Vivian will come with us?'

Purcell reminded Mercado, 'You seem to think that the Holy Spirit has told her to go. So ask him. Or her.'

Mercado smiled.

Purcell suggested, 'Let's talk about something else.'

'All right. I just spoke to my office. Colonel Gann telexed. He can come to Rome right after the New Year and may be able to go to Berini with us.'

'Good. Did he mention Ethiopia?'

'He said he would go if he could get in.'

'Getting in is easy. Getting out, not so easy.'

'I assume he meant getting in without being rearrested.'

The wine came, and Henry poured it himself. He raised his glass and said, 'Amicitia sine fraude – to friendship without deceit.'

'Cheers.'

CHAPTER 20

The Forum bar was crowded when Purcell arrived at 5:30, so he took a table by the window and sat facing the entrance, nursing a glass of red wine.

This wasn't the first time in his life that an ex-lover or estranged girlfriend had wanted to meet in a public place, and sometimes he'd suggested it himself. And maybe with Henry still in the picture, this was a good idea. In fact, he wasn't sure himself what he wanted to happen tonight, except that he wanted Vivian to go with him – and Henry – to Ethiopia. And that, apparently, was what she wanted, though it had to be worked out if she was with him, or with Henry, or with neither.

In any case, despite Henry's toast, Purcell had no guilt about deceiving Henry regarding Vivian's arrival. In fact, Henry probably knew he'd heard from Vivian, and Henry understood that a three-person reunion would not be a good first step toward a return trip to Ethiopia. Purcell had made his separate peace with Henry Mercado, and now he'd do the same with Vivian. Eventually they'd all have a drink together and be civilized – even if Vivian decided to be with Henry. Actually, he was sure Henry would not take her back, even if she wanted that. Henry, like his Italian friends, had a monumental ego – and if he didn't have an inferiority complex before, he'd acquired one in Ethiopia.

It was past 6 P.M., but Purcell knew she'd be late, though he had no idea what time her plane had arrived from Geneva. But the traffic from Fiumicino was always bad, and it was rush hour in Rome, and Christmas, and maybe she was looking for a hotel, which was difficult during the holy season.

He lit a cigarette and looked out at the Colosseum. Or maybe she'd changed her mind. And that was okay, too. Less complicated.

'Hello, Frank.'

He stood and they looked at each other. She hesitated, then put her hand on his arm. He leaned forward and they kissed briefly, and he said, 'You're looking very good.'

'You too.'

She was wearing a green silky dress that matched her eyes, and her long black hair framed her alabaster skin, and he remembered her as he'd seen her that night at the mineral spa when he realized he was taken with her.

'Frank?'

'Oh … would you like to sit?'

A hovering waiter pulled a chair out for her, she sat, and Purcell sat across from her. She said to the waiter, 'Un bicchiere di vino rosso, per favore.'

They looked at each other across the table, then finally she said, 'I'm sorry.'

'You don't need to apologize or explain.'

'But I'd better do that.'

He smiled.

'I just needed to sort things out.'

'How did that work out?'

'Well, I'm here.'

That didn't answer the question, but Purcell said, 'Thank you for coming.'

'Did you throw my stuff out?'

'Tempted.'

The waiter brought her glass of wine and Purcell held up his glass. 'Sono adirato.'

'Why are you angry?'

'I thought that meant, "I adore you."'

She laughed and they touched glasses. She said, 'Ti amo.'

'Me too.'

She put her hand on the table and he took it. They didn't speak for a while, then she asked, 'Did you come to Rome to see Henry?'

'I did.'

She nodded, then asked, 'Does he know I'm here?'

'No.'

She nodded again and asked, 'How is he?'

'Adirato.'

'Well . . . I don't blame him . . . but . . . at least you two are talking.'

'I think he's ready to talk to you.'

'That's good. So he's working for *L'Osservatore Romano*?'

'He is. Seems to enjoy it. Loves Rome.'

'I'm happy for him.'

'Any other feelings for him that I should know about?'

She shook her head.

'All right ... but when you see him, you can work that out with him.'

'I will.' She added, 'I'm sure he's over it.'

'He said he was.'

She changed the subject and asked, 'How long are you staying in Rome?'

'That depends. How long are *you* staying in Rome?'

'As long as you are.'

'All right.' He informed her, 'I've resigned from the AP office in Cairo.'

'Why?'

'Because Charlie Gibson fired me.'

'Good. You hated the job and you hated Cairo.'

'I wasn't fond of either,' he admitted, 'but it was tolerable with you there.'

She smiled. 'I can make any place tolerable, Frank.'

'Even Ethiopia.'

'That may be overstating my powers.' She asked him, 'What about our apartment in Cairo?'

'That's the only home I have at the moment.'

'Me too.'

'We'll keep it awhile.' He asked, 'Where did you stay in Geneva?'

'My old boarding school.' She explained, 'We're always welcome back. Twenty francs a night in the guesthouse. Best deal in Geneva.' She added, 'No men allowed.'

'Can you at least drink?'

'Yes. You *must* drink to stay sane there.'

He smiled.

She told him, 'I'm not a writer, but I did write a sort of diary about what happened in Ethiopia.' She told him, 'I also wrote about us in Cairo.'

'Can I see it?'

'Someday.' She added, 'I'm still angry about losing all my photographs.'

'You can ask Getachu for them when we go back.'

She looked at him for a few seconds. 'Are we actually doing that?'

'Well ... that's the plan.' He asked, 'Are you still interested?'

'I am.' She added, 'I'm surprised that Henry wants to go back.'

'I'm not, and neither are you.' He reminded her, 'He believes he has been chosen by God to find ... it.'

She nodded.

'And you?'

Again, she nodded, and asked, 'And *you*?'

'My motives, according to Henry, are confused at best.'

'But you *do* want to go?'

'I do.' He informed her, 'Henry is working on getting us press credentials with *L'Osservatore Romano*, then we need to get visas. If none of that works, we may consider jumping the border from Sudan.'

'That could be dangerous.'

'No more dangerous than trekking through Getachu territory to find the black monastery.'

She nodded.

He told her, 'Good news. Colonel Gann has been released from prison.'

'Thank God. I thought ... they'd kill him.'

'They would have, but they sold him instead.' He added, 'I don't know where he is now, but Henry got a telex from him and Gann says he's willing to accompany us to Ethiopia.'

'That is insane.'

'He probably had the same thought about us.'

'But he's ... an enemy—'

'Maybe he'll rethink that trip. In the meantime, he's coming to Rome after the New Year, and if you're up for it, all four of us will go to sunny Sicily for holiday. Berini.'

She smiled. 'I would like that.'

He informed her, 'There was a piece in the news ... they shot Prince Joshua.'

'I saw that ... that poor man ... and all those other members of the royal family, and all the former government people ... ' She looked at him. 'How can people do that to other people?'

'It's been going on awhile.'

'I know ... but ... there's such evil in the world ... ' She asked him, 'Doesn't it test your faith in God?'

'Father Armano – and Henry – would tell you it's all part of God's plan.'

'It can't be.'

'The devil, then.'

She nodded, then looked at him and said, 'I always meant to ask you ... that night ... when we were driving, why did you suddenly turn off the road?'

'I don't know.'

'You went right through a wall of bushes. Right where the spa was.'

He'd thought about that himself, and he couldn't recall what had made him suddenly crash the Jeep through those bushes. He smiled. 'A voice said, "Turn right."'

'Be serious.'

'I don't know, Vivian.'

'But don't you think it was beyond strange that you turned off the road exactly where the spa was?'

'Let me think about it.' He changed the subject. 'Henry and I discussed the possibility that Getachu or someone else has already found the black monastery.'

'They haven't.'

'All right . . .' He wanted their first night to be more romantic, so he asked, 'Would you like dinner?'

'No. I want to take a walk.'

'Good idea.' He signaled the waiter for the bill, then asked her, 'Where are you staying?'

'There is not a room to be had in Rome.'

'Sorry to hear that.' He inquired, 'Where is your luggage?'

'In your room.'

He smiled. 'How did you manage that?'

'Really, Frank. We're in Italy.'

He asked, seriously, 'How did you know this would go well?'

'It didn't matter how it went. We're sleeping together tonight.'

He didn't argue with that, and he suggested, 'Let's get you unpacked.'

'I need a walk. It's a beautiful night.'

'Okay.' He paid the bill while she got her coat, and they went down to the lobby and outside into the cool night.

The Roman rush hour had ended, and the streets were

236

becoming more quiet, and pedestrians were strolling on the broad Via dei Fori Imperiali. The Christmas decorations, such as they were, were mostly of the religious type, and there was no sign of Santa or his reindeer.

They held hands and didn't speak much as they took in the city and its people. Vivian said, 'This is what I pictured when I received your romantic letter.'

'I didn't know what tone to use.'

'So you wrote it as a news release. If it wasn't for your PS, I'd still be in Geneva.'

'I know.'

'Well, I don't blame you for being angry.'

'Why should you?'

'I know I shouldn't have left under false pretenses. And I'm sorry for that. But I couldn't face you ... and say ... '

'Drop it.'

She squeezed his hand and said, 'I kept thinking to myself, "Get thee to a nunnery, Vivian. Go think this out."'

'Good. Let's move on. Avanti.'

'I feel cleansed now, and pure.'

'We'll take care of that later.'

She laughed and they continued on. She asked him, 'What is the most romantic spot in the city?'

'My room.'

'Second most.'

'I'll show you.'

They walked around the Vittorio Emanuele monument, then up the steps of the Campidoglio to the piazza at the top of the ancient Capitoline Hill where dozens of hand-holding couples strolled past the museums and around the equestrian statue of Marcus Aurelius.

Purcell led her to a spot at the edge of the hill that looked out over the floodlit Forum below and at the Palatine Hill rising above the Forum ruins, with the Colosseum in the distance.

Vivian said, 'Breathtaking.'

'We'll come back here after Ethiopia.'

'We will come back.'

They descended the long flight of steps down the hill and walked back to the hotel.

CHAPTER 21

Purcell picked up his room phone and called Henry at his office to inform him that Vivian was in Rome, though he didn't say when she'd arrived, or where she was staying, and Henry didn't ask. Had he asked, Purcell would have told him that Vivian was in the shower.

Henry suggested lunch at a restaurant called Etiopia, which he thought would be a fitting place for their reunion. Purcell didn't think so, but he took down the address, which Henry said was near the Termini. Henry further suggested that he, Henry, meet Vivian there at 12:30, and that Purcell join them at one — or even later.

Purcell wasn't sure he liked that arrangement, but he'd leave it up to Vivian.

Later, as he and Vivian began a morning walk, he told her about his call to Mercado, and about lunch.

He thought she might want to return to the hotel to change out of her jeans, sweatshirt, and hiking boots for lunch with her old boyfriend, but she said, 'I'm all right with that. If you are.'

'I'm okay.' He informed her, 'It's an Ethiopian restaurant.'

'That's Henry.'

It was a warm and sunny morning, and it was the Saturday

before Christmas, so traffic was light and the city seemed to be in a holiday mood.

They walked through the Campo de' Fiori, which made Purcell think of his advice to Jean, which in turn made him think of Henry sending Jean to his table under false pretenses. Henry Mercado, Purcell understood, was a manipulator and a man who knew how to compromise other people. But Henry was also a gentleman of the old school, and Henry would not mention Jean to Vivian. Unless it suited his purpose.

They then walked to the Trevi Fountain, made their secret wishes, and tossed their coins over their shoulders into the water, which according to tradition guaranteed that they'd return to Rome someday.

At 11:30, Purcell suggested they head toward Etiopia – the restaurant, not the country.

Their route took them past the Termini, Rome's central rail station, around which was Rome's only sizeable black neighborhood, whose residents were mostly from the former Italian colonies of Ethiopia, Eritrea, and Somalia. The area around the Termini was crowded with African street vendors whose native wares were spread out on blankets.

As they walked, Purcell asked Vivian, 'Are you still all right with this meeting?'

She nodded, but he could see she was apprehensive. The last time Vivian had seen Henry was when they'd gotten off Getachu's helicopter in Addis Ababa. The flight from Getachu's camp to Addis had been made mostly in silence, except for Gann telling them that as foreigners and journalists, the worst they could expect was a show trial, a conviction, and expulsion from the country.

Purcell had realized at the time that Colonel Gann was not speaking about himself — he fully expected to be hanged or shot — and yet he'd put his own fears aside to boost the morale of three people he hardly knew. A true officer and gentleman. And now, according to Mercado, Gann was willing to return to Ethiopia, where he was under a death sentence. Fearless was one thing, but foolhardy was something else. He wondered what was motivating Colonel Gann.

From the helicopter, they had been made to run barefoot across the tarmac, wearing leg shackles, to four waiting police cars. Before they were separated, Vivian had called out to Henry, 'I love you!'

But Henry had not replied — or maybe he hadn't heard her.

Then Vivian had turned toward him, and they made eye contact. She gave him a sort of sad smile before the policeman pushed her into the car.

And that was the last he saw of her until the Hilton, and the last Henry would see of her until about fifteen minutes from now.

He said to her, 'If you're having second thoughts, I'll go with you.'

'No. I just need to put it to rest, Frank. Then get on with what we have to do.'

'All right.' There was no script for this sort of thing — the eternal triangle in the Eternal City — and he supposed that Henry's request for half an hour alone with his former lover was not unreasonable, and that Vivian's acquiescence was meant, as she said, to put it to rest and move on. Henry, on the other hand, had many agendas, and Purcell didn't know which one was on the schedule today.

Vivian was looking at the blankets spread over the open spaces around the Termini, and the street vendors were calling out to her in Italian as she passed. She said something to one of them in Amharic and the man seemed surprised, then delighted.

She stopped and looked at the crafts on his blanket, and the man was speaking rapidly to her in Amharic, then switched to Italian.

Purcell looked at the items. There were a few objects carved out of what looked like teak and ebony, some beadwork, and a few sculptures carved from jet black obsidian, polished to a high gloss, including a model of the distinctive octagon-shaped Saint George Cathedral in Addis Ababa. He smiled. 'We've found the black monastery.'

'Frank, that's Saint George in Addis.'

'Looks smaller than I remember.'

A lady was selling embroidered *shammas* and Purcell suggested, 'Let's wear these to lunch.'

Vivian surprised him by saying, 'The last time Henry saw us in shammas, he didn't like what he saw.'

Purcell had no comment on that. He walked over to another blanket covered with bronze ware, and he spotted a wine goblet that reminded him of the goblets in Prince Joshua's tent. The vendor wanted fifty thousand lire, Purcell offered ten, and they settled on twenty.

Purcell moved back to Vivian, who was negotiating the price of Saint George's, and held up the goblet. 'I have found the Holy Grail.'

She laughed.

'Here. Give it to Henry and tell him mission accomplished.'

She examined the goblet of hammered bronze, which looked ancient, but was probably made last week, and asked, 'How will we know?'

'The thing will speak for itself.'

She nodded, then handed it back to him, saying, 'You give it to him.'

The *polizia* were doing a scheduled sweep through the Termini area, chasing off the street vendors, who rolled up their blankets and wares and moved a few meters behind the sweep, then set up again on the pavement. No one seemed to take things too seriously here, he noticed, and maybe Henry had found the right place to live and die, if he didn't die in Ethiopia. Same for him and Vivian.

Purcell asked a policeman for directions to Via Gaeta, and he walked Vivian part of the way. They stopped and he said, 'See you in half an hour.'

'Don't be late.'

'I might be early.'

She smiled, then said seriously, 'If he's willing to forget the past, and get over his anger, and be with us under these ... I guess, awkward circumstances, then you—'

'I get it.'

'All right ...' She gave him a quick kiss, turned, and walked off.

Purcell checked his watch, then wandered the streets around the Termini. He found a taverna and went inside. The clientele was mostly black, though the taverna itself seemed to be traditional Roman.

He sat at the small bar and ordered an espresso, then changed his mind and asked for a *vino rosso*.

Henry Mercado had a flair for drama and stage setting. He was, in fact, a performer. An illusionist. Purcell could see it in some of Henry's writing. There were never any hard facts — just suggestions of fact, mixed with his profound insights. Henry manipulated words the way he manipulated people. Purcell had no doubt that Henry's epiphany in the Gulag was real, but Henry's inner pagan had remained the same. If Henry Mercado wasn't a Catholic journalist, he'd probably be a magician or a wizard. Purcell didn't think that Vivian would again fall under his spell, but Henry would use her guilt to his advantage.

He had a second wine and looked at the patrons in the bar mirror. Ethiopia was disgorging large chunks of its population, especially the entrepreneurs and the professional class, and also the old aristocracy who had escaped hanging and shooting, as well as the Coptic and Catholic clergy who felt threatened by the god-less revolutionaries. Ethiopia was, in fact, a replay of the French and Russian revolutions; an isolated ruling elite had lost touch with the people, and with reality, so the people had brought reality to the palaces and churches. The three-thousand-year-old established order was crumbling, and for this reason, the Holy Grail was up for grabs.

It was only a matter of time, he thought, before the revolutionaries located the black monastery; it was well hidden, but nothing can be hidden forever, though he knew that the lost cities of the Mayans had remained undiscovered for hundreds of years in jungles far smaller than those of Ethiopia.

But no matter who found the monastery, he was sure that the Holy Grail, or whatever else was there, would be spirited away before the first intruders got over the walls. And yet ...

He took the bronze goblet out of his trench coat and looked at it.

The proprietor, an Italian, looked at it also, then nodded toward his clientele and said in English, 'Ethiopian junk.'

Not wanting the man to think he was a gullible tourist, Purcell informed him, 'This is the Holy Grail.'

The proprietor laughed. 'What you pay for that?'

'Twenty thousand.'

'Too much. Ten.'

'This can turn wine into the blood of Christ.'

The proprietor laughed again, then said, 'Okay, for twenty is good.'

Purcell left a ten on the bar, walked out into the sunshine, and headed for Etiopia.

CHAPTER 22

Purcell spotted Vivian and Mercado sitting in the rear of the dark restaurant. They weren't tête-à-tête, but they did seem at ease, talking and smiling.

He brushed past the hostess, walked to the table, and said, 'Sorry I'm late.'

Mercado replied, 'You're a bit early, actually.'

Purcell did not shake hands with Mercado or kiss Vivian; he sat, still wearing his trench coat. Henry, he noticed, was looking a bit more trendy in a black leather jacket and black silk shirt.

Vivian said, 'Henry has brought me up to date.'

'Good.'

There was a bottle of wine on the table, and Henry poured into an empty glass for Purcell, then raised his glass and said, 'Ad astra per aspera. Through adversity to the stars.'

Purcell wondered how many Latin toasts Mercado had in him.

They touched glasses, and Vivian proposed, 'To peace and friendship.'

Purcell lit a cigarette and scanned the room. The place looked as if it had been decorated with the stuff from the blankets, including the blankets themselves that hung on the walls. The tables were half empty, and the clientele seemed to be mostly African and well dressed, probably, Purcell thought, the cream of Ethiopian society who'd washed up on the banks of the Tiber.

Vivian, trying to keep the conversation going, said, 'Henry told me about the research he's done in the Vatican archives.'

Purcell didn't respond.

Mercado said to her, 'Frank was unimpressed.'

Vivian waited for Purcell to respond, then said, 'Odd that they wouldn't let you into the Ethiopian College.'

Mercado assured her, 'I'll work that out.' He added, 'That is the type of practical research that would appeal to Frank's practical mind.'

Mercado and Vivian continued their two-way conversation, the way they had before Purcell arrived, and Purcell knew he was not being civilized or sophisticated, and this probably pleased Mercado no end. So to avoid a scene later with Vivian and to avoid giving Mercado the satisfaction of seeing him uncomfortable in this situation, Purcell said, 'Henry and I have agreed to disagree about some things, but we agree that the three of us are going back to Ethiopia – if we can get in – and we are going to pick up where we left off when we buried Father Armano.'

Vivian nodded, then reminded Purcell, 'You have something for Henry.'

'I do? Oh …' He reached into his coat pocket and set the bronze goblet on the table.

Mercado picked it up and looked at it.

Purcell announced, 'We have found the Holy Grail.'

Vivian added, 'At a street stall near the Termini.'

Mercado laughed, then turned the goblet upside down and said, 'Indeed you have. Made in Jerusalem, 10 B.C., property of J. Arimathea.'

Vivian laughed.

Mercado said, 'Well done, you two. Now Frank and I can get working on this story, then go our separate ways.'

Purcell thought that would be nice, but to keep the ice from refreezing, he said, 'You need to research this grail, Henry.'

They all laughed, then Mercado picked up the wine bottle and poured into the bronze goblet. He said solemnly, 'We will drink of this and this will be our covenant.' He passed the goblet to Vivian, who put it to her lips and drank, then passed it to Purcell. He drank and passed it to Mercado, who finished the wine and said, 'May God bless our journey.'

Vivian reached out and took both men's hands, though Purcell and Mercado did not join hands. Vivian lowered her head and said, 'God rest Father Armano and all those who suffer and die in his name, in Ethiopia and around the world.'

'Amen,' said Mercado.

The waiter, a tall thin black man wearing a colorful *shamma*, saw that they had completed their prayers and came by with menus, but Mercado stood and said, 'I will leave you to enjoy this wonderful food and enjoy each other's company — after your long separation.'

Purcell forced himself to say, 'Please stay.'

'Yes, please stay, Henry.'

'I've let some work pile up at the office.'

Purcell stood and they shook hands, then Mercado came around and gave Vivian a peck on the cheek and left.

Purcell sat and the waiter left two menus.

Vivian said to Purcell, 'Thank you.'

Purcell perused the menu.

Vivian informed him, 'We've worked everything out.'

'Good. I hope you like lamb. Here's a fish called Saint Peter's fish.'

'He understands what happened and how it happened, and he understands that we are in love.'

'Good.'

'Did you tell him we were in love?'

Purcell put down the menu. 'At the time I spoke to him, I didn't know if we were.'

'Well, you know now.'

'I do.' He looked at her and said, 'A piece of advice, Vivian. Henry Mercado is a charming rogue. He is also a manipulator and a con artist.' He added, 'Don't get me wrong – I like him. But we need to keep an eye on him.'

She thought about that, then replied, 'He's not trying to ... reseduce me.'

'He would if he could. But what I'm talking about is our partnership with him.' He nodded toward the goblet. 'Our new covenant.'

She stayed quiet for a few seconds, then said, with some insight, 'I was easy for him. But I think he knows he's met his match with you.'

Purcell couldn't have said it better, and he smiled at Vivian. 'I have met my match with you.'

'You never stood a chance, Frank.'

'No, I never did.'

She filled the goblet with wine and passed it to him. He drank and passed it back to her. She said, 'If you believe in love, you believe in God.'

Where had he heard that before?

CHAPTER 23

They didn't see Henry again for several days, but he, or a messenger, dropped off an envelope in which were their visa applications partly filled out, awaiting only their passport information and their signatures. A note from Henry said, 'Bring these in person to the Ethiopian embassy, ASAP. Cross your fingers.'

Purcell and Vivian visited the Ethiopian embassy the next morning and spent a half hour waiting for a consulate officer who seemed to be a relative of General Getachu. The former regime's diplomatic staff had been dismissed, of course, and had undoubtedly chosen not to go back to Ethiopia and face a possible firing squad, so they'd probably stayed in Rome and were hanging out with the other expats at Etiopia. The colonial ties between Italy and Ethiopia had been brief and not strong, but they persisted, as Purcell saw around the Termini, and he imagined that Italy would see even more upscale refugees as the revolution got uglier. Meanwhile, he had to deal with the unpleasant consulate officer, who didn't speak English but spoke bad Italian to Vivian, who maintained her composure and smiled. The man didn't seem to believe that anyone wanted to travel to the People's Republic for legitimate purposes, and he was right. The officer took their passports, which he said would be returned to them in a week or so at their place of business, which was *L'Osservatore Romano*, with or without their visas. He also took 100,000 lire from each of them for expedited processing.

The consulate officer's parting advice, which Vivian translated, was, 'If you are denied visas, do not apply again. If you are accepted as journalists, you must refrain from all other activities in Ethiopia.'

Vivian assured him they understood and wished him, 'Buongiorno.'

They spent the next few days before Christmas exploring the city. Vivian said she'd been to Rome twice on school trips, but she didn't know the city as an adult, so Purcell showed her Rome by night, including Trastevere and the fading Via Veneto, where he pointed out the Excelsior where Henry was living and presumably drinking. They didn't go into the hotel bar, but he did take her to Harry's, and after they'd had a drink at the bar, he told her about finding Henry there.

She said to him, 'Thank you for doing that.'

'That's what you wanted.'

'Was it . . . awkward?'

'It was, but we moved on to bigger issues.'

'I knew you would both be mature.'

'I didn't say that.'

She smiled, then leaned over and kissed him at the bar, and the slick bartender said, 'Bellissimo.'

During the day they walked the city and he took her to out-of-the-way places, including the Chapel of Quo Vadis, where Vivian was intrigued by Christ's footprint in the paving stone, and she said, 'This *could* be real.'

252

'You never know.'

A call to Henry had gotten them put on the visitor's list at Porta Santa Rosa, and they walked the hundred acres of Vatican City, and Purcell showed her Henry's office building, and also the Ethiopian College where black-robed monks and seminarians entered and exited. Vivian asked, 'Will I be allowed in there?'

'Good question. I don't think it's coed. But we'll try.'

'I'll wear your trench coat.'

'They're celibate, Vivian, not blind.'

Henry had gotten them passes to Saint Peter's for Midnight Mass on Christmas Eve, and they met Henry at Porta Santa Rosa at eleven and walked to the basilica without having to go through the throngs in Saint Peter's Square.

The Mass looked to Purcell as it had looked on television when he'd seen it sitting in a New York bar one Christmas Eve.

Vivian, as expected, was moved by the pageantry and the papal address, and the pope's announcement that 1975 would be a Holy Year. Purcell, though he spoke neither Italian nor Latin, was also impressed by the history and the grandeur of the Roman Mass. He wondered if they'd keep the Holy Grail at the altar of the basilica or in the Vatican Museums. He'd suggest the altar, and maybe he would make that part of the deal. He smiled at his own absurd thoughts and Vivian whispered to him, 'It's good to see you happy.'

Henry had secured late supper reservations in the Jewish ghetto, explaining, 'There is nothing else open in Rome tonight.'

And there were no taxis or public transportation either, so they walked along the Tiber to the ghetto and entered Vecchia Roma on the Piazza di Campitelli.

The restaurant was standing room only, but the hostess seated them immediately, and Henry confessed, 'I promised them a four-star review in *L'Osservatore Romano*.'

Vivian asked, 'Do you do restaurant reviews?'

'No, and neither does the paper.'

Vivian and Purcell exchanged glances.

Henry asked, 'Red or white?'

'Both,' Purcell replied. He looked around at the fresco walls, seeing nothing that looked particularly Jewish. In fact, the restaurant was decorated for Christmas.

Mercado commented, 'The Jews have been in this ghetto since before the time of Christ and I'd say they are more Roman than the Romans.' He added, 'I'm sure Peter and Paul found comfort here among their fellow Jews.'

Vivian said, 'Amazing.'

The wine came and Henry toasted, 'Merry Christmas to us.'

Vivian added, 'And a happy, healthy, and peaceful New Year.'

Purcell didn't think their immediate plans for the New Year included any of that, so he also proposed, 'To a safe and successful journey.'

Vivian said to Henry, 'And thank you for this night.'

Purcell offered, 'We'll split the bill.'

'No, no,' said Mercado. 'This is my Christmas gift to you both.'

'Thank you,' said Vivian.

Purcell noticed that the table was set for four, and he wondered if Mercado's lady friend was joining him, but he didn't ask. Henry, however, brought it up. 'I have an old friend in Rome – Jean – whom I mentioned to Frank, but she couldn't join us.'

Purcell doubted if the lady was named Jean, and he looked at Henry, who smiled at him. *Bastard.*

Vivian said, 'We'd like to meet her.'

They looked at the menus and Vivian noted that the food didn't seem much different than traditional Italian, but Mercado assured her that there were subtle differences, and he offered to order for everyone, which he did. Mercado then held court for the rest of the evening, and if Purcell didn't know better, he'd think that Henry was trying to re-impress Vivian, who handled the balancing act well, giving equal time to her host and former lover and to her new beau.

They left the restaurant at 3 A.M. and Mercado walked with Vivian and Purcell part of the way to their nearby hotel, then wished them Merry Christmas and continued on to the Excelsior.

Purcell and Vivian strolled hand in hand through the quiet streets and Vivian said, 'I didn't know Henry had a lady friend in Rome.'

'I'm sure Henry has a lady in every city.'

'And you?'

'Only four — Addis Ababa, Cairo, Geneva, and Rome.'

She leaned over and gave him a kiss. They continued on and Vivian said, 'Wasn't that a beautiful Mass?'

'It was.'

'Could you live in Rome?'

'I would need a job.'

She pointed out, 'If we find the Holy Grail, you probably won't need a job.'

'Right. Let's ask ten million. Dollars, not lire.'

'We're not going to steal the Grail or sell it. But you and Henry will write a book, and I'll supply the photographs, and we'll all be famous.'

'Don't forget your camera.'

On the subject of money, Purcell had informed Vivian in Cairo that the AP, which he'd been working for when he went missing inside a Khmer Rouge prison camp, had generously given him a year's back pay on his release. As with Henry's back pay after four years in the Gulag, it wasn't the easiest money Purcell had ever made, but the lump sum came in handy when he'd collected it in New York. He still had most of it, and this was paying for his Roman Holiday, and *L'Osservatore Romano* would pay the expenses for his Ethiopian assignment, sans salary. He assumed Henry would work out something similar for his photographer.

As for Vivian's finances, she'd told him in Cairo that she had a small trust fund, though she never mentioned its source or anything about her family. All he knew about her past was that she'd gone to boarding school in Geneva. If there was anything more she wanted to tell him, she would. Meanwhile they were in Rome and in love. *La dolce vita.*

Most of the restaurants in Rome were closed on Christmas Day, but the concierge booked Christmas dinner for them at the Grand Hotel de la Minerva because he said Vivian was as beautiful as the goddess Minerva. That cost Purcell thirty thousand lire, but Vivian paid for dinner, which was her Christmas gift to him. His to her would be a trip to Tuscany.

Purcell rented a car and they drove to Tuscany and spent the week touring, staying at country inns, then they drove up to Florence for New Year's Eve, where they joined the crowd in the Piazza della Signoria and celebrated the arrival of the New Year on a cold clear winter night.

They drove back to Rome on New Year's Day and returned to the Hotel Forum in midafternoon.

There was a handwritten message at the desk from Henry that said, 'Col. Gann will arrive at Fiumicino Jan. 4. Staying at Excelsior. Dinner at Hassler Roof 8 P.M. Call me when you've returned. Can you go to Berini next week? Good news about our visas.' It was signed, 'Love, Henry.'

Purcell said, 'Well, it seems that we are going to Ethiopia.'

Vivian nodded.

They returned to their room and Purcell called Henry at the office. 'Happy New Year,' Purcell said.

'And to you. Are you in Rome?'

'We are. Got your message.'

'Good, come join me for cocktails and we'll catch up. Excelsior, say five.'

'Six. See you then.' He hung up and said to Vivian, 'I can go alone.'

'I'll come. Lots to talk about.'

'There always is with Henry.'

'Now that it's becoming real ... I'm getting a little apprehensive.'

He looked at her. 'I always feel that way before an assignment into a hostile area.' He assured her, 'It's normal.'

'Ethiopia was my first time in a war zone.' She smiled. 'I was excited and clueless.'

'Now you're an experienced veteran.'

'God will watch over us. He did last time.'

Purcell thought that God's patience with them might be wearing thin, and he didn't reply.

257

CHAPTER 24

The Excelsior bar and lounge, Purcell guessed, was probably Old World when it was brand-new, and Henry was at home here, and everyone seemed to know him. Someday they'd name a drink after him.

They were escorted to a good table by the window, and they gave their orders to a waiter, Giancarlo, who had greeted Signore Mercado by name, of course, and knew what he was drinking.

Purcell thought back to Harry's Bar when Signore Mercado had told him never to darken his doorstep at the Excelsior. They'd come a long way. Purcell noted that Henry was wearing a sharp blue suit with a white silk shirt, and what looked like an Italian silk tie. Apparently Henry had gone shopping. Vivian, too, had gone shopping, in Florence, and she looked good in a white winter silk dress, which Henry complimented.

Purcell was feeling a bit underdressed in the only sport jacket he'd brought from Cairo. He would have gone shopping, too, but they weren't going to be here long.

It was New Year's Day evening, a quiet night back in the States, Purcell recalled, but the Excelsior bar and lounge was full, and Mercado informed them, 'The Italians will take the rest of the week off.'

Purcell inquired, 'And you?'

'The printing presses never stop, as you well know.' He added, 'I'll do half days.'

Vivian asked, 'Will Jean be joining us?'

Mercado replied, 'She had to go to London.'

Purcell lit a cigarette.

Vivian asked him, 'So do we have our visas?'

Mercado pulled two passports from his inside pocket and handed the blue one to Purcell, then opened Vivian's red Swiss passport and said, 'This photo never did you justice.'

Vivian reached across the table and Mercado gave her her passport.

By this time, Purcell thought, he'd have clocked the guy, who was pissing him off, but he decided to see if Henry continued to be an asshole, then take it from there.

Henry said, all businesslike now, 'Same as last time, the visas are stamped inside.' He drew two sheets of paper from his pocket. 'And these are copies of your visa applications, signed and stamped by the consul general.' He handed a visa to each of them.

Purcell glanced inside his passport and saw that the new visa stamp, unlike his last one, had been altered by someone, who'd scratched out the Lion of Judah in red ink. His visa application had the same rubber stamp, similarly altered to show that things had changed in Ethiopia.

Their drinks came and Henry informed them, 'Tonight is on L'Osservatore Romano.'

They touched glasses and Purcell asked, 'Do you have our press credentials?'

'I do.' He handed each of them a press card, and also a larger document written in several languages, including Amharic, Arabic, and Tigrena, which he said was sort of a journalist's safe-conduct pass. He smiled.

Neither Purcell nor Vivian returned the smile.

The waiter brought over an assortment of nuts, olives, and cheese, which Purcell suspected was Henry's dinner on most nights.

Purcell asked, 'Any good news about the Ethiopian College?'

'Not yet.' Mercado explained, 'The college is closed until the Epiphany.'

'Good time to break in.'

Mercado looked at him, but did not respond.

Vivian, too, had nothing to say about that, but she asked, 'Will I be allowed in?'

'No.'

Purcell inquired, 'What do you make of this refusal to let us see their library?'

Mercado pondered that, then replied, 'That depends on your level of paranoia.' He informed them, 'The Ethiopian College is a very cloistered place. I'm sure there is nothing strange or secretive going on there, but they like their privacy.'

'We all do, Henry, but this place is not a monastery on a mountain – or in the jungle. It's on Vatican City property, under the authority of the papal state. Who makes the rules? Them or the Vatican?'

'They are semi-autonomous.' He let them know, 'I'm pushing our cover story that we want to do some research for our Ethiopian assignment – which is actually true. But I'm not pushing so hard that someone would think there is more to my interest.'

'All right.' He asked, 'Is this library worth the trouble?'

'I think the maps will be invaluable. But I may be wrong.'

Purcell nodded. Henry's time in the Vatican Library and his request for access to the Ethiopian College were well within his needs as a reporter for *L'Osservatore Romano*. On the other hand, if someone in the Vatican hierarchy was putting the pieces together – including Henry asking to go back to hell with the same reporter and photographer he'd been with in prison – then a picture was taking shape. Actually, two pictures: one that looked like a reporter doing his job, and one that looked like a reporter who was getting nosy about something he wasn't supposed to know. The thing that would put the picture in focus would be Henry's notifying the Vatican of Father Armano's death, saying in effect that he'd heard the dying words of Father Giuseppe Armano, who once had a papal letter in his pocket telling the good father to grab the Holy Grail from a Coptic monastery.

Mercado asked, 'What's on your mind, Frank?'

'Our cover story.'

'The beauty of our cover story is that it is real.'

'Right.' Up until the point where they went off into the jungle. And even then, they were on assignment, though not necessarily for *L'Osservatore Romano*.

Also, Purcell thought, Henry was driving this bus with a lot more enthusiasm than he'd shown at Harry's Bar. He'd been touched by the Holy Spirit, or he just smelled a good story – the Holy Grail of stories. Plus, of course, Henry wanted to make up for his past poor performance in Ethiopia. It was important to him that neither Vivian nor Frank Purcell thought he had lost his nerve. Henry should take his own advice about going to Ethiopia for the right reasons.

Henry seemed to be done with business, and he inquired about their trip to Tuscany, and Vivian provided most of the answers. Henry said it sounded like a wonderful trip, and added, 'If you are still here in the spring, or the fall, Tuscany is at its best.' He further advised, 'But stay away in the summer. It's overrun with Brits.' He smiled and said, 'The Italians call it Tuscanshire.'

Henry continued with his travel advice, and it occurred to Purcell that he might be lonely. He obviously knew people in Rome, including his colleagues at the newspaper as well as every bartender and waiter on the Via Veneto. And there was also the mysterious lady whose name was not Jean. But Purcell could detect the loneliness – he'd experienced it himself. In a rare moment of empathy, Purcell understood that Henry had lost more than a lover in Ethiopia – he'd lost a friend. Or, considering the age difference, he'd lost a young protégée – someone he could teach. Or was it manipulate?

He looked at Vivian as Henry was going on about Perugia or something, and it seemed to Purcell that Vivian had lost the stars in her eyes for Henry. In fact, Vivian, like himself, had been transformed by her experience in Ethiopia. She had seemed then, to him, a bit … immature, almost childish in Addis and on the road to the front lines, not to mention the mineral baths or Prince Joshua's tent. But she'd grown up fast, as people do who've been traumatized by war. He knew, too, that the encounter with Father Armano had affected her deeply, as had her recent romantic complications. It was a mature decision to get herself to a nunnery, and though he loved the woman who'd left him in Cairo, he liked the woman who'd met him in Rome.

Henry, on the other hand, seemed to be regressing. But Purcell was not going to underestimate the old fox.

Henry had moved on to Milan, and Vivian was nodding attentively, though her eyes were glazing over.

It occurred to Purcell, too, that Henry must hear time's wingèd chariot gaining on him. So for Henry, a return to Ethiopia was a no-lose situation; if he died there, he wasn't missing much more of life. But if he returned – with or without the Holy Grail – he would have stories to tell for the rest of his life. Hopefully to a nice woman, but anyone would do.

For Vivian and Purcell, however, the timeline was different. Especially for Vivian. Henry Mercado was at the end of that timeline, while he, Purcell, was somewhere in the middle, and Vivian was just beginning her life and her career as a photojournalist. By now, she'd figured out that it wasn't easy or glamorous, but it *was* exciting and interesting. Unfortunately, the exciting parts were dangerous and the interesting parts had nothing to do with the job. And it was often lonely.

He didn't know if Henry had ever had this conversation with Vivian, and he would advise against it in any case. Frank Purcell was not going to give her The Lecture. She'd figure it out on her own. Meanwhile, Vivian thought they had something together, and they did, but the future was something else. He'd had a few Vivians in his life, and the odds were that Vivian would have a few more Frank Purcells in her life, and maybe one or two more Henry Mercados.

Or Ethiopia would join them together forever, one way or the other.

'Frank?'

He looked at Henry.

'Are you mentally attending?'

'No.'

Mercado laughed. 'Learn to lie a bit, Frank. You're offensive when you don't.'

'I'm learning from a master, Henry.'

'That you are.' He said to Purcell, 'I was just telling Vivian the terms of her employment. All expenses paid, but no pay.'

'Right. Money is tight at the Vatican.'

Henry laughed, then informed him, 'We try to keep the newspaper self-sufficient.'

'Sell tobacco ads.'

'The assignment is for one month.' He looked at both of them and said, 'That should be enough time ... one way or the other.'

Neither Purcell nor Vivian replied.

Mercado said, 'I have a contract for each of you to sign.'

Purcell informed him, 'I stopped signing contracts in bars years ago.'

Mercado laughed. 'They're in my office, not here.' He let them know, 'Anything you write – or photograph – becomes the exclusive property of *L'Osservatore Romano*.'

'Who gets to keep the Holy Grail?'

'We will see.'

The waiter brought another round along with a plate of canapés. Main course.

Mercado announced, 'By the way, I've informed the Vatican, by letter, of the death of Father Giuseppe Armano of Berini, Sicily, with copies of my letter to several Vatican offices, which is what one does in a bureaucracy, and a copy to the Ministry of War because the deceased was in the army serving the fatherland in Ethiopia.'

Purcell asked, 'Have you had a response?'

'No.'

Vivian asked, 'Did you relate the circumstances of his death?'

'Yes, of course, but I neglected to mention the black monastery or the Holy Grail.'

Purcell asked, 'Did you use our names in the letter?'

'I did.' He explained, 'I didn't want them thinking I was hallucinating at the sulphur baths.'

Purcell said, 'We'd like to see a copy of the letter.'

Mercado took a photostatted page out of his pocket and handed it to Purcell. Purcell read it and saw it was a fairly straightforward account of what had happened that evening, though Father Armano's tale had been condensed to a few lines about his capture by Ethiopian forces – though he'd actually been captured by Coptic monks – and his forty-year imprisonment in a Royal Army fortress. Purcell noticed, too, that Henry had not mentioned the nude bathing.

He passed the letter to Vivian and said to Mercado, 'I would think someone would have replied to this.'

'Communication with the Vatican is usually one-way. Same with government ministries.'

'Yes, but they'd want more information.'

'Not necessarily.'

'How about a thank-you?'

'A good deed is its own reward.' He popped a canapé in his mouth, then said, 'I wasn't actually sure whom to notify, so I copied six Vatican offices, and I admit I am a bit surprised myself that no one from the Vatican has gotten back to me – though someone else did.'

'Who?'

'The order of Saint Francis. And they have no one in their files or records by the name of Giuseppe Armano of Berini, Sicily.'

Vivian looked up from Mercado's letter.

Purcell asked him, 'What do you make of that?'

'I'm not sure. Certainly Father Armano existed. We saw him. Or we saw someone.'

Vivian said, 'A man lying on his deathbed does not make up a lie about who he is.'

Mercado agreed and said, 'It gets curiouser.' He continued, 'I called the Franciscans in Assisi to follow up and someone there said they'd get back to me, though they haven't. Then I tried the Ministry of War, and some maggiore informed me that the 1935 war in Ethiopia was not his most pressing problem. He did say, however, that he'd make internal inquiries.'

Purcell thought about all this, then said to Mercado, 'Things, I'm sure, move slowly in the Vatican bureaucracy, but you may hear back soon.'

'What is the date of my letter?'

Vivian looked at it and said, 'Ten November.'

'Which,' Mercado said, 'is less than a week after I arrived in Rome from London, and which is why, as you'll see in the letter, I didn't apologize for any delay in reporting this death to whomever I thought were the proper authorities.'

Purcell reminded him, 'You told me you didn't notify the Vatican.'

'I lied.' He smiled. 'I didn't like you then.' He added, 'Now we are friends and partners in this great adventure and we have sealed our covenant with blood. Well ... cheap wine. And we are, as they say, putting all our cards on the table.'

Purcell thought Henry was still holding a card or two. He asked, 'What do you think is actually going on?'

Mercado drained his gin and tonic and replied, 'Well, obviously, something is going on. Someone, perhaps in the Vatican, instructed the Franciscans to post a reply, and further instructed them to say there is no Father Armano.'

'Why?'

'Your guess is as good as mine.'

Vivian said, 'The Vatican knows who Father Armano is, and they know what Father Armano was doing in Ethiopia. And now they're wondering how much we know.'

'That's very astute, Vivian. And they will continue to wonder how much we know — what Father Armano's last words were to us.'

Again Purcell thought about this. He wasn't a believer in grand conspiracies or a fan of those who did believe in them. But Father Armano had, in effect, spelled out a Vatican conspiracy to steal the Holy Grail. It would follow, then, that there still existed a conspiracy of silence regarding what seemed to be an ongoing Vatican mission to relieve the Coptic Church of their Holy Grail.

Vivian asked Mercado, 'Will you do any further follow-up?'

'That would not be a wise thing to do.'

She nodded.

Purcell commented, 'It would have been wiser for someone in the Vatican to just say, "Thank you, we will notify next of kin, and God bless you."'

Mercado nodded. 'That would have been the wise thing for them to do. But I suspect my letter caused some worry and they decided to ... what is the expression? Stonewall it.'

Purcell also pointed out, 'Maybe you shouldn't have sent the letter at all.'

'I thought about that. About not tipping my hand. But then the job in Rome came up with *L'Osservatore Romano*, and I thought ahead to writing about this, so I couldn't very well reveal this story in an article months or years later without having to explain why I'd kept this information to myself.'

Purcell suggested, 'Your letter to the Vatican may actually be the reason you're working in and for the Vatican.'

Mercado looked at Purcell. 'Interesting.'

'And,' Purcell pointed out, 'why Vivian and I are now working for the Vatican.'

'Actually, you're working for the Vatican newspaper, Frank, but I won't split hairs with you.'

Vivian was taking this all in, then said to Mercado, 'You did the right thing, Henry, by reporting Father Armano's death.'

'Yes, you can never do wrong by doing right.' He suggested, 'Let's put conspiracy aside and think this could be typical bureaucratic indifference, coupled with bad record-keeping in all departments.' He added, 'The Italians, like the Germans, would just as soon not be reminded of the 1930s and '40s.'

Purcell replied, 'That could explain the indifference of the Ministry of War. But not the Vatican.'

Mercado did not reply.

Vivian said, 'Father Armano was real, and we are going to make sure that his suffering and death are acknowledged by the people who sent him to war.'

Mercado looked at her, and it seemed to Purcell that Henry was just noticing the change in his former playmate.

Vivian continued, 'We will go to Berini and find his family.'

'That is the plan,' Mercado agreed, and ordered another round.

Vivian had two full glasses of red wine in front of her, and Purcell was still working on his last Jack Daniel's, and he wondered where Henry put all that gin.

They spoke awhile about the timing of their trip to Berini, then Ethiopia, and how they'd approach the problem of covering their assignments while actually trying to find the black monastery, which was in Getachu territory.

Vivian surprised everyone and herself by saying, 'I hope Getachu gets arrested and shot before we get there.'

Mercado informed her, 'Men like that do not get eaten by the revolution. They do the eating.'

Vivian nodded, then said, 'Maybe we should not be asking Colonel Gann to come with us.'

Mercado suggested, 'Let's discuss that further when we see him.'

Vivian got up to use the ladies' room and Purcell said to Mercado, 'As I mentioned to you in your office, these entry visas are not necessarily exit visas.'

'And as I said to you, save your paranoia for Ethiopia.'

'I'm practicing.'

Mercado changed the subject and said, 'She looks very happy.'

Purcell did not respond.

'I told you, I'm over it, and I'm over the anger as well.' He asked, 'Can't you tell?'

'We don't need to have this conversation.'

'It's not about us, Frank. And it's not even about her. It's about our ... assignment.'

'We all understand that. That's why we're here.'

'I'd like us to be truly friends.'

'How about close colleagues?'

'I didn't steal her from you. You stole her from me.'

'You sound angry.'

'Put yourself in my shoes. I'm hanging there from a fucking pole, and what do I see? *Fucking*.'

'You're drunk, Henry.'

'I am ... I apologize.'

'Accepted.' Purcell stood. 'And if you mention the name Jean one more time, I am going to clock you.'

'What does that mean?'

'You don't want to find out.'

Mercado stood unsteadily and offered his hand to Purcell. Purcell saw Vivian coming back, so he took Mercado's hand.

Vivian asked, 'Are we leaving?'

'We are.'

She said to Henry, 'We had a long drive from Florence. Thank you for drinks.'

'Thank our newspaper.'

She looked at him and suggested, 'You should turn in.'

He leaned toward her, she hesitated, then they did an air kiss on both cheeks. 'Buona notte, signorina.'

'Buona notte.'

Purcell took Vivian's arm and they left.

As the doorman signaled for a taxi, Vivian said, 'I've never seen him so drunk.'

Purcell did not respond.

She glanced at Purcell. 'Well ... I only knew him a few months.'

The taxi came and they got in. Purcell said, 'Hotel Forum.'

They stayed quiet on the ride to the hotel, then Vivian said, 'If I hadn't met him, I wouldn't have met you.'

Purcell lit a cigarette.

She took his hand. 'Did something happen when I was gone?'

'No.'

'I love you.'

He took his hand out of hers and put his arm around her shoulders. He said to her, 'You once told me to go to hell.'

'I was so angry at you.' She mimicked him: 'I think I could have done this on my own. Can we save this for the Hilton bar?' She said, 'Bastard.'

He drew her closer and she put her head on his shoulder. She said, 'It was my idea to invite you along.'

'I thought it was God's plan.'

'It was. I just went along with it.'

'What's the rest of the plan?'

The taxi stopped. 'Forum.'

She said, 'To get upstairs and get our clothes off.'

'Good plan.'

CHAPTER 25

The golden domes and crosses of the churches caught the first rays of the rising sun, and Purcell watched the dawn spreading over the city.

He looked back at Vivian lying naked in the bed, her skin as white as the sheets, making her appear wraithlike.

'Come to bed, Frank.'

He sat at the edge of the bed and she ran her hand over his back. She said, 'You were talking in your sleep.'

'Sorry.'

She sat up and said, 'I dreamt that we were at the mineral baths, and we were swimming, and we made love in the water.'

Purcell wondered where Henry was, but he didn't ask.

'And then we went back to the Jeep, and Father Armano was there ... and we were still naked ...'

'Sounds like a Catholic schoolgirl's nightmare.'

She laughed, then stayed silent awhile. 'Why did he have that skull?'

'I don't know.'

'Was it a warning?'

'I'm not good at symbolism, Vivian.'

'What did *you* dream about?'

'Henry, in the Vatican archives. A nightmare.'

'Tell me.'

'Henry has solved the mystery of how the Holy Grail wound up in Ethiopia.'

'What difference does it make?'

'That was my point.' He lay down beside her and asked, 'Do you believe that the actual Holy Grail is sitting in a black monastery in Ethiopia?'

'I told you I believe what Father Armano said to us. I believe that God led us to him, and him to us.' She also told him, 'I believe that if we find the Grail, and if we believe in it, it will reveal itself to us. If we do not believe in it, it will not be real to us.' She made him understand, 'It's not the Grail by itself — it is our faith that heals us.'

This sounded to Purcell almost as complex as the doctrine of the Trinity, but he understood what she was saying. 'All right . . . but do you believe that we should risk our lives to find it?'

She stayed silent a moment, then replied, 'If this is God's will . . . then it doesn't matter what happens to us — it only matters that we try.'

Purcell glanced at her. He wondered if Mercado had told her what he'd said to him.

She asked, 'Do you believe in this, Frank?'

'Henry says I do.'

'And you say . . . ?'

'Depends on the day.'

'Then you shouldn't be going to Ethiopia.'

'I am going.'

'Go for the right reasons.'

'Right.'

She moved closer to him and said, 'There is another miracle. Us.'

'That's one I believe in.' He asked her, 'Would you like breakfast in bed?'

'It's early for breakfast.'

'It's two hours to get room service. You're not in Switzerland anymore.'

She laughed and said, 'I want you to fill the tub and make love to me in the water. That's what I wanted you to do at the spa.'

'I didn't know that.'

'You did.'

'Never crossed my mind.'

'Do you think I take my clothes off in front of any man I just met?'

In fact, he'd thought that she and Henry were just being worldly and sophisticated, and maybe trying to shock his American sensibilities.

'Frank?'

'I thought that was a rhetorical question.' He got out of bed. 'I'll run the water. You call for coffee.'

He filled the tub and she came into the bathroom and they got into the steamy water together, facing each other. They moved closer, embraced, and kissed. She pressed her breasts against his chest, then rose up and came down on his erect penis. She gyrated her pelvis as she clung to him in the warm water, and they climaxed together.

*

274

They sat at opposite ends of the tub, and Vivian lay back with her eyes closed, breathing in the misty air.

He thought she'd fallen asleep, but she said softly, 'It doesn't matter what happens, as long as it happens to us together.'

'I believe that ... but I want to make sure we're not choosing death over life.'

'We are choosing eternal life.' She added, 'As Saint Peter did.'

'Right ... but I'm not a martyr, and neither are you. We're journalists.'

She laughed. 'Journalists go to hell.'

'Probably ... and we're not saints either, Vivian.'

'Speak for yourself.'

They sat back in the water with their eyes closed, and Purcell drifted off into a pleasant sleep. He thought he heard Vivian saying, 'Take this cup and drink of it, for this is my blood.'

'Frank?'

He opened his eyes.

Vivian stood over him in a robe, holding a cup. 'Have some coffee.'

He took the cup and drank it.

CHAPTER 26

The Hassler Hotel sat high above the Spanish Steps, offering a panoramic view of Rome and the Vatican. It was Saturday, and the elegant rooftop restaurant was filled with well-heeled tourists, businesspeople, and celeb types, but Mercado had gotten them a choice table by the window.

Purcell had no doubt that Signore Mercado used his connection to *L'Osservatore Romano* all over town. No one actually *read* the paper, of course, but it was widely quoted over the wire, and its name had cachet, especially in Rome.

Henry Mercado and Colonel Sir Edmund Gann had arrived together from the Excelsior, and Gann, thin to begin with, looked like a man who'd been on starvation rations for a few months, which he had, and he hadn't put on any weight in London. His tweed suit hung loosely and his skin had a prison pallor. As Purcell knew from firsthand experience, it took awhile before the body got used to food again.

Gann's eyes, however, were bright and alert, and his demeanor hadn't changed much. His mind had stayed healthy in prison, and his body just needed a few Italian meals. Then back to Ethiopia for another round with fate. Purcell wondered again what was driving Colonel Gann.

Purcell noticed that Henry had slipped into his British accent to make the colonel feel at home away from home, and Colonel Gann had now become Sir Edmund.

Mercado informed them that he'd briefed Sir Edmund over a few drinks at the Excelsior, but Purcell wasn't sure how detailed that briefing had been. Sir Edmund, however, did seem to know that Miss Smith was now with Mr Purcell, and that Mr Mercado was okay with that – so there'd be no unpleasantness at dinner.

Cocktails arrived at the table, and Henry toasted, 'To being alive and being together again.'

Vivian added, 'And thanks to Sir Edmund for keeping us alive.'

They touched glasses and Sir Edmund said modestly, 'Trying to save my own skin, actually, and I was glad for the company – and your assistance.'

Purcell was sure that Gann didn't want to talk about his three months in an Ethiopian prison, so Purcell picked another unhappy subject. 'I assume you heard about Prince Joshua.'

'I did.'

Gann didn't seem to want to talk about that either, so they perused the menu. Purcell remembered that he was buying, and the prices, in lire, looked like telephone numbers. But he supposed he owed this to Colonel Gann for saving their lives, and he owed it to Henry for stealing his girlfriend.

The waiter came and they ordered. Henry found the same amarone at double the price of the Forum.

Mercado said to Vivian and Purcell, 'I've told Sir Edmund that we have our visas, and I took the liberty of telling him that this black monastery may be of interest to us when we return.'

Gann reminded Purcell, 'Last time we discussed this – in that ravine – I believe you said you were never going back.'

'I've changed my mind.' He added, 'Actually, we've all *lost* our minds.'

Colonel Gann flashed his toothy smile. He thought a moment, then replied, 'I grew up with King Arthur and his Knights of the Round Table, Mr Purcell. And when I was a boy, my greatest dream was to join in a quest to find the Holy Grail.'

'So you're crazy, too.'

Everyone laughed, and Gann continued, 'Now, of course, I, like most rational men, do not believe any of this ... but it is a wonderful story – it is the story of our unending search for something good and beautiful ... which is why it appeals to us ... to our hearts and our souls. And I loved those stories of Arthur and his knights, and they affected me deeply. And then I grew up.'

Everyone stayed silent, so Gann continued, 'But those stories have stayed with me ... and they are still part of me.'

Again no one spoke, then Mercado confessed, 'I believe there *was* a King Arthur, and a Camelot. I also believe there was a round table of virtuous knights, and I believe they sought the Holy Grail.' He hesitated, then continued, 'I also believe that Perceval and Gauvain found the Grail Castle in Glastonbury and sailed off into a fog with the Grail and returned it to Jerusalem.'

Again, no one spoke, then Gann said, 'I don't seem to remember the Jerusalem bit.'

Mercado said, 'That's my theory.'

'Yes ... well, I suppose that's possible.'

Mercado took the opportunity to explain to Gann, and also

to Vivian, how the Holy Grail was then taken from Jerusalem to Egypt, then to Ethiopia, a half step ahead of the armies of Islam.

Both Gann and Vivian seemed to agree that Henry's scholarship was impressive and logical.

Purcell said to Gann, 'More importantly, we have been told by this Father Armano, who Getachu was asking us about, that the Grail – or something called the Holy Grail – is sitting in this black monastery.'

'I see.'

'So we're going back to Ethiopia to see who's crazier – us or Father Armano.'

Gann said, 'There is a thin line, Mr Purcell, between bravery and insanity.'

'No argument there.'

'Some people are content to accept things on faith. Others are driven to extraordinary efforts to find and see the thing they want to believe in. Vide et crede. See and believe. And that is where bravery and insanity become one.'

'And that's when you buy a ticket to Ethiopia.'

Gann smiled and suggested to his dining companions, 'And while you are there looking about for the Holy Grail, you might as well try to get a look at the Ark of the Covenant.'

'Is that there too?'

'Apparently, but not in the black monastery. It's in the ancient ruins of Axum.'

Purcell asked Mercado, 'Have you heard of that?'

'I have.'

It seemed to Purcell that Ethiopia had at least two amazing

biblical relics, making him start to wonder about the first one. He asked Gann, 'Has Noah's Ark also shown up there?'

Again Gann smiled, then said, 'Not that I'm aware of. But I have seen the resting place of the Ark of the Covenant.'

Vivian encouraged him to tell them about it, and Purcell wished she hadn't.

Gann explained, 'The Ark of the Covenant is hidden in a small Coptic chapel in Axum, and it is guarded by one monk, a man named Abba who is called the Atang – the Keeper of the Ark.' He further explained, 'This is the most solemn position in the Ethiopian Orthodox Church – the Coptic Church. Abba can never leave the grounds of the chapel and he will hold this position of Atang until he dies.'

Vivian asked, 'And you've seen this man?'

'And I've spoken to him.' He added, 'He is the only living person who has ever actually seen the Ark, but he has never opened this chest to see the stone tablets on which God gave Moses the Ten Commandments.' Gann explained, 'Abba told me that whoever opens the Ark will be struck dead.'

Purcell inquired, 'Did the Ark of the Covenant arrive in Ethiopia along with the Holy Grail?'

Gann smiled again and replied, 'No, the time and the circumstances were quite different.' He explained, 'As you know, the Queen of Sheba, who ruled in Axum three thousand years ago, went to Jerusalem and was impregnated by King Solomon. She returned to Axum and bore a child whom she named Menelik, and this was the beginning of the Solomonic dynasty that has ruled Ethiopia until ... well, a few months ago.' He continued, 'When Menelik was a young man, he traveled to Jerusalem to meet his father. Menelik stayed for three years, and when he left, Solomon ordered that the Ark of the Covenant accompany his son to protect him. Menelik brought the Ark to a monastery called Tana Kirkos on the eastern shore of Lake Tana, which feeds its waters into the Blue Nile. The monastery is still there, guarded by monks, and I have actually been a guest at this monastery.'

Purcell inquired, 'Did the monks insist that you stay forever?'

'Sorry?'

'Please go on.'

Gann went on, 'After Menelik died, the new emperor, Ezana, sent for the Ark, and it was brought to Axum, where it remains to this day.'

Purcell asked, 'Why hasn't the Marxist government grabbed it?'

'Interesting question.' Gann explained, 'They've appropriated some church property, but there is a backlash growing among the Coptic faithful, so the government has backed off a bit.' He added, 'The stupid Marxists have actually stirred a religious revival amongst the peasants.'

Purcell nodded. That wasn't what happened in Russia when the Communists crushed the churches, but it was interesting that it was happening in Ethiopia. More importantly, if the Ark of the Covenant was safe for the time being, then maybe the black monastery and the Holy Grail were also safe for now – at least until the team from *L'Osservatore Romano* arrived.

Mercado had come to a similar conclusion and said, 'The black monastery is also on borrowed time.'

Gann said, 'The new government is trying to consolidate its

power, and it doesn't wish to anger the masses whom it purports to represent. But as you say, it's only a matter of time before they resume their confiscation of church property. For now, they are satisfied with executing the royal family and the rasses, and appropriating their palaces and wealth.'

Purcell asked Gann, 'Are you still working for the Royalists?'

Gann hesitated, then replied, 'I am in contact with counterrevolutionary elements here in Rome, in London, and in Cairo and Ethiopia.'

'How's that counterrevolution looking?'

Gann replied, 'Not very good at the moment. But we are hopeful.'

Their antipasto arrived and Mercado picked at his food, then said, 'I am convinced that the Holy Grail could eventually wind up in the hands of the Marxist government. And if that happens, the Grail may not be sold to the highest bidder – it may be destroyed.'

Purcell looked at Mercado. It was inevitable, he thought, that Henry, or one of them, would find a justification for stealing the Grail from the monastery – for its own protection, of course. And, in truth, Henry had a point.

Mercado went on, 'After three thousand years of relative stability under the Solomonic dynasty, the whole country is in chaos.' He pressed his point. 'And if the black monastery is looted by revolutionary troops – soldiers of Getachu, for instance – the Grail is in jeopardy. Even if it is sold to the highest bidder, that bidder could very well be someone like the Saudi royal family, who have billions to spend on whatever they fancy.' He concluded, 'I don't want the Holy Grail to wind up in Mecca.'

Purcell pointed out, 'You've done a quantum leap, Henry.'

'Perhaps, but you see what I'm getting at.'

'You're making a case for why we should relieve the Coptic monks of their property.'

'I am trying to protect the Grail.'

Purcell inquired, 'And where do you think it would be safe?'

'The Vatican, of course.'

'I thought you might say that.'

Everyone got a small laugh from that.

Vivian said, 'I agree with Henry.'

Gann, too, said, 'I agree that you – we – need to get this relic out of Ethiopia.'

Purcell, too, agreed, but he advised, 'Not permanently. Just until the times in Ethiopia grow less evil.'

Mercado pointed out, 'The Grail has been taken on long journeys over the last two thousand years to safeguard it from evil, and I believe it has fallen to us to do that again.'

Purcell said, 'So we are all agreed that if we find the black monastery and the Holy Grail, we are morally justified in stealing the Grail for its own protection.'

Everyone nodded.

Colonel Gann looked at Mercado, Purcell, and Vivian and said, 'I should tell you that I am not a believer in this relic as the true cup that Christ used at the Last Supper, and neither do I believe that the Ark of the Covenant and the Ten Commandments are in a hidden chapel in Axum. But these artifacts are central to the Coptic Church in Ethiopia, as well as in Egypt.' He continued, 'Egypt may never be Christian again, but Ethiopia will be. And it is important that all the religious objects that are in jeopardy be safeguarded for the time when the Marxists are overthrown and the emperor is restored to the throne.'

Purcell thought that if by some miracle they actually got hold of the Holy Grail and got it to the Vatican – for safekeeping – it wouldn't get out of there until the second coming of Christ. But that wasn't his problem.

Gann asked, 'Can you tell me a bit more about this Father Armano?'

Mercado looked at Purcell and Vivian, who both nodded. Mercado said to Gann, 'I'm sure you know of the Italian spa that Getachu was talking about.'

'I do indeed.' He told them, 'You shouldn't have spent the night there.' Gann explained, 'The Gallas fancy the place. I don't think they bathe there – or bathe at all – but there is fresh water for their horses and for themselves.' He advised, 'It is a place to avoid.'

Purcell commented, 'We had an old guidebook.'

Mercado continued, 'Well, we put up for the night – had a quick wash – and when we returned to our Jeep, we came upon Father Armano, who was wounded and dying.'

'And I'm sure he said more to you before he died than you told Getachu.'

'Correct.' Mercado suggested that Vivian relate the story, which she did.

Gann listened attentively, nodding now and then, and when Vivian had finished, he said, 'Remarkable. And do you believe this man's story about the Lance of Longinus hanging in thin air, dripping blood? Or that this blood healed the priest?'

Vivian said she did, as did Mercado.

She also said, 'We think it was more than chance that we and

Father Armano arrived at the same place at the same time. And now you tell us that the Gallas are usually there, but they weren't that night.' She concluded, 'We think it was a miracle.'

Colonel Gann nodded politely.

Vivian added, 'And it was an eerie coincidence, I think, that Father Armano and Henry were at the same battle of Mount Aradam in 1935.'

'Yes ... striking coincidence.' He looked at Purcell.

Purcell said, 'I believe the substance of Father Armano's story, but I'm a bit skeptical about the Lance of Longinus hanging in thin air, or about the Holy Grail healing Father Armano.'

Gann replied, 'Yes ... that seems a bit unnatural, doesn't it? But we agree that this relic is probably in the black monastery.'

Everyone agreed.

Gann asked, 'Do you have any specific operational plans to find this monastery?'

Mercado replied, 'We hoped you could help us with that.'

'I believe I can.' He informed them, 'I have a general idea where it is.'

'So do we,' said Purcell, 'based on what Father Armano said about his army patrol from Lake Tana to the black monastery, then being taken by foot to the Royalist fortress, then his escape forty years later and his walk that night to the Italian spa.' He suggested, 'Maybe we could triangulate all of that if we had a good map.'

Gann nodded again. 'It's a starting point.' He advised, 'You ought to begin with aerial reconnaissance if you can.'

Purcell informed him, 'We might have access to a light plane in Addis.'

'Good. That will save you time and effort, and help keep you out of the hands of the Gallas – or Getachu.'

Mercado told Gann, 'There are possibly some good Italian Army maps in the Ethiopian College in Vatican City.'

'Excellent. I'd like to take a look at them.'

'I'm working on that.'

Gann also informed them, 'There is a Falasha village in the vicinity, as I mentioned to Mr Purcell at Getachu's parade ground. These Jews may be a key to locating the black monastery.' He explained, 'There seems to be some ... ancient relationship there.'

Vivian asked, 'What is that relationship?'

Gann further explained, 'The royal family, of course, has Jewish blood from Solomon, and they are proud of that. Proud, too, that they, through the Coptic Church, are the keepers of the Ark of the Covenant, which presumably they are keeping safe for the Jews. The Jews there, the Falashas, see Jesus as a great Jewish prophet and they revere him, and presumably they also believe in the Holy Grail – the kiddush cup of Jesus's last Passover meal.' He asked his companions, 'Do you see the connection?'

Everyone nodded.

Gann continued, 'Also, it would appear that the only connection the black monastery has with the outside world is through this Falasha village. Shoan.'

Purcell inquired, 'What sort of connection?'

Gann replied, 'A spiritual connection. But also a practical connection. Food, medical supplies—'

'They have the Holy Grail,' Purcell reminded him. 'Cures what ails you.'

'Yes ... well ... good point.' He continued, 'The monastery, like most monasteries, is self-sufficient, but even a monk needs new underwear now and then. Sandals and candles. And a bit of wine.'

Purcell asked, 'How do you know all this?'

'We can discuss that in Ethiopia.'

'All right.' Purcell said, 'It would seem, then, that the Falashas know how to find the black monastery.'

Gann replied, 'My understanding is that there is a meeting place somewhere between the monastery and the village.'

Purcell nodded. He had this feeling, as he'd had in Ethiopia, that he'd fallen through the rabbit hole. He said to Mercado, 'This is a whole chapter in our book, Henry. Jews for Jesus.'

Gann changed the subject. 'Have you thought about how you will actually get into this walled monastery if you find it?'

Purcell admitted, 'We haven't thought that far ahead – about pulling off a heist in a monastery filled with club-wielding monks.'

Gann nodded. 'Well ... we can discuss that if or when the time comes.'

'Right.' But the more Purcell thought about all this, the more he believed that time might never come. More likely, they'd wind up in Getachu's camp again, or if they were really unlucky, they'd meet up with the Gallas. Henry and Vivian, however, believed they were chosen to find the Holy Grail, and that God would watch over them. As for himself, he half believed half of that.

Purcell asked Gann, 'If you can get back into Ethiopia, will you actually come with us to the monastery?'

'Am I invited?'

Vivian cautioned, 'This would be more dangerous for you than for us.' She asked, 'And how would you get into the country?'

Gann reminded them, 'I am officially a fugitive from Ethiopian justice, so I will not be applying for a return visa. I will acquire another identity and fly in from Cairo on a commercial flight.' He informed them, 'I have access to everything I need in regard to a passport and a forged visa.'

Vivian said, 'Sounds risky.'

'Not too.' He explained, 'The security people at Addis airport are totally inept – except the ones who are corrupt.' He informed them, 'That was how I flew in last time. I was Charles Lawson then, a Canadian citizen, and within a few days I was Colonel Sir Edmund Gann again, up north with Prince Joshua.'

Vivian pointed out, 'They know what you look like now.'

'You, Miss Smith, will not know what I look like when I see you in Ethiopia.'

Purcell inquired, 'What is your motivation, Colonel, in risking your life?'

'I believe we had this discussion on a hilltop.' He informed everyone, 'I *am* being well paid by the Ethie expat community, but even if I weren't, I'd do this because I believe in it.'

'And what is it that you believe in?'

'The restoration of the monarchy and the liberation of the Ethiopian people from Communism, tyranny, and terror.'

'Do you get paid for trying? Or only for success?'

'Both.' He admitted, 'The princely payment comes when the emperor or his successor is back on the throne.'

'Do you get a palace?'

'I get the satisfaction of a job well done – and the honor of having changed history.'

Vivian asked Gann, 'Will you be coming to Sicily with us?'

'I'm afraid not. As I explained to Mr Mercado earlier, I have related business here in Rome.'

Mercado informed Gann, 'Neither the Vatican nor the Ministry of War nor the Franciscans seem to have any record of Father Giuseppe Armano, which is why we need to go to Berini — to establish his existence. And also to notify next of kin of his fate.'

Gann thought about that, then replied, 'Well, I suppose his name could have been lost.' He added, 'But if the Vatican *wants* his name lost, then they've been to Berini before you.'

That thought had briefly crossed Purcell's mind, but it seemed outlandish to believe that Father Giuseppe Armano was disappearing into an Orwellian black hole. But maybe not so outlandish. They'd find out in Berini.

CHAPTER 27

Mercado said, 'In 1868, the Ethiopian emperor Theodore wrote a letter to Queen Victoria. She did not respond, and Theodore, to avenge the insult, imprisoned a number of British nationals, including the consul. The British then landed an expeditionary force on the African coast and marched on Ethiopia to rescue these people.'

Colonel Gann said, half jokingly, 'Now we've got to pay the bastards to get her majesty's subjects released.'

Purcell didn't know if he was actually back in the reading room of the Vatican Library, or if this was a recurring nightmare. Vivian, however, seemed fascinated by the library and impressed with all the documents that Henry had assembled.

Mercado had assured Purcell that this would be a quick visit, to wrap up his background briefing. Next stop was the Ethiopian College, and if they weren't kicked out again, he, Mercado, and Gann had been allowed one hour in the college library. Vivian, because of her gender, was not welcome.

Mercado continued, 'The British Expeditionary Force was led by Sir Robert Napier, and they advanced on the new Ethiopian capital of Magdala. Theodore was beaten in battle and committed suicide on Easter Day 1868.'

Purcell glanced at his watch. Vivian had volunteered to stay in this room and read through Henry's notes. She'd also brought her camera with her, a brand-new Canon F-I, to begin her photographic documentation of their story, starting with this reading room, and ending, Purcell hoped, with cocktails in the papal reception hall, with everyone holding up the Holy Grail like it was the Stanley Cup.

Vivian saw Purcell smiling and took his picture.

Mercado continued, 'Napier, in good imperial tradition, sacked the emperor's palace and the imperial library at Magdala, carrying off a trove of ancient documents. He took four hundred or so of the most promising of them back to England. He also took the ancient imperial crown that wound up in the British Museum.'

Gann said, 'I believe we gave it back.'

'You did,' said Mercado. 'And now it's probably in the hands of the Marxists — or it's been sold or melted down for the gold and gems.'

Purcell said, 'We get the point, Henry.'

Mercado continued, 'Inside the rim of the crown is engraved, in Geez, the ancient language of Ethiopia, which remains the language of the Coptic Church, these words' — he glanced at his notes — 'King of Kings, Conquering Lion of Judah, Descendant of the House of David, Keeper of the Ark of the Covenant, and Keeper of the Holy Vessel.' Mercado looked at his audience and said, 'We can assume that is the Holy Grail.'

No one argued with that translation, but everyone knew that kings and emperors liked to give themselves titles. Theodore may have descended from the House of David, Purcell thought, but he wasn't the conquering Lion of Judah on Easter Day 1868. Nor was he King of Kings. He was dead. As for keeper of the Ark of the Covenant and the Holy Grail, Purcell was sure that Theodore believed it, but that didn't make the relics real.

Mercado continued, 'Napier, now Lord Napier of Magdala, sold some of the looted documents at auction, and a few of them found their way into the Vatican archives, and this' – he took a curled, yellowed parchment out of a velvet folio – 'is one of them.'

Mercado held up the parchment by a corner and said, 'It is written in Geez, and I had one of the Ethiopian seminarians who can read Geez translate it for me.'

Gann was looking closely at the parchment as though he could read it, but he said, 'It's Geez to me.'

Mercado smiled politely and replaced the parchment in its velvet folio. 'The seminarian thought that based on the style of Geez used, and on the historical event described, this is from about the seventh century – about the time that Islam conquered Egypt.'

Mercado referred to his notes and continued, 'This parchment is unsigned, and the author is unknown, but it was probably written by a church scribe or monk and it is an account of a miraculous healing of a Prince Jacob who was near death from wounds sustained in battle with the Mohammadans, as they are called here, who had invaded from Egyptian Sudan. According to this account, Prince Jacob was carried to Axum to die, and was taken to the place – it doesn't say which place – where the Holy Vessel was kept. The abuna of Axum, the archbishop, gave this prince the last rites, then anointed him with the blood from the Holy Vessel, and Prince Jacob, because he was faithful to God, and because he loved Jesus, and also because he fought bravely against the Mohammadans, was healed of his wounds by the sacred blood of Christ, and he rose up and returned to battle.' Mercado said, 'Unfortunately, there is no actual mention of the Lance of Longinus.'

Purcell thought there were other problems with that story. In fact, it sounded like propaganda to rally the troops and the citizens in time of war. But everyone understood that, so he didn't mention it.

Mercado, too, saw the story as a morale builder and possibly a bit of a stretch. He said, 'This proves little, of course, but it does mention the Holy Grail being in Axum at this time, and it is one of the few early references to the Grail having the power to heal.'

Vivian said, 'The power to heal those who believe.'

Mercado nodded at his former protégée, then said to everyone, 'At some point after this time, with Axum being threatened by Islam, the Grail was taken to a safe place – or many safe places – and now we think we know where it is.'

Mercado stayed silent a moment, then said, 'Edward Gibbon, in his *Decline and Fall of the Roman Empire*, wrote, "Encompassed on all sides by the enemies of their religion, the Ethiopians slept near a thousand years, forgetful of the world, by whom they were forgotten."'

Mercado looked at his watch and said, 'We will now go to the Ethiopian College.'

CHAPTER 28

A short, squat Ethiopian monk met them in the antechamber and escorted them, without a word, to a second-floor library. The college appeared to still be closed for the long Christmas holiday, and they seemed to be the only people there.

A very large monk stood inside the entrance to the library, and the two monks exchanged a few words in what sounded like Amharic.

Purcell looked around the library, which was windowless and badly lit. Book-laden shelves extended up to the high ceiling, and long reading tables ran down the center of the room.

The short monk left, and the big one remained in the room. Apparently he wasn't leaving, so Mercado said something to him in Italian, and the monk replied in halting Italian.

Mercado informed Purcell and Gann, 'He's staying.'

Purcell asked, 'Does it matter?'

'I suppose not.' He said, 'There's a map room here somewhere, and that's what we want to see.'

Gann suggested, 'Don't go right for it, old boy. We'll look around here a bit, then find the map room.'

Mercado nodded and moved over to the shelved books and scanned the titles. Gann did the same, so Purcell took a look at the books. Most seemed to be in Latin, some in Italian, and many in what looked like Amharic script.

Mercado said, 'Here's a Bible in Geez.'

Purcell's three minutes of pretending were up and he moved toward the far end of the long room, where there was a closed door, which he opened, expecting to be shouted at by the monk. But the monk didn't say anything, so Purcell entered the room, which was indeed the cartography room.

A long, marble-topped table sat in the center of the room, and hundreds of rolled maps sat stacked on deep shelves, each with a stringed tag attached. He looked at a tag that was handwritten in Italian, Latin, and Amharic.

He heard something behind him and turned to see the monk standing a few feet from him. Purcell asked, 'Mind if I smoke?'

The monk did not reply.

Purcell moved along the shelves, looking at the hanging tags, though he couldn't read any of them.

Mercado and Gann joined him, and they seemed pleased to see all the maps. Mercado began immediately reading tags, and Gann said, 'Here are the Italian Army maps.' As he picked a few dust-covered maps off the shelf, Purcell unrolled them and laid them on the map table, weighting their corners with brass bars that had been stacked there for that purpose.

There didn't seem to be a card catalog, but Mercado soon figured out how the maps were grouped, and he took a few ancient maps, hand drawn on parchment and papyrus, and set them gently on the table.

The monk watched, but said nothing.

Gann was now sitting at the table, studying the unfurled army maps, and Purcell sat to his right and Mercado to his left. Sir Edmund was once again Colonel Gann.

Purcell saw that the army maps were color printed, with shades of green for vegetation, shades of brown for arid areas, and pale blue for water. The elevation lines were in dark brown, and the few roads were represented by black dotted lines. The symbols for other man-made objects were also in black, as were the grid lines and the latitudes and longitudes. The map legend and all the other writing was in Italian. Gann said, 'We used these captured maps in '41, and map words are the extent of my Italian.'

Gann pointed to a map and said, 'This one is a 1:50,000 map of the east bank of Lake Tana. It was partially field checked by the Italian Army's map ordnance section that made it, but most of this map was compiled from aerial photographs. This map here is of the fortress city of Gondar and environs. It is a more accurate 1:25,000, and completely field checked. Everything else seems to be crude 1:100,000- and 1:250,000-scale maps, not field checked.'

Purcell knew how to read aviation charts, but these were terrain maps, and unless you understood what everything meant, it was like looking at paint spills on graph paper.

Gann continued, 'Most of Africa was accurately mapped by the colonial powers. Ethiopia, however, was not a European colony until the Italians invaded, and the Ethies themselves hadn't any idea how to make a map, or what use they were. Therefore, most of what exists is a result of the Italian Army's brief control of the country.'

Mercado asked, 'And nothing since then?'

Gann informed them, 'The former Ethiopian government had a small cartography office, but they mostly reproduced Italian maps, and now and again they'd produce a city map or a road map, though never a proper field-checked terrain map.' He added, 'Both armies in the current civil war are using what we see here from 1935 until 1941.'

Purcell pointed out, 'I assume the black monastery hasn't been moved, so maybe these are better than nothing.'

'Quite so.'

Gann studied the maps closely, then unrolled a few more.

'Here. This is the area where we were, and this is the map I was using then.' He ran his finger in a circle around a green-and-brown-shaded area. 'This is the jungle valley where the spa is located, and this is the unimproved road by which you presumably arrived.'

Purcell asked, 'Where is the spa?'

'Not here, actually. Probably built after the map was done. But right here' – he pointed – 'is where it is.'

Gann bent over the map and said, 'These are the hills where Prince Joshua set up his camp … These are the hills where Getachu's camp was located. And this is the high plains or plateau between the camps where … where the armies met.'

Purcell stared at the map – the same one Gann had shown him – and that unpleasant day came back to him as it had just come back to Colonel Gann.

Purcell said to Mercado, 'Puts me right there again, Henry. How about you?'

'Makes me wonder why we ever left.'

They all got a laugh at that, and Gann continued his map

recon. He glanced at the monk across the room, then joked, 'Don't see the symbol for hidden black monastery.'

Purcell asked, 'Do you see anything that could be a fortress?' He reminded Gann, 'Father Armano's prison for almost forty years.'

'No ... don't see any man-made structures ...'

Mercado reminded everyone, 'Father Armano walked through the night *from* this fortress *to* the spa.'

'Yes ... but what direction?'

Purcell said, 'He mentioned something about Gondar to the north. And I'm assuming the fortress was in the jungle – the dark green stuff.'

'Yes, possibly ... here is something that would be a night's march to the spa ...' He pointed to a small black square identified as '*incognita*' – unknown.

Gann surmised, 'Probably seen from the air and put on the map, but never field checked to identify it.'

Mercado said, 'Could be the fortress. I don't see any other man-made structures in this jungle valley.'

Gann agreed that *incognita* could be the fortress, but he advised, 'The scale of this map is so large that even these hills, which we know are large from being there, look quite small.'

In fact, Purcell thought, those hills had almost killed Henry.

The monk had moved and was now standing across the table, looking at them.

Gann said, 'Don't assume he doesn't speak English.'

Purcell said to Mercado, 'Maybe this guy wants to back off.'

Mercado said something to the monk, who moved a few feet away.

Purcell said softly, 'The priest said he was taken *from* the black . . . place by the monks and handed over to soldiers of this Prince Theodore, who marched him to the fortress.' He thought back to the spa and to Father Armano's dying words. 'The priest didn't remark about the march, so maybe it was a day's march at most.'

Mercado, too, was thinking about what Father Armano had said. 'I don't know if we can make that assumption . . . I wish we'd known we were going to be looking for this place. I'd have asked him to be more specific.'

Purcell replied, 'We knew at some point, but there was a lot going on. He was dying.'

Gann suggested, 'Try to recall all that this man said. He may have given you a clue.'

Purcell and Mercado thought about that, then Purcell suggested, 'Let's back it up. The priest said his battalion had made camp on the eastern shore of Lake Tana.' He pointed to the lake. 'His patrol went out to find the place where the Gallas had ambushed the previous patrol. They found the ambush site . . . maybe the same day . . . then continued on to find the black walls and tower that the sergeant, Giovanni, said he'd seen on the previous patrol.'

Mercado added, 'The priest said this took several more days . . . Three? Four? And they were lost, so they could have wandered in circles.'

Gann said, 'I can tell you that you'd be good to make a kilometer an hour in this terrain. So if we assume a ten-hour-a-day march, from somewhere along this eastern bank of Lake Tana, we can reckon thirty kilometers in three days, perhaps, less if this patrol was moving cautiously, which I'm certain they did.'

Gann took a notebook from his pocket and a pen, which caused the monk to say, 'No!'

Gann said to Mercado, 'Tell him I'm not going to mark his map.'

Mercado spoke to the monk, and Gann measured the kilometers from the map legend on a piece of notepaper that he marked with his pen, then held the paper against the map and said, 'This is ten K. But to find the ambush site, we would need to know where this man's battalion made camp along the lakeshore – which as you can see is about eighty kilometers long – then draw a ten-K radius from there, and somewhere along that radius would be the ambush site. But we don't know where on the lakeshore to start.'

Mercado said, 'And then they wandered around for several more days to find the black wall and tower – the monastery.' Mercado said, 'We've narrowed it down a bit, but that is still a lot of square kilometers of jungle to be walking through.'

Gann said, 'That is why aerial recon would be helpful.'

They studied the terrain map and recomputed their numbers, based on different points along the shore of Lake Tana and different traveling times through the terrain, as well as trying to guess what Father Armano meant by 'several days' from the ambush site to the black monastery. They then approached the problem the other way – from the fixed location of the fortress to the monastery, though Father Armano never said how long his march was from the monastery to the fortress. And what they thought was the fortress could be something else, though '*incognita*' was about five kilometers east of the spa – a night's march.

Mercado and Purcell tried to recall if Father Armano had said anything else that could be a clue, and Purcell pointed out to Mercado that the priest had spoken Italian and that Mercado and Vivian had translated, so Purcell may not have gotten the entire story, or gotten an accurate translation.

Mercado said, 'Perhaps Vivian will recall some further details.'

Purcell said to Gann, 'This man did say something about a rock, a stream, and a tree.'

'No rocks on this map, I'm afraid, and I'm not sure which of the million trees he was referring to, but here is a small, intermittent stream ... and another here, and a larger one here, all flowing downhill to Lake Tana.' He suggested, 'Remember this when you are on the ground. But it's of no help here.'

Purcell asked, 'Where is this Falasha village?'

Gann replied, 'Not on this map ... ' He pulled another map toward him and said, 'Here, on the south adjoining map ... the village of Shoan.' He put the maps together and said, 'About forty K west and south of the suspected fortress.'

Purcell reminded Gann, 'They might know the location of the monastery.'

Gann replied, 'They know where they meet the monks. But they're not going to take us along for company.'

They again looked at the maps, trying to transfer what little they knew to what was spread out in front of them.

Gann pointed out, 'The Italian aerial cartographers saw this unknown structure, and noted it, but they apparently didn't see what we are looking for or they'd have noted that as well.'

Mercado informed him, 'Our friend said it was in a deep jungle valley, with trees that went right up to the walls.'

'I see ... Well, it could have been missed from the air.'

Purcell added, 'He said the area within the walls had trees, gardens, and I think a pond.'

Gann nodded. 'This whole area was photographed and transferred to a map, and the thing we are looking for was on one of those photographs, but the cartographers missed it when they made these maps.' He further informed them, 'Most aerial photography was done in black and white, so things — man-made and natural — are missed in black, white, and shades of gray that would be more apparent in color.' He added, 'What we're seeing here is what the cartographer thought he saw in black-and-white photographs, and there was little field checking. We can also assume the cartographers were a bit sloppy and perhaps overworked and under pressure to get these military maps to Il Duce's army.'

Purcell said, 'Maybe we'll have better luck when we fly over this area ourselves.'

Gann agreed, but advised, 'Don't do too much flying, old boy, or you'll attract attention.' He asked, 'Do I understand that you have an aircraft and pilot?'

Purcell replied, 'We're working on that.' He confessed, 'I'm the pilot.'

'I see. Well, good luck.'

'I thought you were coming with us.'

'I will try my best.'

Purcell said to Gann, 'We are going to do this, Colonel. And we will find what we are looking for.'

'I believe you will.' He added, 'That may be the easy part.'

Henry stood and moved to the antique maps, and Purcell said, 'Henry, you will not find what we're looking for there.'

Gann agreed. 'Those maps are more fantasy than accurate representations of reality, old boy. Dragons and all that.'

Mercado ignored them and unrolled a few parchments on which were hand-colored maps of sorts, showing lakes, mountains, and hand-drawn churches. Mercado said, 'This is written in Geez.'

No one replied.

He said, 'I think this one is showing Axum. I see a crown, and here is a drawing of what looks like the stone tablets of the Ten Commandments.'

Purcell said, 'Well, that proves it.'

'And here, to the southeast of this lake that looks like Tana . . . with the Blue Nile . . . is a drawing . . .' He slid the map toward them and they saw a nice drawing of a golden cup, next to which was a black cross, surrounded by well-drawn palm trees that Gann said would be about a half kilometer tall if they were drawn to scale.

Purcell said, 'We should have started with this map, Henry.'

Gann suggested, 'Offer this monk fellow ten pounds for it.'

Mercado was not enjoying the jokes, and he said, 'Well, this may not be very detailed or accurate, but it is significant that it shows . . . or possibly shows what we are looking for.' He added, 'Cross and cup. Monastery and Grail.'

'We get it.'

Gann said, 'But it does show it southeast of Lake Tana . . . so that may actually be a clue on a real map, and on the ground.'

The monk said something in Italian, and Mercado said, 'Our hour is fini.'

CHAPTER 29

They found Vivian sitting on a bench outside the Ethiopian College, and she informed them, 'I was asked to leave the reading room.'

Mercado seemed surprised. 'Why?'

'No explanation except that the archive materials had been out too long, and the reading room was needed by others.'

Purcell said to Mercado, 'You have been abusing your library privileges, Henry.'

'This is not funny.'

Purcell pointed out, 'You said we were done.'

'We were, but ...' He looked at Vivian. 'Where is my notebook?'

'In my bag.' She gave it to him.

Purcell said to Mercado, 'If I were paranoid, I'd say you should not leave that notebook in your office.'

Mercado nodded.

It was late afternoon, the sky was overcast, and Henry said he had a bottle of Strega in his office to lift their spirits.

On the way, Vivian asked, 'How did you make out?'

Mercado replied, 'We've narrowed it down.'

Gann asked Mercado, 'Is it possible to get back in there?'

'Another request is one too many.'

Gann suggested, 'If you contact the Ministry of War, they will have a complete set of army survey maps of Ethiopia.' He also informed them, 'If you know Father Armano's military unit, you should ask to see his unit logs to see where his battalion made camp on the shore of Lake Tana.'

Mercado thought about that, then replied, 'I will inquire about the maps. But we don't know Father Armano's army unit, and the War Ministry doesn't know Father Armano.'

Vivian said, 'Someone in Berini may have letters from him with a return military address.'

'Good thinking,' said Mercado.

Gann said, 'There is a possibility, however, that these unit logs never made it back to Italy.'

Purcell pointed out, 'Even if they did, the Ministry of War's archives may not be open to us – or what we're looking for may no longer be there.'

No one responded to that.

They continued their walk across the parkland of Vatican City. Purcell looked at Saint Peter's, rarely seen from the rear, and he realized it was much bigger than it appeared from its well-known façade. The basilica and the square with its encompassing colonnades was the public face of the Vatican. But there was more to this place. There were offices and archives, and there were people whose job it was to manage the money, to support charities, to stamp out heresy, to propagate the faith, and to put out the word of God and the word of the pope and the Sacred College of Cardinals – as Henry did at *L'Osservatore Romano*.

Purcell didn't think there were any great conspiracies being hatched behind the closed doors of all those offices — but he did think there was two thousand years of institutional memory that defined the Vatican and the papacy; there was an unspoken and unwritten understanding regarding what needed to be done.

Most times, he suspected, everyone was on the same page — the clergy, the hierarchy, and the bureaucracy who toiled here. But now and then there were quiet differences of opinion. And maybe that was what he was seeing now — assuming, of course, that the people here were on the same quest that he and his three companions were on.

Gann was saying, 'If we can't get access to the military maps here, I know that the Italian Library in Addis has a collection of wartime maps.' He added, 'Problem is, the Provisional Revolutionary government may have confiscated all the maps as a security measure, or to issue to their fighting units in the field.'

Purcell interjected, 'One of the first places we need to find is the village of Shoan.' He asked Gann, 'Do you know how to get there?'

'I have been there.' He continued before anyone could ask him about that. 'As I said, finding the monastery may not be as difficult as we think, given what we know. The problem, as with any military objective, is to get inside the place, get what we want, then get out.'

Purcell liked the way Gann thought. Military minds were generally clear, and geared to practical matters and problem solving. Lives depended on it. Vivian and Henry, on the other hand, were focused on the righteousness of their mission, with only passing thoughts about the logistics and the battle plan — like medieval

Crusaders off to free the Holy Land. But, he supposed, the world needed those people too.

As for himself, he'd had enough of maps, archives, and religious experiences. He was ready to move.

They reached Mercado's office, and Henry produced the bottle of Strega, which he shared with his guests to warm them up. Regarding their trip to Sicily, he consulted his calendar and said, 'The Italians have the most vacation days in Europe. Forty-two, I believe. The fourteenth looks good for me.' He asked, 'Is that good for everyone?'

Purcell and Vivian said it was, and Mercado asked Gann, 'Are you sure you don't want to go to sunny Sicily?'

'I'm afraid I can't.'

Mercado said, 'I won't use the Vatican travel office, and I suggest we all use different travel agencies to book a flight to Palermo. We'll hire a car there and drive to Berini.'

Purcell and Vivian agreed, and Henry poured more of the yellow liqueur into their water glasses.

Purcell said, 'While we're making travel plans, I suggest we pick a date now to fly to Addis Ababa.'

No one responded, and Purcell said, 'As Colonel Gann would agree, we need to stop planning the invasion and we need to have a jump-off date.'

Gann said, 'I'm actually fixed to go on January twenty-fourth – or thereabouts.'

'Good.' Purcell suggested, 'The *Osservatore Romano* team needs to go separately, in case there is a problem at the other end. I will go first – let's say January eighteenth. If I telex all is well, Vivian will follow on January twentieth—'

'We're going together, Frank.'

He ignored her and continued, 'If you don't hear from me, take that as a sign that I may be indisposed.' He said to Mercado, 'You may have the most risk considering your prior conviction for consorting with an enemy of the Ethiopian people. But if I and Vivian are okay, you bring up the rear.'

Gann agreed, 'That is a safe insertion plan.'

Purcell said, 'Unless they're waiting for all of us to get there.'

Mercado said, 'If your paranoia has substance, Frank, then I should go first to see if there is a problem.'

'Your offer is noted for the record.' He added, 'I leave on the eighteenth.'

Gann informed them, 'I have a number of safe houses in Addis. Where will you be staying?'

Purcell replied, 'With all the other reporters at the Addis Hilton.'

'Safety in numbers,' said Gann.

'With the journalistic community, Colonel, it's more like dog eat dog.'

Mercado reminded Purcell and Vivian, 'Alitalia still has daily flights to Addis, and seats are not hard to come by. Same with rooms at the Addis Ababa Hilton. I will notify the newspaper and the travel office of our plans next week.' He added, 'Gives us time to think about this.'

Purcell said, 'There is nothing to think about.'

Mercado nodded.

They discussed a few other operational details, and in regard to their Berini trip on the fourteenth, Mercado consulted an Alitalia flight schedule and said to Purcell and Vivian, 'Book the nine-sixteen A.M. Alitalia to Palermo. I'll meet you at the airport.'

Mercado said he had work to do, and his three visitors left.

Gann said he wanted to wander around the seat of the papacy, and he wished them good day.

Purcell and Vivian exited Vatican City and walked along the Tiber.

Vivian said, 'This has just become real.'

'It gets even more real in Ethiopia.'

CHAPTER 30

They landed in Palermo, rented a Fiat, and bought a road map of Sicily.

There were a few routes to Berini, which was in the mountains near the town of Corleone, and they decided to reverse the route that Father Armano had taken in 1935 from Alcamo to Palermo, though instead of a train, they drove the new highway to Alcamo. There, they took an increasingly bad road into the hills – the same road that the priest had undoubtedly walked forty years before with the other army conscripts who, like himself, were bound for Palermo, then Ethiopia. Father Armano, however, had taken a detour to Rome, and to the Vatican, before his fateful and fatal journey to Africa.

It was a sunny day and much warmer than Rome. The sky was deep blue and white clouds hung over the distant mountains. Lemon and orange groves covered the narrow valleys, and olive trees and vineyards rose up the terraced slopes. Clusters of umbrella pines shaded white stucco houses, and tall cedars stood sentry at the bases of the hills.

This, Purcell thought, was the last that Father Armano had seen of his native land, and he must have realized as he was walking to Alcamo with the other young men that he might never see it again.

Vivian said, 'This is beautiful. Completely unspoiled.'

Purcell noticed there was very little vehicular traffic, but there were a good number of donkeys and carts on the road, and a lot of people walking and biking. The villages, as expected, were picturesque – white stuccoed houses with red tile roofs, and church bell towers in even the smallest town. 'They must pray a lot.'

Mercado said, 'I'm sure they're all in church every Sunday and holy day. And, of course, for weddings, funerals, baptisms, and such, not to mention Saturday confessions.' He added, 'They are a very simple, religious people and there are not many like them in Europe anymore.'

Purcell suggested, 'You should move here, Henry.'

'After you, Frank.'

Vivian said, 'I can see having a summer place in Sicily.'

Mercado reminded her, 'You don't speak the dialect.'

Purcell pointed out, 'You both spoke to Father Armano.'

Mercado explained, 'He spoke standard Italian, a result I'm sure of his seminary training and his time in the army.'

'Are we going to have trouble speaking to the citizens of Berini?'

'Sicilians understand standard Italian when they want to.' He added, 'The priest will understand my Italian. And the younger people as well, because of television and cinema.'

'Then maybe we'll get some answers.'

Mercado informed them, 'Sicilians don't like to answer questions, especially from strangers.'

'We're doing a nice story for *L'Osservatore Romano* on their native son.'

'Doesn't matter. They are suspicious of the outside world.'

'And with good reason.'

Vivian suggested, 'Use your charm, Henry.'

Purcell said, 'We may as well turn around now.'

Mercado ignored that and said, 'The key is the village priest.'

They reached Corleone, consulted the road map and the signs, and headed southwest into the higher hills.

It would not have been too difficult, Purcell thought, to walk downhill to Alcamo. But it would not have been an easy journey home to Berini, on foot, though a soldier returning home would not think about that.

They had spotted a few classical Roman and Greek ruins along the way, and Mercado informed them, 'The Carthaginians were also here, as well as the Normans, the armies of Islam, and a dozen other invaders.' He further informed his audience, 'Sicily was a prize in the ancient world, and now it is the land that time forgot – like Ethiopia.'

'The world changes,' Purcell agreed. 'Wars have consequences.'

'I have an English cousin who served with Montgomery, and he may have passed through here in '43.'

'We'll keep an eye out for anyone with a family resemblance.'

The village of Berini was strategically located at the top of a hill that rose above the valley, and the one-lane road hugged the side of the slope and wrapped around it like a corkscrew until it abruptly ended at a stone arch, which marked the entrance to the village.

Purcell drove through the arch and followed a narrow lane

between whitewashed houses. The few pedestrians stood aside and eyed them curiously as they passed by.

A minute later they entered a small, sunlit piazza, and at its far end was a good-sized stone church, which according to the Vatican directory was San Anselmo. The parish priest, if the information was up to date, was Father Giorgio Rulli. There were no other priests listed.

On the right side of the square was a row of two-story stucco buildings, one of which had an orange awning and a sign that said, simply, 'Taverna.' On the other side of the piazza was a place called 'Caffe,' and next to that was a tabaccheria, a sort of corner candy store. That seemed to be the extent of the commercial establishments, and the other structures appeared to be residences and a village hall. A few miniature Fiats were parked around the perimeter of the piazza, but the main form of transportation seemed to be bicycles. Purcell noticed there were no donkeys.

The outdoor seating under the awning and umbrellas of the taverna and caffe was filled with people, and Purcell noted they were all male. He could also see that their full-sized Fiat had attracted some attention. It was a little past three o'clock and Mercado said, 'This is the riposo – the traditional four-hour afternoon break.'

Purcell inquired, 'Break from what?'

Vivian suggested, 'Park someplace.'

'I'm looking for a parking meter.'

'Wherever you stop the car is a parking place, Frank.'

'Right.'

He moved the Fiat slowly over the cobblestoned piazza and stopped a respectable distance from the church. They all got out and stretched. It was cooler here at the higher elevation, and the air smelled of woodsmoke.

They had been advised by one of Mercado's colleagues to dress modestly and in muted colors. The rural Sicilians, the colleague said, literally laugh at brightly colored clothing, the way most people would laugh at someone coming down the street in a clown outfit. Purcell and Mercado wore black trousers, white shirts, and dark sports jackets, and Vivian wore a black dress, a loose-fitting black sweater, and sensible shoes. She also had a black scarf to cover her head if they entered the church.

A few elderly men and women made their way up and down the steps of the church, and Mercado said to an old woman in a black dress, 'Mi scusi, Signora,' then slowly and distinctly asked her something.

She replied, pointed, and moved on, giving the strangers a backward glance and looking Vivian up and down. Mercado informed them that the rectory was behind the church and he led the way.

The rectory was a small stucco house set in a garden, and they went up the path to the door. They had discussed what they were going to say, and they'd agreed that Mercado would take the lead. There was a doorbell and Mercado rang it. They waited.

The door opened and a very young priest stood there and looked at them. 'Si?'

Mercado inquired, 'Padre Rulli?'

'Si.'

Mercado introduced himself and his companions, and said they were from *L'Osservatore Romano*, then Purcell heard him say, 'Padre Armano.'

The priest didn't slam the door in their faces, but he seemed to hesitate, then invited them inside. He ushered them into a small, plain sitting room and indicated a narrow upholstered couch. They sat, and the priest sat opposite them on a high-backed chair.

The priest, as Purcell noted, was young, and also short of stature, though he had a presence about him. His nose looked like it could have its own mailing address, and his eyes were dark and intelligent. He had thin lips and an olive complexion, and the sum total of his appearance was handsome in an interesting way.

Purcell glanced around the room. A woodstove radiated heat, one floor lamp cast a dim light in the corner behind the priest's chair, and the crude plaster walls were adorned with colored prints of men with beards and women with veils. A white marble Jesus hung from an olivewood cross above the priest's chair.

This was obviously a small and poor country church in a poor parish, Purcell thought; a place where the priest answered his own door. This was not the Vatican.

Mercado said something to the priest, enunciating each word so the Sicilian priest would have no difficulty understanding.

The priest replied, 'You may speak English if it is better than your Italian.'

Mercado seemed surprised, then recovered and said, 'Forgive us, Father, for not making an appointment—'

'My doorbell rings all day. It is the only doorbell in Berini. I am here.'

'Yes ... well, as I said, we are from *L'Osservatore Romano*. Signorina Smith is my photographer and Signore Purcell is my ... assistant.'

'I understand.' He informed them, 'I have taught myself English. From books and tapes. Why? It is the language of the world, as Latin once was. Someday ...' He didn't complete his thought, but said, 'So forgive me in advance if I do not understand, or if I mispronounce.'

Mercado assured him, 'Your English is perfect.'

Father Rulli asked, 'How may I be of assistance?'

Mercado replied, 'My colleagues and I were in Ethiopia, in September, and while there we came across a priest who was dying—'

'Father Armano.'

'Yes.' He asked, 'Have you been notified of his death?'

'I have.'

'I see ... When were you notified?'

'In November. Why do you ask?'

Purcell answered without answering, 'We're writing a newspaper article on Father Armano, so we are collecting information.'

'Yes, of course. But it is my understanding that you have all this information from the Vatican press office.'

Purcell knew that the Vatican press office and *L'Osservatore Romano* were not one and the same, though sometimes they seemed to be. He glanced at Mercado.

Mercado said to Father Rulli, 'I haven't had contact with the Vatican press office.'

'They said they were in contact with *L'Osservatore Romano*.'

'They may be ... but not me.'

Father Rulli admitted, 'I have no idea how these things work in Rome.'

Purcell assured him, 'Neither do we.'

Father Rulli smiled. He then informed them, 'But you do know about the steps toward Father Armano's beatification.'

At first Purcell thought that the priest had mispronounced 'beautification,' and he was confused. Then he understood.

Mercado seemed dumbstruck.

Vivian asked, 'What am I missing?'

Mercado told her, 'Father Armano has been proposed for canonization — sainthood.'

'Oh ...'

'Did you not know this?' asked the priest.

'We ... had heard ...'

'That is the purpose of your visit, is it not?'

'Yes ... well, we wanted to gather some background on his early life. His time in the army ... perhaps letters that he wrote to his family and friends.'

Father Rulli informed them, 'You could have saved yourselves the journey.' He explained, 'A delegation from the Vatican was here in November to let me know of Father Armano's death and his proposed canonization. As you know, if he is entered into the sainthood, and if a church is ever built in his name, a relic is needed to consecrate the church. And also a complete biography of the prospective saint is compiled. So a call was put out in Berini and we also searched the storage cellar of this rectory.' He let them know, 'We found some of his old vestments in trunks, and his family had photographs and letters they had saved. Some from Ethiopia.' He told them, 'The man from the Vatican press

317

office interviewed the family and some childhood friends of Giuseppe Armano. So this has all been done.'

Mercado replied, '*L'Osservatore Romano* likes to do this work themselves.'

'As you wish.' Father Rulli said, 'We had a special Mass when the delegation from the Vatican announced this. The town was very excited, and the bells of San Anselmo rang all day. His family was filled with joy at the news of his beatification. And of the news that he had performed miracles in Ethiopia.'

Mercado nodded, then said, 'We are sorry we missed that day.'

Well, Purcell thought, Colonel Gann had guessed correctly. The Vatican was here first, and it was Henry's unanswered letter that led them here. It was possible, of course, that there was nothing sinister about this; it was just the Vatican doing its job of making a death notification of a priest. And while they were at it, they sent a whole delegation to announce that Father Giuseppe Armano was being considered for sainthood. And they took what they needed. Purcell was impressed.

Father Rulli looked at his guests. 'Did you say you were with Father Armano when he died?'

'Yes.'

The priest nodded, then said, 'I am not clear about the circumstances of his death.' No one replied, so Father Rulli went on. 'Monsignor Mazza from the office of beatification told me that Father Armano had been imprisoned since 1936, and that he escaped and was found dying by three war correspondents from England who did not speak much Italian.' He asked, 'So that was you?'

Mercado nodded.

Father Rulli said, 'Well, that is itself a miracle. After forty years, to be found by ... English people who work for *L'Osservatore Romano*.' He asked Mercado, 'Can you tell me the circumstances of this encounter?'

Mercado related an edited version of what happened that night, and Father Rulli kept nodding with interest. Mercado concluded, 'We buried him in a garden of this Italian spa ... and said prayers over his grave.'

'That is a wonderful story. And wonderful that this man did not die alone.'

Mercado said, 'He was at peace.'

'Yes. Good.' He thought a moment, then asked Mercado, 'Is your Italian good?'

'It is passable.'

The priest thought a moment, then said, 'But Monsignor Mazza said to me he received a letter from one of the people who found Father Armano dying and that this man had little to report about Father Armano's last words – because of the language difficulties and because he died soon after he was found.'

'He ... was unconscious most of the time.'

'I see.' Father Rulli stayed silent awhile, then said, 'As you know, there must be three miracles for a person to enter into the sainthood, and I am wondering how they in Rome would know of a miracle.'

Mercado replied, 'I'm not sure.'

'Perhaps these miracles took place when he was serving in the army during that terrible war.'

'Probably.'

'And they were reported by the survivors of his military group.'

'That's possible.' Mercado added, 'That's what we are investigating. For our story.'

Purcell inquired, 'Do you have any information as to Father Armano's military unit?'

'Well, his return address would have been on his letters, but that is all in Rome now.' He looked again at his guest and said, 'It seems to me that all this information is available to you in Rome.'

'Of course.'

Father Rulli informed them, 'I was told not to speak of this to outsiders. Why is that?'

Mercado replied, 'I have no idea.' He added, 'Rome is Rome.'

Father Rulli nodded, then changed the subject. 'The most important relic of a saint is part of his body. Monsignor Mazza said that he was going to send a mission to Ethiopia to locate this spa and recover the remains.'

Mercado, wanting to appear more knowledgeable than he had been, replied, 'Yes, we know that. In fact, we may return to Ethiopia ourselves.'

The priest advised them, 'It has become dangerous there.'

Purcell reminded him, 'We've been there.'

'Yes, of course.' Father Rulli looked at his watch and said, 'I am to perform a burial Mass in half an hour.'

Purcell asked him, 'Can you put us into contact with any of Father Armano's family? Or anyone else who is still alive from his time? He mentioned a brother and two sisters.'

'Yes, Anna is still alive. A widow. And I can have her and other family members, and perhaps some friends, meet you here if you wish.'

'That would be very good of you.'

'Anna would find some comfort in speaking to you who last saw her brother alive.' He added, 'She grieved for his loss, but now she has been delivered a miracle.'

The priest rose and his guests also stood. Father Rulli showed them to the door and said, 'Five o'clock. I will have coffee.'

They thanked him, left the rectory, and walked along the side of the church and entered the piazza. The afternoon break seemed to be over and the taverna looked quiet, so they crossed the piazza and found a table under the awning.

Mercado said, 'We were scooped by the Vatican press office.'

Purcell added, 'And they made off with all traces of Father Armano.'

Vivian said, 'This is hard to believe ... I mean, is this canonization ... legitimate?'

Mercado replied, 'It could be.'

Purcell lit a cigarette and looked at him.

Mercado met his stare and said, 'It *could* be, Frank.' He explained, 'They'd want his army letters to see if he mentioned anything that could be construed as a miracle.'

'They wanted his army letters to see if he mentioned anything about the letter he was carrying from the pope.'

'We don't know that.'

Purcell asked, 'Aren't there supposed to be eyewitnesses to these miracles?'

Mercado replied, 'I'm impressed with your knowledge of the steps to sainthood.' He added, 'The Vatican office of beatification will be trying to find and interview men who served with Father Armano in Ethiopia.'

Vivian said, 'Even if he didn't *perform* a miracle, he experienced the greater miracle of ... being healed.'

Purcell inquired, 'Does that count?'

Mercado surprised him by saying, 'Even doubting Thomas had a place among the apostles.' He assured Purcell, 'We need a skeptic.'

Vivian smiled. 'I look forward to being there, Frank, when you are in the black monastery in the presence of the Holy Spirit.'

'I will eat my words. Or drink them.'

Vivian thought a moment, then said, 'Father Armano asked us to tell his sister Anna of his death.'

No one responded.

'Why did he say Anna? Why didn't he mention his other sister or brother?'

The obvious answer, as they all knew, was that Giuseppe Armano had indeed gone home to Berini, then returned to Ethiopia with the happy knowledge that Anna was still alive, and that she would be waiting to hear from them about his last hours on earth.

Purcell said, 'The rational side of me says that Anna was closest to him.'

No one responded.

Purcell continued, 'But I like the other possibility better. He went home.'

The proprietor saw they were still sitting in his chairs and he came out to see why. Mercado greeted him and asked politely for three glasses of *vino rosso* and *acqua minerale*. The man seemed all right with that and disappeared inside.

Mercado said, 'The last strangers he saw were wearing British Army uniforms.'

'He looks the right age to be your cousin.'

Vivian returned to the subject. 'Father Rulli seemed a bit confused, or even suspicious, that we didn't know about the Vatican delegation or much else.'

Mercado assured her, 'Catholic priests know better than anyone that the Vatican moves in mysterious ways.' He added, 'Rome is Rome.'

Purcell said, 'The Roman Church, in my opinion, is a continuation of the Roman Empire, also not known for openness or enlightenment.'

Mercado replied, 'The Church of Rome preaches and practices the word of God.'

Purcell thought that every time Henry Mercado heard the word 'God,' he also heard a choir of heavenly angels. He said to Mercado, 'You lied to the priest.'

Mercado replied, 'I was as confused as he was and I may have misspoken.'

'You need to go to confession.'

Mercado changed the subject. 'We may be able to get some information on Father Armano's military unit from his family. But to be honest with you, the Ministry of War is not going to be cooperative in regard to providing us with maps or logbooks.' He added, 'We have been shut down.'

Purcell agreed. 'This is not a productive trip. But it could be good background for our story – though not the one we write for *L'Osservatore Romano.*'

Vivian reminded them, 'We also came here to inform his family – to tell Anna – of his death and to tell them we were with him at the end.'

Purcell pointed out, 'The Vatican beat us to the death notification.' He added, 'And whatever else we tell them might contradict what the Vatican delegation has already told Father Rulli and the family.' He advised, 'Keep it short, general, and upbeat.'

Mercado reminded Vivian, 'He was unconscious most of the time.'

Vivian replied, 'Lies just breed more lies.'

Purcell said, 'When in Rome.'

Their wine and water came with a bill written on a slate board, and Mercado gave the proprietor a fifty-thousand-lire note. He said to his companions, 'It's pay as you go.'

'We look shady,' Purcell agreed.

The proprietor made change from his apron and Mercado took it, explaining, 'Overtipping is in poor taste.' He left some coins on the table.

Mercado raised his glass, 'God rest the soul of Father Giuseppe Armano.'

'San Giuseppe,' said Purcell.

Mercado pronounced the wine drinkable, then informed them, 'Sainthood moves very slowly. We will not see his canonization in our lifetime.'

'Well, not your lifetime, Henry.'

Mercado pointed out, 'None of us knows how much time we have left here, Frank.' He nodded toward San Anselmo, where men, women, and children, dressed in black, were climbing the steps as the church bells tolled slowly and echoed through the piazza.

Vivian said, 'Let's go to this burial Mass.'

Purcell inquired, 'Did you know the deceased?'

'I want to see Father Armano's church.'

Purcell and Mercado exchanged glances, then Mercado said, 'All right.' He went inside to say *arrivederci* to the proprietor, then came out and informed his companions, 'You never leave without saying good-bye.'

Purcell said, 'I'm impressed with your rustic etiquette.'

Vivian said, 'I think I could live in Sicily.'

Purcell informed her, 'Half the Italians in America are Sicilian. They couldn't live here.'

'Maybe summers.'

They walked across the piazza to the church and Vivian draped her scarf over her head as they climbed the steps.

The church of San Anselmo was big, built, Purcell thought, when more people lived here. The peaked roof showed exposed beams and rafters, and the thick stone walls were plastered and whitewashed. The altar, though, was of polished stone and gilded wood, and looked out of place in the simple setting, as did the intricate stained glass windows.

A white-draped coffin sat at the Communion rail and Father Rulli stood beside it, blessed it, then went up to the altar.

There were no pews, but a collection of wooden chairs were lined up in rows, and most of them were filled with the people of Berini and the surrounding farms. The three visitors took empty seats in the rear.

Father Rulli stood in the center of the altar, raised his arms, and greeted his flock in Italian. Everyone stood and the Mass of Christian burial began.

Purcell looked at Father Rulli, and he saw Father Armano,

forty years ago; a young priest from this village who'd gone to the seminary and returned to his village, his family, his friends, and his church where he'd been baptized. In a perfect world, where there was no war, Father Giuseppe Armano might have stayed here until the burial Mass was for him. But the new Caesar in Rome had much grander plans for the Italian people, and the winds of war swept into Berini and carried off its sons.

Father Rulli was now at the lectern, speaking, Purcell imagined, of the mystery of death and of the promise of eternal life. Or maybe he was speaking well of the departed, because people were crying. Even Vivian, who had no clue who was in the coffin, was dabbing her eyes with a handkerchief.

Purcell returned to Father Armano, and wondered if the priest saw his life as wasted or as blessed for having seen and experienced a miracle. Probably, Purcell thought, the priest had had moments of doubt in his prison cell, but his faith and his experience in the black monastery had sustained him. And in the end, as he was dying, he had probably thought he was again blessed to be ending his life a free man, in the company of at least one, maybe two believers who would tell his family and the world of his fate and of what he had seen and experienced. He seemed at peace, Purcell recalled, ready for his journey home.

It occurred to Purcell that they didn't have to come to Berini, but it was the right thing to do; it was the right place to begin their own journey back to where this all began.

— PART III —

Ethiopia

The longest journey
Is the journey inwards
Of him who has chosen his destiny,
Who has started upon his quest
For the source of his being ...

— Dag Hammarskjöld, *Markings*

CHAPTER 31

Frank Purcell stood with his back to the bar, a drink in one hand and a cigarette in the other.

The Addis Ababa Hilton cocktail lounge was filled with the usual clientele that one finds in times of war, pestilence, and famine, though it seemed to Purcell that there were far fewer news people here than in September – though more UN relief people and embassy reinforcements. And, as always, there were some shady-looking characters whose purpose here was unknown, but it had to do with either money or spying.

Another difference from the last time was that the rich Ethiopians seemed to have disappeared. The ones that weren't dead or in prison were at Etiopia in Rome. The Italian expats and businesspeople had also disappeared.

Purcell was happy to see that the newly arrived Soviet and Cuban advisors were not drinking in the Addis Hilton. The hotel demanded hard currency, which kept out the riffraff and the Reds.

He'd sent his telex to Vivian at the Forum Hotel, and to Mercado at the newspaper two days before, informing them he was alive and well at the Hilton. Now he was waiting for Vivian to arrive.

A few of his former colleagues had approached him in the two days since he'd been here, but they'd observed the unspoken rule of not asking any questions of a fellow reporter. He had, however, volunteered a few details about his trip to the front in September, his arrest and imprisonment, and his expulsion from the country. He was back, he said, on assignment for *L'Osservatore Romano*. This was old news and didn't rate getting bought a drink, but they wished him good luck.

One reporter, a nice lady named Fran from AP, had informed him, 'The crazy fun phase of the revolution is over. Almost everyone they wanted dead is dead or in jail, or on the run. Now they have to govern and they can't deal with the famine or the Eritrean separatists.'

Purcell had asked her about the Gallas, but she didn't know or care much. The Gallas were not on the radar screens of anyone in the capital; they were like marauding lions, somewhere out there, with no political agenda. Plus, they were not available for comment.

He also asked, 'How about the Royalist partisans?'

'They're finished.'

He thought about Colonel Gann, who was returning to fight a lost cause. Colonel Gann would wind up dead this time.

Fran also informed him that the Falasha Jews were beginning an exodus, to Israel, and that was a good story.

Purcell looked up at the huge stained glass window that diffused the dying afternoon sunlight throughout the modern bar, and which would do credit to a European cathedral. The window was the work of a contemporary Ethiopian artist, done in a neo-primitive style, and told the story of the founding of the

Ethiopian royal line. The first panel showed the black queen, Sheba, visiting Jerusalem with her attendants. The next panel showed them being received by King Solomon. The queen then returns to her homeland, and there she gives birth to a son, Menelik, the ancestor of the present emperor, who would also be the last emperor of Ethiopia, unless Colonel Gann could perform a miracle. Purcell wondered if the new government would allow that window to stay there. The hotel guests liked it.

He looked at his watch: 4:36. Vivian's plane had landed. Lovers meet at the airport. Reporters and their photographers do not if they are also lovers and don't want to advertise that relationship to the security apparatus, who might make use of the information. So for that reason, and also because *L'Osservatore Romano* was a Catholic enterprise, Vivian had her own room.

Purcell had, however, sent a hotel car and driver to meet her, and to report by telephone that the hotel guest had arrived and was safely through passport control.

Purcell informed the bartender that he was waiting for this call.

He ordered another Jack Daniel's and perused an English-language newspaper on the bar. A small item tucked away inside the paper reported that the former monarch, Mr Haile Selassie, remained under the protective custody of the Provisional Revolutionary government.

If Mr Selassie was a younger man, Purcell knew, they'd have already executed him. But one of the advantages of advanced age – if there were any – was that people who wanted you dead only had to wait patiently. Also, the now Mr Selassie was still popular in the West and killing him would further strain relations with Europe and America. Even the Soviet and Cuban advisors would argue against regicide in this case. The murdered Romanovs had become martyrs, and the modern Marxists wanted to avoid that this time.

Purcell thought back to Berini. Coffee and cannoli at the rectory of San Anselmo had not been as awful as he'd expected. The sister of Father Armano, Anna, was a sweet woman and she had taken to Vivian, despite Vivian's exotic appearance.

Vivian had told Anna that her brother had mentioned her by name, which made Anna weep. Anna told them that she had seen her brother in a dream, last year when there was much news of Ethiopia, and her brother was smiling, which according to Sicilian belief meant he was in heaven. Unfortunately, Anna couldn't recall the exact date of the dream, though with Vivian's prompting she agreed it could have been in September.

Coincidence? Not according to Vivian or Mercado, who took this as a further sign of divine design. Even he, Frank Purcell, found himself wanting to believe that Father Armano had traveled home for a last visit.

Father Rulli's small rectory had become filled with the near and distant relatives of the late Giuseppe Armano, and as Father Rulli explained, unnecessarily, 'Sicilian families are large.'

There were some language difficulties, but mostly everyone understood each other, and Mercado and Vivian repeated the story of how they and Signore Purcell, who spoke no Italian, had found Father Armano, mortally wounded, and how the priest had asked them to tell his family that he was thinking of them in his last moments. Everyone was very moved by the story, and no one asked why it had taken so long for the three *giornalisti* to come to Berini, though Mercado mentioned he'd been in an Ethiopian prison. An older man, who'd fought in Ethiopia, and was a cousin of Father Armano, said, 'Ethiopia is a place of death. You should not return.'

Vivian informed him and everyone that they were going to find the grave of Father Armano and bring back a mortal relic of the saint-to-be. Purcell thought this custom was ghoulish, but no one else there did.

The women disappeared at about 6 P.M., and cordials were served. At seven, the men excused themselves and Father Rulli invited his three guests to stay for dinner. Vivian wanted to stay, but it was obvious that Father Rulli wanted his guests to clear up some inconsistencies between their story and that of the Vatican beatification delegation, so Mercado reminded Vivian of their flight to Rome – which was actually the next day.

They thanked Father Rulli for his hospitality and assistance and promised to return to Berini after their assignment in Ethiopia. The priest blessed them and their work and wished them a safe journey.

Outside, on the way to the car, Vivian said, 'That was a very moving and wonderful experience.'

Mercado agreed, and so did Purcell, though he'd had to rely on translations for the experience.

In the car, Vivian announced, 'I got Father Armano's military address from Anna. She knew it by heart.'

They drove to Corleone and spent the night in a small hotel, then caught a noon flight from Palermo back to Rome.

Mercado wrote to the Ministry of War on *L'Osservatore Romano* letterhead, saying he was doing an article on the Ethiopian war and requesting information such as unit logs on the battalion or regiment whose military designation he specified in his letter.

The response, unusually fast, informed him that all records of this regiment had been lost in Ethiopia.

And that was that.

As for Italian Army maps, which would be critical for their mission, Colonel Gann had informed them that he had a source in London for captured Italian maps. He also advised them not to visit the Italian Library in Addis Ababa, which he'd discovered was under some sort of state surveillance. So now they needed Colonel Gann and his maps before they could begin their journey, and Gann was scheduled to arrive on the twenty-fourth. He said he'd contact them at the Hilton, but if they didn't hear from him by the twenty-eighth, they were on their own.

Purcell looked at the telephone on the bar. He'd checked for telexes twice already, to see if Vivian – or Mercado – had tried to contact him. He picked up the phone, called the front desk, and asked again. The clerk informed him, 'We will deliver any telex to you in the lounge, Mr Purcell.'

'And forward my phone calls here.'

'Yes, sir.'

He knew he should have gone to the airport to meet her, but they'd all agreed in Rome not to do that. Sounded good in Rome.

He ordered another drink and lit another cigarette. It was now 5:24, long past the time when she'd be through airport security. But probably the Alitalia flight from Rome was late.

He turned and looked at the patrons at the cocktail tables. People gravitated toward the hotel bars in times of stress. They came to get news, or hear rumors, or because there actually is safety in numbers. Some of the patrons were quiet and with-drawn, and some were hyper. A feeling of unreality always permeated these softly lit islands of comfort, and sometimes a feeling of guilt; there was death and famine out there.

He looked up at the stained glass window again. The mid-January sun was almost gone, and when the light struck the huge window at this angle, Purcell could make out in the modern scene of the panorama, as well as in the ancient scene, a church or monastery. The artist chose to use black glass for the depiction of the church, and around it were dark green palms. Purcell won-dered if the church was black by design or by the random choice of the artist. The dark green glass of the palms made the black church almost impossible to see except in a certain light, yet the remainder of the panorama was a contrast in light and dark. He stared at the glass as the sun sank lower and both the modern and ancient depictions of the same church – or monastery – disap-peared, and the soft glow of the lounge lighting gave the stained glass an altogether different appearance.

The phone rang and the bartender answered it, then gave it to him.

'Purcell.'

A woman with an Italian accent said, 'This an Alitalia cus-tomer servizio.'

'Yes?'

'I hava deliver to your room a young a lady.'

He smiled and asked, 'Is she naked?'

'Due minuto.'

'I'll be right there.'

CHAPTER 32

Purcell and Vivian spent the next two days re-familiarizing themselves with the city, and reestablishing some press contacts and local contacts.

L'Osservatore Romano had no office in Addis, but the paper shared space in the old Imperial Hotel with other transient reporters and freelancers who paid a small fee for a place to hang their hats and use the typewriters and telexes.

They also visited the American embassy to register their presence, and to see Anne, the consulate officer who'd come for Purcell in prison, and also for Vivian. Vivian gave Anne a pot of black African violets she'd picked up from a street vendor, and Anne gave them some advice: 'You should not have returned.'

Purcell assured her, 'We'll try not to get arrested this time.'

Purcell also wrote and filed a story about Ethiopian Catholic refugees from the fighting on the Eritrean border. He knew nothing about this, so in Mercado style, he made up most of it. But to give it a little twist, he mentioned his visit to the Ethiopian College in the Vatican, and praised the Catholic brothers there for their hospitality and their blessing of his journey to Ethiopia.

Vivian read his piece and asked, 'How much of this is true?'

He reminded her, 'The first casualty of war is the truth.' He added, 'We need to earn our keep. Take a picture of a beggar and caption it "Catholic Refugee."'

They checked for telexes twice a day to see if Henry Mercado had decided that Rome was a better place to be. But Mercado's only telex, that morning, said: ARRIVING ALITALIA, 4:23. CONFIRM.

Purcell sent him a telex confirming they were still alive and well, and looking forward to his arrival.

Purcell left a note for Mercado at the front desk saying he'd be in the bar at six, and now he and Vivian sat at a cocktail table waiting to see if Henry had made it past the security people at the airport. It was 6:35.

Vivian looked up at the stained glass window and asked him, 'Where are they keeping the emperor these days?'

'They're not saying.'

'Do you think he's still alive?'

'If he was dead, they'd announce he died of natural causes.' He reminded her, 'He's the reason the rasses are still fighting.'

'Who is the successor to the throne?'

'Crown Prince Afsa Wossen. He escaped to London. Probably a pal of Gann.'

She nodded.

Purcell glanced at his watch: 6:46. Henry was very late.

He said to Vivian, 'Do you know that the Rastafarians in Jamaica consider Haile Selassie to be divine?'

'No, I didn't.'

'We need to fly to Jamaica next and do a story on that.'

She forced a smile.

Clearly she was worried about Henry, but she was reluctant to say that in case he misinterpreted her concern.

He pointed to the long bar and said, 'Right over there. That's where I was sitting, minding my own business, when you and Henry came up to me.'

She again forced a smile.

He mimicked Henry's slight British accent, 'Hello, old man. Have you met my photographer?'

Her smile got wider. 'I was immediately taken with you.'

'You wanted my Jeep.'

'I didn't even know you had a Jeep.'

'Well, I don't anymore. The Gallas probably have it now. Pulling it around with their horses.' He added, 'I have to find the guy I rented it from and get my three-thousand-dollar security deposit back.'

'Why should he give it back? You lost his Jeep.'

'Wasn't my fault.'

'It wasn't his fault either. Where did you get the Jeep? We need another one.'

'An Italian resident of Addis. Probably gone by now.'

'You need to find him.'

'I think he's out of Jeeps.' He informed her, 'There's another guy here, Signore Bocaccio, who owns or owned a small plane. I've asked around, but no one seems to know if he's still here.'

She nodded, then glanced at her watch. She said, 'I'll go to the front desk to see if he's checked in. Or see if the flight is late.'

'All right.'

She got up and left the lounge.

Purcell sipped his drink. He had an after-hours emergency number for the British, American, and Swiss embassies.

It occurred to him that without Mercado and without Gann, the quest for the Holy Grail was going nowhere. He and Vivian could, of course, press on, but that would be crossing the line from brave to crazy. And yet . . . now that he was here, something was telling him that it was going to be all right – that what they'd felt and believed was correct; they had been chosen to do this.

He understood, too, that they had not necessarily been chosen to succeed, or even to live. But they'd been chosen to find the Holy Grail that was within themselves. And that was what this was always about; the Grail was a phantom and the journey was inward, into their hearts and souls.

Vivian and Henry walked into the lounge, smiling, arm in arm, and Purcell stood, smiled, and said, 'Henry, have you met my photographer?'

'I have indeed. She's going to buy me a drink. And buy one for yourself.'

CHAPTER 33

Purcell walked across the windy airstrip. The rising sun began to burn off the highland mist that still shrouded the valley floor. In the distance, along the same mountain chain, Addis Ababa was becoming visible as the ground fog dropped back into the valley.

Purcell noticed the condition of the concrete as he walked. Like much of the civil and military engineering in this country, this old airfield was an Italian legacy. The Italians were good builders, but forty years was a long time. The concrete runways were patched with low-grade blacktop and the hangar roofs were mended with woven thatch. A platoon of soldiers was forming up near the hangar. The Royalists may have been beaten, but the Eritreans, who were now trying to win independence from the new Ethiopian government, were winning, and the whole country was on a war footing.

The Ethiopian Air Force kept a wing of American-made C-47 transports here, and Signore Bocaccio, the Italian coffee dealer, whom Henry had found, also kept his American-made Navion here. He told Mr Purcell, however, that he used to hangar it at the Addis Ababa International Airport, but the Ethiopian Air Force made him keep the ancient Navion within their grabbing distance in the event they should need it. It had in fact already been used as a spotter for jet fighters in the Eritrean conflict, and as a consequence of that, the Navion sported a rocket pod under its fuselage that Signore Bocaccio pointed out to Mr Purcell. The rocket pod was used to fire smoke markers at the Eritrean rebels, the Royalist forces, or anyone else they didn't care for. The few French Mirage jets that the Ethiopians possessed would then try to place their bombs and rockets on the smoke markers, with varying degrees of success.

Purcell walked up to the stoutly built, low-wing craft and did a quick walk-around. Its black paint was not holding up well, and bare spots of aluminum were everywhere, except for the red-painted name of the plane – *Mia*. The nose wheel of the tricycle gear needed air and the plane pitched forward. Purcell noticed that the sliding canopy was pushed halfway back on its tracks, and a bullet hole was visible in one of the rear panes. He asked Signore Bocaccio, 'Am I paying extra for the rocket pod?'

Signore Bocaccio made a classic Italian shrug. 'What am I to do about it? You think this is America? Italy? Here, they do what they want. There is no war today, so you can have the plane. If you fly her well, perhaps they will make you a colonel in the air force. This is Ethiopia.'

'Yes, I know.'

'If you were not a journalist, they would not let me rent her to you at all. There was trouble as it was. I had to pay them to allow this.'

'That's why they make trouble.' He walked around the craft again. There were at least six bullet holes in it. 'Do you file a flight plan?'

'Yes. You must. Before the trouble they did not care. But now they insist. They think everyone is a spy for the emperor. So they want a flight plan. There are ten airstrips in the whole country. They want a flight plan. Hah!' He assured Purcell, however, 'Today we are doing only the check out. So we need no flight plan, but when you go to Gondar, you must file for Gondar.'

The flight plan was an unforeseen problem. This morning he was just logging in some flight time with Signore Bocaccio, to see if the Navion was airworthy. But when he was with Vivian, Mercado, and Gann – if he showed up – they'd be doing aerial recon, and he did not want to land in Gondar, which was Getachu's Northern Army headquarters. He could, however, file a flight plan for Khartoum, where they could conceivably have business. He asked Signore Bocaccio, 'Can I fly to Khartoum?'

'You can if you want to get arrested.'

'They're not getting along with the Sudanese, I take it.'

'They are not. Anyway, I would not want you to take Mia that far.' He tapped the fuselage where the name appeared. 'Khartoum is the limit of her cruising range. But if you come upon head-winds or bad weather, you will run out of fuel.' He smiled as his hand did a nosedive.

'All right . . . ' Purcell informed Signore Bocaccio, 'Tomorrow, or the next day, I'll have one passenger. Perhaps two or three.' He asked, 'Are the rear seats in place?'

'Unfortunately, no.' Bocaccio explained, 'I took them out for the beans.'

'Right, but—'

'I sometimes take samples from the plantations. I carry items to trade. And things to eat. You cannot find Italian food outside of Addis.' He added, 'In fact, with the famine, sometimes you cannot find any food at all.'

'Sorry about that. Can you replace the seat?'

'It was stolen.'

'Of course. Well, my passengers can sit on your bean bags.' He asked, 'How does Mia handle with four?'

'How would you handle with four people on your back?' He inquired, 'Who are the others?'

'Giornalisti.'

'They are friendly with the government, I hope.'

'Of course.' Purcell could see that Signore Bocaccio was having second thoughts, so he distracted him with technical questions. 'When was she built?'

'Twenty years ago. She is a young girl, but an old aircraft.' He smiled. 'She is American made, as you know, and all measurements are in feet, miles, and gallons.'

'What is her stall speed?'

'She stalls at any speed. So go as slow as you please. She will stall when she wants. Just give yourself enough altitude to recover.'

'What speed, Signore Bocaccio?'

He shrugged. 'The airspeed indicator is inaccurate. And the needle jumps. The airplane is, how you say in English, out of trim. The leading edge is banged up.'

'I noticed.'

'Well, so, the stall speed is perhaps sixty. But when she was young, she could go forty-five. But what difference does that make? You must just give yourself the altitude to recover – and why would you want to approach stall speed?'

'I want to go low and slow. I want to make steep banks and turns. Will she do that?'

Signore Bocaccio looked at him closely. 'That is not the way to Gondar, my friend. Gondar is three hundred miles due north. There are no steep banks or turns to be made.'

'We are looking for the war, Signore.'

'This is not a plane for that. She knows the way to Gondar as a straight line. She does not like to be fired at.' He put his finger into a bullet hole, then patted his plane and dusted off his hands. He also informed Purcell, 'The government does not want you looking for the war from the air. That is their job. If you do that, they will think you are spying for the Royalists. Or the Eritreans. Or the British or the Americans—'

'Cruising speed? Altitude?'

'This airfield is already at eight thousand feet. You will get the best cruising speed if you climb to perhaps twelve thousand. To go much higher would take too long. Especially with four people. As you go over the valleys you can drop down if you wish, but you must remember that at eight thousand feet, you may meet a nine-thousand-foot mountain. You understand?'

'Si. And what will she make?'

'Perhaps you can get a hundred fifty out of her. I make Gondar in two and a half hours, normally.'

'How's the prop?'

'She wanders. Sometimes a hundred – two hundred rpm. Give it no thought.'

'It can wander all it wants as long as it doesn't wander off the airplane.'

'The hub is solid. It has no cracks.'

'Let's hope so.'

'Do you think I am' – Bocaccio tapped his head – 'pazzo?'

'Well, Signore Bocaccio, if you are, so am I.'

He laughed, then looked at Purcell and said seriously, 'Do not try tricks with Mia, my friend. She will kill you.'

'Capisco.' He said to Signore Bocaccio, 'Are you ready to teach me how to fly Mia?'

He smiled. 'After all I have said, you still want to fly her?'

'If the Ethiopian Air Force can fly her, I can fly her.'

Again Bocaccio looked at Purcell. 'Whatever is your purpose, it must be important to you.'

'As important as your coffee beans.'

Apropos of nothing, Signore Bocaccio said, 'This has become a sad land.'

'You should leave.'

'I will ... ' He smiled and said to Purcell, 'Perhaps *L'Osservatore Romano* would like to buy Mia.'

'I will ask.' He looked up at the cockpit. 'Ready?'

'I fly, you watch, then you fly and I watch you. Next time, you fly and I watch you from the ground.'

'Let's hope for a next time.'

Signore Bocaccio laughed, and they climbed into the aircraft.

CHAPTER 34

Henry Mercado, wearing a bathrobe and undershorts, sat on the balcony of his top-floor room sipping coffee. The fog was lifting, and in the distance he could see a single-engine black aircraft rising off a hilltop airstrip. He said, 'That must be Frank.'

Vivian, sitting next to him, replied, 'He said to look for him about seven.'

Mercado glanced at her. She was wearing a short white *shamma* that she'd picked up somewhere, and she had obviously worn it to bed. The *shamma* reminded him of Getachu's camp. The parade ground. The pole. He wondered if she'd thought about that.

Vivian told him, 'Frank said he'd do a flyby and tip his wings.'

He supposed that meant she had to leave and get to her own room – or Purcell's room – so that Purcell would not see both of them having coffee on Henry Mercado's balcony at 7 A.M. But she didn't move.

To make conversation, he said, 'This is a squalid city.'

'It is not Rome.'

'No. This is the Infernal City.'

She laughed.

He had developed a strong dislike for Addis Ababa in 1935, and forty years later nothing he'd seen had changed his opinion.

Even the Ethiopians disliked it. It was like every semi-Westernized town he'd seen in Africa or Asia, combining the worst aspects of each culture. Its only good feature was its eight-thousand-foot elevation, which made the climate pleasant — except during the June-to-September rainy season when mud slid down the hills into the streets.

He poured more coffee for both of them. Vivian put her bare feet on the balcony rail and her *shamma* slipped back to her thighs.

He was surprised that she had accepted his invitation for coffee on the balcony, and more surprised when she came to his door wearing only the *shamma* and little else. Or nothing else.

On the other hand, Vivian was of another generation. And sometimes he thought of her as a child of God: naturally innocent while unknowingly sensuous.

He looked out at the black aircraft in the distance. It was circling over the hills and making steep, dangerous-looking turns. He said, 'I hope he's a good pilot.'

She was staring at the aircraft and didn't reply.

He looked out again into the city. Like all the cities of his youth, he hated this place because it reminded him of a time when he was hopeful and optimistic — when he believed in Moscow and not Rome. Now he was burdened with years and disappointments, and with God.

If he looked hard enough into the swirling fog below, he could see Henry Mercado dashing across Saint George Square to the telegraph office. He could hear the roar of Italian warplanes overhead. He could and did remember and feel the pleasure of making love to the nineteen-year-old daughter of an American diplomat in the blacked-out lobby of the Imperial. Why the lobby? He had a room upstairs. What if they'd snapped on the lights? He smiled.

'What is making you smile, Henry?'

'What always makes me smile?'

'Tell me.'

So he told her about having sex in the lobby of the Imperial Hotel during an air raid blackout.

She listened without comment, then stayed silent awhile before saying, 'So you understand.'

He didn't reply.

'We do things when we're frightened.'

'We were not frightened of the air raid.'

'We want to hold on to another person.'

'I didn't follow this person to Cairo.'

She didn't reply.

He looked out at the Imperial Hotel. Its surrounding verandas seemed to sag. He had the nostalgic idea of checking in there instead of here, but maybe it was enough to visit once a day when he went to the press office. In fact, the places that once held good memories were best left as memories.

The aircraft was climbing to the north, and Mercado saw that it cleared a distant peak by a narrow margin. Vivian didn't seem to notice, but he said to her, 'I hope you're prepared to do some aerial photography in a small plane with a novice pilot.'

'You should stay here, Henry.'

'I don't care if I die, Vivian. I care if you die.'

'No one is going to die. But that's very ... loving of you to say that.'

'Well, I love you.'

'I know.'

He didn't ask the follow-up question and stared out at Addis Ababa. It was dirty and it smelled bad. Old men with missing pieces of their bodies were a walking reminder of old-style Ethiopian justice. Adding to the judicial mutilations were the wounded of recent and past wars. And then there were the deformed beggars, the diseased prostitutes, and the starving bare-foot children running through donkey dung. A quarter million already dead from the famine. How was he supposed to believe in God? 'How can this be?'

'How can what be?'

'*This.*' He swept his arm over the city.

She thought a moment, then replied, 'It's good that you still care.'

'I don't care anymore.'

'You do.'

He said to her, 'Sometimes I think I've been around too long.'

'I think you told me that once before.'

'Did I? What did you say?'

'I don't remember.'

But *he* did. She'd said to him, 'How can you say that when you have me?'

He looked at her and his heart literally skipped a beat.

The aircraft was now directly over the city, making tight bank-ing turns as they'd have to do when they were shooting photographs of the ground. He thought she should leave before Purcell decided to do a flyby. But she just sat there, her feet on the rail, with her legs parted too wide, sipping coffee, watching her lover fly. Finally he said to her, 'You should go to your own balcony. Or his.'

Again, she didn't reply.

Mercado stood, but did not go inside.

The sun was coming over the eastern hills, burning off the last of the ground mist. The capital of the former empire was a straggly city of empty lots with gullies and ridges everywhere. The few high-rise buildings were separated by miles of squalid huts that sat in clusters like primitive villages. Banana trees and palms shaded the corrugated metal roofs of the huts from the blazing sun. Vermin and insects swarmed through the city, and at night hyenas howled in the surrounding hills. Whatever hope there had been for this city and this country under the emperor's half-hearted reforms was now drowned in a sea of blood. A long night was descending on this ancient land, and if a new dawn ever arrived, he would not see it in his lifetime.

'Are you all right?' she asked.

'I see things more clearly now. And I am feeling sorry for myself, and for these people.'

'You're a good man, Henry.'

'I was.'

'We will find that good, happy, and optimistic man. That's why we're here.'

He nodded. This was the last quest. He hoped for salvation, but was prepared for the final disillusionment.

He looked down into the square dominated by the city's only beautiful building, the octagonal Cathedral of Saint George. The square was filled with beggars by day and prostitutes by night. To further desecrate the great Coptic cathedral, it had been built by

Italian prisoners of war captured at Adowa during the first Italian invasion of 1896. He found that an irony of sorts, or maybe a great cosmic joke.

Vivian said, 'Here he comes.' She pointed.

The black aircraft was coming in from the east so that the pilot's side would be facing the hotel as it passed by. Mercado noticed the aircraft was flying dangerously low and slow as it approached the hotel. If he stalled, he had no altitude to recover.

Vivian seemed not to understand the danger, and she was smiling and waving.

Mercado could not take his eyes off the aircraft, expecting it to nosedive any second. What was Purcell thinking? That's what happens when you show off for a woman, Mercado thought. You die. And if Frank Purcell died . . . He looked at Vivian.

She was standing on her toes now, waving wildly. 'Frank! Over here!' She jumped up and down.

The aircraft dipped its wings about a hundred yards from the balcony, indicating he'd seen them. Mercado gave a half wave, and as the plane passed by he could see Purcell's face, looking at them.

Vivian shouted, 'He saw us! Did you see him, Henry?'

He didn't reply. Mercado watched the aircraft as it gained speed and continued west. He expected that Purcell would come around for another flyby, but he continued on and disappeared against the background of the tall western mountains.

Vivian remained standing at the rail, looking at the fog-shrouded hills.

Mercado was going to ask her to leave now, but he didn't. Finally he said, 'I trust this will not cause a problem.'

She turned her head toward him. 'We had coffee. Waiting for Frank.'

He nodded.

She turned and put her back against the rail. 'You were not the jealous type.'

'No.'

'We all bathed together.'

'Yes ... well, bathing together and sleeping together are different things.'

'One is a prelude to the other. And you knew that.'

'Don't try that argument on me, Vivian.'

She walked past him into his bedroom.

He stood on the balcony for a few seconds, then went through the sliding door.

She was lying on his unmade bed, her *shamma* still on, but pulled back, revealing her jet black pubic hair.

He looked at her, but said nothing.

She said to him, 'This will make everything right between us.'

He understood what she meant. This was her way of saying, I'm sorry. I'm giving you back your pride. I'm taking away your anger.

He dropped his robe to the floor, then slipped off his shorts and got into the bed. He knelt between her wide-spread legs, bent forward, and started to pull off her *shamma*, but she said, 'No. Like this.'

He looked at her.

'Like this, Henry. You understand.'

He nodded.

She reached out and took his hard penis in her hand and pulled him toward her. He lay down on top of her and she guided him in, then wrapped her legs around his buttocks and pulled him in tighter.

He began thrusting against her tight grip, and within a minute she climaxed and let out a long moan – the same moan he'd heard that night hanging from the pole. He kept thrusting inside her and she climaxed again, then he felt himself coming into her.

They lay side by side, holding hands, gazing at the paddle fan spinning slowly on the ceiling.

She asked him, 'Do you understand this?'

'I do.'

'And you understand that this is between two friends.'

He didn't reply.

'I hurt you, and now I feel better, and I want you to feel better. About me. And about ... all of us.'

'I understand.'

'I hope you do. If not right now, then later.'

He knew that she meant when he next saw Purcell. When the three of them sat together having a drink, the score was even, even if Purcell did not know that. But Henry Mercado did.

And actually he did feel better already. The anger wasn't there any longer, or if it was, it was not helpless anger. But what remained was a sense of loss. He wanted to be with her.

He said to her, 'At least tell me you enjoyed it.'

'I always did.'

'Encore?'

She glanced at the clock. 'I'd better get moving.'

'Rain check?'

'No. This will not happen again.' She sat up and started to swing her legs out of the bed, but he put his hand on the back of her head and gently pulled her toward him.

She hesitated, then let him bring her head and face down on his wet penis, which she took into her mouth.

She knelt between his legs and her long, raven black hair fell across his thighs as her head bobbed up and down.

He came and his body arched up, and she stayed with him until there was nothing left inside him.

Vivian sat back on her haunches, and he looked at her, his semen running down her chin. Their eyes met and she smiled, then pulled off her *shamma* and stood on the bed. She turned completely around for him, and he watched her but said nothing.

Vivian jumped off the bed, wiped her face with a tissue, slipped on her *shamma*, and moved toward the door. 'Thank you for coffee.'

'Anytime.'

She left, and he stared up at the rotating fan. 'I love you.'

CHAPTER 35

Purcell took a taxi from the airstrip to the hotel and called Mercado in his room to meet him for coffee. The two men sat in the Hilton cocktail lounge, which doubled as the breakfast room.

Mercado had hoped Vivian would be there so he could have that post-coital moment that she suggested would make him feel better. It wasn't the same, somehow, with only the two cuckolded men having coffee. He asked, 'Where is Vivian?'

'I called both rooms, but she's not answering.'

Mercado wanted to say, 'Well, she's not still in my room.' Instead he said, 'Probably napping. She was up early.' He suggested, 'Try her again.'

'She'll be down.'

A waiter came by with breakfast menus and Mercado said, 'Every time I eat, I think about the famine.'

'Order light.'

'That's very insensitive, Frank.' He added, 'You wouldn't say that if Vivian was here.'

Purcell looked up from his menu, but didn't respond.

Purcell ordered a full breakfast, saying, 'Flying makes me hungry.'

Mercado ordered orange juice and a *cornetto* with his coffee. He asked Purcell, 'How did it fly?'

'Not very agile. But it seems safe enough.' He asked, 'How did it look to you?'

'Well, I can't tell, of course, but you seem to know what you're doing.'

'What did Vivian think?'

'She was excited when you did your flyby.' He added, 'You saw her.'

'I did.'

'Yes. And we could see you in the cockpit.'

'And how did I look, Henry?'

'Sorry?'

'Did I look happily surprised to see Vivian on your bedroom balcony?'

Mercado did not answer the question, but said, 'Hang on, Frank. We had coffee, waiting to see you. I hope you don't take that as anything other than what it was.'

Purcell stared at him, but didn't reply.

Mercado was not enjoying this moment as much as he'd thought he would. It would have been much better if Vivian and Purcell had already had a tiff about this, followed by Purcell being sulky at cocktails or dinner.

Mercado didn't want to protest too much, but he said, 'We're all civilized, aren't we?' He reminded Purcell, 'We're going to be in close quarters when we get into the bush.' He immediately regretted his choice of words. *Get into the bush.* Freudian slip? He suppressed a smile.

'All right.' Purcell let him know, 'It's nothing.'

Nothing? Mercado wanted to tell him, 'I fucked her, actually,' but that would wreck the whole deal. So instead, he said, 'She's very attached to you, Frank.'

'End of discussion.'

'In fact, you should have this discussion with her.'

Purcell didn't respond, but he was getting annoyed with Mercado. The subject of Vivian was not a happy one between them, and Mercado's familiarity would have earned him at least a punch in the gut, as he'd told him in Rome. But Purcell didn't want to upset the mission. Also, he liked Henry.

Mercado said to him, 'I'm not sure, but I think you were flying too slow as you passed by.'

'Let me pilot the aircraft, Henry.'

'I'm thinking about *me*. Your passenger. And Vivian.'

'Don't worry about it.' Purcell informed him, 'If it makes you feel better, Signore Bocaccio was impressed with my flying skills.'

'Good. But will he let you fly it again?'

'He's thinking about it.'

'We need that plane.' Mercado asked, 'And how is Signore Bocaccio? Is he trying to pretend that the Marxists haven't taken charge and that his privileged life will continue as usual?'

'No, I think he gets that it's over.'

'He sounds more realistic than many of my colonial compatriots around the world.'

'Right.'

'The old world order is finished.'

'Indeed it is.' Purcell informed Mercado, 'Signore Bocaccio wants to know if our newspaper wants to buy Mia.'

'Who?'

'The airplane. Mia.'

'Oh … I don't think so.'

'Please ask.' He explained, 'Signore Bocaccio wants to get out.'

'He should. And you should tell him we're considering buying his aircraft so he will let us continue renting it.'

'I may have led him to believe that.'

'You are devious, Frank.'

'*Me?* You just told me to con him.'

Their breakfast came and Purcell said, 'On the taxi ride to the airstrip, I saw children with distended stomachs.'

Mercado stayed quiet a moment, then said, 'Sometimes I weep for this land.'

'If you'd seen what I saw in Cambo, you'd weep for that land, too.' He looked at Mercado. 'We could weep for the whole world, Henry, but that won't change the world.'

Mercado nodded. 'When you get to be my age, Frank, you start to wonder … what the hell has gone wrong?'

'It's all gone wrong.'

'It has. But then you see … well, Father Armano. And these UN relief people. And all the aid volunteers and missionaries who come to places like this to do good. To help their fellow human beings.'

'That is a hopeful thing.'

'For every Getachu, there is a decent human being trying to soften the world's suffering.'

'I hope so.' Purcell asked, 'When will the good guys win?'

'When the last battle is fought between the forces of good and evil. When Christ and the Antichrist meet at Armageddon.'

'Sounds like a hell of a story. I hope I get to cover it.'

'We cover it every day, Frank.'

Purcell nodded.

Purcell wasn't as hungry as he'd thought, and he drank his coffee and lit a cigarette.

Mercado was looking up at the stained glass and said, 'It doesn't actually show Solomon and Sheba in the act.'

'You have to use your imagination.'

'I think that scene would bring in the customers.'

'Or the police.' Purcell asked, 'Have you heard anything about Mr Selassie, as he is now called?'

'I have heard a rumor that they are gently grilling him about his assets here and abroad, and that he's giving them a little at a time in exchange for the lives of some of his family.'

'And what happens when he's given them everything?'

He informed Purcell, 'They've smothered a few old royals with pillows and announced a natural death. That will be his fate. Or something similar.'

Purcell nodded. He asked, 'Do you think the emperor knows the location of the black monastery?'

'That is a good question. The royal court used to travel throughout the kingdom to dispense justice, give pardons, give money to churches, and so forth. They would always visit the Ark of the Covenant at Axum. So it is possible that the emperor has visited the black monastery, but my instincts say he has not. And even if he had, he could not give his captors the grid co-ordinates.'

'Right. I'm sure he wasn't driving the tour bus.'

'More likely the Grail was brought to him at some location away from the monastery.'

'Like the village of Shoan.'

'Possible.' Mercado informed him, 'The royal court has been shrouded in secrecy for three thousand years. They make the emperor of Japan's court seem like an open house party.'

'And the Vatican makes every other closed institution look like a public information office.'

'Your anti-papist views are annoying, Frank.' He reminded him, 'You work for the Vatican newspaper.'

'God help me.'

'In any case, the imperial court of Ethiopia is no more.'

'Unless Gann gets his way.'

'That will not happen. There is no going back.'

'I think you're right, Henry. And on that subject, where is Sir Edmund?'

'I'm beginning to wonder myself.'

'He said he'd arrive on the twenty-fourth, which was yesterday. But we were to wait four days before we gave up on him.'

'Then we will wait. But if he doesn't show, we will press on. Without him.'

'We need those maps.'

'We have an aircraft.'

'Aerial recon is not a substitute for terrain maps. One complements the other. Also, Colonel Gann has skills we don't have.'

'I believe we can do this without him. But I can't do this without you and Vivian.'

Purcell looked at Mercado and asked, 'Why are we actually doing this? Tell me again.'

'My reasons, like yours, Frank, change every day. There are days

I think of my immortal soul, and other days I think how nice it would be to become rich and famous on a world Grail tour. The only thing I'm sure of is that we — all three of us — were chosen to do this, and I believe we will not know why until we are in the presence of the Holy Grail and the Holy Spirit.'

Purcell nodded. 'All right. If Gann doesn't show up, I'm still in. I'll ask Vivian.'

'You don't have to ask.' Mercado looked toward the lobby. 'But if you'd like to, here she is.'

Vivian came into the room carrying a tote bag and wearing khaki trousers, a shapeless pullover, and walking shoes. She spotted them and came toward the table, smiling.

Mercado rose, smiled at her, and pulled out a chair.

Vivian gave them both a peck on the cheek, then sat and said, 'I thought I might find you both in the bar as usual.'

Mercado replied, 'It is now the breakfast room. But I can get you a Bloody Mary.'

'No thank you.' She asked, 'What have you two been talking about?'

Purcell replied, 'Aerial recon.'

She took his hand. 'Frank, you were absolutely magnificent. What other skills do you have that you haven't told us about?'

'I can tie a bow tie.'

She laughed, then took Purcell's toast. 'I'm famished.'

Mercado said to her, 'I was telling Frank that we were impressed with his flyby.'

Vivian glanced at Purcell, who was trying to get a waiter's attention, then she looked at Mercado and their eyes met. He smiled. She gave him a look of mock annoyance.

The waiter came and Vivian ordered tea and fruit, then ate one of Purcell's sausages. Mercado told her, 'We were feeling guilty about the famine.'

'Did you cause it, Henry?'

'I'm having only a cornetto.'

'Well, you should keep up your strength. You're going to need it.'

'Excellent point.' Mercado was not getting the full satisfaction from this moment, so he suggested, 'Perhaps we should clear the air about this morning.'

Vivian responded a second too late. 'What do you mean?'

'Frank was wondering why we were having coffee together on my balcony.'

She looked at Purcell. 'What were you wondering about?'

'I think Henry misconstrued my question.'

She looked back at Mercado, who said to Purcell, 'Sorry – I thought you were showing a bit of jealousy.'

Purcell looked at him and said, 'I was actually wondering how you got your old ass out of bed so early.'

'I set my alarm to see you, Frank. And then I thought, What if Vivian oversleeps? So I rang her up and asked her to join me for coffee while you buzzed by.' He joked, 'If you hadn't seen either of us, then perhaps you should have wondered where we were.'

Purcell was not amused, and Vivian kicked Mercado under the table and said, 'Can we change the subject?' She asked, 'Have we heard from Sir Edmund?'

Mercado replied, 'We have not.'

'Should we be worried?'

'Frank thinks not.'

'Can we do this without him?'

'Again, Frank thinks not.' Mercado added, 'The maps.'

Vivian reached into her bag, withdrew a thick manila envelope, and put it on the table. 'This was at the front desk.'

Purcell saw that it had been hand-delivered, addressed to 'Mercado, Purcell, Smith, *L'Osservatore Romano*, Hilton Hotel.' There was no sender information.

Vivian asked, 'Shall I open it?'

Purcell glanced around the room. 'Okay.'

Vivian used a knife to cut through the heavily taped flap, then peeked inside. 'M-A-P-S.'

Purcell said, 'See if there's a note.'

She slid her hand in the envelope and pulled out a piece of paper. She read, 'I am in Addis. Will contact you. Good flying, Mr Purcell.' Vivian told them, 'It is unsigned.'

Mercado said, 'Thank God he's here and safe.'

Purcell pointed out, 'Being here is not being safe.'

'Well, in any case, we have the maps, and if he does not contact us, we three can continue on.'

Vivian asked Purcell, 'How did he know you were flying?'

'I suppose we're being watched by the Royalist underground.'

Vivian said, 'This is exciting.'

Purcell assured her, 'It gets more exciting when the security police knock on your door.'

They finished their breakfast and Purcell said he'd call Signore Bocaccio to see if they could get the airplane for seven the next morning. He advised Mercado, 'We don't need you on board, but another set of eyes would be good.'

Mercado hesitated, then replied, 'I wouldn't miss the experience, Frank.'

'Good.'

Mercado said he was going to the Imperial to check telexes and catch up on rumors and gossip. He added, 'I will also write a story on the famine.' He told Purcell, 'I saw that story you filed about the Catholic refugees, saying that the Provisional government was not helping them.'

'Hope you enjoyed it.'

'Was *any* of it based on fact?'

'I'm taking a page from your notebook, Henry, and being creative.'

Mercado did not reply to that, but said, 'It is true that newspapers are a rough draft of history. But not a rough draft of historical fiction.'

Purcell was getting annoyed. 'Looking forward to your factual coverage of the famine.'

'My story will stress the government's selling of national treasures to buy food for the people.'

'That is not what is happening. They are buying guns.'

'My point, Frank, has nothing to do with truth or fiction – it has to do with not writing anything that will get us expelled from the country. Or arrested.'

'I think I know that, Henry.'

'Good. We can tell the truth when we get out of here.'

'When you're in Ethiopia, it's *if*, not *when*.'

'Meanwhile, I've told the paper to hold your story.'

Vivian, who had stayed quiet during this exchange, said, '*When* we get out of here, we will have a much bigger story to tell.' She said to Mercado, 'We have agreed to work together, Henry, and to be friends and colleagues, and to forget the past.' She looked at him. 'Didn't we?'

He smiled. 'We did.' He wished them a good day and left.

Vivian stayed quiet a moment, then said to Purcell, 'I'm sorry.'

'About what?'

'You know.'

'Look, Vivian, I know you're still fond of him, and that's all right.' He recalled what Mercado said and reminded her, 'We're going to be in close quarters when we get out of Addis, so we all need to put aside the ... jealousies.'

She smiled and asked, 'So can we all bathe together in the nude?'

'No.'

'See? You *are* jealous.'

'What do you want to do today?'

'I want to take pictures of everything I lost when I was in jail and those bastards ransacked my room.'

'Sounds good.'

'I need to get my camera.' She stood and said, 'Will you come upstairs with me, Mr Purcell? I want to show you my new F-1.'

He smiled and stood. 'Remember that we work for the Vatican, Miss Smith.'

'I will shout, "Oh, God!" at the appropriate moment.'

He picked up the envelope and they went to her room.

As he was getting undressed, he noticed the white *shamma* she had been wearing, draped over a chair. He also noticed the hotel bathrobe lying on her bed. It was a very cool morning and he thought she should have worn that on Henry's balcony.

CHAPTER 36

The small Fiat taxi climbed the fog-shrouded hills with Purcell and Vivian in the rear and Mercado in front with the driver.

They reached the airstrip, where a swirling ground mist obscured the runway and the hangars. Purcell said to Mercado, 'It's okay if you want to go back.' He added, 'It's not a bad idea to have a potential survivor.'

Mercado did not reply.

'Someone to carry on with the mission. Or tell our story.'

Mercado opened the door and got out of the taxi.

Purcell told the driver to wait, and to Vivian he said, 'In case there's a problem with the authorities. Or with Henry.'

'He's not good in the mornings.'

'I wouldn't know.' He got out of the taxi and walked to the hangar to file his flight plan. He found, to his surprise, that he was still annoyed with Henry – and with Vivian – about their coffee date. There was no reason for her to be alone with him. But as they all knew, there would be more such moments in the weeks ahead.

A young air force lieutenant sat behind a desk in the hangar office, smoking a cigarette. Signore Bocaccio had given Purcell a few flight plan forms and advised him how to fill them out, which Purcell had done in English, the international language of flight – except here, apparently.

The lieutenant looked at the flight plan, and it was obvious he couldn't read it.

'Where go you?'

'Gondar.' Purcell pointed to the destination line of the form.

'Why?'

Purcell showed him his press credentials and his passport. 'Gazetanna.'

The man pointed outside. 'Who go you?'

'Gazetanna.' He held up two fingers.

The lieutenant shook his head. 'No.' He waved his hand in dismissal.

Purcell took the carbon copy of the flight plan out of his pocket and put it on the desk. The Ethiopian birr had collapsed, but there was a fifty-thousand-lire note – about forty dollars – paper-clipped to the form.

The lieutenant eyed the money – about a month's pay – then picked up his rubber stamp and slammed it on Purcell's copy of the flight plan, then wrote the time on it. 'Go!'

Purcell took his copy and exited the hangar.

Henry hadn't taken the taxi back to the hotel, and he was talking to Vivian near the Navion. Purcell paid the cabbie, then walked to the aircraft.

Mercado asked, 'Any problems?'

'Are we reimbursed for bribes?'

'There are no bribes in the People's Republic. Only user fees.'

Vivian had her camera bag and said, 'I was telling Henry that

I dug up a wide-angle lens at the Reuters office, and they have a good lab for blow-ups.' She added, 'And they don't ask questions.'

'Good. Are we ready? Pit stop? Henry? How's your bladder?'

'Everything down there works well.'

Purcell tapped his canvas bag and said, 'I have an empty water carafe from the hotel if anyone needs to use it.' He asked Mercado, 'Did you remember to buy binoculars?'

'I borrowed a pair from the press office.'

As Purcell walked to the wing, Mercado asked him, 'What is this?' He pointed to the rocket pod.

'What does it look like, Henry?'

'A rocket pod. Are we attacking?'

As Purcell was explaining about the rocket pod, Mercado noticed bullet holes in the fuselage and pointed them out to everyone.

Purcell assured Vivian and Mercado, 'Lucky hits.' He climbed onto the left wing from the trailing edge, unlatched the canopy, and slid it back. The odor of musty leather and hydraulic fluid drifted out of the cockpit. He reached down for Mercado, who took his hand and vaulted up onto the wing. Purcell said, 'Pick any seat in the rear.'

'There are no seats.'

'Sit on the bean bags.'

Mercado climbed unhappily into the rear as Purcell reached down for Vivian and pulled her up. She squeezed into the cockpit and crossed over to the right-hand seat.

Purcell got in and slid the canopy closed. 'All right, Henry, there is a seat belt back there.'

'I'm working on it.'

Purcell fastened his belt and Vivian did the same. He said, 'The time written on our flight plan is six thirty-eight. We are supposed to be in Gondar in under three hours. Anything longer will raise questions from the guy who takes our flight plan at the other end. But we need to make some unauthorized detours, so it might be after ten when we land. I will blame headwinds.'

Mercado asked, 'What if they know there are no headwinds?'

'They only know what is reported to them by other pilots who have landed. And I don't think there is much traffic from Addis to Gondar.'

Purcell opened Signore Bocaccio's chart and glanced at it. He said, 'What I will do is run her up to twelve thousand feet, and try to get a hundred and fifty out of her. When we see Lake Tana, I will go as low and slow as I can around the areas where we think the black monastery could be located.' He added, 'We'll also take a look at the spa and the thing marked incognita. Vivian will take wide-angle photos, then at some point we need to climb to six thousand feet, which is Gondar's elevation. With luck we will land in Gondar no later than ten A.M.'

Vivian said, 'If anyone asks, what are we supposed to be doing in Gondar?'

'We're doing an article on the ancient fortress city.'

Mercado said, 'That's a stretch, Frank.'

'Okay. We're looking for an interview with General Getachu.'

Vivian said, 'I like your first idea better.'

Purcell reminded them, 'We're reporters. We have no idea what we're doing.' He looked at his watch: 6:52. 'Ready?'

Vivian said, 'If you are, I am.'

He turned on the master switch, then pulled the wheel, and

Vivian was startled when the wheel in front of her moved in concert with his. He pushed on the rudder pedals, and hers moved under her feet. He said to her, 'This is dual control, but that does not mean that two of us are going to fly this. Keep your hands off the wheel and your feet off the pedals.'

'Yes, sir.'

He pumped the throttle a few times, then hit the starter. The engine coughed, and a black puff of smoke billowed out from under the cowl. The propeller went by once, twice, and the engine caught.

Vivian noticed a Saint Christopher medal that Signore Bocaccio had pinned to the headliner above the windshield. She touched it, and said, 'Patron saint of travelers. He will watch over us.'

'Good.'

Purcell looked at the disarrayed and mostly inoperative gauges. Under the control panel was a new switch, marked in English, 'Safety,' and 'Fire.' A separate red button was the actual trigger for the smoke rockets. A round, clear plastic sighting device was mounted in front of him on a swivel near the windshield. He had noticed that there were still four smoke rockets left in the pod. According to Signore Bocaccio, this was not unusual; the Ethiopian ground crews minimized their workload. Signore Bocaccio had advised Purcell not to demand that the rockets be taken out. He also advised him not to fire them for sport.

Purcell glanced at the distant windsock, then released the handbrake and rolled toward the runways. He saw that a C-47 was sitting on the edge of the long runway that he had used with Signore Bocaccio the previous day. He had no time to wait for the

C-47 to move, so he taxied to the shorter runway, which Signore Bocaccio had said was all right to use, depending on winds, fuel load, and cargo load. The fuel gauge said full, but Vivian was light and Mercado had skipped breakfast.

Purcell taxied to the end of the shorter runway. The noise level in the cockpit was tolerable and speech was possible if they raised their voices. He asked, 'Everyone okay?'

Vivian nodded. Mercado did not reply.

Purcell checked the flight controls and the elevator trim position. He did a quick engine run-up and noticed that the magneto drop was neither good nor bad. He'd go with it.

He cycled the propeller through its range, then wheeled onto the runway, where the ground fog had mostly blown off. He lined up the nose on what was once a white line. The expanse of broken concrete was a little disturbing. He hesitated, then pushed the throttle in and the Navion began its run.

The aircraft bounced badly over the broken concrete. The control panel vibrated, the Plexiglas canopy rattled, and the controls shook in his hands. The thumping sound of the nose gear strut filled the cabin as it bottomed out. He glanced at Vivian and saw that she was playing with her camera.

The Navion ate up the runway at the rate of fifty miles per hour, then sixty. The end of the runway was shrouded in fog, but he knew it was also the end of the flat-topped hill that he'd noticed when he'd flown over it with Bocaccio. Purcell saw that the land dropped away to his sides into fog banks. He was on a ridge and there was no aborting this takeoff anymore.

'Frank!'

It was Mercado, but there was nothing to discuss.

Vivian looked up from her camera, but said nothing.

Purcell glanced at his airspeed indicator and noticed that the balky instrument read zero. The throttle was fully open, but Mia showed no signs of lifting.

The runway suddenly ended and Vivian let out a startled sound, then reached out and put her fingers on Saint Christopher.

The control wheel felt light in Purcell's hands and the Navion hung for a moment, as though trying to decide whether to fly or drop into the valley.

The nose dipped down, and Purcell pulled back slowly on the wheel and pulled the hydraulic landing gear lever. Mia lifted slightly. The adjoining hill went by off his left wing, and he noticed that it had more elevation than the Navion. The sound of the landing gear banging into its wells gave Vivian a start, and Mercado said, 'Oh!'

The aircraft began to climb. Purcell glanced at the altimeter. He was at seventy-eight hundred feet, which was not good considering he had started at seventy-nine hundred. Around him, the mountains rose ten and twelve thousand feet and seemed to hem him in. A peak rose up to his front.

The aircraft continued to climb, and at twelve thousand feet he relaxed a bit. He turned to a northwesterly heading and asked, 'Mind if I smoke?'

No one seemed to mind, so he lit up. He asked, 'Anyone need that carafe?'

Vivian replied, 'Too late for that.'

Purcell asked, 'How you doing, Henry?'

No response.

Vivian turned her head. 'Are you all right?'

'I'm fine.'

'Would you like some water?'

'I'm fine.'

Vivian asked Purcell, 'Did you do that yesterday?'

'Yesterday we used the longer airstrip.'

'Can we do that next time?'

'We can.'

'How did the landing go?'

'Don't worry about it.'

'Can I have a puff?'

He handed her the cigarette.

They continued on a northwesterly heading and Purcell said to Mercado, 'You should familiarize yourself with those terrain maps.'

'I thought you had them.'

'Are you joking, Henry?'

'Oh ... here they are.'

Vivian laughed.

Purcell settled back and scanned the instrument panel. He was happy to see that the airspeed indicator was now working.

Mercado said, 'The next time, I will volunteer to be the potential survivor.'

'Happy to shed the takeoff weight.'

They continued on and Purcell looked out his left side. It was a beautiful country from the air. This is what God had given the human race. In fact, the earliest remains of a human ancestor, over three million years old, had been found in the Awash Valley. And since then, it had been a long, hard climb toward ... something.

Vivian snapped a picture of him, then of Henry sitting on the coffee bean bags in the rear. Henry took her camera and said, 'Turn around.'

She turned, smiled, and Mercado took a picture of her.

Vivian said to her companions, 'We have begun our journey.'

Mercado replied, 'We almost ended it on takeoff.'

Vivian assured him, 'I felt Saint Christopher and the angels lifting our wings.'

Purcell was about to say something clever, but when he thought about that takeoff, there was no aeronautical reason why it should have happened.

Vivian again touched the Saint Christopher medal over the windshield. 'Thank you.'

'How about me?'

'Next time, use the longer runway.'

They continued on in silence as Ethiopia slid by beneath their wings. Somewhere down there, Purcell thought, was the thing they were looking for. And maybe that thing was waiting for them.

CHAPTER 37

An hour out of Addis, Purcell spotted the great bend in the Blue Nile. He banked right and followed it north. Their airspeed was one hundred fifty, and the flight so far had been smooth except for some mountain updrafts. The smell of the coffee beans in the burlap bags was pleasant.

Purcell had been thinking about the logistics of their quest, the devils that were in the details. He said to Vivian, 'If there is any problem when we land in Gondar, they may confiscate your film. And if they see we've been shooting wide-angle photos of the terrain, we will have some explaining to do.'

'I will hide the exposed rolls on my person.'

'They may look at your person.'

Mercado confided to them, 'I once hid a roll of film in a place where the sun does not shine.'

'Don't tempt me, Henry.' He added, 'We don't want the film found on us.' He suggested, 'Maybe the coffee bags.'

Mercado replied, 'The ground crew at Gondar will help themselves to a bag or two.'

Purcell noticed a taped rip in the headliner above the windshield where the Saint Christopher medal was pinned. He pulled back the tape and said, 'We can also put the maps in there.'

Mercado pointed out, 'Even if there is no trouble in Gondar, the authorities will do a thorough search of the cockpit when we leave the aircraft, and they will probably find that.'

Purcell did not reply.

Mercado continued, 'If we deny any knowledge of the maps or the film, which together may look suspicious, then Signore Bocaccio will be down at police headquarters in Addis answering questions, while we are answering questions at Getachu's headquarters in Gondar.'

Purcell thought about that. Henry made some good points. 'What do you suggest?'

'I say we take a chance that there will be no problems at the Gondar airfield, and we should carry the exposed film and maps with us.' He added, 'If there *is* a problem in Gondar, it is already waiting for us, and the film and the maps will be the least of our problems.'

Purcell's instincts still told him not to carry around incriminating evidence in a police state. Especially with prior arrests hanging over their heads. But Henry Mercado had been at this game far longer than Frank Purcell. And there seemed to be no good choices.

Vivian said, 'I will carry my exposed film in my bag.' She added, 'Naked is the best disguise. As soon as you try to hide something, you get in trouble.'

Mercado commented, 'You should know.'

Vivian ignored him and continued, 'Frank will carry the maps.' She pointed out, 'It's not as though we're carrying guns or a picture of the emperor.'

Purcell nodded. 'Okay. We land in Gondar and take our things with us. I need to give our flight plan to the officer on the ground, then we take a taxi to town.'

Mercado, too, had some thoughts about their destination. 'If Getachu somehow knows we have returned to his lair, I believe he will not reveal himself to us. He will watch to see what we are doing back in Ethiopia.'

Purcell replied, 'I don't think he's that bright. I think he acts on his primitive impulses.'

'We will find out in Gondar.'

Vivian asked, 'Can we change the subject?'

Purcell said, 'Here's another subject. When we begin our search for the black monastery, we should not drive from Addis to the north again. Agreed?'

Vivian agreed. 'I would not do that again.'

'So,' Purcell said, 'at some point, after we've finished our aerial recon, and when we think we have a few possible locations for the black monastery, we need to fly to Gondar, ditch the aircraft, and buy or rent a cross-country vehicle to go exploring.' He pointed out, 'From Gondar to the area we need to explore is about four to six hours — rather than three or four days cross-country from Addis.'

Mercado agreed. 'Gondar should be our jump-off point.'

They continued on in silence. Purcell followed the Blue Nile north and maintained his airspeed and altitude.

Vivian announced, 'I need to go.'

Mercado passed her the empty water carafe. She said, 'Close your eyes. You too, Frank.' She pulled down her pants and panties and relieved herself.

Purcell said, 'My turn. Close your eyes, Henry.' He unzipped his fly.

Vivian offered, 'I'll hold it for you so you can fly.' She laughed. 'I mean the *carafe*.'

Purcell suspected that Henry was not amused. He held the wheel with his left hand and himself with the other, and Vivian held the carafe for him.

'Finished.'

She snapped the hinged lid of the carafe in place and passed it to Henry, who also used it. Indeed, Purcell thought, they would be in close quarters in the days and weeks ahead with many more close bonding moments. It was good that they were all friends.

At 8:32, Purcell spotted Lake Tana, nestled among the hills. The altimeter read eleven thousand eight hundred feet, and the lake looked like it was about six thousand feet below, which put the lake's altitude at about a mile high. In the hazy distance, about twenty miles north of the lake, would be Gondar.

He pointed out the big lake to his passengers and said, 'We've made good time, so we may be able to snoop around for an hour.'

Purcell began his descent. Within half an hour they were about a thousand feet over the terrain, and the altimeter read sixty-three hundred feet above sea level.

He made a slow banking turn over the lake's eastern shore, and Henry, who had a map spread out in the rear, said, 'I can see the monastery of Tana Kirkos that Colonel Gann mentioned. See it on that rocky peninsula jutting into the lake?'

Vivian saw it and took a photo through the Plexiglas.

Mercado said, 'Somewhere along that lakeshore is where Father Armano's battalion made camp, almost forty years ago.'

The lake was ringed with rocky hills, which Purcell knew was very defensible terrain for Father Armano's decimated battalion.

The monastery of Tana Kirkos, he thought, was also defendable because of its position on a rocky peninsula. The black monastery, however, was safe because it was hidden. Even from up here.

He made another slow banking turn and said, 'We will see if we can find the spa.'

Mercado peered through the canopy with his binoculars and Vivian had her nose pressed against the Plexiglas. 'There! See it?'

Purcell lowered his right wing and reduced his airspeed. Below, off his wingtip, he could clearly see the white stucco spa complex and the grassy fields around it. He saw the main building where they'd parked the Jeep and found Father Armano, and he spotted the narrow road that they'd driven on to get there. He wondered again why he'd turned off that bush-choked road at exactly that spot.

Vivian said excitedly, 'There's the sulphur pool!'

Purcell stared at the pool, then glanced at Vivian. A whole confluence of events had come together down there on that night, and from up here, in the full sunshine, it was no more understandable than it was in the dark.

Vivian said, 'It looks so beautiful from here.' She took several pictures and said, 'We will go back there to find Father Armano's remains.' She reminded them, 'The Vatican needs a relic.'

Purcell had no comment on that and said, 'We will continue our walk down memory lane.'

He turned the aircraft north and said, 'The scene of the last battle.'

Below were the hills where the last cohesive Royalist forces, led by Prince Joshua, had camped and fought, and died. Purcell dropped to two hundred feet. All the bright tents of the prince's army were long gone, and all that remained were scattered bones and skulls in the rocky soil.

Mercado said, 'A civilization died there.'

Purcell nodded.

The hills still showed the cratered shell holes on the bare slopes, and those scars and the bones were all the evidence left of what had happened here while he, Vivian, and Henry were bathing at the Italian spa. If they had arrived a day earlier – or a day later – who knows?

They flew farther north to Getachu's hills. The army had decamped long ago, and only the scarred earth of trenches and firing positions remained to suggest that thousands of men had been there.

Purcell could not determine where Getachu's headquarters tent had been, but then he saw where Getachu had hanged the soldiers with commo wire, and he spotted the ravine where they had all been shackled, and the helipad where they had been lifted out of this hell.

Purcell got lower and slower and they could see the natural amphitheater – the parade ground – and Purcell was certain that Vivian and Henry saw the ten poles that were still sticking out of the ground. But no one pointed this out. And neither did anyone point out the wooden platform where he and Vivian had clung to each other in what they both believed was their last night on earth.

Unlike the spa, this scene, from this perspective, made the events of that night more understandable.

Vivian did not take photographs and she turned away from the Plexiglas.

Henry, of course, had nothing to say, but Purcell would have liked to know what he was thinking.

Purcell circled around toward the plateau between the two camps. To their left he spotted the ridgeline that they'd all climbed to get away from the Gallas, and the peak where Henry and Colonel Gann had picked the wrong time to take a nap. He banked to the right, and the wide grassy plateau spread out before them between the hills.

Vivian asked him, 'Is that where we were?'

'That's it.'

'It looks very nice from up here.'

'Everything does.' He pointed. 'That's the ridge we climbed to go get help from General Getachu.'

It sounded funny in retrospect and Vivian laughed. 'What were we thinking?'

'Not much.'

He turned east and flew the length of the plateau between the hills where the armed camps had once been dug in.

Something caught his eye in the high grass ahead: a dozen Gallas on horseback riding west toward them.

Mercado saw them, too, and said, 'Those bastards are still here.' He suggested to Purcell, 'Fire your rockets at them.'

'They're not my rockets. And they're only smoke markers.'

'Bastards!'

Henry, Purcell thought, was recalling Mount Aradam, where the Gallas had almost gotten his balls.

The Gallas saw the aircraft coming toward them, and Purcell was about to bank right to get out of rifle range, but he had a second thought and put the Navion into a dive.

Vivian asked, 'What are you doing? Frank?'

Mercado called out, 'For God's sake man—'

Purcell got as low and slow as he dared, and the Gallas sat placidly on their horses, staring at the rapidly closing airplane. They must have seen the rocket pod, Purcell thought, because they suddenly began to scatter. A few horses reared up at the sound of the howling engine, and a few riders were thrown off their mounts.

Purcell got lower and gunned the engine as he buzzed over them. He banked sharply to the right to avoid giving them a retreating target, then flew over the Royalist camp and dropped lower toward the valley to put the hills between himself and the line of fire of the very angry Gallas.

Mercado shouted above the noise of the engine, 'What the hell are you doing?'

'Looking for my Jeep.'

'Are you insane?'

'Sorry. I lost it.'

Vivian took a deep breath. 'Don't do that again.'

Purcell headed southeast along the jungle valley and said, 'We will look for Prince Theodore's fortress.'

He reduced his airspeed and his altitude as he followed the valley, which widened into a vast expanse of green between the neighboring hills.

Mercado leaned between the two seats with the map of the area and said, 'Here is incognita.' Purcell glanced at the map, then looked through the surrounding Plexiglas to orient himself. He made a slight right turn and said, 'Should be coming up in a few minutes at about one o'clock.'

He pulled back on the throttle and the airspeed bled off, and the Navion sank lower above the triple-canopy jungle. He was starting to recognize the warning signs of a stall in this aircraft, but its flight characteristics were still unpredictable.

He got down to two hundred feet and Vivian said, 'It's all going by too fast.'

He explained, 'If we go low, we can see things in better detail, but everything shoots by fast no matter how slow I go. If we go high, the ground looks like it's going by slower, but we can't see smaller objects.'

'Thank you, Frank. I never realized that.'

'I'm telling you this because you are in charge of photography. What do you want?'

'I need altitude for the wide-angle lens. I'll get the photos enlarged and we can go over them with a magnifier.'

'Okay. Meanwhile, if you'll look to your one o'clock position, I see something.'

Henry learned forward and they all looked to where Purcell was pointing. He picked up the nose to slow the aircraft, and up ahead, to their slight right, they could see a break in the jungle canopy, and inside the clear area were broken walls and burned-out buildings. If they hadn't known it was intact five months before, they'd have thought it was an old ruin – except that the jungle had not yet reclaimed the clearing.

Purcell thought of the priest. He'd escaped death here, then walked out of his prison into the jungle. And something – God, memory, or a jungle path – led him west, to the Italian spa. But he wasn't heading for the spa. It hadn't been built when he'd been captured, according to Gann and to the map, which did not show

383

the spa. So what was it that took him west to that spa and to his rendezvous with three people who themselves did not know about the spa? Probably, Purcell thought, a jungle path, or a game trail. If he asked Vivian or Henry, the answer was simple: God led Father Armano to them. Purcell thought he'd go with the game trail theory.

Vivian shot a few photos as they approached, then the ruined fortress shot by and she said, 'Can we come around higher?'

'We can.' He climbed as he began a wide, clockwise turn.

In a few minutes, the fortress came into view again off their right side at about a thousand feet.

As Vivian took photos, she asked, as if to herself, 'Can you imagine being locked in a cell in the middle of the jungle for forty years?'

Purcell wanted to tell her that if they found the black monastery, she might find out what that's like.

More importantly, he had confirmed another detail of Father Armano's story. Also, they'd fixed a few points of this tale – the east shore of Lake Tana, the spa, and the fortress. Now all they had to do was find the black monastery which they believed was in this area.

He looked at the thick, unbroken carpet of jungle and rain forest below. He'd once ridden in an army spotter plane in Vietnam, and the pilot had told him, 'There are enemy base camps under that triple canopy. And thousands of men. And we can't see anything.'

Right. Which was why the Americans defoliated and napalmed the jungle. But here, there were hundreds of thousands of acres of thick, pristine jungle and rain forest, and there could have been a city under that canopy and no one would ever see it. Also, they had only a vague idea where to look.

Mercado was having similar thoughts and said, 'This is a rather large area of jungle.'

'You noticed?'

'A clue might be that old map we saw in the Ethiopian College.'

'Henry, please.'

'And the stained glass window at the Hilton.'

'You're sounding oxygen-deprived.'

'What they have in common is that they show palm trees. And if you look, you won't see many clusters of palms down there.'

Purcell glanced out the canopy. True, there weren't many palm trees, but ... that wasn't a very solid clue. He said, 'Okay, we'll keep an eye out for palms. Meanwhile, we have about a half hour before we need to head for Gondar, so I'll make ascending corkscrew turns and Vivian will begin shooting everything below as we climb.' He suggested to her, 'Try to overlap a bit—'

'I know.'

'Good. Up we go.' He pushed in the throttle and the Navion began to climb. Purcell said to Mercado, 'Use the field glasses, and if you see any abnormalities below, bring it to my and Vivian's attention.' He told them, 'I'm going to slide open the canopy so Vivian can get clear shots.' He unlatched the canopy and slid it open a few feet, and the roar of the engine filled the cabin.

Vivian unfastened her seat belt, leaned forward, and pointed her camera through the opening.

They circled the area east of Lake Tana – the forested land that matched up with Father Armano's story, which began on the east shore of the lake and ended at his fortress prison. The lakeshore was known, though not the exact location of the priest's starting point along the eighty-mile shoreline. And the fortress was no longer incognita. What *was* incognita, however, was everything under that jungle canopy, including the black monastery.

Purcell looked down at the land below. There seemed to be no man-made break in the green carpet of jungle. But they knew that.

Vivian, believing in Henry's inspiration about the palm trees, took lots of photos of palm clusters. There were a few small ponds below, and she also focused on them because the priest had mentioned a pond within the walls of the monastery.

As for the tree, the stream, and the rock, as Gann had pointed out, there were lots of trees, and a rock would not be visible unless it was huge, or sat in a clearing. Purcell and Mercado saw streams on the map, but they were not visible through the thick jungle.

Purcell thought about the Italian Army cartographers who'd created dozens of terrain maps based on their aerial photography. They'd spotted the fortress, and a few other man-made objects on their photographs that they'd transferred to their maps. But they had not spotted the black monastery, or anything else they might have labeled 'incognita.'

Needle in a haystack. Monastery in a jungle.

The key, he thought, might be the village of Shoan. He looked at his watch. It was almost 10 A.M. and they needed to head for Gondar, or they'd be unexplainably late on a flight from Addis.

He let Vivian take a few more photos, then shouted, 'That's it!' He slid the canopy closed and latched it. The cockpit became quieter, but no one spoke. If they were disappointed in their aerial recon, they didn't say so.

Purcell picked up a northwesterly heading and began climbing to Gondar's elevation.

He had no idea what awaited them in Gondar, away from the relative safety of the capital. But if their last trip to Getachu territory was predictive, their search for the Holy Grail could be over in half an hour.

He had enough fuel to turn around and go back to Addis, but then he'd have no explanation for this flight.

He said, 'We land in about twenty minutes.'

No one replied, and he continued on.

CHAPTER 38

Lake Tana was coming up on their left, and beyond the lake were the mountains of Gondar.

Purcell said, 'We'll catch Shoan on the way back.'

Mercado informed him, 'You may not see anyone down there.' He explained, 'There is a mass exodus of Falasha Jews under way.'

'I heard that. But why?'

'They feel threatened.'

'I know the feeling.' He reminded Mercado, 'Gann said the Falashas have a special place in Ethiopian society.'

'Not anymore.'

Vivian asked, 'Where are they going?'

'To Israel, of course. The Israelis have organized an airlift.' Mercado informed them, 'Every Jew in the world has the right to emigrate to Israel under the Law of Return.'

It seemed to Purcell that everyone who could leave was leaving. Soon the only people left would be the Marxist government, the Russian and Cuban advisors, the peasants, and idiot reporters. And for all he knew, the monks of the black monastery were gone, too, along with the Holy Grail.

Mercado continued, 'The Falashas are the only non-convert Jews in the world who were not part of the Diaspora. They are

Ethiopians who have been Jewish since before the time of Sheba. Their ethnic origins are here, not Israel or Judea, so the Law of Return does not technically apply to them. But the Israeli government is welcoming them.'

'That's good. But I hope they're still in Shoan, because we're going to put that on our itinerary.'

'I think you're placing too much hope on Shoan for our mission.'

'We'll see when we get there.'

At 10:20, Purcell spotted the fortress city of Gondar rising from the hills. It looked like some movie set from a fantasy flick that featured dragons and warlocks. The reality, however, was worse; it was General Getachu's army headquarters.

The civilian-military airfield was perched on a nearby plateau, and without radio contact, Purcell had to swoop down to see the windsock, and for the tower to see him, making him feel like an intruder into enemy airspace.

The control tower turned on a steady green light for him, the international signal for 'Cleared to land.'

He lined up on the north–south runway and began his descent.

Mercado said, 'I don't see a firing squad waiting for us.'

'They're behind the hangar, Henry.'

Vivian suggested, 'Can we stop with the gallows humor?'

As the Navion crossed the threshold of the long runway, Purcell snapped the throttle back to idle, and the aircraft touched down. 'Welcome to Gondar.'

He let the Navion run out to the end of the runway as he looked around for any signs that they should turn around, take off, and fly to Sudan, or to French Somaliland, about two hundred fifty miles to the east.

Henry, too, was looking toward the hangars, and at the military vehicles nearby.

The Navion came to a halt, and Purcell taxied toward the hangars.

Vivian lifted her camera, but Mercado said, 'You cannot take photos here.'

She put the camera in her bag.

Purcell noticed a C-47 military transport parked near one of the hangars, and he wondered if it was the same one that had blocked him from using the longer runway at the Addis airstrip. The tail number seemed to be the same, but he couldn't be sure.

He taxied up to the hangar and killed the engine. The cockpit became quiet after four hours in the air, and it was easy now to speak, but no one had anything to say.

Purcell unlatched the canopy and slid it back, letting the cool mountain air into the stuffy cockpit. He said, 'Take everything. Leave the carafe.'

He climbed onto the wing, then helped Vivian and Mercado out.

Four men in olive drab uniforms, wearing holsters, were watching them.

They knew the Navion, of course, and Purcell could see they had expected Signore Bocaccio to come out of the cockpit, or maybe Ethiopian pilots who had commandeered the Navion to shoot smoke rockets at the enemies of the state.

Purcell said to his companions, 'The good news is that they seem surprised to see us.'

They all jumped down to the concrete apron and walked toward the four military men. One of the men, a captain, motioned them inside the hangar office. He took his seat behind a desk and looked at them.

Purcell noted that the captain was wearing the red star insignia of the new Marxist state, but he had probably worn the Lion of Judah six months ago. Hopefully, this guy was not Getachu's nephew, and hopefully he spoke the international language of flight, and also believed in the international brotherhood of men who took to the skies. Or he was an asshole.

The captain asked, in good English, 'Who are you?'

Purcell replied, 'We are journalists from Addis and friends of Signore Bocaccio.'

'What is your business here?'

'We are here to see the ancient city of Gondar.'

'Why?'

'Because it is famous.'

The captain thought about that, then said, 'Your flight plan, passports, and credentials.'

Purcell gave him the flight plan, and everyone gave him their passports and press cards. He studied each passport, then checked their names against a typed list. Purcell, Vivian, and Mercado glanced at each other.

The captain looked at their press cards, then handed everything back to Purcell and informed him, 'There is a landing fee.'

'What is it today?'

The captain stared at him, then asked, 'What do you have?'

'Lire.'

'Fifty thousand.'

Purcell said to Mercado, 'Pay the gentleman, Henry.'

Mercado looked both relieved and annoyed. He took a fifty-thousand-lire note out of his wallet and gave it to the captain.

The captain asked, 'How long are you here?'

'A few hours.'

'A long flight for a few hours in Gondar.'

Vivian replied, 'I am a photographer.' She tapped her camera bag. 'We are taking preliminary photographs today, and if our newspaper likes them, we will be back to do a photographic essay of the ancient city.'

The captain stared at her, and he seemed to be processing that information. He asked Purcell, 'What other business do you have here?'

'None.'

'Do you know anyone here?'

'No one.' Except General Getachu, of course, but that wasn't worth mentioning.

The captain looked at them for a long time, then said, 'If a military situation develops, the Provisional Revolutionary Air Force has the right to make use of your aircraft, as I am sure Signore Bocaccio told you.'

'We understand.'

'Are you here to report on the war?'

'Not today.'

'What is your next destination?'

'Addis.'

The captain informed them, 'Your fuel tanks will be filled in your absence and you will pay for the fuel in Western currency.'

He reminded them, 'You will file a flight plan for Addis, and there will be a takeoff fee.'

'I understand.'

'You will see me – Captain Sharew – before you take off.'

'All right.'

'You may leave.'

They walked toward the door.

'Wait!'

They turned and Purcell saw that Captain Sharew was looking at their flight plan. He said to Purcell, 'It has been over four hours since you left Addis.'

'We had headwinds.'

Captain Sharew pointed to the C-47 outside his window and informed them, 'That aircraft left from the same airstrip after you. He arrived two hours ago and reported no headwinds.' He asked, 'Did you deviate from your flight plan?'

'Actually, I misread the chart, and I'm unfamiliar with the terrain, so I was lost for about an hour.'

'So, headwinds *and* lost. You are an unlucky pilot.'

'Apparently.'

'I will be taking note of your total fuel consumption from Addis.'

'Note that we started with only three-quarters fuel.'

'Perhaps someone at Addis will remember that.'

'I'm sure they will.'

The captain kept staring at them, then said, 'You may leave.'

They turned and exited the hangar.

Mercado said, 'He is not buying headwinds and lost, Frank.'

Purcell had spotted the small commercial aviation terminal

from the air, and as they walked toward it to get a taxi, he assured everyone, 'My explanation, as a pilot, was logical and believable.'

Vivian replied, 'I think my explanation as a photographer for what we're doing here for two hours was more believable than your explanation about what took us over four hours to get here.'

'You're a better liar than I am.'

Mercado also reminded them, 'They may borrow our aircraft while we're gone.'

'They'll return it if it doesn't get shot down.'

Vivian asked, 'Is there a hotel in this town?'

Mercado replied, 'There were a few good ones last time I was here.'

'When was that?'

'Nineteen-forty-one.'

They reached the passenger terminal and entered through the rear. The small, shoddy terminal building looked deserted, and Vivian asked, 'Are there any commercial flights to Addis?'

Mercado replied, 'There used to be one a day. Now, from what I've heard, perhaps one a week.'

Purcell observed, 'Obviously we missed that one.'

Vivian said, 'We could get stuck here.'

Purcell replied, 'That would be the least bad thing that could happen here.' He noted that the only car rental counter was closed and he suggested, 'While we're in town, let's see if we can find a cross-country vehicle to rent.'

They exited the front of the terminal, where a single black Fiat sat at the taxi stand. Mercado woke the driver and they climbed in, with Mercado in the front. 'Gondar,' he said.

The driver seemed confused, as though he hadn't had a customer since the revolution.

Purcell said to Mercado, 'Give him twenty thousand.'

'That's about fifteen dollars, Frank. He makes about a dollar a day.'

'That's more than *L'Osservatore Romano* is paying me. Let's go.'

Mercado reluctantly gave the driver a twenty-thousand-lire note, and the man stared at it, then started his car and drove off.

On the way down the plateau, Mercado attempted a few words of conversation with the driver in Amharic, Italian, and English.

Vivian said to Purcell, 'I don't think we should fly the Navion back here. That would be one trip too many.' She suggested, 'We'll take the commercial flight here when we're ready to begin our journey.'

'We need one more recon flight to check out anything that looks interesting on your photographs.'

'I'm not even sure we're getting out of here.'

'We have been chosen to get out of here.'

She didn't reply.

As they climbed the steep, narrow road toward the walls of the city, Mercado turned and said, 'This driver was actually waiting for a Soviet Air Force general.'

Vivian laughed. 'Then why did he take us?'

Purcell replied, 'Because Henry gave him a month's pay.'

Mercado said, 'Nothing has gone right today.'

Purcell disagreed. 'I didn't crash, and we didn't get arrested.'

'The day is not over.'

CHAPTER 39

Mercado directed the driver to the Italian-built piazza in the center of Gondar. They stood in the cool sunshine and looked around at the shops, cinema, and public buildings designed by Italian architects in 1930s modern Fascist style.

Mercado said, 'This looked better in 1941.'

'So did you,' Purcell pointed out.

Mercado ignored that and said, 'Gondar is where the Italian Army made its last stand against the British in '41.' He stayed quiet awhile, then continued, 'I was traveling as a war correspondent with the British Expeditionary Force by then ... we'd taken Addis from the Italians six months before, and Haile Selassie was back on the throne.'

Purcell looked at Henry Mercado standing in the piazza. The man had seen a great deal of life, and death, and war, and hopefully some peace. He had, in fact, seen the twentieth century in all its triumphs and disappointments, its progress and failures.

It was a wonder, Purcell thought, that Mercado had anything left in him. Or that he could still believe in something like the Holy Grail. Or believe in love.

Purcell glanced at Vivian, who was looking at Henry. Purcell hadn't meant to take Henry's lady.

Mercado nodded toward the cinema. 'The British soldiers watched captured Italian movies, and I stood on the stage and shouted the translations.' He laughed. 'I made up some very funny sexual dialogue.'

Vivian laughed, and Purcell, too, smiled.

Mercado pointed to a large public building. 'That was where the British Army put its headquarters. The Union Jack used to fly right there.' He informed them, 'Gann told me he was here as well, but we never met. Or if we did, it was in a state of intoxication and we don't remember.'

Purcell wondered if thirty-five years from now he'd be here, or in some other place from his past, telling a younger companion about how it was way back then. Probably not. Henry had been exceedingly lucky at cheating death; Purcell felt lucky, too, but not *that* lucky.

Mercado continued, 'The Italians carried on a surprisingly strong guerrilla war in the countryside against the Brits for two more years before they finally surrendered this last piece of their African empire. By then I was traveling with the British Army in North Africa.' He stayed quiet a moment, then said, 'I always meant to come back to Ethiopia, and especially to Gondar. And here I am.'

Vivian said to him, 'Show us around, Henry.'

They left the piazza and walked into the old city, which was as otherworldly as it appeared from the air: a collection of brick and stone palaces, churches, fortifications, an old synagogue, and ruins. It looked almost medieval, Purcell thought, though the architecture was unlike anything he'd seen in Europe or elsewhere.

Vivian took photographs as Mercado pointed out a few

buildings that he remembered. He observed, 'There seem to be fewer people here than I remember.' He informed them, 'Gondar and the surrounding area is where most of the Jewish population in Ethiopia lives. I think, however, the Jews have left, along with the nobility, the merchant class, and the last of the Italian expats.'

Vivian pointed out, 'If you lived where General Getachu lived, you'd get out, too.'

Mercado also told them, 'The Falashas, along with the last of the Royalists, and other traditional elements in the surrounding provinces, have formed a resistance against the Marxists. So Getachu is not completely paranoid when he sees spies and enemies all around him.' He added, 'The countryside is unsettled and dangerous.'

Vivian asked, 'Does that include the area where we will be traveling?'

'We will find out.'

Most shops and restaurants were closed, including an Italian restaurant that Mercado remembered. Soldiers with AK-47s patrolled the nearly deserted streets and looked them over as they passed by.

Vivian said, 'This is creepy.'

Purcell suggested, 'Tell them you know General Getachu.'

They found a food shop that sold bottled water and packaged food and they noted its location for when they needed to buy provisions.

There was an open outdoor café in a small square near a church, and they would have stopped for a beer, but six soldiers, who were undoubtedly Cuban, were sitting at a table watching them approach. One of them called out to the senorita, and Vivian blew them a kiss. They all laughed.

Purcell wanted to find the English missionary school where young Mikael Getachu got his ass whipped, but an old man who spoke Italian told Mercado, 'It is now the army headquarters.'

Mercado suggested they skip that photo, and Purcell said, 'Mikael is trying to work through some childhood issues.'

Inquiries about the best hotel in town led them to the Goha, near the Italian piazza. They asked for an English- or Italian-speaking person, and were escorted into the office of the hotel manager, Mr Kidane, who spoke both languages.

They inquired about rooms for the near future, though the hotel seemed deserted, and also asked about renting a cross-country vehicle. Mr Kidane informed them he could get his future guests a British Land Rover, but unfortunately, due to the unsettled situation, the price would be two hundred dollars American, each day. A driver and security man would be extra, and he recommended both. Mr Kidane also required a two-thousand-dollar security deposit in cash — just in case the vehicle and his guests never returned, though he didn't actually say that.

They took Mr Kidane's card with the Goha's telex number. Purcell gave him a twenty-dollar bill for his trouble, and Mr Kidane called them a taxi.

Purcell, Vivian, and Mercado headed back to the airport.

Vivian said, 'That was fascinating.'

Mercado replied, 'Someday, Gondar will be a tourist attraction. Now it is Getachu's prize, if he can hold on to it.'

Purcell said, 'It looks like we have our vehicle, and we can also get provisions in Gondar. But we have to act fast in case the fighting starts again.'

Mercado agreed. 'These mountains have always been a place of desperate last stands.'

Purcell suggested, 'We'll make one more recon flight tomorrow or the next day, and if we still haven't heard from Gann, we need to decide our next move.'

Everyone agreed, and they continued on to the airport, where Captain Sharew awaited them.

The Navion was still there, but Captain Sharew was happily not, so another kleptocrat took their fifty-thousand-lire takeoff fee, which Mercado paid while Purcell quickly filled out the flight plan.

Purcell didn't mind the bribes; it was when the authorities stopped taking bribes that you had to worry.

The new officer wrote their takeoff time as 1:30 P.M., and advised them, 'Do not deviate.' He then presented them with an outrageous bill for fuel, which needed to be paid in Western currency. Purcell said, 'Your turn, Vivian.'

They got quickly into the Navion and noticed that two bags of coffee beans were missing, as well as the urine-filled carafe. Purcell hit the ignition switch and said, 'I hope they left the spark plugs.'

The engine fired up and he taxied at top speed to the north end of the runway. He got a green light from the tower and pushed the throttle forward.

The Navion lifted off and he continued south, toward Addis Ababa.

A half hour out of Gondar, he took an easterly heading and said to Mercado, 'Pass me the map that shows Shoan.'

'I do not want to be late into Addis.'

'We have tailwinds.'

Mercado passed him the map and Purcell studied it. He asked Mercado, 'Do you have any interest in flying over Mount Aradam?'

Mercado did not reply, and Purcell did not ask him again.

Purcell found Shoan on the map, and looked at the terrain below, then turned farther east. He picked out the single-lane north–south road that they'd used when they were looking for the war and found the spa. He noticed on the map that Shoan was only about thirty kilometers east of the road, located on high ground that showed on the map as agricultural, surrounded by dense vegetation. If Gann was correct about the village supplying the black monastery with candles and sandals, then Shoan should be a day or two's walk to the meeting place. The monastery, too, could be a day or two's walk to this meeting place. Therefore, Shoan could be a four-day walk to the monastery. But in what direction?

He looked again at the terrain map. They had narrowed it down a bit, but the area was still thousands of square kilometers, and most of it, according to the maps, was covered with jungle and forest.

Vivian asked, 'What are you looking at?'

'I'm looking for a black dot in a sea of green ink.'

'It's down there, Frank. And we will find it.'

'We could walk for a year and not find it. We could pass within a hundred yards of it and miss it.'

'I'll have the photographs developed and enlarged before noon tomorrow.'

'Good. And if we don't see anything . . . then we need to start at a place we can easily find. Shoan.' He looked out the windshield. 'In fact, there it is.'

He made a shallow left bank and began to descend.

As they got closer, they could see white farmhouses with corrugated metal roofs sitting in fields of crops. There were also what looked like fruit orchards, and pastures where goats roamed and donkeys grazed. There was also a horse paddock built around a pond. It looked peaceful, Purcell thought, an island of tranquility in a sea of chaos.

The village itself was nestled between two hills, and they could see a cluster of houses around a square. There were a few larger buildings, one of which Purcell thought could be the synagogue. Another large building at the edge of the village was built around a courtyard in which was a round pool and palm trees.

Mercado was looking through his binoculars and said, 'Amazing.'

Purcell asked, 'Do you see any people?'

'Yes . . . and I see . . . a vehicle . . . looks like a cross-country vehicle . . . maybe a Jeep or Land Rover.'

'Could it be military?'

'I really can't say, Frank. Get closer.'

He glanced at his watch, then his airspeed. The phantom headwinds he'd reported on the northbound flight were real now, and they needed to get back to the flight plan and head directly toward Addis. 'We're heading back.'

He looked at his chart and compass and took a direct heading toward Addis Ababa with the throttle fully opened. He said, 'If there's a vehicle in the village, then there is a passable road into the village. Probably from the one-lane road we took.'

Mercado replied, 'I don't remember seeing any road coming off that road.'

Purcell said, 'There wouldn't be a road sign saying, "Shoan, population a few hundred Jews."' He speculated, 'The road might be purposely hidden.'

Mercado agreed. 'They don't want visitors.'

'Well, they are about to get three.' He said, 'From what I see below, and from what we've experienced ourselves, most of this terrain is impassable, even for an all-terrain vehicle. What I suggest is that we have a driver in Gondar take us as far as the spa, and from there we'll walk to Shoan. Should be a few hours.'

No one replied.

'I suggest we use Shoan as our base of operation and explore out from there.'

Mercado said, 'I'm not sure the Falashas would welcome our intrusion. Nor would they be keen on us looking for the black monastery.'

'Gann was telling us something. And I think what he was saying was, "Go to Shoan."'

Mercado informed him, 'The English are not that subtle, Frank. If he wanted us to go to Shoan, he would have said, "Go to Shoan."' He further informed Purcell, 'That's the way we speak.'

'I think he was clear.'

'What is clear to me is that we should avoid all human contact

403

as we're beating about the bush. Nothing good can come of us trying to get help from friendly natives.'

'I hear you, Henry. But as we both know, you can usually trust the outcasts of any society.'

'The Falasha Jews are not outcasts – they are people who just want to be left in peace as they have been for three thousand years.'

'Those days are over.'

'Apparently, but if Sir Edmund is correct about the Falashas and the monks, and if we engage the Falashas, we may find ourselves as permanent residents of the black monastery.'

'There are worse places to spend the rest of your life, Henry.'

Vivian had stayed silent, but now said, 'I think you are both right to some extent.'

'Meaning,' Purcell replied, 'that we are both wrong to some extent.'

She pointed out, 'We could clear this up if Colonel Gann shows up.'

No one responded to that.

They continued south, toward Addis.

Vivian said, 'I think we are missing something.'

'The carafe?'

'There was something that Father Armano said ... He gave us a clue, without knowing it.'

Purcell, too, had had the same thought, and he'd tried to drag it out of his memory, but couldn't.

Vivian said, 'It's something we should have understood.'

Mercado reminded them, 'He didn't want us looking for the black monastery or the Holy Grail, so he wasn't giving us an obvious clue to where the monastery was located. But Vivian is correct and I've felt that as well. He told us something, and we need to understand what it was.'

No one responded to that and they fell into a thoughtful silence. The engine droned, and the Navion bounced and yawed in the highland updrafts. Purcell scanned his instruments. This aircraft burned or leaked oil. The engine probably had a couple thousand hours on it, and the maintenance was probably performed by bicycle mechanics.

He glanced up at the Saint Christopher medal, which may have been the only thing that worked right in Signore Bocaccio's aircraft.

He tried to figure out if he'd taken leave of his senses, or if this search for the black monastery and the so-called Holy Grail was within the normal range of mental health. A lot of this, he admitted, had to do with Vivian. *Cherchez la femme.* His libido had gotten him into trouble before, but never to this extent.

And then there was Henry. He not only liked Henry, but he respected the old warhorse. Henry Mercado was a legend, and Frank Purcell was happy that circumstances — or fate — had brought them together.

And, he realized, the sum was more than the parts. He wouldn't be here risking his life for something he didn't believe in with any other two people. Also, they all had the same taste in members of the opposite sex. That ménage, however, was more of a problem than a strength.

Vivian was sleeping, and so was Henry, curled up on the remaining two coffee bean bags.

*

Within three hours of leaving Gondar, he spotted the hills around Addis Ababa, then saw the airstrip. The southern African sky was a pastel blue, and streaks of pink sat on the distant horizon.

Vivian was awake now, and she glanced in the rear to see Mercado still asleep. She said to Purcell, 'I had a dream ...'

He didn't respond.

'You and I were in Rome, and I was the happiest I've ever been.'

'Did we have the Grail with us?'

'We had each other.'

'That's good enough.'

He throttled back and began his descent.

CHAPTER 40

Vivian came out of the Reuters news office carrying three thick manila envelopes in her canvas tote, which contained a total of ninety-two eight-by-ten photographs.

Purcell and Mercado met her outside and they walked toward Ristorante Vesuvio, which claimed to be the best Italian restaurant in Africa, and probably the only one named after an Italian volcano.

To add to the surreal and almost comic quality of Addis Ababa, the street was lined with Swiss Alpine structures, which seemed to fit the mountainous terrain, but which Mercado thought were grotesque parodies of the real thing. He explained, 'The Emperor Menelik II, who founded Addis, commissioned a Swiss architect to design the city, and I think the Swiss chap had a bit of fun with the emperor.'

'You get what you pay for,' Purcell said.

They went into Vesuvio and took a table in the back. Mercado said, 'This place has been here since the Italian Army conquered the city.'

Purcell observed, 'The décor has not changed.'

'They took down the portrait of Mussolini. It used to be right above your head.'

'Where was the portrait of the emperor?'

'Also above your head.'

'What's above my head now?'

'Nothing. The proprietor is waiting to see who survives the Derg purges.'

'The Italians are very practical.'

Vivian gave an envelope to Purcell and one to Mercado, and they slid out the enlarged photographs. They all sat silently, flipping through the matte-finish color prints.

A few of the photos showed part of the wing, and some were almost straight-down shots, showing only a green carpet of jungle without wing or horizon, and these were not easy to orient, but they did penetrate into the jungle. All in all, Vivian had done a good job, and Purcell said, 'You could work for the Italian cartography office.'

'And you could work for the Italian Air Force.'

Purcell looked closely at a few photos, studying the sizes, shapes, tones, and shadows of the terrain features. He said, 'We'll look at these with a magnifier and good light in one of our rooms.'

Mercado looked up from his photos and said, 'We did not see anything that could be a man-made structure when we were in the air, and I don't think we will see anything more in these photographs than the Italian cartographers did forty years ago.' He pointed out, 'The monastery is *hidden*. By overhanging trees.'

Purcell reminded him, 'Father Armano said that sunlight came through the opaque substance used in the roof of the church. If sunlight came through, then the roof can be seen from the air.'

Mercado nodded reluctantly, but then said, 'That was forty years ago. Those trees have grown.'

'Or died.'

Vivian was looking closely at the photos in her hands. 'Father Armano also mentioned green gardens, and gardens do not grow well under a triple-canopy jungle. So what I think is that the monastery is hidden by palms – palm fronds move in the breeze and block the sun, but they also let in some sunlight.'

Purcell observed, 'We're back to palms.'

'Makes sense.'

'All right. But I don't remember Father Armano saying anything about palms.'

Vivian reminded him, 'He did say that on the doors of the church were the symbols of the early Christians – fish, lambs, palms.'

'That's not actually the same as palm trees overhead.'

'I know that, Frank, but . . .' She studied a photo in her hand.

Purcell thought, then said, 'All right . . . in Southeast Asia, from the air, or in aerial photographs, palm fronds were a good camouflage. They create a sort of illusion because of their shape, movement, and the shadows they cast. They break up the image on the ground and fool the eye. Photographs, though, capture and freeze the image, and if you're a good aerial photo analyst, you might be able to separate the reality from the optical illusion.'

Vivian looked at him. 'Did you make that up?'

'Some of it.' He said. 'Okay, let's concentrate on clusters of palms. Also, there is something called glint.'

Vivian asked, 'What is glint?'

'If you buy me lunch, I'll tell you.'

'I'll buy you two lunches.'

The waiter came by, an authentic Italian who, like Signore Bocaccio, hadn't bought his ticket to Italy yet. Most of what his customers wanted on the menu was no longer available, but pasta was still plentiful, he assured them, though the only sauce today was olive oil. There was also a small and diminishing selection of wine, and Mercado chose a Chianti that had tripled in price. He said to his luncheon companions, 'I miss Rome.'

Purcell asked, 'What makes you say that?'

Vivian reminded them, 'There is a famine out there. Get some perspective, please.'

Purcell admitted, 'I hate eating in restaurants when there's a famine.'

Mercado admonished, 'That is insensitive.'

'Sorry.' He reminded Mercado, 'I almost starved to death in that Khmer Rouge prison camp. So I can make famine jokes.' He asked, 'What do you call an Ethiopian having a bowel movement? A show-off.'

'Frank. Really,' said Vivian. 'That is not funny.'

'Sorry.' He said to Mercado, 'You can use that as a Gulag joke.'

Purcell lit a cigarette and said, 'This famine is mostly man-made by a stupid, corrupt government that has instituted stupid policies.' He continued, 'Half the famine relief food coming in is stolen by the government and sold on the black market. The birr is worthless and you can't buy food at any price unless you have hard currency. The UN relief workers are being harassed, and the military uses all the available transportation to move soldiers around instead of food.' He told Mercado, 'That's my next article for *L'Osservatore Romano*.'

'You can write it, Frank, but it will not run. And if it does, you will be lucky if you only get expelled.'

'The truth will set us free, Henry.'

'Not in Ethiopia. Save it for when we are out of here.'

'What is worse — me not demonstrating the proper guilt about eating during the famine, or you not letting me write the truth about it?'

Mercado stayed silent awhile, then replied, 'Your point is made, and well taken.' He smiled, 'Someday you will make a good journalist.'

Vivian asked, 'Is the pissing match over?'

Purcell said, 'Pass the bread.'

The wine came and they drank as they flipped through the photographs.

Purcell looked around the restaurant, which, if it could talk, would have some stories to tell. The clientele was mostly Western European embassy staff, though he spotted four Russians in bad suits at a table. Vesuvio, unlike the Hilton and other hotels, was not in a position to demand only hard currency, but the proprietor and staff did not go out of their way to welcome the Russians or Cubans who paid in birr.

This country was in bad shape, Purcell thought, and the worst was yet to come. The old Ethiopia was dead, and the new Ethiopia should never have been born.

Vivian said, 'I assume there was no message from Colonel Gann at the hotel.'

Mercado replied, 'None.'

'Do you think something has happened to him?'

Mercado replied, 'If he's been arrested, and being held in Addis, someone in the press community would have heard through sources.' He added, 'But if he's been killed in the hinterlands, we may never know.'

Purcell said, 'We will hear from him.'

Vivian reminded Purcell, 'You were going to tell us what a glint is.'

'It is what you see in my eyes when you walk into a room.'

Purcell thought that was funny, but Vivian did not, though she might have if Henry was not at the table. Clearly she was still uncomfortable with the situation, but no more so than he was. Henry, too, was not amused, though he smiled for the record.

Purcell said, 'A glint is what it sounds like — a quick reflection of light off a shiny surface. Pilots in combat look for the glint of an enemy aircraft, or the glint of a metal target on the ground.' He picked up his wineglass. 'Glass, too, can give off a type of glint. Glass roofs, even if opaque, may give off a glint.' He drank his wine.

Mercado was nodding, and Vivian was flipping through the photographs again, looking for a glint.

Purcell continued, 'Obviously, the sun has to strike the object, and the object has to be reflective enough to produce a glint.'

Mercado nodded again, and Purcell continued, 'Father Armano said he thought the roof could have been alabaster, and he said it let in the sunlight and bathed the church in a glow that made his head swim and hurt his eyes.' He speculated, 'It could also have been quartz, or, despite what the priest thought, it could have been a type of stained glass that was rippled and mostly clear, and that might account for the strange light.' He concluded, 'In any case, this substance did not let all the sunlight in, and that means it had to reflect some sunlight back.'

Mercado asked, 'So do we now believe in palm trees and glints?'

Purcell replied, 'I can make a stronger case for that than I can for the existence of the Holy Grail.'

Mercado did not respond to that, but said, 'If we see a glint coming through palm trees, then I think we've found the black monastery.'

Vivian said, 'I see palm trees, but I'm not seeing any glints.'

Purcell said, 'We'll have the photographs done again in a high-gloss finish, and we'll go over them inch by inch in our rooms.'

Vivian informed them, 'The Reuters photo lab guy is very taken with me, but if I ask him to reprint ninety-two photographs in a different finish, I'll have to have a drink with him.'

'Have several,' Purcell suggested.

She smiled, then said, 'He also asked me why I was taking aerial photos of jungle.'

Mercado said, 'He is not supposed to ask questions. What did you tell him?'

'I told him I was trying to find the right green for my drapes.'

Mercado asked, 'Is Father Armano's mention of this roof the unintended clue he gave us as to the location of the monastery?'

Purcell replied, 'It *is* an unintended clue, but there is something else. Something keeps nagging at my mind, and it will come to me.'

Vivian poured him more wine. 'This might help.'

'Can't hurt.'

Their lunch came and Purcell said, 'Buon appetito.'

CHAPTER 41

They laid the photos out on the bed in Mercado's room. Each photograph was now in matte and gloss finish, and Vivian had also borrowed two lighted magnifiers from the smitten lab tech.

The drapes were open and they knelt around the bed, studying the photographs. Purcell was at the foot of the bed, and Vivian and Mercado on opposite sides. Vivian looked up to say something to Mercado and saw him looking at her across the bed that they'd shared a few days before. She met his gaze for a second, then looked down at the photograph in front of her.

They each had a grease marker that they used to circle palm clusters. Next, they looked closely for a glint, or a reflection of light, or anything that could be an anomalous source of light.

Purcell advised them, 'Consider the position of the sun when looking for a glint or sparkle, and consider the direction we are looking at.'

They also had the terrain maps spread out so they could match the photos with the maps, but this turned out to be difficult unless there was an identifying feature in the photo that was represented on the map. Real aerial photographers, Purcell knew, had methods of printing grid coordinates on their photos, but he,

Vivian, and Mercado were trying to match the photo to the maps, then mark the maps, which they would use on the ground.

Mercado said, 'This is more difficult than I thought it would be.'

'It was never going to be easy or fun.'

Vivian found what she thought was a glint close to the destroyed fortress, and they all took a look at it.

Mercado said, 'It is definitely a reflection of some sort, but there are no palms around it.'

Purcell added, 'It's also too close to the fortress — maybe five hundred meters.'

Vivian agreed that the monastery would not be that close to the fortress.

Mercado said, 'It could be a pond, or one of the streams that run through the area. We will check it out when we get there.'

Vivian pointed out the sulphur pool of the spa and said, 'That is what a body of water looks like in these photographs. It is more reflective than ... glinting.'

Purcell agreed. 'We are looking for something that ... if we saw it from the air, we'd say something sparkled down there. Or maybe flashed. The problem with still photography is that you need to capture the glint at the moment it happens. And even then, it might not register on the film.'

Vivian said, 'I used both high- and low-speed film, but I'm not sure which would be better for capturing a quick glint of light.' She added, 'The matte finish actually seems better for showing a light anomaly.'

Purcell also pointed out, 'It was a mostly sunny day, but there are a few cloud shadows on these photographs, and when the sun is blocked, you won't get reflected or refracted sunlight.'

Mercado said, 'We will pray for clear skies on our next flight.'

Purcell replied, 'Remind God that we are chosen.'

'We are being tested.'

'Right. But tell him clouds are not fair.'

They continued to study the photographs.

After half an hour, Purcell said, 'I'm going blind and nuts.' He stood and retrieved the photographs that Vivian had taken in Gondar for her bogus photographic essay.

He sat in a chair and flipped through the photos. One was an artistic shot of a palace garden with a reflecting pool, and the plants around the pool were reflected in the water of the pool, which was the idea. He thought a moment, then said, 'Depending on what that church roof was made of, it might reflect what is above and around it.' He suggested, 'Look for a palm frond or maybe a tree branch that has an exact mirror image.'

Vivian looked up at him, 'All right ... would you like to join us?'

'I'm just the pilot. Also, you have the only two magnifiers.'

Vivian smiled. 'I can get another one from the lab guy, but it will cost me.'

'Go for it.'

Vivian and Mercado continued to study the photos, then Mercado stood and said, 'I need a break.'

'I'm surprised your old eyes lasted this long.' Purcell stood and took Mercado's place at the side of the bed, and Mercado sat and looked at Vivian's pictures of Gondar.

Vivian said, 'I have three possible ... glints. But I could be looking at ground water, or even moisture on leaves or palm fronds.'

'That is another problem with photographs. They are two-dimensional, and depth of field can only be interpreted from what we know of the image.' He added, 'This is not an exact science.'

'Thank you, Frank.'

'Anytime.'

He moved a photograph to the side and noticed something on the bedspread. He looked closer and saw that it was a long, straight jet black hair, and he didn't need the magnifier to tell whose it was.

He looked up at Vivian, who was bent closely over the magnifier. He glanced at Mercado, who was looking at the Gondar photos. He tried to remember if Vivian had knelt at this side of the bed, but he knew she hadn't. Not today, anyway.

He had two choices: pick up the hair and bring it to everyone's attention – or forget it.

He looked again at Vivian. If he asked her what happened here, she would tell him the truth. But he already knew the truth. Or did he? It would not be unlike her to make herself comfortable on a male friend's bed and chat away while the poor guy was trying to talk his dick down.

On the other hand ... but why would she have sex with Henry Mercado? He thought he knew, and thinking back to Henry's changed demeanor since that morning, he could imagine what Vivian's purpose was.

Or was he misinterpreting all those images the way he might misinterpret a photograph?

Vivian said excitedly, 'I think I see a double image. Two palm fronds that are the mirror image of each other.' She put a circle on the photograph and flipped it to him.

He looked at the circled image under the magnifier and said, 'These are not exact doubles. These are two very similar palm fronds.'

'Are you sure?'

'I am sure.'

'Damn it.'

He said to her, 'Things are not always what they seem.'

She looked at him, then some instinct, or prior experience, made her look at where his hand was resting on the light yellow bedsheet. She looked up at him again and said, 'Sometimes things *are* what they seem.'

He nodded and went back to his magnifier and the photograph in front of him.

At 5 P.M., Mercado determined that there was nothing else to look at, and he suggested a cocktail in the lounge.

They stopped at the front desk for messages, and the desk clerk gave them a hand-delivered letter-sized envelope addressed to 'Mercado, Purcell, Smith, *L'Osservatore Romano*, Hilton Hotel.' The handwriting was different from the writing on the manila envelope that had contained the maps, but they had no doubt who this was from.

Purcell carried the envelope into the lounge and they sat at a table.

Vivian said, 'He's alive and well.'

Purcell pointed out, 'He was when he sent this.'

'Don't be a pessimist. Open it.'

'We need a drink first.'

Mercado signaled a waiter and ordered a bottle of Moët,

saying to his companions, 'We're either celebrating something, or we need to drown our troubles in champagne.'

'I like the way you think, Henry.'

Vivian said, 'Out of ninety-two photographs, there are only six circled locations that fit our criteria.' She listed the criteria: 'Palm trees, and/or a glint, in a location that is not too close to the fortress or to the spa, or the road, or to any place that would not be a likely location of a hidden monastery.' She continued, 'Only one photo has all three — palms, a glint, and a likely location.'

Mercado suggested, 'But we may have our criteria wrong.'

'In fact,' said Purcell, 'we may have talked ourselves into palms and glints, so we need to look at the photos with a fresh eye in the morning.'

Mercado informed them, 'I need to go to work tomorrow to justify our existence here.'

Purcell reminded him, 'You're on the payroll. The rest of us are working for room and board.'

They discussed photo analysis for a while, and their next recon flight over the area.

Purcell looked at Vivian, then at Mercado. There had definitely been a new spring in Henry's step since that morning. But interestingly, Vivian seemed the same. In fact, at breakfast on the morning of his flight with Signore Bocaccio, which would have been soon after Vivian had sex with Henry, she had seemed herself — as though she'd put the encounter in a file drawer and forgot about it.

And then she'd invited Purcell to have sex with her.

It was possible, however, that nothing of a penetrating nature had happened. He was certain he would not have been happy to see what did happen in Henry's bedroom, but it might have fallen short of a legal definition of cheating on your boyfriend.

Henry, however, seemed to be happy with whatever had happened, even if the object of his affection didn't seem so moved by the experience.

He looked again at Vivian, who was chatting happily with her old friend.

In Vivian's mind, all was now right with her world, and they could *all* be friends, and continue with their mission here, which to Vivian was far more important than two horny men. No doubt she loved Frank Purcell, and he loved her, so now he had to decide what to do about what she had done.

Two waiters appeared with a wine bucket, fluted glasses, and a bottle of Moët & Chandon, which one of them displayed to Mercado. He pronounced the year *magnifique*, and told his companions, 'This is on the newspaper.'

Purcell suggested, 'Tell them you entertained a member of the Derg.'

'I always do.'

The headwaiter popped the cork, which caused some heads to turn, then filled the flutes.

Henry held up his glass and proposed, 'To us, and to Sir Edmund, and to our journey.'

They drank and Vivian said, 'Ooh. I love it.'

Mercado suggested, 'We will take a bottle with us on the road, and pop it when we see the black monastery in the jungle.'

Purcell warned him, 'That might be the last alcohol you ever see.'

'Nonsense. The monks drink wine.'

They finished their glasses and Mercado refilled them.

Purcell said, 'Okay, one more flight to Gondar, and on the way we will check out whatever we've circled on the photographs. With any luck, we will be able to narrow the circles down to a few, or we will see something else that may be of interest. In any case, we will land in Gondar and go to the Goha Hotel. We'll shop for provisions without attracting too much attention, then we will spend the night, then get in the Land Rover with the driver and security man, and tell them we are hiking. We'll get dropped off near the spa, tell the driver to meet us there in six hours, and we are off on our quest. First stop is Shoan.'

Mercado and Vivian processed all that, and Mercado said, 'I think we should go first to the places in the photographs that are possibly what we're looking for.'

'I don't want to traipse around the jungle for a week or two.' He reminded Mercado, 'That is rough country, and I don't just mean the terrain. We want to minimize the walking, and not use up our provisions.'

Mercado replied, 'I've done this sort of thing before, Frank.'

'Good. Then you agree.' He continued, 'The Falashas may be more helpful than those photographs.'

'They may be the opposite of helpful — or they may all be gone.'

Vivian said, 'Our first objective should be the spa.' She reminded them, 'We said we'd bring back a relic … a bone of Father Armano.'

'You carry the bone.' He also said, 'I will call Signore Bocaccio tonight about the availability of the plane. I'd like to go tomorrow.'

Mercado thought about that, then asked, 'Are you saying that we're leaving the aircraft in Gondar?'

'Well, it's not going to fly itself back.' He assured Mercado, 'I'll telex Signore Bocaccio from the Goha and let him know he can pick up his plane in Gondar, and keep our security deposit.'

Neither Mercado nor Vivian replied.

'I don't think we'll be needing Mia one way or the other after we leave Gondar on our journey.'

Again, no one responded.

Purcell further explained, 'There is no reason for us to return here. We don't need any more photographs developed, and it is time we moved forward – before we get shut down by the authorities or by something outside our control.' He looked at Mercado and Vivian. 'Caesar crossed the Rubicon and burned his bridges behind him. And that is what we will do tomorrow.'

Mercado said, 'We should see what Sir Edmund has written to us. That may influence what we do next.'

'Let's first have our own plan.'

'All right, Frank. We have a plan. Now please open the envelope.'

Purcell glanced around to see if anyone was paying too much attention to them, then tore open the envelope. He extracted a single piece of paper and looked at it.

Vivian asked, 'What does it say?'

'It is … a poem.' He smiled, then said, 'Titled, "The Explorer."'

Mercado said, 'That's Kipling, if you don't know.'

'Thank you.' He read, 'Something hidden. Go and find it. Go and look behind the Ranges – Something lost behind the Ranges. Lost and waiting for you. Go!'

He looked up at Mercado and Vivian.

They stayed silent, then Vivian asked, 'Is that it?'

'That is it – except for the signature.'

Mercado asked, 'Did Sir Edmund sign it?'

'Actually, no, and neither did Rudyard Kipling.' He glanced at the signature and said, 'It is signed, I. M. N. Sloan.'

'Who?'

'You gotta say it fast, Henry.'

Vivian said, 'I am in Shoan.'

Purcell passed the note to her. 'You win.'

She looked at it, then gave it to Mercado.

Purcell said, 'We will join Sir Edmund in Shoan.'

Mercado had a dinner date and left them in the lounge. They sat without speaking for a while, then Vivian said, 'I don't want dinner. Let's have a bottle of wine sent to our room.'

Purcell replied, 'You can have one sent to your room.'

She didn't reply.

He stood and said, 'Good night.'

'Frank . . .'

He looked at her in the dim light and he could see tears running down her face.

She looked at him. 'Do you understand?'

'I do.'

'I'm sorry.'

'We will all stay friends, until we leave Ethiopia.'

She nodded.

He turned and left.

CHAPTER 42

The Navion was available the next day for an overnight stay in Gondar and a return to Addis on the following day. Signore Bocaccio met them at the airport at noon to collect his rental fee and deliver the news. 'This is unfortunately your last flight.' He explained, 'This is causing me worry.'

'I'm the one flying this thing.'

Signore Bocaccio smiled, then said seriously, 'I want no trouble with the government.'

'I understand.'

He advised, 'You, too, should be careful with the government. They will be curious about your flights to Gondar.'

'We are journalists.'

'There is a commercial flight once a week. So perhaps they will want to know why you need my aircraft.'

'We don't want to spend a week in Gondar.' Purcell asked, 'How does that sound?'

'To me, it sounds good. To them ... who knows?' He motioned toward Vivian and Mercado, who were standing near his aircraft. 'You are nice people. Please be careful.'

'We're not actually that nice.' Purcell paid him in dollars for the two-day rental and informed him, 'Some of your coffee was stolen in Gondar.'

'It is there to be stolen.'

'Right.' He suggested to Signore Bocaccio that he meet them at the Hilton for dinner on their return from Gondar so that the Signore Bocaccio could release their security deposit.

'But you must let me buy you dinner, and I will keep the security deposit for the down payment on Mia.' He smiled.

Purcell returned the smile and suggested, 'Seven P.M., but check at the desk for a telex from us in case we are delayed getting out of Gondar.'

The Italian looked at him. 'Be careful.'

'See you then.'

Signore Bocaccio would actually be dining alone, but he had their two-thousand-dollar security deposit to keep him company — and also to pay for his commercial flight to Gondar to retrieve his aircraft.

Purcell was about to say *arrivederci*, but then said to Signore Bocaccio, 'I have seen expats and colonials all over the world waiting for the right time to leave a place that has become unfriendly.' He advised him, 'That time has arrived.'

Signore Bocaccio, the owner of coffee plantations and other things in Ethiopia, nodded. 'But it is difficult. This is my home.' He told the American, 'I love Africa.'

'It doesn't love you anymore.'

He smiled. 'It is like with a woman. Do you leave the woman you love because she is having difficulties with life?'

Purcell did not respond.

Signore Bocaccio informed Purcell, 'My wife is Ethiopian. And my children. Would they be happy in Italy?'

'I saw many Ethiopians in Rome.'

'Yes, I know.'

'At least take a long vacation.'

'As soon as I leave, the government will take all I have.'

'They'll take it anyway.'

'This is true ... so perhaps a long vacation.' He smiled. 'I will fly to Rome with my family in Mia.'

'Bad idea.' He suggested, 'Bring your wife to dinner.'

'That is very kind of you.'

They shook hands and Signore Bocaccio wished them, 'Buona fortuna.'

'Ciao.'

Purcell had already filed his flight plan for Gondar, and as a repeat customer with fifty thousand lire clipped to the form, he got his red stamp without attitude. The duty officer had written 12:15 as the departure time on the form, and that was fifteen minutes ago, so Purcell said to his flight mates, 'Let's hit it.'

Mercado and Vivian had loaded the luggage, which contained more than they needed for an overnight in Gondar, and most of what they needed for a few weeks in the bush, including a bottle of Moët for when they found the black monastery. Henry had also sent a hotel employee out early in the morning with three hundred dollars and a shopping list that included three back-packs, flashlights, and other camping equipment, all of which could be found in Addis's many secondhand stores that were bursting with items sold by people who were getting out or who needed hard cash to buy food. The young hotel employee had found nearly everything on the list, including a compass. The only thing they needed now was food, which they could buy in Gondar, and luck, which could not be bought anywhere.

Purcell jumped on the wing and helped Mercado up, then took Vivian's hand and pulled her onto the wing. They looked at each other a second, then she released his hand and climbed into the cockpit and over to the right-hand seat.

Purcell got in, hit the master switch, and checked his flight controls, then pumped the throttle and hit the starter. The engine fired up quickly, and he checked his instrument panel. Oil pressure still low.

Mercado said, 'It's a bit tight back here with the luggage.'

Vivian said to him, 'Do not disturb the pilot when he is doing his pilot stuff.'

Purcell said, 'Seat belts.'

He released the handbrake and brought the Navion around. He saw Signore Bocaccio standing beside his old Fiat, waving to them. He returned the wave, then slid the canopy closed and taxied toward the end of the longer runway, which was clear of traffic this afternoon.

Vivian asked him, 'Do I need to pray to Saint Christopher?'

He didn't reply.

Vivian had been trying to engage him in light banter all morning, but he wasn't in the mood. She'd been good enough not to call him in his room last night, or knock on his door, and he was fairly certain she hadn't spoken to Mercado about the new sleeping arrangement because Henry seemed himself.

Purcell ran the engine up, checked his controls and instruments again, then wheeled onto the runway. 'Ready for takeoff.' He pushed the throttle forward and the Navion began its run.

The aircraft lifted off and Purcell began banking right, north toward Gondar. To his right lay Addis Ababa, a city he would

427

probably never see again, or if he did, it would be from a prison cell – unless they gave him the same view of the courtyard and gallows.

Purcell steered the Navion between two towering peaks, then glanced back at what he hoped was his last look at Addis Ababa.

Henry, as it turned out, had not gone to the press office that morning, but he'd sent a telex from the hotel to *L'Osservatore Romano* telling his editors that the team was going to Gondar for a few days to report on the Falasha exodus.

Purcell, Vivian, and Mercado had spent the morning in Henry's room, giving the photos a last look and marking the terrain maps with a few more suspected hiding places for the black monastery. The other suspicious thing in Mercado's room, the strand of black hair, was still there. Henry should speak to the maid. But they would not be returning to their hotel rooms ever. It was time, as Colonel Gann suggested, to go and find it.

Regarding where to go next if they did find it, Colonel Gann, in the maps he'd sent them, had included contiguous terrain maps from Gondar and Lake Tana to French Somaliland on the coast. Clearly Gann was suggesting an exit plan for them.

So, with or without the Holy Grail, they would make their way to French Somaliland, the closest safe haven, where many Westerners and Ethiopians on the run had gone. The French officials were good about providing assistance to anyone who reached the border. All they had to do was get there.

Vivian said to him, in a soft voice, 'You told me we would be friends.'

'We are.'

'You've barely spoken to me all morning.'

'I'm not good in the morning.'

She glanced back at Henry, who was concentrating on a photograph with the magnifier. She said to Purcell, 'It will never happen again. I promise you.'

'Let's talk about this in Gondar.' He added, 'I'm flying.'

She looked at him, then turned her head and stared out the side of the canopy.

They continued on, and Mercado said, 'We have reached the point of no return on our journey.'

Purcell replied, 'Not yet. We have burned no bridges, and I can still fly back to Addis and say we had engine problems.'

Mercado did not reply, but Vivian said, 'Avanti.'

CHAPTER 43

Purcell spotted the single-lane road and followed it north. Off to his right front, he could see Shoan about ten kilometers away. He banked right and began descending, saying to his passengers, 'I want Colonel Gann to know we are on the way.'

As they got lower and closer, Mercado leaned forward with his binoculars. 'I don't see the vehicle.'

Purcell replied, 'We don't know if that vehicle had anything to do with Gann.'

Purcell flew over the village at four hundred feet and tipped his wings.

Mercado said, 'I saw someone waving.'

'Did he have a mustache and a riding crop?'

'He was wearing a white shamma ... but it could have been him.'

'Going native.'

They flew over the spa, then Purcell banked right, to the area east of the single-lane road where most of their photographs had been taken of the jungle and rain forests that lay between Lake Tana and the area around the destroyed fortress – an area that Purcell estimated at more than a thousand square miles.

Vivian had the large-scale maps on her lap, and Purcell asked her to hold up the one of the area below.

She held the map for him, and he glanced at the circled sites, then banked east toward the first circle on the map. He dropped down to three hundred feet and slowed his airspeed as much as he could.

Mercado was leaning between the seats, dividing his attention between the map and the view from the Plexiglas canopy.

Purcell dropped lower as he approached the first site, marked Number One on the map, which had shown a light reflection in the corresponding photograph. He made a tight clockwise turn, then dipped his right wing so that it was not obstructing their view. Mia shuddered to warn him she was about to stall, and Purcell pushed in the throttle as he leveled his wings.

Mercado lowered his binoculars. 'I think I saw a pond ... or maybe swampland.'

Vivian agreed, 'It was water. Not a glass roof.'

Purcell said, 'At least what we saw in the photograph was not an illusion, and we've also marked the map position correctly. That's the good news.'

Vivian agreed. 'One of these circles will be the black monastery.'

'If not, we have at least eliminated some locations.'

They continued on to the next closest circle that showed a large cluster of palm trees in the photographs, and Purcell repeated his maneuvers. No one saw anything, so he made another pass, and this time Vivian said, 'I definitely saw a body of water through the palms.'

'Any shiny roofs?'

'No.'

Purcell moved on to the next circle on the map, Number Three, which Vivian pointed to on the corresponding photograph. He glanced at the photo and saw a very large cluster of palms, surrounded by much taller growth. This looked more promising and he pulled off some power and lowered his flaps as if he intended to land. The airspeed indicator bounced between sixty and sixty-five miles per hour.

The cluster of palms was coming up fast at his one o'clock position and he dropped his right wing, causing the Navion to shudder, but giving Vivian and Mercado an unobstructed view as they passed by.

Vivian shouted, 'I saw something! A glint of light ... not water.'

Mercado agreed, and Purcell, too, had seen something, and it was definitely not water.

He climbed as fast as he could, got to six hundred feet, and came around again, this time from the west so that the afternoon sun was at their back. He was higher than last time, so he could keep his nose down as he flew straight toward the cluster of palms.

Vivian had taken the binoculars from Mercado and she was unbuckled and leaning over the instrument panel, staring through the front windshield.

Purcell continued his dive until the last possible second, then pushed the throttle forward, pulled back on the wheel, and raised his flaps. The Navion continued downward for a few more seconds, then the nose slowly lifted and they leveled out over the jungle canopy at about two hundred feet, then began gaining altitude.

Mercado said, 'That was a bit close.'

'Right.' Purcell glanced at Vivian, who was sitting back in her seat with the binoculars in her lap. He asked, 'See anything?'

She nodded. 'It was ... black rock. Just rock.'

Purcell nodded. That was what he thought he'd seen, too. A shiny outcropping of black rock – probably obsidian. 'Well, there is black rock in this area.'

Vivian said, 'Father Armano mentioned a rock, a tree, a stream ...'

'Right. Lots of that down there.' He added, 'We'll check this out on the ground tomorrow.'

He glanced at his watch. It had been three hours since they left Addis. They could keep flying over the area for maybe another half hour, and they should be able to recon all the sites marked on the maps, with maybe some time left over to look at anything else that seemed promising. They'd be late into Gondar again, but not two hours late as they'd been last time. He'd worry about that when they landed. The goal now was to complete the aerial recon, which, if they were very lucky, would reveal the location of the black monastery.

He said to Vivian, 'Map.'

She held the map toward him, and he looked at it, trying to determine what heading to take to get to the next circle on the map.

Vivian was glancing out the windshield, then suddenly shouted, 'Look!' She dropped the map.

Purcell looked quickly through the windshield. Passing across their front was a helicopter, about a half mile away. 'Shit!'

Mercado said, 'I think he may have seen our maneuvers.'

'You think?' Purcell had no way of knowing if the helicopter just happened to be in the area, or if it was sent to track them. He said, 'If he has a radio, and I'm sure he does, he has radioed ahead to Gondar Airport.'

Vivian said, 'Maybe he didn't see us.'

'We saw him, he saw us.'

Purcell watched as the helicopter turned northwest, toward Gondar, which was where they were supposed to be heading. So Purcell took the same heading, but stayed to the left of the helicopter, and kept his distance at about half a mile.

Vivian asked, 'How will he know it was us?'

Purcell informed her, 'There are not too many black-painted vintage Navions in East Africa, Vivian. Probably one.'

She nodded.

Mercado said, 'We actually have done nothing illegal.'

Purcell reminded him, 'We didn't do anything illegal last time we wound up in jail here, and this time we are suspiciously diverting from the flight plan.'

'Quite right.' Mercado asked, 'What do we do?'

Purcell watched the helicopter. He was flying at the same altitude, and he had definitely slowed his speed relative to the Navion, and the distance was closing. Purcell throttled back and the Navion slowed.

'Frank?'

'Well … what we don't do is continue on to Gondar Airport where a reception committee will be waiting for us.'

No one replied to that, then Mercado announced, 'We need to fly to French Somaliland.' He asked, 'Can we do that?'

Purcell glanced at his fuel gauge. 'The fuel should not be a problem.' But they could have other problems with that idea.

Purcell saw that the helicopter had also reduced its speed to maintain the distance between the aircraft. He understood that the helicopter pilot wanted the Navion to follow him into Gondar.

Mercado suggested, 'You may want to turn east now.' He reminded Purcell, 'French Somaliland is that way.'

'Right.'

Vivian was slumped in her seat. She said softly, 'It's over. We never got a chance …'

Mercado said comfortingly, 'We will come back.'

Purcell noticed that the helicopter had slipped to the right and was higher now, so that Purcell had a side view of it, and the pilot had a better view of the Navion.

Mercado said, 'We have to turn east.' He asked, 'Can we outrun this helicopter?'

'Depends on too many unknowns …' Purcell said to Vivian, 'Give me the binoculars.'

She gave them to him and Purcell focused with his left hand while he flew with his right. The helicopter was olive drab, definitely military, and on the side of the fuselage was a red star. He said, 'It's a Huey … UH-ID … saw a million of them in 'Nam …' In fact, this was the same type of helicopter that Getachu had used, and maybe it was the same one that had taken them to prison in Addis. He added, 'His top speed would be about the same as ours.' He lowered the binoculars and said, 'Also, I can see a door gunner.'

'A what?'

'A fellow sitting in the door opening with a mounted machine gun. Probably an M-60, and there is probably another one on the other side.' He added, 'I don't see anyone in the cabin, so General Getachu is not on board.'

No one replied.

Purcell noticed that the distance between him and the helicopter was again closing. He was barely doing seventy miles per hour, and the helicopter pilot, of course, could do zero if he wanted to, so Purcell was going to pass alongside that machine gun unless he turned.

Mercado said again, 'You really need to turn, Frank.'

'Right ... but I'm thinking this guy will follow us toward French Somaliland, and even if I can outrun him, I can't outrun a stream of 7.62-millimeter machine-gun rounds.'

Vivian drew a deep breath. 'Oh, God ...'

Purcell continued, 'Also, even if I could stay out of his machine-gun range, he will radio for support, and the Ethie Air Force might scramble some kind of fighter aircraft.'

Mercado processed all that and said, 'We have no choice then ... we must continue on to Gondar.'

Purcell told them, 'I don't think we're going to be as lucky in General Getachu's headquarters as we were last time.'

No one replied, but then Mercado said again, 'We've done nothing illegal.' He had an idea and said firmly, 'We will jettison everything that is incriminating – the camera, the maps, the photographs, the film ... our camping gear – everything.'

Purcell replied, 'That goes without saying, Henry. But I have to tell you both – Getachu knows, or will know, what we are doing here, and he will not hesitate to use any means that comes into his sick mind to get us to tell him everything he wants to know.'

Vivian put her hands over her face. 'Oh my God ...'

Purcell continued, 'And if he also asks us about Colonel Gann, one of us will eventually say Shoan.'

Vivian was visibly shaken, but she sat up in her seat, took a deep breath, and said, 'I would rather die trying to get away.'

Purcell agreed. 'That would be preferable to what awaits us in Gondar.' He asked, 'Henry?'

Mercado did not respond.

Purcell looked out the windshield and saw that he was only about five hundred yards behind and to the left of the helicopter. He could now see the left door gunner leaning out, attached to his harness, looking back at them, with the machine gun pointed at the Navion.

He slid the Navion to the right to get directly behind the helicopter, but the pilot also slid to the right, so his door gunner could keep them in sight. Purcell knew he couldn't play this game with a highly maneuverable helicopter, so he maintained his position, but reduced his airspeed as low as he could without going into a stall. He needed time to think.

Vivian said to him, 'Frank ... we have to get away from him. Can you do that?'

He was already considering his options. If he made a sudden dive left or right, one or the other door gunners could easily blow them out of the sky. If he climbed, he could possibly pass over the helicopter, and if he kept directly in front of him and got some distance, the door gunners might not be able to swivel their guns that far to the front — but the helicopter pilot only had to swivel his aircraft to give one or the other of his gunners an easy shot at the retreating Navion.

His only chance was to go into a dive – to get into the blind spot below the pilot and the door gunners. He'd have the dive speed he needed to possibly get beyond the accurate range of the machine guns before the helicopter pilot could position his aircraft to give one of his gunners a shot.

Vivian put her hand on his shoulder. 'Frank?'

He asked Mercado, 'Have you come to a decision, Henry? Run or follow this asshole to Gondar?'

Again, Mercado did not reply.

Purcell looked at the distant horizon. Lake Tana was coming up, and so was Gondar. It was possible, he thought, that the Ethiopian Air Force had already scrambled fighters or more helicopters to make sure they didn't lose them. He was a few minutes away from having no options left.

Mercado said, 'Run.'

'Okay …' He looked at his airspeed and altimeter and considered what to do, and how best to do it. His rate of descent in a dive would be greater than the Huey's, and his airspeed, too, would be greater. But, as he said, he couldn't outrun a bullet.

The helicopter was nearly hovering now, about three hundred yards away, and he saw the left door gunner making a sweeping motion with his arm, indicating that the Navion should pass and get in front of the helicopter on the approach into Gondar.

That was not what Purcell wanted to do, and it suddenly became clear to him what he needed to do. And he'd known this almost from the beginning.

He reached up and moved the plastic aiming disc on its flexible arm so that it was in front of his face.

Mercado asked in a forcibly controlled voice, 'What are you doing?'

'What does it look like I'm doing?'

'Are you insane?'

Purcell moved the switch under the instrument panel to the 'Fire' position.

Vivian watched him, but said nothing.

The helicopter was less than two hundred yards away, and the door gunner kept waving his arm for the Navion to pass.

Purcell dipped his right wing as though he were going to bank right, and the helicopter pilot, who'd either seen this or heard from his left door gunner, slid his helicopter to the right to keep the Navion on his left.

Purcell pushed forward on the throttle and shoved his rudder hard right, causing the Navion to yaw right, with its nose now pointed at the helicopter. He lined up the helicopter in the red concentric circles of the plastic disc and pushed the firing button, praying that the electrical connection to the rocket pod was working.

The rocket shot out of the pod with a rushing sound and trailed a white smoke stream toward the Huey, less than two hundred yards away now.

Vivian let out a startled sound and Mercado shouted, 'Oh God!'

The rocket went high over the helicopter, just missing the rotor shaft.

The door gunner seemed frozen behind his machine gun.

Purcell fired the second rocket, which went low, passing between the landing skids and the cabin, right under the door gunner's feet.

The door gunner fired a long burst of rounds at the Navion and the tracers streaked over the Plexiglas canopy. Vivian screamed and dove onto the floor.

The helicopter pilot made the instinctive mistake of taking evasive action, which threw off the aim of his gunner and gave Purcell a better shot at the Huey as it tilted away from him and slipped sideways and downward. Purcell again kicked the rudder to yaw farther right, and pushed hard on the control wheel to lower the Navion's nose. He kept looking through the plastic disc as the Huey again passed into the concentric circles. The door gunner fired again, and Purcell heard the unmistakable sound of a round impacting the aircraft. He pushed the red button once, then again, firing his last two rockets.

The first smoke rocket sailed through the open cabin, past the head of the door gunner, and the second rocket hit the Plexiglas bubble and burst inside the cockpit. Billows of white smoke poured out the hole in the bubble and through the open doors of the Huey.

The pilots were either injured or blinded by smoke, or something critical was damaged in the cockpit, and the Huey's tail boom began swinging left and right.

Purcell did not change course and continued to fly straight at the unstable helicopter. He could see the door gunner through the billowing smoke, but the man, undoubtedly terrified, had let go of his machine gun and the barrel was hanging loose.

The Huey began a slow roll to the right, then suddenly

inverted and dropped like a stone into the jungle canopy below, just as the Navion passed through the airspace that the helicopter had occupied a second before. There was a barely audible explosion behind them as Purcell gave it full throttle and began to climb hard.

Purcell turned off the firing switch, slapped away the plastic aiming disc, then said to Vivian, 'It's over.'

She rose slowly back into her seat.

He asked, 'Mind if I smoke?'

No one replied, and he lit a cigarette, noticing that his hand was shaking.

He glanced at Vivian. Her skin, already pale, was now stark white. 'Are you okay?'

She nodded.

'Henry?'

No reply.

Vivian turned in her seat. 'Henry? Henry?' She leaned farther into the rear compartment. 'Are you all right? Did you get hit?'

'By what?'

Vivian watched him awhile, then turned around.

Purcell kept the throttle open and the Navion continued to climb.

Mercado asked, 'What happened?'

Vivian replied, 'The helicopter ... crashed.'

He didn't reply.

Vivian looked at Purcell. 'Now what?'

'Well ... the French Somaliland option is again open. But that's over two hours from here ... and the Ethiopian Air Force may be looking for us shortly.'

Mercado seemed to be fully aware now, and he cleared his voice and asked, 'Do you think the helicopter pilot had time to radio anyone?'

Purcell didn't think the pilot even had time to piss his pants after the first smoke rocket went over his head. He replied, 'I don't think so. But the helicopter is now obviously out of radio contact, so Gondar will be looking for him, and for us.'

Mercado stayed silent, then said, 'I don't see that we have any option other than French Somaliland ... or perhaps Sudan. How far is that?'

Purcell glanced at his flight chart. 'The Sudan border is less than two hundred miles – maybe an hour-and-a-half flight. But the Ethie Air Force won't hesitate to pursue over the Sudan border, though they probably won't pursue over the French territory's border.'

Mercado seemed to be thinking, then said, 'I will vote for the French border.' He reminded everyone, 'We will receive a better reception there than in Sudan.'

Purcell nodded, then glanced at Vivian. 'Your vote?'

She had already thought about it and said, 'Shoan. Can you land there?'

Purcell thought about that. The single-lane road was too narrow, with towering trees on both sides. The open pastures, however, were a possibility.

Mercado said, 'I'm not sure I'm following you, Vivian.'

'You are, Henry.' She let them both know, 'We are not leaving Ethiopia. We came here to find the Holy Grail.'

Mercado pointed out, 'We are now hunted fugitives. We have just committed murder.'

Purcell corrected him. 'I engaged a hostile aircraft.'

'Call it what you will, if it makes you feel better as they put the noose around your neck.' He said to Vivian, 'We need to get out of here.'

'We will, when we finish what we came here to do.'

Purcell was still heading east, toward French Somaliland, and if they decided to change course to Sudan, they had to do it soon, before Sudan became a longer flight than the French territory. He said to Vivian, 'You have two choices, and landing in Shoan is not one of them.'

'How do you know you can make it to a border before the Ethiopian Air Force shoots us down?'

'I don't know.'

'Then *land*. In Shoan. How far is it?'

'Maybe ... twenty or thirty minutes.'

She pointed out, 'Colonel Gann is there. Waiting for us. The black monastery is down there, also waiting for us.'

Purcell thought about that. Vivian was crossing the thin line between bravery and insanity – or obsession at best. But she made good arguments.

He was about three thousand feet above the ground and climbing. Airspeed was a hundred miles per hour in the climb, but he could get a hundred fifty in a descent. He banked right and the Navion began turning south.

Mercado asked, 'What are you doing?'

'We are landing in Shoan, Henry.' To be completely honest, he added, 'Or we will die trying.'

'No!'

Vivian turned in her seat. 'Yes!'

443

Vivian and Henry looked at each other for several seconds, and Purcell could imagine Vivian's green eyes staring into Henry's soul.

He heard Henry say, 'Yes ... all right.' He added, 'We have come a long way to find the Grail, and we are too close to turn back.'

Vivian reached out and touched Henry's face, then turned in her seat and stared out the windshield as the Navion picked up a southwesterly heading toward Shoan and began descending.

She turned her head toward Purcell and looked at him until he looked at her. She said softly, 'I love you.'

'You love anyone who gives you your way.'

She smiled. 'What is best for me, is best for us.'

He didn't reply.

They continued their rapid descent and Purcell said, 'Shoan, about ten minutes.' He added, 'I will *attempt* a landing.'

Vivian said, 'That's all I ask of you.' She let him know, 'You can do it.'

'We are about to find out.'

He cut his power and began a gradual descent toward the village, which was now visible in the distance.

If he let his imagination go, and if he excluded the surrounding jungle, the fields of Shoan could be upstate New York where he first learned to fly as a young man. His mother had said flying was dangerous and urged him to pursue something safer, like writing.

'I am glad to see you smiling.'

'I used to write for my high school newspaper and the hometown weekly. I majored in journalism in college. My mother wanted me to have a safe job.'

She smiled and said, 'I've read only one article that you wrote. Are you any good?'

'My mother thinks so.'

'I lost my parents when I was twelve. A plane crash.'

'Sorry.'

'Maybe I should have picked a better moment to say that.'

Purcell didn't know how many moments they actually had left, but he said, 'We have a lot to tell each other in Rome.'

She unpinned the Saint Christopher medal from the fabric over the windshield and stuck it on his shirt. 'Christopher saved a child from a river, and though he was a big and strong man, the surprising weight of the small child almost made him stumble and fall into the raging water, but he would not let go of the child – and when they reached safety, the child revealed to him that he was Jesus who carried the weight of the world.'

'I know the feeling.'

He eased the throttle back and continued their descent.

CHAPTER 44

Purcell looked for an open pasture among the hundreds of acres of orchards and planted fields. He thought he needed about a thousand feet of unobstructed, mostly level terrain, but stone and wooden fences separated many of the fields, and trees grew in most of the pastures.

Purcell wanted to do a wheels-down landing, but if the ground was too wet, rocky, or potholed, he might have to do a belly landing, though he had the rocket pod to contend with.

Most importantly, he had too much fuel on board – about half a tank – and he couldn't risk staying in the air to burn it off. He instructed Vivian and Henry to clear the aircraft quickly after it came to a stop.

He circled around the periphery of the fields, and he could see a few people near the village looking up at him. Hopefully, Gann was one of them.

Vivian asked, 'Do you see a place to land?'

'Only one. That pasture ahead.'

Mercado asked, 'Is that long enough?'

'I'll make it long enough.'

The pasture was slightly sloped, and he decided to land upslope so that the land came up to meet the Navion, and the aircraft would slow sooner uphill and hopefully come to a stop before he ran out of pasture.

He lined up the aircraft with the pasture, which looked to be about a thousand feet long. He now noticed there was a stone fence at the end of the rise, but no trees or water holes.

He had no idea what the winds were doing, but it didn't matter; this was the landing strip, and upslope was the direction.

Purcell lowered his landing gear and flaps and pulled back on the throttle. His airspeed was barely sixty miles per hour, and he estimated his altitude at five hundred feet, then four, three ... He looked out at the approaching pasture of short brown grass. The goats had scattered, but now he could see rocks and sinkholes. 'Hold on.'

He cut the power back to idle, pulled the nose up, and the Navion touched down hard and bounced high, then down again and up again across the rocky pasture. He shut down the engine and applied the brakes. Up ahead he could see the stone fence. He worked the rudder, making the aircraft fishtail, and he began to slow, but the stone fence was less than a hundred yards away, then fifty yards.

'Frank ...'

'Brace!'

He kicked the rudder hard, causing the Navion to go into a sideways skid. He expected the landing gear to collapse, but the old bird was built well and the gear held as the wheels traveled sideways across the grassy pasture. The Navion came to a jolting, rocking halt less than twenty feet from the stone fence.

Vivian said, 'Beautiful.'

Mercado said, 'Good one.'

Everyone grabbed their canvas bags that held the maps, camera, and film, as Purcell slid the canopy open and scrambled onto the wing. Vivian followed quickly and jumped to the ground, followed by Mercado. Purcell joined them and they put some distance between themselves and the Navion in case it decided to burst into flames.

Purcell stood looking at Signore Bocaccio's aircraft, which landed a bit better than it flew. Vivian unpinned the Saint Christopher medal from Purcell's shirt, kissed it, then shoved it in his top pocket.

He heard a noise behind him and turned to see a Land Rover coming toward them. The vehicle stopped a distance away and the door opened. Colonel Gann, wearing a white *shamma* and sandals, came out of the driver's side and walked toward them. He called out, 'Was that a landing, or were you shot down?'

Mercado replied in the same spirit of British lunacy, 'Just dropping in to say hello.'

Gann smiled as he continued toward them. 'Just in time for tea.'

Gann's hair was now very short, Purcell noticed, and jet black, and he'd lost his red mustache somewhere, and also lost his riding crop if he'd had one. Also gone was his prison pallor, replaced by a nice tan.

Gann walked up to Purcell. 'Good landing, actually. Frightened the goats a bit, but they'll get over it.'

'So will I.'

Gann flashed his toothy smile, then took Vivian's hand. 'Lovely as always.'

'You look good in a shamma.'

'Don't tell.' He took Mercado's hand. 'Is Gondar closed today?'

'It is to us.'

'Well, you must have a good story to tell. But first meet my friend.' He waved at the Land Rover, and the passenger-side door opened.

A young woman wearing a green *shamma* came out of the vehicle, and they all followed Gann as he walked toward the lady.

Gann announced, 'This is Miriam.'

She nodded her head.

Purcell looked at her. She was about early thirties, maybe younger, with short curly black hair. Her features were distinctly Semitic, though her skin was very dark, and her eyes were a deep brown. All in all, she was a beautiful woman.

Gann introduced his friends who'd dropped in unexpectedly, and she took each person's hand and said, 'Welcome.'

Gann didn't say this was his girlfriend, but it was, and that explained a few things. Always *cherchez la femme*, Purcell knew.

Gann asked his visitors, 'Are you being pursued?'

Purcell replied, 'Possibly by air.'

'All right then … we will bury the aircraft in palm fronds.' He looked at Miriam, who said in good English, 'I will see to that.'

Gann let them know, 'Miriam is … well, in charge here.' He explained, 'She's a princess of the royal blood.'

Purcell had had a few experiences with Jewish princesses, but he understood that this was different.

Mercado said to Princess Miriam, 'We are sorry to intrude, your highness.'

'Please, I am just Miriam.'

Mercado bowed his head in acknowledgment.

Purcell reminded everyone, 'Sir Edmund actually invited us.'

449

Gann replied, 'I did, didn't I? Glad you understood that. Well, here you are. So let's be off.' He opened the door of the Land Rover for his princess, and said to everyone, 'If the aircraft doesn't blow up, your luggage will be along shortly.'

Purcell, Mercado, and Vivian squeezed into the rear of the Land Rover. Gann got behind the wheel and turned toward the village, saying, 'I'm afraid Shoan will look a bit deserted, as you may have noticed when you flew by a few days ago. Most everyone has gone to Israel. Just a dozen or so left, and they'll be heading off soon.'

No one responded to that, and Gann put his hand on Miriam's shoulder and said, 'But they'll all be back. You'll see. A year or two.'

Miriam didn't reply.

They entered the small village of about fifty stucco houses, and except for the tin roofs and unpaved streets, Purcell thought he could be back in Berini. No church, however, but he did see the building on the small square that he'd seen from the air, and indeed it was the synagogue, with a Star of David painted in blue over the door.

The square was deserted, and so was the narrow street they turned down, which ended at the edge of the village. Purcell saw the large house he'd also seen from the air, which turned out to be the princess's palace.

Gann stopped the vehicle under a stand of tall palms and said, 'Here we are.'

Everyone got out and Gann opened a small wooden door in the plain, windowless façade. Miriam entered, then Gann waved his guests in.

It wasn't that palatial, Purcell saw, but the whitewashed walls were clean and bright, and the floor was laid with red tile. Niches in the walls held ceramic jars filled with tropical flowers. They followed Miriam and Gann through an open arch into a paved courtyard where the round pool that Purcell had seen from the air sat among date palms. Black African violets grew beneath the palms, and bougainvillea climbed the walls of the other wings of the house.

Gann indicated a grouping of teak chairs and they sat.

A female servant appeared and Miriam said something to her and she left, then Miriam said to her guests, 'I can offer you only fruit drinks and some bread.'

Purcell informed her, 'We have about a hundred pounds of coffee beans in the aircraft. Please consider that our houseguest gift.'

Miriam smiled, turned to Gann, and said something in Amharic.

Gann, too, smiled, and Purcell had the feeling that Colonel Gann had briefed the princess about his friends.

Vivian said, 'This is a beautiful house.'

'Thank you.'

Purcell went straight to the obvious question and asked Gann, 'So, how did you two meet?'

Gann replied, 'I was a friend of Miriam's father back in '41. Met him in Gondar after we kicked out the Italians.' He explained, 'The Falashas own most of the weaving mills and silver shops in Gondar, and the bloody Fascists took everything from them because they are Jews, and arrested anyone who made a fuss about it. I found Sahle in a prison, half dead, and gave him a bit of bread and a cup of gin. Put him right in no time.' He continued, 'Well, Sahle and I became friends, and before I left in '43, I came to Shoan to see the birth of his daughter.' He looked lovingly at Miriam. 'She is as beautiful as her mother.'

Vivian smiled and asked Miriam, 'Are your parents ... here?'

'They have passed on.'

Gann said, 'Miriam has an older brother, David, who unfortunately went to Gondar on business a few months ago, and has not returned.' He added, 'He is said to be alive in prison.' He added, 'Getachu has him.'

The servant returned with a tray of fruit, bread, and ceramic cups that held purple juice. Everyone took a cup and the servant set the tray on a table. Miriam spoke with the woman, then said to her guests, 'The aircraft is being hidden, and your luggage has arrived.' She also assured Mr Purcell that the coffee beans were with the luggage, and coffee would be served later.

Gann raised his cup and said, 'Welcome to Shoan.'

They all drank the tart juice, which turned out to be fizzy and fermented.

Gann said, 'You must tell me everything.'

Purcell replied, 'Henry is good at telling everything.'

Mercado started with their separate arrivals in Addis, and his finding Signore Bocaccio and his aircraft. Gann nodded, but he seemed to know some of this, and Purcell was impressed with the Royalist underground, or whatever counterrevolutionaries Gann was in touch with.

Mercado then described their aerial recon, and Vivian's wonderful photography, and remembered to thank Gann for the maps, but forgot to compliment Purcell on his flying. Purcell noted, too, that Henry didn't tell Sir Edmund that he, Henry Mercado, had recently fucked Frank Purcell's girlfriend. But that wasn't conversation for mixed company, though Henry might mention it later to Sir Edmund, man to man.

Purcell looked at Gann, then at Miriam, then at Mercado and Vivian. He hoped he was as lucky when he hit sixty. He thought, too, of Signore Bocaccio with his Ethiopian wife and children. If all went well – which it would not – they'd be in Rome in a few weeks; he, Vivian, Henry, Colonel Gann, Miriam, and the Bocaccio family, sitting in Ristorante Etiopia, drinking wine out of the Holy Grail. That was not going to happen, but it was nice to think it.

Henry was getting to the good part – the part where Frank Purcell shot down an armed Ethiopian Air Force helicopter. Henry said to Purcell, 'Perhaps you'd like to tell this, Frank.'

Purcell understood that this was a good story for a bar, far away from Ethiopia. But here, it was not a good story. In fact, he had put them all in mortal danger. Though in Ethiopia, that was redundant.

'Frank?'

'Well, I think this chopper was looking for us, and I think our old friend General Getachu had sent him. So the game was up, one way or the other, and we – I – decided to take this guy out.'

Gann asked, 'Do you have weapons with you?'

'No.' He explained about the rocket pod, and his creative use of the smoke markers. He didn't go into detail, but he did say, 'I rode in a lot of Hueys in 'Nam, covering the war, and I saw them using smoke rockets.' He added, 'Looked easy.' He also explained, 'We were dead anyway. Or worse than dead if we landed in Gondar.'

Gann nodded. 'Quite right.'

Vivian let Gann know, 'They fired a machine gun at us. Frank was very brave. I was petrified.'

Mercado admitted, 'I was a bit anxious myself.'

Gann thought about this, then asked, 'Did you see any other aircraft?'

Purcell replied, 'No.'

Gann said, 'They're probably looking for you on the way to the French territory.'

'We thought about heading there, instead of here. Or Sudan.'

'Well, good that you didn't.' He informed them, 'You wouldn't have made it.' He let them know, 'The Ethies don't have many jets – just a few Mirages – but they are getting Russian helicopter gunships with Russian pilots, and you would probably have met them on your way to Somalia or Sudan.'

Purcell nodded, then said, 'Sorry, though, if we've put you in a difficult situation.'

It was Miriam who said, 'We are already in a difficult situation. You are most welcome here.'

'Thank you.'

Vivian assured her, 'We won't be here long.'

Miriam looked at Vivian and said, 'You are welcome to stay, and you are welcome to leave for French Somaliland, and we can help you with that journey.' She continued, 'But I would prefer if you did not go to the place where you wish to go.'

Vivian replied, 'We have come a long way to find this place.' She assured Miriam, 'We mean no harm to these monks, or to their religious objects.'

'I understand that from Edmund. I understand, too, that you think you have been chosen to find this place. And I respect your beliefs. But I can offer you no assistance with your search.'

Purcell asked, 'Why not?'

She looked at him and replied, 'We here in Shoan have a sacred covenant with the monks of the black monastery.'

Purcell reminded her, 'You're Jewish. They're Copts.'

'That does not matter. We are of the same tradition for two thousand years.'

'Right. Well, all we're asking then is a good night's sleep and food to take on our journey.'

'I will gladly give you that, but I wish you would reconsider that journey.'

'Can't do that.'

Miriam didn't reply.

Purcell said, 'And we may have to return here at some point.'

'You are welcome to do that, but we may not be here when you return.'

Purcell looked at Gann and reminded him, 'You let us know you were here.' He asked, 'Why?'

Gann hesitated, then replied, 'I would like to go with you.' He explained, 'I've spoken to Miriam, and she understands that we believe that the object you are looking for is in danger, and it must be taken to a safe place, though she believes the monks themselves could do that.'

'Maybe they can.' He asked, 'But if *we* took it, where would we take it?'

Gann glanced at Mercado, then said, 'It's not my decision to make.' He let them know, 'We need to discuss this.'

Purcell pointed out, 'We don't have it yet, and to be honest with you, we probably never will. So maybe this is moot.'

Vivian said, 'When we find it, we will know what to do.'

Purcell thought that Henry had undoubtedly promised the Grail to the Vatican, and Gann may have promised it to the British Museum, to take the place of the Ethiopian royal crown the British had snatched and given back. But in either case, the Grail, if it existed, and if they found it, was to be held in custody until Ethiopia was free again. At least that was the promise.

Mercado asked Gann, 'What is the situation in the country-side?'

'A bit unsettled.' He explained about the counterrevolutionaries, and the Royalist partisans, both of whom he was in touch with. He also said, 'The Gallas have mostly gone east where the Eritreans are fighting for independence from Ethiopia. But there are some left to see if the fighting here resumes.'

Purcell told him, 'We saw some Gallas from the air.' He said to Gann, 'I meant to ask you — what do they do with all those balls?'

'They eat them, old boy.' He further explained, 'Not the Christian or Muslim Gallas, of course. But the pagan Gallas.' He added, 'Gives them courage.'

'Right. You'd need a lot of courage to do that.'

'Never thought of that.' Gann further addressed Mercado's concerns and told them, 'The Israelis have smuggled in some firearms for the Falashas, to be sure the exodus goes off without a problem.' He reached into an empty urn and retrieved an Uzi submachine gun. 'Nice piece of goods.' He handed it to Purcell and told them, 'We'll take that with us.'

Purcell looked at the compact weapon with a magazine longer than the barrel. 'This should scare the hell out of those monks.'

Gann smiled. 'I was thinking more of the Gallas – or anyone else who we may meet in the jungle.' He also informed them, 'Getachu has sent some units down this way, but they've gotten a bad reception from the Royalist partisans and the anti-Marxist counterrevolutionaries.'

'Good.' Purcell asked, 'Do you have three more Uzis?'

'I'm afraid not.' He let them know, 'The few men left here need them.'

Purcell passed the Uzi to Mercado, who said, 'Reminds me of the old British Sten gun,' and gave it to Vivian.

Gann said to his guests, 'It's a simple weapon, and I'll show you how to use it in the event . . . I'm not with you.'

Miriam looked at her lover, but said nothing.

Mercado asked Gann, 'Is Shoan safe?'

'It is to the extent that the Provisional government has agreed to let the Jews leave, unhindered.' He added, 'So far the exodus has gone well all over the country, though there have been a few incidents, and thus the Uzis.'

Purcell asked Gann, 'How do you communicate with the Royalists here, and in Addis?'

'I have a shortwave radio. I keep it outside the village, so as not to compromise the people here.'

'Can you show it to us?'

'Of course. But my batteries have died, and I'm waiting for replacements.' He added, 'My Kipling poem to you was my last transmission.'

'We would have brought batteries if they'd been left for us at the hotel.'

'If you're found with a shortwave battery, you are shot. After being tortured.'

'Right.' Maps and photographs were maybe explainable. Shortwave radio batteries were as hard to explain as a gun. He'd rather have the gun, which could explain itself.

Gann took the gun from Vivian and said, 'We should push off tomorrow.' He asked them, 'Do you have any idea where you would like to look?'

Purcell replied, 'I hoped you – or Miriam – could suggest something.'

'I'm afraid I can't, old boy.' He said, 'I thought perhaps you'd seen something from the air.'

'We did. But we don't want to see all those places on the ground.'

'Well, we may have to do that.' Gann stayed silent for a moment, then glanced at Miriam and said to his guests, 'As I mentioned to you in Rome, the people of Shoan have some contact with the monastery. However, those who had this contact are gone.'

Purcell looked at Miriam. She told them, 'The secret is with the elders who have left, and they took their secret with them.'

Gann looked at his guests. 'A relationship . . . a friendship, that has lasted four hundred years, since the monastery was built, is now severed.' He told them, 'The last meeting took place two weeks ago, and the monks have been told.'

Purcell again had the feeling he'd slipped into an alternate universe. He asked Miriam, 'When the people who went to this meeting place left, how long were they gone?'

She looked at him but did not reply.

He asked, 'Which way did they go?'

She replied, 'They went in a different direction each time, and they were never gone for the same number of days.'

'Well, that narrows it down.'

Vivian said to him, 'Frank, you are being rude.'

'Sorry.' He explained his rudeness. 'I just want to find this place and get out of here.'

Miriam said to him, and to her other guests, 'Let me think about what you have asked.'

'Thank you.'

Miriam said softly, 'This is a difficult time for everyone. This civilization – Christian and Jewish – has come to an end. But we look to the future, which will be better. We must all leave here, but when we return, we must return as we were, with our customs and traditions, and our covenants unbroken.'

Purcell nodded. 'I understand.'

Vivian said to Miriam, 'We are here to do what you are doing. To take with us what cannot be left here. To keep things safe until this nightmare is over.'

Miriam replied, 'You should let the monks do that.' She stood. 'I must see to your comforts. I will return shortly.'

The gentlemen stood, and the princess left.

Gann said to his guests, 'Miriam and I have had this conversation, as you can well imagine, and I assure you, she knows nothing more than she has told you.'

Mercado said, 'I'm sure she'd have told you if she knew more.'

Purcell wondered if Henry really believed that women told their men everything. If he did, he'd be cuckolded every year.

Vivian told Gann, 'Tomorrow, we'd like to go to the spa.' She explained that this was not a nostalgia trip, but a bone-hunting expedition.

Gann replied, 'Rather odd custom, don't you think?'

Mercado, former atheist, now a believer working for the Vatican newspaper, explained, 'This is very important to the Church of Rome when a person is proposed for sainthood.' He further explained, 'A mortal remain is considered a first-class relic. A piece of a garment is second-class, other objects—'

'Yes, well, we can stop at the spa and look about for a bone or two.' He added, 'Short walk. Half a day at most.'

Vivian continued, 'And we'd like to see the fortress where Father Armano was imprisoned for forty years.'

Mercado told Gann, 'We spotted incognita from the air and it was, indeed, Prince Theodore's fortress.'

'Good recon.' He asked Vivian, 'Is this part of the sainthood thing?'

She replied, 'It is part of Father Armano's story. It is something I need to see.'

'I see ... Well, I'm sure it's on the way to something.'

Mercado said, 'Most of the suspected locations of the black monastery are a day or two walk from the fortress.'

Vivian added, 'There may be a clue there.'

Gann nodded. 'We'll take a look.'

They had more fermented fruit juice as they discussed a few items on everyone's agenda. They agreed they'd be gone a week — or less if they found what they were looking for. If not, they would return to Shoan, and as Colonel Gann said, 'Regroup, refit, and strike out again.'

Vivian asked Gann, 'Will anyone be here when we return?'

He didn't reply for a moment, then said, 'Everyone will be gone.' He told them, 'Miriam and I will meet in Jerusalem.'

Vivian smiled. 'That's very nice.'

Mercado, who was again thinking about exit strategy, asked Purcell, 'Could you get that aircraft out of here?'

'We could carry it out.'

'Why can't you fly it out?'

'It has to take off first, Henry. That's the hard part.'

'If you land, you can take off.'

'I may have blown the tires. I'll look at it later.' He asked, 'Where would you like to go?'

'French Somaliland.'

Gann interjected, 'I think we will need to walk out of here.' He assured them, 'A number of Royalist partisans have been to Somalia and back. I have a few chaps who will come along.'

Miriam returned and announced that dinner would be served in an hour, and she offered to show everyone to their rooms.

They all stood and Miriam led them to an arched loggia, along which were wooden doors. She indicated a door and said, 'For Mr Mercado.' Miriam thought she knew the sleeping arrangements and indicated another door. 'For Mr Purcell, and Miss Smith.' She added, 'I hope we have gotten your luggage correctly placed.'

Gann pointed to the end of the loggia and said, 'Bath down there.' He suggested, 'Let's say cocktails in one hour, on the patio.'

Purcell, Vivian, and Mercado thanked their hosts, and entered their rooms.

Purcell looked around the small, whitewashed room with a beamed ceiling. There were no windows, but narrow wooden louvers sat high in the wall to let in air and light, and to keep out wildlife and uninvited guests.

There were two gray steel beds against one wall that looked like they'd come from an institution. Against the opposite wall was a wooden table, on which sat their luggage and an oil lamp. In one corner was a chair, and in another was a washstand with a bowl and pitcher. He said, 'Looks like a monk's cell.'

'This will look good after a week in the jungle.'

'It will look like a palace.'

She asked him, 'Are you all right with this?'

He didn't reply.

'I can ask for a separate room.'

'Let me do that.'

'Frank. Look at me.'

He looked at her.

'I am sorry, and I love you.'

'We'll discuss this in Gondar.'

'We are not going to Gondar.'

'Right.'

She changed the subject and said, 'I didn't think Sir Edmund had so much romance in his soul.'

Purcell admitted, 'I was a bit surprised.'

'Love conquers all.'

'Any good news?'

'I'm going to find the bath.' She left.

He stood there awhile, then decided he needed a bath.

He found the door at the end of the loggia and went inside a roofless enclosure in which was a sunken pool against the far wall. The face of a black stone lion was embedded in the wall, and a stream of water poured from the lion's mouth. Vivian's clothes lay on a stone bench, and Vivian herself was floating full frontal nude in the pool.

He took off his clothes and slipped into the water, which was unheated but warm.

She said to him, 'No one would believe a village of Jews in the middle of the Ethiopian jungle.' She added, 'Or a Roman spa. Or a monastery of Coptic monks.'

'Don't forget the Jewish princess.'

'Maybe this is a dream.'

With a bit of nightmare, for sure, he thought.

She stayed silent awhile, floating with her eyes closed. She said, 'We're very close.'

'Closer than I thought we'd get.'

'Do you think Miriam will help us?'

'She's thinking about it.'

Neither of them spoke for a while, then Vivian said, 'Thank you for staying with this.'

He didn't reply.

'You could have left, and I wouldn't have blamed you.'

'It's a good story.'

The door opened, and Mercado said, 'Oh … sorry …' He asked, 'Mind if I join you?' He explained, 'I'm a bit rushed for time.'

Vivian did not reply, but Purcell said, 'You don't need to ask. We're all friends.'

CHAPTER 45

Purcell, Vivian, and Mercado, all fresh from their communal bath, joined the princess and the colonel for cocktails on the patio. Vivian wore her best khaki pants and green T-shirt, and the two gentlemen wore khakis, top and bottom.

The sun was setting and the night had grown pleasantly cool. The purple African sky above the date palms was magnificent, Purcell thought, and if it wasn't for Colonel Gann's Uzi on the table, he could imagine he was someplace else.

Colonel Sir Edmund Gann had gone unnative, and he wore his paramilitary khakis to cocktails, though he'd kept his afternoon sandals.

Princess Miriam wore a purple evening *shamma*, trimmed with lion's mane, the sign of royalty in old Ethiopia.

Cocktails were limited to Boodles gin, a half bottle of which Colonel Gann had been saving for a special occasion, and this was it – which pleased Henry. The gin could be had with or without fruit juice.

The cocktail chatter had mostly to do with the Falasha exodus and the local security situation. Gann explained, 'Getachu and his army control the Gondar area and the surrounding Simien Mountains. Here, to the south, which is nearly unpopulated, there are counterrevolutionaries operating in the jungle valleys, as I've said, as well as the remnants of the Royalist forces.' He further explained, 'These two groups have far different agendas – an elected government on the one hand, and a return to an absolute monarchy on the other.' He told them, 'I'm trying to get them to pull together to get rid of the Marxists. I explained to both sides how we in Britain have a monarch and an elected parliament. But they're not understanding the concept.'

Purcell admitted, 'Neither do I.'

Cocktails were brief, and they were escorted into the palace, where dinner was served in a room that held a long table which would seat about twenty; suitable for large family meals, except that everyone was gone. The floor, Purcell noticed, was laid with black stone.

The teak table was set simply, though the silverware was real, Purcell noticed, and each piece was decorated with the Lion of Judah. The dishes, too, had the heraldic lion hand-painted on them. The dinner theme, Purcell saw, was lions.

Fading sunlight came through the high louvers, and oil lamps flickered on the table.

On the menu was grilled goat, some sort of root vegetable, and flatbread, with bowls of dates scattered around the table. Fermented fruit juice was poured into bronze goblets that looked like the ones Prince Joshua once owned, and the one that he, Purcell, had overpaid for in Rome.

Two ladies in middle age served the simple meal and kept the fizzy fruit juice flowing. Miriam promised fresh coffee at the end of the meal.

She was an intelligent and interesting lady, Purcell saw, and he could see why the other old goat in the room – Sir Edmund – was taken with her.

Dinner conversation began light, and in answer to Vivian's question, Miriam explained, 'Most of the Solomonic line are Christian, of course, but some are Jewish, and some are even Muslim. The line from Solomon and Sheba is well recorded, but over the centuries, the three religions have influenced the faith of some families.' She added, 'The Jews are not the oldest religion in Ethiopia – the pagans are. If you call that a religion.'

Purcell had just learned that the pagan Gallas ate human testicles, but he didn't know how to work that into the dinner conversation – or if he should try.

Purcell also wanted to ask Miriam why, in her early thirties, she was not married yet with ten kids, but to be more subtle and polite, he asked, 'So do you have to marry within the Solomonic line?'

She stayed silent for a few seconds, then replied, 'I was married at sixteen, to a Christian ras, but we produced no heirs, so my husband divorced me. This is not unusual.' She added, 'Most of the rasses are now dead, or they have fled, so I have few prospects for marriage.' She looked at her boyfriend and said without cracking a smile, 'So I have settled for an Englishman.'

Everyone got a laugh at that, and Gann said, 'Could do worse, you know.'

Vivian asked boldly, 'Do you two plan to marry?'

Miriam replied, 'We have no word for knight, so here they call him Ras Edmund, which makes him acceptable.'

Again everyone laughed, but clearly this was a touchy subject, so the nosy reporters did not ask follow-up questions.

Miriam switched to another touchy subject – her benighted country. 'This is an old civilization in the middle stage of history – a medieval anachronism. The Muslims keep harems and slaves. The Christians dispense biblical justice, and men are made eunuchs, and women are sold for sexual purposes. The Jews, too, have engaged in Old Testament punishment. The pagans practice unspeakable rites, including castration and crucifixion. And now the Marxists have introduced a new religion, the religion of atheism, and a new social order, the mass killing of anyone who is associated with the old order.'

Purcell needed another drink after that. When he was first here, in September, living at the Hilton in Addis, he had almost no idea what life was like outside the capital, which itself was no treat. Their trip out of Addis to the northern front had opened his eyes a little to what Ethiopia was about. Gann, however, had known this place since 1941, and Mercado even longer. And yet they'd returned, and in Gann's case, he found something compelling about this country – something that drew him to it the way some men are drawn to those places on the map marked 'terra incognita – here be dragons.' And Signore Bocaccio … he'd forgotten there were better places to do business.

Vivian, like himself, had come here clueless and freelance, but she had discovered that she was chosen by God to be here, which was better than being chosen by the Associated Press.

And then there was Frank Purcell. He needed to think again about why he was still here.

In his mental absence, the subject had again turned to dark matters. Miriam said, 'Mikael Getachu's father worked for my father in Gondar in the weaving shop. My father treated the family well, and paid for Mikael's education at the English missionary school.'

Purcell informed everyone, 'Getachu's biography says his parents went without food to pay for his education.'

Miriam replied, 'They went without nothing.'

Gann said, 'Miriam's brother, David, was actually lured by Getachu to come to Gondar with the promise that Getachu would release two young nieces and a nephew of the family if David would identify and sign over the family's assets to Getachu.' Gann added, 'Getachu knows he can't violate the ancient sanctity of Shoan, or more importantly the international agreement protecting the Jews during the exodus. But he has sent a message to Miriam saying that if she voluntarily comes to Gondar, then he will release David, and the nieces and nephew.' He added, 'The children's parents, who are Sahle's sister and brother-in-law, have already been shot.'

Purcell looked at Miriam, who seemed stoic enough on the outside, but he could imagine the conflicts and pain inside her.

Gann said, 'Getachu's goal all along was to get hold of his princess.'

Miriam said bluntly, 'He will not have me.'

Vivian was looking at her, but said nothing.

Mercado suggested in a quiet voice, 'You should leave here as soon as possible.'

'I will be the last to leave. That is my duty.'

Gann said, 'We're hoping for a UN helicopter pickup here next week.'

Purcell would have liked them all to be on that helicopter, but he knew that would jeopardize not only the Falashas, but also the

UN mission. In fact, just their being here did all of that, plus some. He said, 'We are leaving at daybreak, and we won't return until everyone here is safely gone.' He also suggested to Gann, 'Set fire to the aircraft so it looks like we crashed and burned. Lots of fuel on board.'

Mercado did not like that, but he understood it.

Gann assured everyone, 'I'll have that done in the morning.'

Miriam wanted to know about Purcell, Mercado, and Vivian, and they filled her in on some of the details, though she seemed to know most of this from her boyfriend, Purcell thought, including the fact that they'd had the pleasure of Mikael's company.

She warned them, 'He has a long memory and a great capacity for cruelty and revenge. Do not fall into his hands again.' She added, 'But you know that.'

As for Prince David, Miriam had no illusions that Getachu would be treating him well, but she felt or hoped that after she was out of Getachu's reach, and she was in Israel, Getachu would release her brother, and the nieces and nephew, under pressure from the Israelis and the UN, and hopefully under orders from his own superiors in Addis. Purcell thought that was a possibility, but he was sure that David, if he ever did arrive in Israel, would be a broken man. As General Getachu himself had indicated, shooting a man is easy; breaking a man is more fun — especially if the man or woman was an arrogant aristocrat, or an annoying journalist.

Miriam suggested to her guests, 'Perhaps you can write about what you have seen here. And perhaps you will mention my brother and my nieces and nephew. That could be helpful for their release.'

They all promised they would do that when they left Ethiopia. And they would keep that promise — if they left Ethiopia.

Miriam thanked them, and then painted for them a grim picture of post-revolutionary Ethiopia for their lead story. 'The land is laid waste by war, and by locusts and drought, sent by God. Famine has killed too many to count, and millions more hang by a thread. Pestilence is spreading across the land and the people have withdrawn into themselves. Churches are looted and monks lock themselves in their monasteries. All this is punishment by God for what we have allowed the godless men in Addis to do. God is testing us, and we must show him that we remain true to him. Only then will we be saved by God.'

No one spoke, and Gann, Purcell thought, looked both embarrassed and proud of his princess. Clearly, there was a great cultural divide between them, but they were both righteous and decent people, and what separated them was not as great as what divided them. Love conquers all, as Vivian said.

Coffee was served with some sort of concoction of goat's milk, honey, and almonds.

Miriam said, 'Trade with Gondar and other cities has been greatly reduced since the troubles began. So we have only what we have. But that is more than they have in the places where the drought and the locusts have killed the land.' She forced a smile and added, 'In any case, we are all going to the land of milk and honey.' She asked if anyone had been to Israel, and Mercado and Purcell had, and they painted a bright picture for Miriam that seemed to comport with what her English knight had already told her.

Purcell had encountered a few former aristocrats or landed

gentry and former capitalists in the bars of Hong Kong and Singapore, and in the capitals of Western Europe, and most of them were indignant that they'd been innocent victims of some revolution or another. Almost all expressed a sense of loss, and what they all had in common was a stunned disbelief that the world had changed so much, or had gone so mad. Born to rule or born to great wealth, these refined refugees could not understand or accept that the lowest elements of society – the Getachus – were the most recent mutation of social Darwinism, and that the former lords and masters were the dodo birds in the process of natural selection and extinction.

Princess Miriam, Purcell thought, was a nice person, and he was sure that she and her family had never knowingly hurt anyone. In fact, they'd sent Mikael Getachu, and probably other poor children, to school. But the two greatest scapegoats in the history of the world were the nobility and the Jews – and if you were both, you had a serious problem.

Gann switched to another subject and informed everyone, 'Obsidian was quarried in these mountains since ancient times and sent down the Nile on barges to Egypt, where it was prized for its strength and its ability to be polished to a high black luster. We've all seen the Egyptian statuary carved from obsidian in museums. It's difficult to work with, and it is rarely seen as a building material, except in floors, such as the one in this room, which could be a thousand years old.'

Purcell wasn't sure where this was going, but then Gann said, 'The quarries in this area have not been worked for hundreds of years, and they are mostly overgrown and lost to memory. But there are a few that I've identified, and on the theory that this black monastery is built of obsidian – which is so heavy that it can't be transported too far – I think we should have a look around these three ancient quarries which I've identified on a map.'

Everyone nodded, except Miriam, who clearly didn't want to participate in any discussion about finding the black monastery.

It occurred to Purcell that, as Vivian said, they were close, and with some luck and brains they could actually be seeing what Father Armano saw forty years ago – high black walls rising out of the jungle in front of them. But was the monastery now deserted? He suspected that it was, especially after the Jewish elders of Shoan told the monks that they were all leaving. Gone, too, would be the Grail, of course. But if he, Vivian, Mercado, and Gann found the monastery, that would be enough for him and maybe for his companions. The journey would be over, and the Grail – as it had a history of doing – would be gone, but safe from the world which had grown evil.

But if they reached the walls of the monastery and a reed basket was lowered ... well, forewarned was forearmed.

Dinner was over, and everyone stood. The long night had begun, and at dawn they would begin their quest for fame, fortune, salvation, a good story, a Grail rescue mission, inner peace, or whatever was driving them into the dark interior.

If, indeed, they had been chosen for this journey, then the answer to why they'd been chosen was waiting for them.

— PART IV —

The Quest

We shall not cease from exploration
And the end of all our exploring
Will be to arrive where we started
And know the place for the first time.

—T. S. Eliot,
Four Quartets 4: Little Gidding

CHAPTER 46

They rose before dawn and met in the courtyard, where Miriam had coffee, fruit, and bread for them.

They carried their backpacks and equipment, and what was left behind would be burned along with the Navion, to hide any traces that they'd been in the village.

Vivian and Purcell had slept in the same room, but not in the same bed. So they were friends.

The sky was beginning to lighten, and Purcell could see it was going to be a clear day. No one spoke much, because there was little to say that hadn't already been said, and also because there were no words equal to the moment of heading off into the unknown.

Purcell, Vivian, and Henry thanked Miriam for her hospitality and promised to meet again under better circumstances. She seemed sorry to see them go, Purcell thought, but probably relieved, too. She didn't hand them a map to the black monastery, but she did say, 'If God wants you to find this place, you will.' She also assured them, 'Edmund will be your guide in the jungle. Please be his guide in the ways of God.'

Henry and Vivian said they would.

They left Colonel Gann to say his own good-bye to his lady, and they went through a back door and into a flower garden.

They had as much food with them as they could carry, which consisted mostly of boiled eggs, bread, dates, and dried meat, all of which Gann assured them was high in nutrition, and would last a week. They each carried two canteens; one of water, one of the purple juice, which Purcell had come to enjoy. Henry had his Moët, of course, and Vivian had her camera. Purcell was in charge of the maps.

Colonel Gann came out into the garden, and it was obvious that his parting had been difficult. Purcell had never known that feeling himself, or if he had, the sense of loss was always made easier by a larger sense of relief.

Purcell looked at Vivian in the dawn light and saw she was looking at him, and probably thinking the same thing: How will we part? Hopefully, as friends.

Colonel Gann gave everyone a five-minute lesson on the Uzi, which indeed was a simple weapon to load and fire. Gann then led them through a fruit orchard and across a pasture toward the thick rain forest that surrounded the fields and village of Shoan.

He knew his way, and within fifteen minutes he'd found the head of a trail that none of them could have found, even in full sunlight. They entered the rain forest, going from human habitation to a world of flora and fauna that had barely been disturbed since the beginning of time.

The trail was narrow, and the jungle growth encroached on all sides. They walked silently, single file, and crouched most of the way. Gann had a machete with him, but he didn't want to use it and leave evidence that the trail had been traveled.

Their first stop, after about ten minutes, was a huge gnarled tree that was mostly dead, and which Gann said was a baobab. A few paces from the tree was the shortwave radio, wrapped in plastic and covered with palm fronds.

Gann had hoped that the Royalist partisans had delivered new batteries, but the radio was still dead.

He said in a whisper, 'This trail will take us to the spa. The road would be faster, but we're more likely to come upon someone on the road – a vehicle, an army patrol, or Gallas on horseback.' He also told them, 'I know some of these trails, but so do others. We need to remain silent, and we need to listen to the jungle. I will take the point, and Mr Purcell will take the rear. If anyone hears anything, you will quickly and silently alert everyone, and point to where you've heard the sound. We will then take cover off the trail.' He asked, 'Any questions?'

'Can I smoke?'

'No.'

They continued on, and the trail became more overgrown. They were heading generally north, paralleling the narrow road that they had driven in September. Purcell hadn't much enjoyed driving the creepy road through the dark jungle, and he wasn't enjoying walking through that jungle now.

The ribbon of sky above the narrow trail was getting lighter, and somewhere out there, the sun was shining.

Vivian was walking ahead of Purcell, and now and then she glanced back and gave him a smile, which he returned. It was hard to stay angry when each step could be your last, and when you were just hours or days away from the greatest religious discovery since Moses found the Ten Commandments – which, as it turned out, were in Axum, inside the Ark of the Covenant.

Purcell still didn't believe in any of this, but he would be happy to be proven wrong.

After about an hour, Gann stopped and motioned everyone to the right side of the trail where an outcropping of black obsidian lay among the ground growth between towering trees. They sat on the rock and took a break. Gann and Purcell looked at one of the maps and estimated where they were. Gann said quietly, 'The spa will be another two or three hours.'

They both studied the map and agreed that their next objective after the spa would be Prince Theodore's fortress, which was about five or six kilometers east of the spa.

Gann said, 'The map does not show a trail between the fortress and the spa, and if we can't find one on the ground, and if there is thick underbrush between the trees, as there is here, we will have to cut a trail.' He informed them, 'That could take more than a day to travel that five kilometers.'

Vivian reminded them, 'Father Armano walked from the fortress to the spa, and we saw him at about ten at night.'

Gann inquired, 'What time did he start from the fortress?'

Vivian replied, 'I don't know ... but we have to assume he started sometime that evening ... he could not have traveled far with that wound.'

Purcell reminded them, 'Getachu said that his artillery bombarded Prince Theodore's fortress — and this is probably how Father Armano got out of his cell.'

Gann nodded and said, 'That would have been about seven-fifteen.' He told them, 'I took note of the time, and I wondered what the idiot was shooting at, because he wasn't shooting at me or Prince Joshua's camp.'

So, with a little simple math, everyone agreed that Father Armano was freed from his cell – probably by a lucky artillery round – after 7:15 P.M., and he appeared at the spa about three hours later, meaning there was a good and direct trail between the fortress and the spa. All they had to do was find it.

Vivian looked at the rock they were sitting on and asked, 'Could this be the rock that Father Armano mentioned?'

Gann replied, 'There are many rock outcroppings in this area, and there is nothing remarkable about this one.' He suggested, 'I think you should forget the rock, the tree, and the stream, which may have had some meaning to the priest, but that meaning is obscure to us.'

Vivian did not reply.

They all stood and continued on. It was becoming warmer, and more humid, and the thick, rotting vegetation gave off noxious vapors, which reminded Purcell of the jungles of Southeast Asia. There was a reason that few people lived in the lush tropical rain forests of the world; it was a hostile environment to humans, and a paradise for insects, slithering snakes, and animals with fangs and claws. In fact, he thought, the jungle sucked.

They continued on.

Colonel Gann walked easily, like he did this every day before breakfast, Purcell thought. And Vivian had youth on her side, but about sixty pounds of gear on her back, and Purcell could see she was dragging a bit. Henry, too, seemed a bit fatigued, and if physical exhaustion is mostly mental, then Henry should be thinking about their last trek when he'd run out of gas at a bad time, which led to a series of events that nearly got them all killed. Henry now wanted to redeem himself, and impress Vivian, of course, or at least not pass out in front of her, and that should keep him moving. If not, he should think about Gallas coming for his balls.

They continued on through the jungle, or rain forest, as Purcell's editors now wanted it called. The insects and birds made a lot of noise, which covered the sound of danger. But as Purcell had learned in Vietnam when traveling with army patrols, if the birds become quiet, they've heard something. It could be you they've heard, or something else.

Purcell considered himself in fairly good shape, despite the cocktails and cigarettes, and this hike, even with all the carried weight, was so far like a walk in the park. But after a week of this, and sleeping on the ground, and the scant rations, he could imagine that they'd all be having some problems. It was obvious why the Gallas rode horses, and why many armies used mules as pack animals. But Colonel Gann had vetoed both for a variety of practical reasons, mostly having to do with noise discipline, and water and forage for the animals. Purcell did not usually defer to anyone in his business, which was why he was freelance and mostly between jobs; but he would defer to Colonel Gann in *his* business, as long as he thought Gann knew what he was doing.

About two hours later, Gann motioned everyone together and said, 'The spa is about fifty meters ahead. I will go first and recon.' He borrowed Mercado's binoculars, then handed Purcell the Uzi and three extra magazines and said, 'You will cover me.' He pulled a long-barreled revolver from under his bush jacket and headed down the trail. Purcell motioned Vivian and Mercado to stay put, and followed Gann.

The trail ended at the clearing around the spa, and fifty yards ahead was the side of the white stucco hotel, sitting in the sunlight. Gann was scanning the area around the building, then moved toward it.

Purcell took the Uzi off safety and followed Gann through the tall grass. Gann went around to the front of the hotel, and Purcell kept about twenty yards behind him. Gann climbed the steps and disappeared into the building, and Purcell waited. A few minutes later, Gann reappeared and signaled all clear.

Purcell looked back to the edge of the jungle and saw Mercado and Vivian making their way through the chest-high grass. He motioned them to join him, and together they walked quickly to the front of the spa hotel.

They stood at the base of the steps that they'd climbed with the Jeep and looked at the crumbling ruin.

Vivian said, 'We are back.'

Purcell looked across the field toward the narrow road they'd driven that night, and he could see the place where he'd crashed the Jeep through the thick wall of high brush that blocked the spa from the road. He looked back at the hotel. He must have seen the dome, he thought, or it registered subconsciously, and that was why he'd suddenly turned off the road.

Vivian saw what Purcell was looking at and said, 'Fate, Frank. Don't try to understand it.'

Mercado agreed, 'I see God's hand in this.'

Hard to argue with that, so he didn't.

Vivian walked halfway up the steps, and Mercado and Purcell joined her.

She looked around and asked, 'Can you believe this?' She turned to Purcell. 'We are back where it began.'

Actually, Purcell thought, this all began in the Hilton bar, with

Henry inviting him to come with them to the front lines. A simple 'No' would have been a good answer. But Henry's invitation was flattering. And Vivian had smiled at him. And he may have had one cocktail more than he needed.

Ego, balls, alcohol, and a restless dick; a sure combination for glory or disaster.

Vivian said, 'We will begin here, where Father Armano ended his life. We have been to Berini, and we have been to Rome, and we will follow the priest's footsteps to his prison. And with his help and God's help we will also follow his footsteps to the black monastery, and the Holy Grail.'

Vivian took both their hands, and they continued up the steps to the place where Father Armano's fate had intersected with theirs.

CHAPTER 47

They found Colonel Gann standing in the rubble-filled lobby. It looked the same as when they'd last seen it, except that along the frescoed wall where Purcell had parked the Jeep, and where they had heard Father Armano's story, there were bones and skulls strewn over the marble floor.

Gann said, 'Firing squad.'

Vivian stared at the skulls and bones, put her hand over her mouth, and said, 'Oh my God ...'

Purcell moved closer to the execution wall. Some military gear and rotted *shammas* confirmed that this was a mass slaughter of Prince Joshua's soldiers. Jackals and ants had nearly cleaned the bones, but some desiccated brown tissue remained, and dried blood covered the marble floor.

The plaster fresco on the wall was shattered where fusillade after fusillade had cut down the condemned men. Purcell noticed that splashes of blood and perhaps brain stained the remnants of the fresco, as high as ten feet off the floor, adding a grisly touch to the pink bathing nymphs.

Mercado, too, was staring at the scene, and he said, 'This is evidence of a war crime.'

Purcell, trying not to sound too cynical or unfeeling, replied,

'Henry, this country is drowning in blood. What difference does this make?'

'This is inhuman.'

'Right.' They'd both seen battle deaths, but that was what passed for normal in war. Mass executions, on the other hand, had a special ugliness.

Purcell counted skulls, but stopped at about fifty.

Gann was poking around the lobby, gun in hand.

Vivian had walked away and was standing at the back of the lobby, which opened out onto the courtyard and gardens.

Mercado stared at the corner where they had laid the priest and covered him with a blanket – the now desecrated spot where he and Vivian felt a miracle of sorts had taken place.

Mercado said, as if to himself, 'The blood of the martyrs gives nourishment to the church.'

Purcell could not completely understand how people like Henry Mercado, and to some extent Vivian, persisted in their belief in a benevolent power. But he'd come to see that there was a special language used to explain the simultaneous existence of God and human depravity. You would need the right words, Purcell thought, evolved over thousands of years, to keep your faith from slipping.

Vivian had unexpectedly returned to the scene, and she had her camera out now. She took a deep breath and shot a few pictures of the grisly carnage. She moved closer to the corner where the priest had lain and died, to shoot photographic evidence of both sainthood and mass murder.

Mercado stood close to her, to give her moral support and silent encouragement. It occurred to Purcell that Vivian and

Henry might well be better suited to one another than Vivian and Frank could ever be. It bothered him to think that, but that may have been the truth. Henry and Vivian were, in a way, kindred spirits, eternally joined at their souls, whereas he and Vivian were connected only once a night. Well . . . but there was more there between them.

Gann had joined them and inquired, 'I don't suppose any of these bones are that of the priest?'

Vivian replied, 'No. We buried him.'

'That's right. Well, lead on.'

They exited the lobby through the rear and walked quickly across the paved courtyard, with Vivian and Mercado in the lead and Purcell and Gann on the flanks with their weapons at the ready.

Gann pointed out horse droppings, obvious evidence of Gallas, but he assured them that the droppings looked to be months old. Maybe weeks.

Purcell thought back to when they'd first walked through this spa complex without too much concern about Gallas, soldiers, partisans, or armed and desperate outlaws who roamed the countryside. God, indeed, watched over idiots.

Gann was being both security man and tourist, and remarked, 'Incredible engineering.' He added, 'Rather a waste, though.'

They found the garden where they'd buried Father Armano. Getachu's soldiers had exhumed the body, and jackals had scattered the bones in the garden and on the paths. The grave itself had caved in and a colony of red ants had taken residence.

Gann seemed pleased for Vivian at all the bones, and Purcell thought Gann was going to pick one up for her and say, 'Here we go. Nice one. Let's move on.' But in fact he stood patiently and reverently, staring at the grave. Vivian took photographs of the grave and of the scattered bones, while Mercado again stood beside her.

The time had come to pick a bone as a relic of the saint-to-be, and Mercado informed everyone, 'The skull is considered the most important mortal relic.'

But there was no skull in sight, so that set off a search through the overgrown gardens. Gann let everyone know, 'The jackals will often take a bit of their find to their lairs.'

Indeed, Purcell had noticed that there were not enough bones to make a complete skeleton. But there were some good-sized bones, including a femur and a pelvis, and he would have pointed this out to Henry and Vivian, but he wasn't sure of the protocol.

Vivian was about to settle for the femur, but then Henry exclaimed, 'Here it is!' and retrieved a skull from the underbrush. He held it up, sans jawbone.

Purcell was standing closest to Henry, so he could see that, thankfully, the skull had been picked clean by jackals and red ants, and that the rains and the sun had contributed to the job, though the white bone was stained with red earth.

Vivian hesitated to take a photograph of Henry holding the skull, which might be considered macabre back at the Vatican, so Henry set the skull on the stone bench, then thought better of that, and set it beside the grave. Vivian took six pictures from different angles and elevations. Gann glanced at his watch.

So now, Purcell knew, they needed to take the skull with them, for eventual delivery to Vatican City. Purcell also knew that if he ever made it back to Rome, he would not be with Henry or

Vivian when they presented their relic to the proper church authorities. And when they got to Berini, they'd bring photographs.

Vivian had taken a plastic laundry bag from the Hilton, which was in her backpack, and which she could use to hold Father Armano's skull in a safe and sanitary manner. She opened the bag, and Mercado took a last look at the skull, as though hoping it had something to tell him. He deposited the skull in the bag and they crammed it in her backpack.

Next, the priest's bones needed to be reinterred, and Purcell helped Mercado hand-dig the loose earth from the grave, evicting the red ants and other things from the pit. Gann contributed his machete, which they used to loosen the soil. They went down only about two feet because there were just bones to bury now, and not many of them.

They gathered up the bones and carefully placed them in the shallow grave, in no particular order. The three men refilled the grave and Vivian took photographs. Purcell supposed that as with photos taken on an exhausting holiday, say to the Mojave Desert, these scenes would be more appreciated when viewed at home.

The time had come for a prayer and Mercado volunteered. He said, 'Earth to earth, ashes to ashes, dust to dust; in sure and certain hope of the Resurrection unto eternal life.' He added, 'Rest in peace,' and made the sign of the cross, and everyone did the same.

Purcell sat on the stone bench, wiped his sweating face, and recalled that Father Armano's death had compelled him into thoughts of his own mortality. But for some reason, seeing and reburying the priest's bones had filled him with a far deeper sense of mortality. The difference between then and now, he understood, was what he'd seen in Getachu's camp, and what he'd just witnessed in the lobby of this haunting ruin. He had already seen firsthand in Southeast Asia that life was cheap, and death was plentiful. But here ... here he was looking for something beyond the grave. And he wanted to find it *before* the grave. *In sure and certain hope of the Resurrection unto eternal life.*

Vivian put her hand on his shoulder and asked, 'Would you like a bath?'

He stood and smiled. They found the sulphur pool, but Colonel Gann, in the interest of security, and perhaps modesty, forbade any skinny dipping and suggested, 'Mr Purcell and I will stand watch, and Mr Mercado and Miss Smith will bathe fully clothed. Five minutes, then we will switch.'

So they did that, and it felt good to be submerged in the warm water, which was cooler than the hot, humid air. Purcell made eye contact with Vivian, who was sitting on a stone bench next to Mercado, and she winked at him.

After Purcell got out of the pool, Gann gave him the revolver with a box of ammunition, which Purcell stuck in his cargo pocket, and Gann took the Uzi submachine gun, which was a far more deadly weapon.

They made their way to the back end of the spa where a wide, overgrown field stretched a hundred yards out and ended at a wall of jungle growth. They began crossing the field, and as they walked, Vivian said, 'This is where Father Armano walked when he came out of the jungle.'

She turned and looked back at the white spa. 'I wonder what he thought when he saw that? Or did he know it was there?'

Gann reminded everyone, 'It was not built when he was imprisoned.' He also told them, 'The road was also not yet improved, as we saw on the map in the Ethiopian College.'

Purcell assured him, 'It is not improved now.'

'Well, it has deteriorated over the years. But in '36 or '37, the Italian Army widened it, put in drainage ditches, and paved it with gravel and tar, all the way to Gondar. Then they built the mineral spa for their army and administrators in Gondar. That's what I saw when the British Expeditionary Force came through here in '41 on the way to taking Gondar from the Italians.'

Mercado said, 'So we know that Father Armano was not looking for this spa – or perhaps not even the road.'

Purcell said, 'For sure not the spa. But he may have remembered the Ethiopian dirt highway from his travels with his battalion, or from the patrol he was on.' He added, 'He may have been thinking of following the dirt track to Gondar.'

Gann again reminded them, 'Gondar was still in Ethiopian hands at the time of Father Armano's imprisonment, and his knowledge of the world was frozen at that moment, and remained so until his escape forty years later.'

Purcell said, 'Right. So where was he going?'

Mercado suggested, 'He had no idea where he was going. He was just running. And if he did know of that dirt road he may have intended to go north to Lake Tana where his battalion had made camp forty years ago. Or he could have taken the road south, toward Addis, where the main units of the Italian Army were pushing north to Tana and Gondar.' Mercado added, 'As

Colonel Gann said, his knowledge was frozen in time, and he was acting on what he knew, or thought he knew.'

Everyone seemed to agree with that theory, except Vivian, who said, 'He was coming to find us.'

Purcell knew better than to argue with that, but he couldn't help pointing out again, 'The spa was not here in 1936.'

Vivian assured him, 'That does not matter. We were here.'

They continued on and reached the towering tree line, then separated to look for a trailhead. Gann, who seemed to have a knack for finding openings in the jungle, found it.

They gathered at what seemed at first a solid wall of brush, but Gann parted the vegetation and showed them the narrow path that led into the dark interior of the rain forest. He said, 'Game trail. But suitable for human use.'

Purcell took out his map, and also the photograph that showed the destroyed fortress. He took a compass reading and assured himself and everyone that this trail led almost due east, toward the fortress, though there was no way of knowing if it turned at some point.

They made their way through the brush and onto the narrow overgrown trail, and began moving through the deep jungle.

Purcell had no doubt that this trail would lead them to the fortress that they'd seen from the air. And from there, there would be many jungle trails converging on the fortress. But Father Armano had picked this one, and Purcell now thought he knew why.

CHAPTER 48

The game trail had not been traveled by humans in a very long time — except perhaps Father Armano five months ago — and at some point they thought they'd lost the trail. Gann still refused to use his machete, so there were times when they had to get on all fours and crawl through the tunnel of tropical growth.

The five or six kilometers that showed on the map should have taken about two hours to travel, but they'd been walking and crawling close to three hours because of the slow progress.

They'd drunk most of their water and were now into the fruit juice. Sweat covered their bodies and the insects were becoming annoying. Gann had assured them that the lions in this region were nearly extinct, but something big roared in the deep jungle, which made everyone stop and listen. Snakes, however, were plentiful, and Purcell spotted a few in the trees, but none on the ground, so far.

They stopped for a break and Mercado wondered out loud if the trail had gone off in another direction and if they'd missed the fortress.

Purcell assured him, 'My compass says we've been heading generally due east.'

Gann concurred and added, 'It always seems longer on the ground than on the map.'

Purcell looked at Vivian, whose white skin was now alarmingly red, and asked her, 'How are you doing?'

She nodded her head.

He looked at Mercado, who also seemed flushed. The jungle, Purcell knew, sucked the life out of you. Theoretically, according to a Special Forces guy he'd interviewed in Vietnam, the jungle was not a killing environment, the way a frozen wasteland was. The jungle had water and food, and the climate, though unpleasant, would not kill you if you knew what you were doing. Snakes and animals could kill you, but you could also kill them. Only disease, according to this SF guy, could kill you, and if you got malaria or dengue fever, or some other fucked-up tropical disease, then you were just an unlucky son of a bitch. End of story.

Gann stood and said, 'Press on.'

The trail seemed to be getting wider, and there was more headroom now, so they were able to walk upright. Within fifteen minutes Gann held up his hand, then he pointed up the trail. He got down and crawled the last ten yards, then raised Mercado's binoculars and scanned to his front.

Gann got up on one knee and motioned everyone forward. The head of the trail was wide enough for everyone to kneel shoulder to shoulder and they looked out across a clearing to Prince Theodore's fortress – a blasted mass of stone and concrete sitting under the noon sun.

Gann was looking through his binoculars again and said, 'Don't see any movement.' He handed the binoculars to Mercado, who agreed, and he gave the binoculars to Vivian, who said, 'It looks so dead.' Purcell took the binoculars and focused on a section of collapsed wall that allowed a peek into the fortress. If anyone was in there, they weren't moving around much.

Gann wanted to go in first, with Purcell covering, but Purcell said, 'My turn.'

Vivian grabbed his arm, but didn't say anything.

Purcell stood and began walking the fifty yards across the clearing to the fortress walls.

There were wooden watchtowers at intervals along the parapets, and he kept an eye on them as he was sure Gann was doing with his binoculars. As he got closer, he could see more clearly through the opening in the wall, and there didn't seem to be anything living within the fortress.

He reached the pile of rubble from the collapsed wall, pulled his revolver, and climbed to the top. Inside the fortress he could see stone and concrete buildings with corrugated steel roofs in various states of ruin. The whole compound seemed to cover about two acres, which was not large for a fortress, but it looked imposing here in the jungle.

He satisfied himself that the place was deserted, and signaled everyone to join him.

Gann, Mercado, and Vivian began crossing the clearing quickly, and Purcell came down from the rubble pile.

He said to them, 'No one home. There's an open gate around the corner.'

He led them along the wall and they rounded the corner, where large iron gates stood open in the center of a long stone wall.

They passed cautiously through the gates and into the fortress. In front of them was an open area, a parade ground, where grass now grew. As they moved farther into the compound, they saw bleached white bones and skulls lying in the brown grass. The smell of the dead was barely noticeable after five months, but it still clung to the dusty earth.

Gann looked around and said, 'This is what a half-hour artillery barrage will do.' He looked at the collapsed section of wall where Purcell had stood atop the rubble, and said, 'Gallas probably came through that breach.' He added, 'Nasty combination of Getachu's modern artillery and primitive, bloodthirsty savages waiting like jackals to get in.'

Purcell could imagine the artillery rounds falling into this tight compound, blasting everything to rubble as the sun set. He could also imagine Prince Theodore's soldiers being blown to pieces by the explosion, or ripped apart by shrapnel. And when the barrage ended, there would be a minute or two of deadly silence before the Gallas came screaming over the walls.

Gann, too, was imagining it and said, 'The Gallas who got in first on foot would have opened those gates, and the mounted Gallas would have come charging in.' He added, 'A Galla war cry is something you don't want to hear more than once in your life – in fact, if you hear it once, you will not hear it again.'

Purcell saw Mercado looking over his shoulder at the open gates, as though expecting a horde of Gallas to come charging in. Also, Henry's face had gone from ruddy to pale. Henry was remembering Mount Aradam again.

Purcell shifted his attention to the field of bones. Indeed, it must have been terrifying, he thought, for the soldiers here who had survived the barrage to see Galla horsemen pouring through the open gates with their scimitars raised. Death on horseback.

Gann said, 'I don't see any horse bones, so it wasn't much of a fight.' He let them know, 'Even if your walls are breached and your gates are open, you must maintain discipline and put up a good resistance. Better than being slaughtered like lambs in a pen.'

Purcell didn't think that was information he could ever use, but he was glad to see that Colonel Gann was wearing his brass military balls.

Purcell said, 'The question is, how did Father Armano survive this slaughter?' He said quickly to Vivian, 'Do not say it.'

'Well, I will. God spared him.'

Purcell was getting a bit impatient with her divine explanations for everything, and he pointed out, 'God wasn't looking out for the Coptic Christian soldiers of Prince Theodore.' He suggested, 'Maybe God is Catholic.'

Vivian seemed annoyed and didn't respond.

Mercado said, 'It does seem a bit of a miracle that Father Armano escaped this.'

Purcell speculated, 'It might have something to do with his prison cell. Certainly the Gallas did not spare him.' He suggested, 'Let's look around.'

They walked through the small fortress which held only about twenty buildings, consisting mostly of barracks and storage structures. A large water-collecting cistern had been shattered by an explosion and it was dry. An ammunition bunker had been hit, and the secondary explosions had flattened everything around it. The headquarters was identified by the Lion of Judah painted in fading yellow over an open doorway. They looked inside and saw that whatever had been there had been burned, and a fine layer of ash lay on the floor and on the skeletons of at least a dozen men.

Gann drew everyone's attention to the pubic bones of the men, and pointed out the hack marks, saying, 'They use their scimitars to do their nasty business. Sometimes the poor buggers aren't even dead.'

Purcell said, 'Thanks for that.'

They continued on between the shattered structures and came to an almost undamaged building that measured about ten feet on each side. It was the only building whose door was intact and closed. The door was rusted steel and there was a hasp on it, but the lock was gone. At the bottom of the door was a steel pass-through with an open bolt.

Purcell said, 'Looks like a prison to me.'

Purcell stepped over several disjointed skeletons that lay near the door and pushed on it, but it would not give. Gann joined him and together they put their shoulders to the door, but it was stuck, probably rusted shut.

Vivian suggested using the pass-through at the bottom, and Purcell knelt and pushed on it until it squeaked open.

Vivian, too, knelt and said, 'I'll go.' No one objected, so she shucked her backpack but kept her camera, and squeezed her slim body into the opening. Her legs and feet disappeared and the door fell shut.

They all waited for her to call out, but there was only silence.

Finally, Purcell banged on the door. 'Vivian!'

'Yes . . . come in.'

Purcell went first, followed by Mercado and Gann.

They all stood in the middle of the dirt floor and looked around at the small, stone prison cell. The floor was covered with debris, and the roof was gone except for a single sheet of corrugated steel. There was a small opening high up one wall, and under the opening was a cross that had been etched into the stone.

Vivian said, 'Forty years ... my God.'

She reached up and touched the cross. 'What incredible faith.'

Purcell and Gann looked at each another. Mercado said, 'Indeed, this man was a saint and a martyr.'

Purcell wanted to point out that it was other Christians who'd put the priest here, but he'd exhausted his theological arguments.

Vivian took a dozen photographs of the cell, then suggested they all observe a silent minute of prayer.

They had been mostly silent anyway, and Purcell had no problem with this as long as they could do it standing, which they did.

Vivian said, 'Amen.'

Purcell said, 'This, I think, solves the mystery of how Father Armano escaped the Gallas.'

They looked around the sparse cell in case they missed something, like a note scratched in the wall or, Purcell hoped, a map or instructions directing them to the black monastery. He reminded everyone that Getachu's soldiers had been here five months ago, and said, 'This place has been picked clean.' Purcell suggested, 'We should get out of this cell.'

Gann agreed. 'This is not a good place to be if anyone comes round.'

Gann crawled out first with his Uzi, followed by Mercado, Vivian, and Purcell. Gann suggested, 'We can take a short lunch break, then move on to our next objective.'

They found a shady spot along a wall and sat on the ground. They broke out some bread and dates, but no one seemed to want the dried meat, perhaps because of the smell of death on the bones all around them.

Gann said, 'We need to find a stream. Shouldn't be too difficult, but sometimes it is. Don't drink from the ponds. But a wash is all right.'

Mercado said, 'I saw some berries on the trail. And fruit of some sort.'

'Yes, some are good. Some will kill you.'

Vivian asked, 'Do you know which is which?'

'Not actually.' He admitted, 'Never could get them right.'

Purcell suggested, 'Henry can be our taster.'

'After you, Frank.'

Gann asked Purcell for the area map. He studied it and said, 'I see you've got six numbered circles here.' He asked, 'Are they numbered in order of importance?'

Purcell replied, 'Sort of. But not really.'

'All right, then ... we'll do them geographically.' He studied the map again and said, 'Unfortunately, I don't see any marked trails, but all of these places are within fifty kilometers of this fort ... and there will be trails converging on this fort. We need to find the various trailheads, then decide which one to take.' He looked up from the map. 'But these six points are not necessarily connected by trails, or by open terrain. So if we have to cut brush and vines, this could take ... well, I'm afraid a month. Or more.'

'Unless,' Mercado pointed out, 'we get lucky on the first try.'

'Yes, of course. But you understand, old boy, none of these little circles here could be the place we are looking for.'

'In fact,' Purcell said, 'I don't think any of them are.'

No one responded to that, and Purcell continued, 'As you said,

Colonel, there would be a number of trails converging on this fortress, so the question is, why didn't Father Armano take one of the other trails? Why did he choose and continue along that bad game trail? Was his choice pure chance? I don't think so. How would he have ever found that small game trail? Unless he came to this fortress on that trail.'

Again, no one responded, then Vivian said, 'He was going back to the black monastery – back to the Grail.'

'Where else would he want to go?'

Gann said, 'By God, that's it.'

Mercado, too, agreed. 'It was staring us in the face.'

Purcell pointed out, 'All of our recon was based on a lot of speculation and false assumptions, all of it wrong. Everything we looked at from the air was east of the road. But in fact, if Father Armano was going back to the black monastery, then the monastery is west of the road, and west of the spa.'

They all thought about that, and Mercado stated the obvious. 'We have no photos . . . no idea what is west of the road.'

'No,' Purcell agreed, 'we do not. But we have a map that shows part of the area, and we have two points of reference – this fortress and the spa.'

Mercado said, 'Any two points will make a straight line . . . but that line does not necessarily give us the third point.'

'Right. But we need to go back to the spa, cross the road, and head west.'

Mercado thought about that, then said, 'So you're suggesting we abandon all we've done and head into a new, unknown area.'

'Only if we all believe that Father Armano was walking to the black monastery.'

They all thought that over and Gann said, 'You also need to believe he remembered the way he came here from the monastery.'

Purcell replied, 'I believe it was burned in his mind. And when he escaped from here and walked through those open gates, he knew exactly which way to go.'

Gann agreed. 'I've heard stories of that.'

Vivian spoke. 'I think we all believe that Father Armano was going to the black monastery, and that he knew the way.'

Everyone nodded in agreement.

They packed up and stood. Vivian asked Purcell, 'When did you think of this?'

'Halfway here.'

'Why didn't you say something?'

'You needed a photo op.' He added, 'We needed to be here.'

She nodded.

They left the ruins of Prince Theodore's fortress by the gates that Father Armano had entered forty years before and had exited five months ago. They walked across the clearing toward the game trail, which they now saw was marked by a towering and distinctive cedar.

As they walked, Vivian came up beside Purcell and said with a smile, 'That was a divine inspiration, Frank. Don't deny it.'

He smiled in return. 'I like to think of myself as a rational genius.' He added, 'But I could be wrong about that and about this, too.'

'You're not wrong.' She also said to him, 'Prepare yourself for a miracle.'

They'd already had several of those, mostly having to do with flying. He said, 'I am open to miracles.'

'And while you're at it, open your heart to love.'

He didn't respond.

'We could die here in the blink of an eye. So you need to tell me now that you forgive me, and that you love me. Before it's too late.'

He stayed silent a few seconds, considering this, then said, 'I love you.'

'Forgive me.'

'I cheated on you before you came to Rome.'

'I forgive you.'

He took her hand. 'All is forgiven.'

CHAPTER 49

They reached the spa in the late afternoon, and though there were hours of daylight left, Gann made the decision to stop for the day, saying, 'I don't want any of us to overdo the first day.'

Clearly, Purcell thought, Gann was concerned about Henry, and maybe Vivian. He was a good officer. Purcell also pointed out, 'We have no idea where we're going after we cross that road, so we should stop and think about it.'

'Quite right.'

Vivian reminded Gann, 'You said Gallas stop here.'

'Yes, well, they've mostly gone east, and their horse droppings look rather old. Also, this is a large place, and we will pick a dark corner of it and be quiet during the night.' He added, 'I have my Uzi, and Mr Purcell has my service revolver.'

They found the bathhouse, which still had fresh spring water flowing into large sunken pools from the mouths of black stone faces embedded in the marble walls – similar to Miriam's bathhouse, Purcell noted, except these faces were not of lions, but Roman gods and goddesses, one of which looked suspiciously like Benito Mussolini.

Gann again marveled at the engineering, saying, 'Reminds me

a bit of the Roman baths in Bath. Water's still flowing there after two thousand years.'

And that, Purcell thought to himself, was the last decent plumbing installed in England.

They drank from the mouths of the gods and goddesses, hoping the water was potable, then filled their canteens. The spring water was cold, but they bathed privately, and washed their clothes.

Not a bad first day, Purcell thought, and in the morning they'd cross the road and strike out into terra incognita.

They reconnoitered the spa complex and found a wing off the main lobby where the guest rooms had been. Gann explained, 'This is where the Italian soldiers, administrators, and men of business came from Gondar for the weekend after a long week of exploiting the Ethiopians.' He added, 'Built mostly by slave labor — captured Ethiopian soldiers. And staffed by young Ethiopian women.'

Purcell commented, 'Sounds very Roman Empire-ish.'

'Indeed. It's in their blood, you know.'

Purcell resisted any comments about the British Empire, but Gann said, 'At least we brought order, education, and law.'

'Thank God you didn't bring your plumbing.'

Gann smiled.

They found a guest chamber that looked fairly clean, and went inside the whitewashed room. All the furniture had been carried off, of course, but a chair sat in the corner in an advanced state of rot.

The spa once had electricity, undoubtedly from a generator, and Purcell noticed electrical outlets, and a ceiling fan that hadn't turned in forty years.

The room also had a large arched window that faced east and would let in the dawn sun. The window had never been glazed, but sagging louver shutters were still fixed to the stone arch. The view from the window was of a garden that had become a miniature jungle, which Gann pointed out as a place to go if anyone came through the door. Conversely, if anyone showed up at the window, they could exit through the door and retreat into the large hotel complex.

They sat on the red tile floor and Purcell broke out the maps. He told Gann, 'We've flown over this area west of the road, on our way to and from Gondar, but as you know, we were not doing an aerial recon of this area. From what I remember, however, this is thick jungle, not much different from the area east of the road.' He added, 'This map seems to confirm that.'

Gann glanced at the map. 'Yes, this whole area south of Tana is carpeted with dense growth.'

Mercado asked him, 'Do you remember any of that terrain from when you were here in '41?'

'I'm afraid not. We pushed up from the road and avoided the jungle.' He explained, 'The Italian Army, too, avoided the jungle and kept mostly to the roads and the towns. When we took Gondar from them, they retreated into the hills and mountains to the north, not to the jungle.' He asked Mercado, 'Did you experience the pleasure of jungle warfare when you were here?'

Mercado replied, 'I was an army war correspondent.' He confessed, 'I fought mostly in the bars and brothels.'

Vivian laughed, Gann smiled, and Purcell was afraid that Henry and Edmund were on the verge of swapping Gondar 1941 war stories, trying to discover if they knew the same bartenders and prostitutes, so he changed the subject and said, 'What I do recall from our flyovers was that there was some high terrain to the west of here — what looked like rocky ridgelines coming through the treetops.'

Gann nodded. 'Two of the three obsidian quarries I've identified from speaking to the people in Shoan are west of here.' He informed them, 'The villagers still visit the quarries for small pieces of obsidian to use for carvings or house ornamentation.'

Vivian asked, 'Could you find the quarries?'

'I have a general idea where they are.'

Mercado asked, 'And you think the black monastery could be in proximity to these quarries?'

Gann replied, 'Perhaps.' He pointed out, 'We don't have much else to go on.'

Purcell looked at Gann and asked, 'Is it possible that Miriam said something to you, which if you thought about it ...?'

Gann considered the unfinished question, then replied, 'The villagers who went out to meet the monks would always return with sacks of carved obsidian, which they would take to Gondar for sale.' He explained, 'Crosses, saints, chalices ... occasionally a Star of David, and now and then a carving of Saint George Cathedral in Addis.'

Purcell informed him, 'Vivian almost bought one of those in Rome.'

Gann smiled and said to her, 'You should have bought the one with the map etched on the bottom.'

'I wish I'd known.'

Mercado said, 'So what you're saying is that you think the

monks carved these objects and gave them to the villagers in exchange for provisions.'

'It would seem so.' He asked rhetorically, 'What else do monks have to do all day?'

Pray and drink, Purcell thought. He said to everyone, 'Well, it seems that this quest has taken on some of the aspects of Arthur's knights running around without a map or a clue looking for the Grail Castle.'

Gann replied, 'They actually found it, you know.'

Purcell pointed out, 'There are no jungles in England.'

Vivian glanced at Purcell and said, 'If we are meant to find it, we will find it. If we are not, we will not.'

'Right.' Purcell asked, 'If the monks' sandals and candles have been cut off from Shoan, how long do you think these monks are going to last in the black monastery?'

'Good question,' Gann replied. 'I believe the monks are fairly self-sufficient in regards to food, though the villagers of Shoan would always bring something that the monks didn't have. Wine, of course, but also grain for bread.' He surmised, 'I don't think there would be a lot of grain grown in the monastery or surrounding rain forest. So they will soon be needing their daily bread.'

Purcell suggested, 'I'd think a single loaf would do, and one fish.'

Gann smiled.

Mercado asked Gann, 'Where do you think these monks come from? I assume they don't reproduce there.'

Gann replied, 'No, they don't. All gentlemen, as far as I know.' He told them, 'It's my understanding that the monks are chosen from monasteries all over Ethiopia. They understand that if they go to the black monastery, they will never leave there.' He reminded them, 'Like the Atang who guards the Ark of the Covenant in Axum.' He concluded, 'It's a job for life.'

Purcell said, 'I have two observations about Ethiopia. One is that this place has been caught in a time warp, and the other is that with the emperor gone, they are free-falling into the twentieth century, and not ready for the landing.'

'Perhaps.'

He asked Gann, 'What has drawn you to this place? I mean, aside from your princess.'

Gann smiled, then replied, 'It gets into your blood.'

Purcell looked at Mercado, who said, 'It is the most blessed and most cursed land I have ever been in.' He added, 'It has biblical magnificence, complete with an apocalyptic sense of doom.' He concluded, 'I hate the place. But I would come back.'

'Send me a postcard.' Purcell returned to the earlier subject and said, 'I think time is running out for the monks of the black monastery. They, unfortunately, can't multiply the loaves and fishes, and history in the form of General Getachu is breathing down their burnooses. I would not be surprised if they are already gone, but if they're not, they will be soon.'

Everyone agreed with that, and Mercado said, 'I would be content with just finding the black monastery.'

Vivian said, 'I would not.'

They looked at the map in the fading light as they ate some bread and dates, and Gann asked, 'Do you know how long the priest was marched from the black monastery to his fortress prison by the soldiers of Prince Theodore?'

Mercado replied, 'As I mentioned, the priest did not comment on it, so I'm assuming it was a day or two's march.'

'All right. We now know that the travel time from here to the fortress is at most four hours. Therefore, let's say the monastery is no more than a day's march west of here. In open country, or on a good trail, either of which would be known by the soldiers, that would be ... let's say a ten-hour march at a brisk pace of four K an hour, will give us forty K to the monastery.'

Vivian reminded them, 'The monks brought Father Armano to the soldiers. The soldiers were not at the monastery.'

'Quite right. And we don't know where the soldiers were in relation to the monastery. But let's use fifty K total.' He drew a half circle on the map, with the center of the radius starting at the spa and ending at the road. 'There we are.' He asked, 'What is that formula to find the area of a circle?'

There was an embarrassed silence, then Mercado said, 'If that were a rectangle and not a half circle, it would be five thousand square kilometers ... so if we nip off the curved part of the semi-circle, it would be about ... let's say, four thousand square kilometers ... give or take.'

'All right.' Gann stared at the map. 'That's a good amount of territory to be walking.'

Purcell suggested, 'It's not really the square kilometers that are important. It's the trails and the few clues we have, including maybe the quarries, that will determine where we look.'

'Quite right,' Gann agreed. 'And we can't be sure that the priest was marched for only one day. It could have been two.'

Purcell asked Gann, 'How long were the villagers actually gone when they left Shoan to go to the meeting place?'

Gann stayed silent, then said, 'I have heard it was two days. A day there, and a day to return.' He added, 'No part of the walk would be made in the dark, so let's say it was a ten-hour walk, an overnight rest, and ten hours back to Shoan.'

Purcell produced the adjoining map that showed Shoan, and they tried to extrapolate from these two known locations – the village and the spa – walking times and distances west of the road, to see what intersected or overlapped.

Purcell was concerned that they were once again making false assumptions, misinterpreting clues, and being too clever, but this time, based on his conclusion that Father Armano was heading for the black monastery when they found him at the spa, he felt a bit more confident that they were narrowing it down.

Gann asked an interesting question. 'Did the priest comment in any way about the spa? Did he say anything such as, "What is this?"'

Everyone thought about that, and Mercado said, 'Now that you mention it, he did not, which in retrospect seems a bit odd.'

Vivian said, 'He did say something ... that Henry may have been asleep for.' She thought a moment, then said, 'He asked, "Dov'è la strada?" Where is the road?'

No one responded, and Vivian continued, 'I didn't think anything of it. He seemed to be delirious.'

Purcell said, 'Well, if nothing else, that confirms he was looking for the road he remembered. The question is, which way was he going to take it? North? South? Or was he just going to cross it and continue west to the monastery?'

Gann said, 'We don't know, but we do know that he had come from the monastery to the fortress on a trail that ended at or crossed the road, and that is what we'd like to find tomorrow.' He added, 'I would put my bet on this trail being either close to here, or farther south, toward Shoan. And I base that on the traveling time of the villagers.'

Again, everyone seemed to agree and they all looked at the maps, and Gann penciled in a few more marks.

Purcell suggested they'd done enough mental exercise, and that they should sleep on it. He lit a cigarette and passed around his canteen of fermented fruit juice.

They made small talk about other things and Purcell told Gann about the Navion and Signore Bocaccio, whose Mia was now a heap of burned and twisted metal. Purcell said, 'I hope he and his wife had a good meal at the Hilton.'

Vivian said, 'I feel awful that we couldn't telex him.'

'I think he got the message that we were not returning.' He asked Gann, 'Would two thousand dollars compensate him for the aircraft?'

Gann assured everyone, 'People are selling what they can for whatever they can get, and they are fortunate to get any buyers.' He added, 'Something such as an aircraft has no buyers, and the government would have expropriated it anyway.'

Purcell said, 'That's what I thought.' He assured Vivian, 'Signore Bocaccio is happy.'

Gann asked Purcell, 'How did you learn to fly?'

'Private lessons. I started in high school, in upstate New York. There was an aerodrome there. Lessons were fourteen bucks an hour, and I made fifteen a week working for the weekly newspaper.' He added, 'Had a buck left over for cheap dates and cheap wine.'

Gann smiled. 'How many hours did you have to invest in this?'

'The flying or the dates?'

'The flying, old boy.'

'Well, twenty dual would allow you to solo. Then twenty solo would allow you to take the test for a license.'

'I see. And why didn't you get into something along those lines?'

'Well . . .' Purcell looked at Vivian and Mercado. 'Well, I never actually took the test.'

Mercado asked, 'Do you mean you don't have a license?'

'Didn't need one here. No one asked.'

'Yes, but . . .'

'I ran out of money.' He said, 'I'll bet you couldn't tell.'

Vivian laughed and said to everyone, 'Can't you tell he's joking with us?' She looked at him. 'Frank?'

'Right. Just kidding.'

Mercado pointed out, 'It's moot in any case. We've burned the plane, and we will not be renting another.'

'But I'll take you flying in New York.'

'No, thank you.'

Purcell stood and said to Vivian, 'Take a walk with me.'

Gann cautioned, 'Do not go far, and be back no later than dark. And don't forget your revolver.'

'Yes, sir.'

Vivian stood and Mercado looked at her. 'I don't think this is a wise thing.'

'Don't fret, Henry.'

Purcell led Vivian into the hallway and back to the lobby, then out to the courtyard. They walked along the colonnade then down the steps to the gardens.

The sky was deep purple now, with streaks of red and pink, and night birds began to sing. A soft breeze blew down from the mountains and they could smell the tropical flowers.

Purcell said, 'I thought we would make love here.'

'I know exactly what you are thinking.'

'Sometimes I think about a cocktail.'

'You're rather basic, you know.'

'Thank you.'

They continued their walk and Vivian asked him, 'Who was it?'

'Who was who . . . ? Oh . . . in Rome.'

'Yes, in Rome.'

'Well . . . I'm not sure who it was. An English lady.'

'How did you meet her?'

'In her hotel bar.'

'Did you go to her hotel, or yours?'

They were actually the same place, but he could imagine that Vivian would not like to think they'd all used the same bed. He replied, 'Hers.' He also said, 'I thought you had left for good.'

'You should have known better. But I understand, and I forgive you.'

'Thank you.'

'And when we get back to Rome, if I go off shopping, I hope you don't think I've left you for good, and go off and fuck another lady you've met in the elevator or somewhere.'

'Right. That won't happen.' He glanced up at the sky. 'It's getting dark.'

She took his arm and led him around the statue of the two-faced Janus. She said, 'For security reasons, we must keep our clothes on, but I suggest you drop your pants.'

He liked that suggestion and pulled his pants and underwear down as she knelt in front of him. Vivian said, 'We will learn a new Italian word today. Fellatio.' She put his now erect penis in her mouth and showed him the meaning of the word.

On the way back to the spa hotel, she said, 'There is a romance in classical ruins – something hauntingly beautiful about a great edifice returning to nature.'

'Right.' He said to her, 'We need to find some privacy tomorrow night.'

'I don't think that will happen again out in the bush.'

'Well … let's see.'

'I'm embarrassed as it is that Henry and Colonel Gann know what we've been up to.'

'I don't think they do.'

'I don't think they could have missed hearing your moaning echoing through the colonnade.'

'Really?'

They got back to the lobby, which was very dark now. At the far end of the big room lay the bones of the slaughtered men, where Father Armano had also lain dying.

Vivian said to him, 'Tomorrow we go to where Father Armano was going. Do not be cynical – he will show us the way.'

'I'm counting on it.'

'Do you know what that statue was?'

'The two-faced guy?'

'That was Janus, the Roman god of the New Year – he faces back and forward.'

'I get it.'

'This is January.'

'Right.'

'Which reminded me of something. When I was in boarding school, which was English-run, I read a very beautiful passage — something that George VI said in his Christmas message to the English people, in the darkest year of the war. He said to them, "I said to the man who stood at the gate of the year, Give me a light that I may tread safely into the unknown. And he replied, Go out into the darkness and put your hand into the hand of God. That shall be to you better than light and safer than a known way."'

'That is very beautiful.'

'Put your hand into the hand of God, Frank.'

'I'll try.'

'You will.'

They rejoined the others.

CHAPTER 50

They rose before dawn and had some bread and boiled eggs as they waited for better light.

The night had been long and uncomfortable, and the jungle sounds had kept them awake. Purcell began to wonder if anything short of the Holy Grail was worth getting eaten by mosquitoes and listening for Gallas.

Vivian seemed cheerful, and that annoyed him.

Gann, too, seemed ready to get moving, but Henry didn't look well, and Purcell was a bit concerned about him. But if Henry complained, Purcell would remind him whose idea this was. Or was this his own idea?

The dawn came and they left the relative comfort of the spa hotel and walked down the steps. They moved quickly across the field and through the brush, then looked up and down the road. Gann said in a whisper, 'I will cross first, then one at a time.'

Gann crossed the narrow road and knelt in the brush on the far side. Mercado followed, and then Vivian and Purcell brought up the rear.

They beat the bush on the side of the road, looking for an obvious trail – a trail that Father Armano might have taken to his imprisonment forty years ago, and which he may have been looking for again before he died in the spa. *Dov'è la strada?* But even Gann couldn't find an opening in the wall of tangled vegetation that lined the road.

Gann said, 'We will walk on the road, though I'd rather not.' He instructed them, 'The drainage ditch here is partially filled with dirt, as you see, and choked with brush. But we will dive into it if we hear a vehicle, or the sound of hoofbeats.'

Especially hoofbeats, Purcell thought.

'We will continue until we've found a trail that will take us into the interior of this rain forest.' He said, 'I suggest we try south, toward Shoan.'

They began their walk south on the old Italian road that Purcell, Mercado, and Vivian had driven from Addis what seemed so long ago. The road, as Purcell recalled, was hard-packed, and he could now see evidence of the tar and gravel that the Italian Army had laid forty years before. But when Father Armano had walked the road – if he had walked it – the Italian engineers had not yet gotten this far. More important, any trails intersecting this road may have been more obvious forty years ago, before this area had become less traveled and less populated.

Gann stepped off the road now and then and smacked the brush with the side of his machete. After half an hour, Purcell said, 'We're going to wind up in Shoan soon.'

'That will be another two hours, Mr Purcell.'

Up ahead was a huge gnarled tree, and Purcell picked up his pace. He got to the tree and said to his companions, 'I am going to do some aerial recon.' He took the binoculars from Mercado, dropped his backpack, and shimmied up the wide trunk, then got hold of a branch and pulled himself up.

Gann said, 'Watch for snakes, old boy.'

Purcell continued to climb the twisted branches and got about forty feet off the ground.

He sat on a bare branch and scanned the area around him with the binoculars. The trees near the road were not tightly spaced, though there was very dense brush between them. As he looked west, he could see the beginning of a great triple-canopy rain forest.

He turned his attention to the road and looked north, toward Tana and Gondar, but he saw no one approaching. The road was probably better traveled before the revolution and civil war, he thought, but now only armed men roamed the countryside, and he didn't want to meet any of them — unless they were friends of Colonel Gann.

Purcell scanned the road to the south, and it was also deserted, though he saw some sort of catlike animals crossing a hundred yards up the road. He watched them go into the bush, then he focused closely on the area where they'd disappeared.

Gann called up softly, 'See anything?'

'Maybe.' He made sure he knew where the cats had disappeared, then climbed down and jumped onto the road.

Gann asked, 'How was your view?'

'Lots of trees out there.'

'What type of trees, old boy?'

Purcell described the terrain and suggested to Gann, 'You can climb the next tree.' He told everyone, 'The good news is I saw some sort of ... medium-sized cats going into the bush. So maybe there's a game trail. '

'Excellent.' Gann guessed, 'Some sort of lynx, I would think.'

Mercado asked, 'Are they dangerous?'

Gann replied, 'Only if they have something better than my nine-millimeter Uzi.'

Purcell led them up the road, and over the drainage ditch, to the ten-foot-high wall of tropical vegetation. He said, 'Right about here.'

Gann got on all fours, like a cat, and said, 'Here is the trailhead.' They all crawled through the tangled brush onto a shoulder-wide trail, overhung with branches that formed a natural ceiling above their heads.

The trail itself was clear, and it was obvious that this was a well-used route.

Purcell said, 'This could be the trail used by the villagers.'

Gann agreed. 'Someone is using it on a regular basis.'

Vivian asked, 'Does anyone but me think that those cats were sent by God to show us this trail?'

Purcell assured her, 'Only you, Vivian.'

'Well.' She smiled. 'I don't think that either.'

But Purcell thought she did. And maybe this time she was right.

Gann said, 'We will travel about twenty feet apart, but always within sight of one another. Maintain sound discipline, no smoking, and alert everyone if you hear something.'

Mercado asked, 'Where are we going?'

Gann replied, 'I don't know, but we'll make good time getting there.' He took Purcell's map and looked at it. 'Don't see this trail.' He said, 'We'll see what we see, and we will fly by the seat of our pants.' He added, 'We're in the right area, and if we read the land correctly, I feel confident we can find at least one of the abandoned stone quarries, which may be a clue to the location of the black monastery.'

Purcell was impressed with Colonel Gann's outdoor skills, and he asked him, 'Can we live off the land? I mean if the food runs out.'

'I don't much fancy jungle pickings, old boy.'

'Me neither.'

'Let's make certain we can get back to Shoan before the victuals run out.' Gann informed them, 'If everyone's gone, there will be a food cache there for us.'

Purcell said, 'If *you're* gone, where would we find that cache?'

'You should look in the stone cisterns which are high up. This is the dry season, and they will be suitable for food storage.'

'Which cistern?'

'Don't know, old boy. Each house has one. You'll find the right one.'

'Couldn't they have left the food in the palace kitchen?'

'We don't know who will be coming around after the last person has left.' He explained, 'Goats, chickens, and such will be left behind, and that draws hungry people.'

'Well, let's hope the Gallas don't come around.'

'More likely soldiers or partisans.' He added, 'We need to be careful when we enter the village.'

Mercado asked, 'How will we actually get out of here after we've completed our mission?'

'There is a Royalist partisan point about fifty K west of Shoan, and I can find it without a map. Been there. Chaps there will guide us to the French Somali border, as I mentioned.'

Purcell asked, 'And if you're not with us to find that place?'

'Dead, you mean?'

'Or just not feeling well.'

Gann smiled, then said seriously, 'I'd advise you to walk to Gondar. You should be able to blend into the population, though it's a bit tricky with all the Western tourists and businesspeople gone, and the soldiers everywhere. But it's not impossible to do that.'

Purcell suggested, 'We could pose as journalists.'

'There you are.'

'What do we do after we blend?'

'You should try to get to Addis by plane, or get someone with a truck to drive you over the Sudan border.' He handed the map back to Purcell and asked, 'Have we covered everything?'

'We have.'

'Miss Smith? Any questions or concerns?'

'No. Let's go.'

Gann, in military style, restated their mission objective. 'We are looking for two things. One is the place where the Falashas meet the monks. We will look for signs of human presence – food waste, campfires, footprints, and all that. Our primary objective, not completely dependent on the first objective, is to find the black monastery.' He reminded them, 'From Shoan, which is a few hours' march south of here, give or take, to the meeting place is, as we know, a day's march. From the meeting place to the monastery is, we believe, or assume, another day's march.' He concluded, 'If we find the meeting place, then we know we are a day's march to the monastery – though we don't know in which direction.' He added, 'It's possible, of course, that we don't find the meeting place, but do find the monastery.'

Gann looked at Purcell, Mercado, and Vivian and asked, 'Is that clear?'

Purcell thought it had already been clear why they were in Ethiopia. But to be a good soldier, he said, 'Clear.'

Mercado nodded.

Vivian said, 'A rock, a tree, and a stream. And maybe a cluster of palms.'

Gann looked at her. 'Yes, all right.' He glanced at his watch, then said, 'We will let Mr Purcell take point and I will bring up the rear.' He smiled. 'Follow those cats.'

Purcell began walking up the trail. Somewhere between here and where they wanted to go lay a vast expanse of unknown. And the end of the trail was also unknown. From the unknown, through the unknown, to the unknown. *Put your hand into the hand of God.* It will be all right.

CHAPTER 51

What started as a hopeful beginning was becoming a long day in the jungle.

The trail remained wide, but it was soon obvious that it was not the only trail; many smaller trails intersected the main one, though none had any signs of recent footprints or hoofprints, or signs of cut vegetation.

Gann stated the obvious. 'There seems to be a network of trails in this area.'

Purcell had checked his compass as they moved, and they were headed generally west, but also veering south.

Mercado inquired, 'What are we actually doing?'

Gann explained, 'We are trail walking, following the paths of least resistance to cover as much ground as possible.'

Purcell recalled an army ranger once saying to him on patrol, 'We don't know where we are or where we're going, but we're making really good time.'

Gann and Purcell looked at the map to try to determine where they were, but the Italian Army maps showed no trails under the dense overhanging canopy. And with no landmarks visible on the ground, it was nearly impossible to determine their position on the map. All they had to go by was the compass and their traveling time.

Gann put his finger on the map and said, 'I believe we are here.'

Purcell asked, 'Where is here?'

'Where we are standing. Give or take a kilometer.'

'I'm not even sure we're on the right map.'

'I believe we are.' He said, 'All we can do is continue to run the trails.'

'Right. But I can see now that we could pass within fifty meters of the monastery and walk right by it.' Purcell added, 'We can assume the monastery is not directly on a trail.'

'That is a good assumption.'

Mercado said, 'I think we should have stuck to the original plan and checked out what we saw in the photographs east of the road.'

Vivian said, 'No, I am convinced that Frank was right – Father Armano was headed this way to return to the black monastery.'

Mercado did not reply.

Purcell reminded Gann, 'You said you thought you could find one of these stone quarries.'

'Yes, I did say that. Unfortunately, now that I'm here, I see the difficulties.' He added, 'No soldier or explorer has ever had a good experience in the jungle.'

'And we're not going to be the first.'

'We need to just push on, trust our instincts, look for a clue or two, and pray that fortune is with us.'

Vivian reminded them, 'Also, we are meant to find the monastery.'

Gann said, 'The good thing is that we are not restricted by

time, as we would be with a military objective.' He added, 'We have all the time we need.'

Purcell reminded him, 'The monks may be packing their suitcases right now.'

'Yes, but the monastery is not going anywhere.'

'Right. But we are restricted by our supplies and stamina.'

'That is always a problem,' Gann conceded.

Vivian said, 'Let's move on.'

Mercado cautioned, 'We need to be sure we can find and reach Shoan before our provisions run out. I say three more days of this, then we need to start back.'

Gann agreed. 'But by a different route so we can explore new territory.'

They moved on and came to a fork in the trail. They explored down both paths, and for no particular reason decided on the left fork.

They continued on, and saw that the trail was getting narrower.

Vivian had taken a few photos, but there was not much to photograph on the tight trails, and she seemed to lose interest in recording their quest to find the Holy Grail. If you've seen one jungle trail, Purcell knew, you've seen them all.

After an hour, Purcell spotted a tall cedar off the trail and made his way through the brush to get to it. He climbed the trunk to the first branch, then climbed branch by branch until he was about thirty feet off the ground. He scanned the terrain with his binoculars and saw that they were a few kilometers away from the higher ground to the west and the triple-canopy jungle he'd seen from the other tree on the road, and seen when he flew to Gondar. The sun would be below the tree line in about an hour.

He climbed down from the tree and made his way back to the trail. He informed them, 'Farther west is triple-canopy jungle, and I suggest we head there.'

Gann nodded. 'That is also where I'm told an old quarry exists.'

Mercado pointed out, 'We've been traveling the better part of the day, and the villagers apparently traveled one day to the meeting spot, and we are at the end of that time period.'

Gann informed him, 'Traveling time is not distance, nor vice versa. If you know where you are going, you probably know how to get there by the quickest and most direct route.'

Purcell assured everyone, 'We can't be lost if we don't know where we're going.'

They continued on the trail, which now turned to the south, and they saw no intersecting trails to the west. Gann did not want to do any backtracking, which he said was a waste of time and energy, and also a sign of desperation that would lead to bad morale.

Vivian said, 'Avanti.'

The sun was below the highest trees and the jungle light took on that strange quality of shadowy darkness before dusk.

They knew they needed to stop for the night, but there was no suitable clearing, so they set up camp on the narrow trail.

Gann posted a guard – Mercado, Vivian, Purcell, and himself – for two hours each, until first light, when they would move on.

They had not found water, and their canteens were nearly empty. Gann said, 'Our first goal tomorrow is water. Without water we will have to sample some of these fruits we see, and edible and poisonous often look similar.' He smiled. 'It's the jungle trying to kill you.'

They spent a restless night sleeping on the bare ground of the path, head to toe, listening to the night sounds of the jungle.

The second day was more or less a repeat of the first, but they found a small, vine-choked stream and filled their canteens.

Purcell noticed that the trails seemed to meander, and most of them headed north, south, or east. Every time they picked up a trail to the west, it turned in another direction, as though the god of the jungle did not want them heading west into the higher ground and the great triple-canopy jungle.

Purcell thought that Mercado was starting to drag, and he suggested to Gann that they slow their pace, which Gann did, but then an hour later Gann picked up his pace. Gann, Purcell thought, was driven, but maybe not the way Vivian and Mercado were driven to find the monastery and the Grail; Gann was driven by Rudyard Kipling — something hidden. Go and find it. If they'd told Gann they were looking for a basketball court in the jungle, he'd have been as enthused as he was to find the Holy Grail. Well ... maybe not that enthused. But this had become a challenge for Colonel Sir Edmund Gann. Also, of course, he wanted to save the Grail from the godless Marxists. Then he could meet his princess in Jerusalem, and have a whiskey at the King David Hotel. Next stop, his club in London, where his friends would have to coax the story out of him. Bottom line, Purcell was glad they had Gann with them, but he was starting to wonder if Gann was with them or if they were with Gann.

As for himself, Purcell sometimes felt he was just along for the ride, though he knew there was more to his motives. Vivian was one reason he was here in this godawful place, and Vivian might also be his second and third reason. He wasn't normally that good a boyfriend. So there were other and more complex reasons for this journey into the literal heart of darkness.

The tropical dusk spread over the rain forest, and they again set up camp on the trail they were on.

Purcell was one of the few war correspondents in Vietnam who had been allowed to travel with a team of the Long Range Reconnaissance Patrol – the Lurps, as they were called. The sergeant of the ten-man team had told him, 'Short patrol. Ten days.'

Ten days, deep inside enemy territory in a very hostile environment. He was younger then, and the Lurps had every advanced piece of field equipment known to man, plus enough dried rations to last twice as long as the patrol. They also carried the best weapons the army could offer, and they had three radios if the feces hit the fan, as they said.

Here, however, in the jungles of Ethiopia, they were very much on their own, and none of them knew the jungle, except maybe for Gann, and Purcell was beginning to have doubts about that. Also, the goal here was not recon; it was to find the Holy Grail of Holy Grails – *The* Holy Grail – and that was the only reason they were not heading for the French Somaliland border, which in any case was the other way.

Days three and four were more trail walking, except now they had made their way west, and the jungle had become triple canopy, and it was hotter, more humid, and darker. The only good difference was that the underbrush had thinned out and they could wander off the claustrophobic trail if they wanted to and walk between the towering trees.

Purcell told Gann, 'As I said, the monastery would not be at the end of a trail. It could be that we need to walk off the trail and through the rain forest to find it.'

Gann replied, 'If that's true, then what we are dealing with is a trackless expanse, in which any direction is possible, but only one direction will lead us to where we wish to go.'

'Right. But maybe that's the best way to cover some of these four thousand square kilometers.'

Gann suggested a break and they sat and looked at the map, which showed the same sea of green ink as it had last time they looked at it.

Gann was trying to determine what ground they had already covered, and he drew pencil lines on the map, saying, 'We've gone in circles a bit, I think.'

'In fact, that snake back there looked familiar.'

'Hard to tell with snakes, old boy.'

Vivian reminded everyone, 'A rock, a tree, a stream. And perhaps a cluster of palm trees.'

No one had been talking about those possible clues since Vivian mentioned them four days ago, but everyone had been at least alert to what seemed so important back in Addis.

Here in the bush, however, the reality changed, or reality became altered. The mind played tricks, as it does in the desert or at sea. The eye sees, and the ear hears, but the mind interprets. They had been so thirsty the day before that they all kept spotting things that were not there, especially water.

Also, they had not seen any signs of human presence since the first day when they'd found the wide trail. This was a good and bad thing. Humans were the most dangerous animals in the jungle, but the Grail seekers needed to go where other humans – Falashas and monks – had gone to meet. They had not even found evidence of a campfire or a dropped or discarded item made by man.

Henry pointed out, 'Father Armano did not walk for four or five days from the monastery to the fortress.'

Gann said, 'This priest was with soldiers who obviously knew the terrain, and they quick-marched this chap directly to the fortress and into his little cell.' He added, 'But I am certain we are still within the area that we agreed at the spa would be the most likely territory for this monastery.' He further added, 'That comports, too, with the travel time of the villagers to the meeting place.'

Purcell commented, 'I didn't realize how big four thousand square kilometers was.'

Mercado also pointed out, 'For all we know, the monks picked a meeting place that was very far from their monastery. Maybe three or four days away.'

Gann replied, 'Well, I hope not.'

Purcell said, 'Let's stick with the logical theory that the monks do not want to walk more than a day to meet the Falashas.' He added, 'The monks are carrying *stone* knickknacks, for God's sake.'

'Quite right,' Gann agreed.

Vivian was not much into theory or speculation, Purcell noticed, and she didn't contribute to the men's attempts to over-think and outthink themselves.

Gann noticed this and said to her, 'Should we be waiting for divine inspiration?'

Vivian replied, 'You can't wait for it. It comes when it comes.' She added, 'You can pray for it, though.'

'I've done that.'

'Try again,' she suggested.

As for the other group dynamics, Purcell had noticed that Henry seemed to have lost interest in Vivian – or in impressing her. There is nothing like exhaustion, thirst, hunger, and fear to get the old libido and weenie down, Purcell knew.

He hoped Henry would hold up, and that Vivian would not have to nurse her ex-lover again. But if it happened, that was all right.

They discussed security and possible run-ins with dangerous people.

Gann said, 'The Gallas don't much fancy the jungle, and we've seen no hoofprints or horse droppings. The Gallas' home is the desert, and they only drop by places such as this after a battle.' He let them know, 'The Royalist partisans are operating to the west, and the counterrevolutionaries are mostly in the Simien Mountains around Gondar, so there is no reason for Getachu's soldiers to be here either. He has his hands full elsewhere.' He assured them, 'We have the jungle all to ourselves.'

Purcell reminded him, 'We've seen three army Hueys fly over.'

'I actually counted four. But these are normal north–south flights from Gondar to Addis, and vice versa.' He assured them, 'The army has neither the fuel nor the helicopters for reconnaissance.'

Purcell reminded him, 'They have one less helicopter than they used to have.'

'Quite right.'

He also reminded Gann, 'Yesterday, a helicopter was going east—west.'

'Well, as long as they keep going, and don't hover about, then they're not looking for anything.'

'I think they're looking for us, Colonel.'

'I doubt that. They think you've flown off to Somaliland.' He asked, 'Why in the world would you stay here after you've shot down an army helicopter?'

'I've been asking myself that very question.'

Gann smiled and said, 'Well, let's press on.'

On day five, Mercado said, 'We need to head to Shoan.' He reminded everyone, 'We are running out of food.'

And Henry was running out of gas, Purcell knew. And they were all dehydrated and covered with insect bites and heat sores.

Mercado reminded Gann, 'Regroup, refit, and strike out again.'

Gann nodded, but not very enthusiastically. He said, 'I feel we should push on just a bit more ... perhaps to the south, to a line parallel with Shoan. We might have more luck that way.' He added, 'Then we can head east toward the road, and Shoan.'

Mercado had no reply.

Purcell said, 'We could be south of Shoan already.'

'That's possible.'

Mercado pointed out, 'If we just head due east, we will intersect with the road.'

Gann reminded him, 'We can't go due *any* direction, old boy.' He pointed out, 'This is not the desert or the tundra.' He reminded Mercado, 'We're in the bush, you know.'

Mercado insisted, 'We have passed the point of no return in regards to food.'

'Not quite yet. But we're close.'

'This is how people die.'

'Well,' Gann agreed, 'that is one way. There are others.' He belatedly asked Mercado, 'How are you feeling, old boy?'

Mercado hesitated, then said, 'I can make it back to Shoan.'

'Good.' Gann also said, 'We must be careful not to get injured or ill.'

Purcell agreed, 'Let's try not to do that.' He asked Vivian, 'How are you feeling?'

'I'm all right.'

Purcell looked into the dark, triple-canopy jungle. 'Let's get off the trail and walk between the trees.' He took a compass heading to the south.

They left the trail, and headed south through the rain forest. The terrain had looked deceptively open between the trees, but as they traveled it, it became clear that they had to cut brush and vines, and the carpet of undergrowth, that had looked low, was actually knee-high in most places.

After about an hour, they realized they weren't making good progress, and they also realized that by leaving the trail, they'd effectively lost it, and also lost any trail in the trackless expanse. It was like walking through a great columned building, Purcell thought, with a green-vaulted ceiling and a carpet of wait-a-minute vines. Rays of sunlight penetrated the triple canopy in places, and they found themselves unconsciously walking toward the spots of sun-dappled ground cover.

The darkness was getting deeper, and the sun was no longer

penetrating into the forest. It was jungle dusk, and they began looking for a place to stop for the night.

Vivian said, 'Look. A cluster of palms.'

They looked to where she was pointing to the west and they saw the distinctive trunks of palms, with their fronds buried in the surrounding growth.

They made their way to the palms, where the ground was more clear, and they sat with their backs to the palm trunks.

Gann looked up and said, 'Doesn't seem to be anything edible up there.'

Purcell handed him a cloth bag. 'Have a date.'

They drank the last of their water and took stock of their food, which they estimated would last one more day.

Gann and Purcell looked at the map and they both agreed they were between twenty and thirty kilometers west of the road, though they couldn't determine if they were north or south of Shoan. And Shoan was another thirty kilometers east of the road.

Gann said, 'We are a long day's march to Shoan.' He added, 'Unless we run into rough country.'

Purcell said, 'That was encouraging until "unless."'

They all agreed they'd head back to Shoan in the morning.

Vivian stood and said, 'Be right back.'

Everyone assumed she'd gone off to relieve herself, but she kept walking, and Purcell was concerned that she was becoming delirious and had seen another mirage. He couldn't call out to her because they needed to be quiet, so he stood and caught up with her.

'Where are you going?'

'I saw a glint.'

'Really?'

'Right over here.'

He let her lead him farther into the tight undergrowth.

The ground was rising, he noticed, and he recalled the high, rocky ground he'd seen when he flew over this area, returning from Gondar.

The undergrowth began to thin, and he felt rocks beneath his feet.

He was looking where he stepped, and also looking left and right to be sure no one was there, and Vivian was ahead of him again. He drew his pistol from his cargo pocket and stuck it in his belt.

Vivian stopped and said, 'There is the rock.'

He caught up to her and looked west into the setting sun. Spread out to their front was a deep depression in the ground that covered acres of land. There were a few trees growing in the sunken ground, but it was mostly open. In the deep, wide depression grew brush, crawling vines, and tropical flowers, but he could also see acres of black rock coming through the ground growth. An old stone quarry.

Vivian pointed, 'The rock.'

On the far side of the abandoned quarry, about a hundred yards away, was a great black monolith – a quarried slab of rock, about twenty feet high and ten feet wide, that had been shaped by human hands, but never transported from here. The late afternoon sun highlighted the black luster on its top edge. Purcell didn't understand how Vivian could have seen it from where they were sitting.

He heard a noise behind him, pushed Vivian down, drew his revolver, and knelt facing the sound.

Gann and Mercado came up the rise and saw them.

Gann said, 'There you are. Don't shoot, old boy. We're still friends.'

Purcell put the revolver in his cargo pocket and waved them up the slope.

Gann asked, 'What have you found?'

'A quarry.'

Vivian said, 'We have found Father Armano's rock.' She pointed.

Mercado and Gann looked across the quarry and Gann said, 'Yes, a quarry. Good scouting.'

Mercado was staring at the black monolith on the far edge of the rock quarry. He looked at Vivian and asked, 'How do you know?'

'Henry, that is the rock.'

Gann spotted the carved rock and said, 'Let's have a look, shall we?'

The sun slipped below the tall monolith, and a shadow spread across the expanse of the ancient quarry.

Purcell said, 'It's not going anywhere. Let's camp here, and we'll take a look in the morning.'

Vivian nodded. 'I knew it was here, Frank.'

Purcell looked at her, then looked downslope from where they'd come. *Impossible.*

She put her hand on his arm. 'No, not impossible.'

CHAPTER 52

They awoke before dawn and ate the last of their bread and dates, leaving only some dried goat meat, which Purcell thought would taste like steak when they were near starvation.

Purcell knew they would run out of food before they got to Shoan, but he wasn't sure they would be starting back today. Not with that black monolith staring them in the face. He looked out across the quarry. It was still too dark to see the black slab – but it was there.

They would have to make a decision; should they look next for Father Armano's tree? Then his stream? Purcell was almost certain that Vivian was right – this was *the* rock.

Purcell asked the question on everyone's minds. 'Do we press on from that rock, or do we head back to Shoan and return here when we're reprovisioned.'

No one replied, except Vivian, of course. 'We did not come this far to turn back.'

Purcell reminded her, 'We're about to eat the last goat.'

'We need only water.'

'Easy to say on a stomach full of dates.' He asked, 'Henry?'

Mercado looked at Vivian. 'We continue on.'

Gann agreed and said, 'We won't starve to death.' He informed them, 'Snakes. Easy to lop their venomous heads off with a machete.' He further informed them, 'You squeeze the buggers and get a good half pint of blood into your cup. Meat's not bad, either.'

Purcell suggested, 'Let's talk about water.' He told them, 'In the gypsum quarries where I grew up, there was lots of ground water. In fact, it needed to be pumped out.'

Gann agreed, 'Should be good water down there.'

'So,' Purcell asked, 'are we all agreed that we've found the rock?'

Everyone agreed.

'And that we have to now look for a tree — which could be long gone after forty years?'

Vivian said, 'We will find the tree. And the stream. And the black monastery.'

'Good.' Purcell said, 'Father Armano did not let us down.' He said to Mercado, 'Cool the champagne.'

Mercado smiled weakly. The man did not look well since they began this hike in Shoan, a week ago, Purcell thought. In fact, his face was drawn and his eyes looked dark and sunken. Purcell handed Mercado his last piece of bread and said, 'Have this.'

Mercado shook his head.

Purcell threw the bread on his lap, and Vivian said, 'Eat that, Henry.' She picked it up and held it to his lips, but he shook his head. 'I'm all right.'

Vivian put the bread in his backpack.

Purcell and Gann looked at the map in the dim light. Gann said, 'I can see nothing on this map that indicates an abandoned quarry, so I'm not quite sure where we are . . . but I would guess here . . .' He pointed to the map where the dark green was a little lighter, an indication that the cartographers had noted the more sparse vegetation shown on the aerial photographs.

Gann continued, 'The elevation lines indicate that beyond the quarry, the ground becomes lower and sinks into a deep basin, with dense growth.'

Purcell said, 'Regarding Father Armano's stream, I don't see any streams.'

Gann reminded him, 'You will only see on the map what could be seen from the aerial photographs.' He added, 'Which is not much.'

Vivian let them know, 'I don't care what is on the maps. We need to see what is out *there*.' She pointed at the black rock.

'Good point,' Purcell agreed. He stood. 'Let's go.'

Everyone slipped on their backpacks and they began picking their way down the terraced slope of the rock quarry. The black obsidian was slippery in places, and the vines were treacherous on the downslope.

Purcell glanced at Mercado, who seemed to be doing all right downhill.

The rocky floor of the quarry was about twenty feet down, and near the bottom they saw water flowing out of the rocks. They stopped and washed their faces and hands in the cool ground water, and drank it directly from its source, then filled their canteens. They sat on a rock ledge and waited, as Gann suggested, for the water to rehydrate them.

Vivian looked out at the black slab at the far edge of the quarry. The sun had peeked over the trees behind them, and the rays now illuminated the east-facing side of the rock. Vivian pointed. 'Look.'

They all looked at the twenty-foot-tall slab, and they could now see that the face of it had been etched with a cross.

Vivian said, 'We are close.'

They all stood, except for Mercado, who was still sitting, looking at the cross on the rock.

Vivian said to him, 'Come on, Henry. We're almost home.'

He nodded, stood, and smiled for the first time in days.

They continued down to the floor of the quarry, then began making their way across the uneven rock and tangled growth.

Gann said, 'By the look of this place, I'd say it has been abandoned for a very long time.'

Purcell wondered if this was where the black stone had come from to build the monastery. He assumed it was. Or had they done again what they were good at – making false assumptions, misinterpreting evidence, and tailoring the clues to fit their theories? Maybe not this time. Somewhere inside him, Purcell felt that they had arrived at the threshold of the black monastery.

They reached the opposite side of the quarry and began climbing the terraced rock. It was not a difficult climb, but they all realized they were weaker than they thought.

The black monolith was set back from the edge of the quarry, and they stood looking at it, and at the cross that they could now see had been deeply cut into the stone by a skilled stone carver. It wasn't a Latin cross, Purcell noted, but a Coptic cross.

At the edge of the quarry, they could see freshly cleaved faces of obsidian, evidence that people had been here to cut small pieces of the stone.

Gann said, 'I would guess that this is where the monks get their stone to carve their little doodads.'

Purcell agreed. 'Better than chipping away at the monastery.'

Mercado had wandered off a few feet and said, 'Look at this.'

They walked to where he was standing, and on the ground was evidence of campfires, and what looked like chicken bones, and eggshells.

It didn't need to be said, but Gann said, 'This could be where the Falashas meet the monks, and set up for the night before returning to Shoan.'

Everyone agreed with that deduction, and Purcell added, 'Shoan then must be a day's walk from here.' He also pointed out, 'It took us five days to get here.'

Gann replied, 'It appears we took the long route.' He added, 'There is obviously a quick and direct route to Shoan. We'll need to find that.'

'Right. Meanwhile, I think it's safe to say that the black monastery is a one-day hike from this meeting place.'

Mercado asked, 'But in which direction?'

Gann replied, 'Probably not east, on the way back to Shoan. So perhaps north or south, or farther west.'

Vivian had walked off, and she called back to them, 'West.'

They moved toward where she was standing on an elevation of rock. The area around the quarry was mostly treeless, covered with rock rubble from hundreds of years of quarrying, but surrounding the open area was thick jungle. To the west, where Vivian was looking, stood a dead cedar about a hundred feet away, and about forty feet in height. The towering trunk of the decay-resistant cedar had turned silver-gray, and all the branches had fallen, or been cut off, except for two that stretched out like arms, parallel to the ground, giving the tree the appearance of a giant cross.

Vivian said, 'The tree.'

Purcell looked at the giant cedar, which could have been there, alive and dead, for hundreds of years.

Gann and Mercado were also staring at the towering tree, and Gann looked back at the monolith and said, 'I believe we have two points in a straight line.'

Purcell had his compass out, and with his back to the monolith, and facing the tree, he took a compass reading. 'A few degrees north of due west.'

Vivian said, 'Now we need to find the stream.'

Purcell replied, 'That should be the easiest thing we've done this week.' He said to Mercado, 'Henry, get the champagne ready.'

Mercado smiled.

Purcell gave Vivian a hug, then Vivian hugged Henry, then Colonel Gann. The men shook hands all around.

Everyone's spirits seemed to be revived, and they forgot their fatigue and jungle sores.

Purcell now noticed, about a hundred feet off to the north, a roofless hut built with scraps of the black rock. The hut sat among flowering bushes, and the branches of a tall gum tree hung over the abandoned structure.

Gann said, 'A shelter for the nasty overseer, I would bet.'

They all walked toward the hut to check it out, and when they got within ten feet of it, a man suddenly appeared in the shadow of the open doorway and stepped quickly out of the hut, followed by another man, then three more.

Purcell counted five men, dressed in jungle fatigues, carrying AK-47 rifles, which were pointed at them.

Vivian let out a stifled scream and grabbed Purcell's arm.

One of the soldiers shouted something in Amharic, and all the soldiers were pointing their automatic rifles at Gann, shouting, and gesturing for him to drop the Uzi.

Gann hesitated, and one of the soldiers fired a deafening burst of rounds over his head.

Gann let the Uzi fall to the ground.

Vivian pressed against Purcell.

Someone else appeared at the door of the hut, and General Getachu stepped out into the morning sunshine. With him was Princess Miriam, whom he pushed to the ground.

Getachu looked at Purcell, Mercado, Gann, and Vivian. 'I have been waiting for you.'

CHAPTER 53

Frank Purcell drew a deep breath and tried to take stock of the situation, which didn't need, he admitted, too much interpretation.

His mind registered that there were five soldiers, and a Huey held seven in the cabin. So if that's how Getachu and Miriam had gotten here, there were no more soldiers – unless there were.

Getachu had a holster strapped to his waist, but his pistol wasn't drawn.

Purcell glanced at the Uzi on the ground, about five feet away, between him and Gann. Was it on safety? Probably. Could he get to it before he was cut down by five AK-47s? Probably not.

Purcell glanced at Mercado, who he saw had tears in his eyes. Vivian had her head buried in Purcell's chest now, her back to the soldiers. Gann was looking at Miriam, who had remained on the ground at Getachu's feet, lying facedown in the dirt. He saw that she wore a white *shamma* that was ripped and stained with blood.

Getachu said, 'Colonel Gann does not seem happy to see his princess.' He stared at Gann. 'I was not happy to hear that they released you in Addis. Now you will wish they had shot you there.'

Getachu knew not to expect a reply from the insolent

Englishman, so he continued, 'I paid a brief visit to Shoan, to pay my respects to my princess before the UN people came to take her away.'

Getachu looked at Gann, then Purcell. 'And what do I find there? I find an aircraft that has been burned. Your aircraft, Mr Purcell. The very aircraft that my helicopter pilot radioed had fired a rocket at him. And now the helicopter is missing, and presumed lost, with all the men on board.' He let Purcell know, 'I have concluded my court-martial, and you will be shot.' He added, 'Within the next five minutes.'

Purcell felt the weight of the revolver in his cargo pocket. He was sure the opportunity would come to pull the revolver and shoot Getachu before the five soldiers cut everyone down with their automatic rifles. At least they'd all die knowing that Getachu was dead.

Getachu lit a cigarette and continued what appeared to be a rehearsed speech. 'I promised you a cigarette, Mr Purcell, before I was going to shoot you in my camp. But I am sorry to break this promise. I will promise you, however, a quick bullet in the brain.'

Purcell made the same promise to Getachu, but kept that to himself.

Getachu continued, 'So the people of Shoan sheltered a murderer. And they also admitted to me that Mr Mercado and Miss Smith came from that aircraft, and that the princess gave them all shelter. Therefore, Mr Mercado will share Mr Purcell's fate, and Miss Smith ...' He smiled at her, 'Miss Smith – Vivian – will belong to me for a time. Then she will belong to my soldiers.' He said something to his men in Amharic and they smiled and looked at Vivian.

Vivian was shaking now and Purcell held her tightly.

Gann was looking at Miriam, but spoke to Getachu. 'What did you do in Shoan?'

'Ah! You speak.' He said to Gann, 'What do you think I did?'

'You will hang for that.'

'For what? Because the Gallas attacked the village and killed everyone, and burned it all? What has that to do with me?'

'You bastard.'

'Yes, yes, Colonel Gann. Getachu is a bastard. And you are a knight. A knight for hire. A man who sells himself to kill.' He said to Gann, 'The prostitutes in Saint George Square charge less, and are better at their profession than you.'

Gann looked at Getachu. 'You are the most incompetent commander I have ever faced.'

'Do not provoke me into putting a bullet into your head. I have something special for you to see before you die.' He looked at Miriam lying at his feet and kicked her in the side.

Miriam let out a moan, but remained facedown on the ground.

Gann took a step toward her, but the soldiers leveled their rifles at him and he stopped.

Getachu said, 'When I was a young man, and when this princess became a woman – about fourteen, I think – I thought of her in that way. Mikael Getachu, the son of a weaver who worked in the shop of their royal highnesses. I told my father of my desire for the princess, and he beat me, of course. But if he were now living, I would say to him – you see? I have got my princess.' Getachu put the toe of his boot under Miriam's *shamma* and pushed it up over her bare buttocks.

He said something to his soldiers in Amharic, and they laughed. He said to Gann, 'So we have this lady in common at least.'

Gann took a deep breath, and Purcell knew he was thinking of diving for the Uzi, and Purcell said to him, 'No.'

Gann took another breath, then stood straight, as though he were in parade formation, and said to Getachu, 'You are not a soldier. You are an animal.'

'Do *not* provoke me. You will die when and how I want you to die. And I will tell you how you will die – by crucifixion, as you watch me having sport with your lady.'

Getachu looked at Vivian, then said, 'And perhaps I will have sport with you both. Yes. I think I would like seeing you, Miss Smith, and the princess enjoying the company of each other.'

Vivian was still clinging to Purcell, her body shaking.

Getachu turned his attention to Mercado, who had stood silently, his eyes closed and his head down. Getachu said to him, 'Will you now tell me that you will write nice words about me?'

Mercado did not answer.

Getachu barked, 'I am speaking to you! Look at me!'

Mercado raised his head and looked at Getachu.

'I will spare your life, Mr Mercado. We will do the interviews, and you will write kind words about General Getachu, a man of the people.' He looked at Mercado. 'Yes?'

Mercado stared at Getachu. 'Go fuck yourself.'

Getachu seemed surprised at the response. 'What do you say?'

'Go fuck yourself.'

Getachu put his hand on the butt of his pistol. 'What do you say, Mr Mercado?'

Mercado said something in Amharic, and the five soldiers seemed almost stunned, and leveled their rifles at him.

Getachu waved them off, then said to Mercado, 'I had planned a quick death for you, who are of no consequence. But I will rethink that.'

Mercado, recalling what Gann had done in Getachu's tent, turned his back on the general.

Getachu looked at Mercado's back, then shifted his attention to his surroundings. He said, 'So this is the place where the Falashas and the monks come to meet, and to exchange goods.' He looked around again. 'I am told this has gone on for several hundred years, which is a very nice thing.' He said to his prisoners, 'I have heard of this arrangement, and I wished to see this place for myself. And now I am told that this arrangement has ended because the Falashas have gone. So I came here to bring food to the monks, and I have waited for them — and for you, who I hoped would come here.' He looked down at Miriam. 'She is a stubborn woman, Colonel. But she did reveal to me the location of this place, but not to you, I think, or you would have been here much sooner.' He let them know, 'I have been waiting for you for six days now, and I had given up hope. But the princess has been kind enough to keep me amused.'

Again, Purcell thought that Gann would go for the Uzi, and he knew that Getachu had left it lying close to Gann to further torment the man.

In fact, Getachu said, 'Why is it that none of you brave men will take up that weapon?' He asked, 'Is that not a better way to die? Please, gentlemen. Show me your courage.'

Purcell moved slightly so that Vivian was blocking Getachu's view of his right arm, and he began to move his hand toward the cargo pocket. He was sure he could kill Getachu, and he hoped that Gann would then dive for the Uzi — or if he didn't, and Purcell was not dead yet, he could go for it himself, and maybe get off a burst. But whatever scenario played out, he, Vivian, Gann, and Mercado would be cut down by bursts of automatic rifle fire. And that was better than what Getachu had planned. He put his hand on Vivian's thigh, close to his cargo pocket.

Getachu also let them know, 'When I am finished with you here, I will find the monastery of the monks, which I know is close by, and I will relieve these holy men of their treasure — and perhaps their lives.' He said, 'Men have died to protect this thing called the Grail, and men have died looking for it — as you will. You have found death.'

Purcell could hear Vivian saying softly, 'No, no, no ... Frank.' He held her tighter.

Getachu turned his attention to Miriam and pressed his boot into her bare buttocks. She sobbed and said something in Amharic.

Getachu said to her, 'Do not be sad, my princess. I will take care of you. Are you sad at losing your English lover? Do you want to speak to him? To tell him that you betrayed him? He will understand. You were in pain. He will understand that pain very shortly. And he will forgive you, because he will understand what pain can do.'

Purcell had his hand in his pocket now, and he wrapped his fingers around the butt of the revolver. No one noticed. He hoped he'd live long enough to see Getachu bleeding his life out.

Gann suddenly let out a strange noise, and Purcell glanced at him. Gann had his hands over his face, and he was crying, and his body was shaking. He called out, 'Miriam! Miriam!'

She turned her head toward him and said softly, 'Edmund ... I am sorry ...'

Gann reached out his arms to her and took three long steps toward Miriam, and almost reached her, but two soldiers grabbed him and pushed him back. He struggled with them, and kept shouting, 'Miriam!'

Purcell understood instantly that Gann was up to something, and Purcell knew this was the moment. He pulled his revolver. Then something suddenly flew through the air and came to rest on the ground, and Purcell saw it was the safety handle of a hand grenade. And he realized what Gann had done.

Getachu was screaming in Amharic at his two men, and he didn't see the grenade in Gann's hand that Gann had pulled from one of the soldier's web belts, and he also didn't see Gann dropping the live grenade on the ground.

The seven-second fuse had been cooking for at least three or four seconds, Purcell knew, and he should have thrown himself and Vivian on the ground and yelled for Mercado to do the same. But he wanted to kill Getachu himself. He pushed Vivian to the ground, facedown, raised the revolver, and pointed it directly at Getachu's heart.

Getachu saw two things in a quick succession – the grenade, and Purcell taking aim at him. His eyes widened.

Purcell fired, and Getachu was knocked back into the stone wall of the hut.

Purcell threw himself on top of Vivian, who was trying to stand, and he yelled at Mercado, 'Down!'

The grenade exploded.

The sound was literally deafening, and Purcell's eardrums felt as though they were going to burst. The ground shook under him.

And then there was complete silence. He felt a burning in his right calf where a piece of hot shrapnel had sliced into him. He whispered in Vivian's ear, 'Do not move.' He told her, 'Getachu is dead.' But he wasn't sure of that.

He rolled off her quickly and rose unsteadily to one knee, with his revolver pointed toward the hut.

No one was standing.

He stood and drew a deep breath, then took a few steps toward the hut. The air was filled with dust and the smell of burned explosives.

The two soldiers who'd been grappling with Gann were gushing blood from multiple wounds where the burning shrapnel had torn into their bodies.

Gann, too, was a mass of blood, and his khakis were soaked red. He was still breathing, but frothy blood was running from his mouth.

Purcell moved toward the three soldiers who'd been standing near the hut, near Getachu. They hadn't caught the full blast of the grenade, but they were down, bleeding and stunned by the concussion. One of them looked at him.

Purcell raised his revolver and put a bullet into each of their heads.

He moved over to where Miriam lay on the ground. He saw no blood, and thought she'd been low enough to escape the flying shrapnel. He knelt beside her and shook her. 'Miriam.' Then he saw the wound in the side of her head where a single piece of shrapnel had entered her skull. He felt her throat for a pulse, but there was none. He reached out and pulled her *shamma* over her buttocks.

He stood and looked at Getachu, who was sitting against the wall where he'd been thrown by the impact of the bullet. His face had caught some shrapnel, and one of his eyes was a mass of blood.

Blood also ran out of his mouth from the bullet wound in his chest. His one eye was following Purcell.

Getachu seemed to be trying to speak, and Purcell knelt near him, though he still could not hear. Getachu spit a glob of frothy blood at him.

Purcell wiped the blood from his face, put the revolver to Getachu's good eye, and pulled the trigger.

Purcell stood and turned, and looked at Vivian, whose body was still shaking, though he saw no blood, and she seemed all right.

He looked at where Mercado had been standing, and saw him lying facedown on the ground.

Purcell knelt beside Vivian and put his hand on her shoulder. 'Are you all right?'

Her face was buried in her arms, and she gave a small nod.

'Do not move.'

He stood and walked to Mercado and knelt beside him. Mercado's backpack had caught a lot of shrapnel, and he had taken shrapnel in his legs and buttocks, and blood was seeping through his khakis. His shirt was also wet, Purcell saw, but not with blood. The champagne bottle had broken. 'Henry. How are you, mate?'

No response.

'Henry.' He shook him.

Purcell heard and felt a rushing in his ears; his hearing was returning. 'Are you all right?'

'I said I've been hit. I've been hit.'

Purcell couldn't tell if the wounds were serious, but the blood was not gushing. It came to him that Henry, by turning his back on Getachu, may have saved his own life. He said to Mercado, 'Just lie still. You'll be all right. I'll be right back.'

He went back to Vivian, knelt beside her, and again put his hand on her shoulder. 'Can you stand?'

She nodded, and he helped her to her feet, keeping her back turned to the carnage around the hut. She put her arms around him. 'Frank ... oh my God ...' She began crying, then took a deep breath and asked in a quiet voice, 'What happened?'

He told her again, to reassure her, 'Getachu is dead.'

She tried to turn to look toward the hut, but he held her against him.

He said, 'The soldiers are dead. Listen to me – a hand grenade exploded. Colonel Gann is dead. Miriam is dead.'

She let out a long cry, then got herself under control and asked, 'Henry ...?'

'Henry is ... he will be okay.' Maybe.

She turned her head to where she'd last seen Henry, and saw him facedown on the ground with blood on his pants. 'Henry!' She pulled loose from Purcell and he let her go.

She ran over to Mercado and knelt beside him. 'Henry!'

Mercado turned his head toward her and smiled. 'Thank God you are all right.'

Purcell didn't recall Henry asking him about Vivian, but he supposed Mercado was in shock.

Vivian was caressing his hair and face. 'You will be fine. You *are* fine. Just lie still ... are you in pain?'

'A bit. Yes.' He turned his head toward Purcell. 'Am I going to live?'

Purcell knelt opposite Vivian and put his fingers on Henry's throat to feel his pulse, which seemed strong. 'How is your breathing?'

'All right ...'

He felt Henry's forehead, and it was not cool or clammy. He informed Mercado, 'Gann is dead. Miriam is dead.'

'No ... oh, God ... what happened ...?'

'Gann got hold of a grenade.'

Purcell stood and walked over to one of the soldiers he'd executed. There was a US Army first aid kit on the man's web belt, and he snapped the canvas kit off and carried it to Vivian. He put it in her hand. 'There should be a pressure bandage in there, and iodine. Get his clothes off and we'll patch him up.'

She nodded and asked Mercado, 'Can you sit up?'

She helped him roll onto his back, which seemed to cause him pain, then she pulled him up into a sitting position, took his backpack off, and began unbuttoning his shirt.

Purcell went back to the other two executed soldiers and retrieved their first aid kits, which each held a pressure bandage. He checked the two soldiers who'd taken the full brunt of the grenade blast, but their web gear was as shredded as their bodies, and he saw that one of them had a protruding intestine.

He went back to Gann, and he knelt beside him and felt for a pulse, but there was none. Purcell pushed his eyelids closed and said, 'You did good, Colonel.'

Henry was naked now, on all fours, and Vivian was dabbing iodine on his legs and butt, which caused him to cry out in pain.

Purcell walked over to them and knelt on the other side of Henry. He counted three shrapnel wounds in his left leg and two in his buttocks. He could see the shrapnel sticking out of one wound and he pulled it out, which made Henry yell in pain. Purcell said, 'I think you may be very lucky.' He took his penknife from his pocket and said, 'This will hurt, but you will remain still and quiet.'

He managed to get all but one piece of metal out of Mercado's flesh, and Henry kept relatively still, as Vivian kept talking to him.

He gave Vivian the other two first aid kits. 'Bandage the ones that look the worst.'

He looked at her kneeling on the other side of Mercado and she looked at him. He said, 'Be quick. We need to get out of here.'

'Where are we going?'

'You know where we're going.'

She nodded, then started opening the first aid kits.

He stood and again surveyed the scene, then lit a cigarette. 'My God. Oh my God.'

He wanted to bury Colonel Gann and Miriam and not leave them for the jackals, but he didn't see a shovel, and he didn't want to stay here any longer than he had to.

He walked over to Gann and hefted him onto his shoulder, then carried him to Miriam and laid Gann down beside her. He crossed their arms over their chests. Hopefully Getachu's men, looking for their general, would know that someone had respected the bodies, and maybe they'd do the same. Maybe, too, they'd be happy to find their general with a bullet in his brain.

Purcell watched Vivian help Henry into his clothes. Henry seemed all right.

Purcell pulled up his pant leg and looked at his wound. A piece of metal protruded from his calf and he pulled it out.

Shrapnel from an exploding grenade or shell was a random thing, he recalled from his time in Southeast Asia – hot metal shards or pieces of spring-loaded wire, killing and maiming some, leaving others untouched. It really didn't depend too much on where you were standing or lying when it went off – close, far, standing, or prone as Miriam was – it didn't matter. When it was your time, it was your time. When it wasn't, it wasn't. It was Colonel Gann's time, and Miriam's time. It was not Henry Mercado's time. Or Vivian's, or his. Indeed, they had been chosen.

He walked over to them and said, 'We are going to the black monastery. We are going to see the Holy Grail.'

CHAPTER 54

Purcell had the Uzi, and he gave Vivian his reloaded pistol, and Henry retrieved one of the AK-47s. They slipped on their backpacks and walked away from the rock quarry, down the slope toward the giant cedar, and continued on toward the wall of tropical growth in front of them.

No one spoke, but then Mercado asked Purcell, 'Did you take any food from the soldiers?'

'No.'

'We should go back.'

Purcell replied, 'Put your hand into the hand of God, Henry. That's why we're here.'

Mercado stayed silent as they continued on, then said, 'Yes … I will.'

Vivian said, 'We are all in God's hands now.'

Purcell did not have to look at his compass to know he was heading due west, with the cedar and the monolith behind him.

There was a worn black rock lying on the ground at the edge of the wall of trees, and beyond the rock he saw a trailhead. They crossed over the black threshold and entered the rain forest. Limbs and vines reached out overhead and immediately blocked out the sunlight.

The land sloped gently down, and the trees became taller, and the canopy became thicker. After a while, Purcell noticed that the ground was becoming soft and spongy as though they were entering a marsh or a swamp.

The trail was no longer defined by walls of vegetation, but it was discernible if you looked ahead and saw the slight difference in the ground where it had been walked on.

Mercado said, 'I don't see a stream.'

Purcell did not reply, and neither did Vivian. They continued on.

The ground was definitely spongy now, and Purcell could see changes in the landscape. Huge banyan trees started to appear, as well as swamp cedar and cypress, which he remembered from the swamps of Southeast Asia.

The land was sloping more steeply now, and Purcell guessed they were entering the bottom drainage basin from the Simien Mountains, which he'd noticed in the air and on the map but which they had not thought to consider as a place where the black monastery could be.

In retrospect, he realized that they had been ... maybe mesmerized by Father Armano and his story, and the priest had given them information, but not knowledge. He had told them enough to put them on the trail, but not enough to bring them to the end of it. They had to do that on their own. And if indeed they were chosen, then they would be guided on the right path.

Purcell looked around him. The terrain appeared deceptively pleasant and sylvan, but he could now see pools of water filled with marsh fern on both sides of their disappearing path. Marsh gasses rose in misty clouds, and the air was becoming hot and fetid. Wispy strands of gray moss hung from the tree limbs, and he noticed that there were a lot of dead trees, and creeping marsh-wort ran over the deadwood on the wet ground. Huge, silent black birds sat on bare tree limbs and seemed to be watching them as they passed. He realized that the marsh was much quieter than the jungle, and there were almost no sounds from insects or birds. A sense of foreboding came over him, but he said nothing and they pressed on.

The land seemed to be bottoming out and becoming a true swamp, and Purcell wondered if this was passable. He also wondered if they were going in the right direction. The path had disappeared, but there was a meandering ribbon of spongy higher ground that passed through the swampy expanse of terrain. The mud was sucking at their boots, and Vivian took off her boots and socks and walked barefoot through the muck. Purcell and Mercado did the same.

Vivian noticed now that Purcell had blood on his pant leg, and she asked him, 'Did you get hit there?'

'I'm fine.'

'Let me see that.'

'I've already seen it.'

She insisted they stop, and Purcell sat on the trunk of a fallen tree while Vivian knelt in the mud, extended Purcell's leg, and examined his wound.

He said, 'It's really okay.'

She had an iodine bottle in her pocket and she dabbed some of it on his wound, then sat beside him on the tree trunk.

They looked around at the swamp. Without saying it, they all knew that Father Armano had never mentioned a swamp.

Vivian said to Mercado, 'Sit down, Henry.'

He sat slowly on the tree trunk and grimaced in pain.

Purcell said, 'I think I left a piece of metal in you.'

'Indeed you did.'

They all smiled, but it was a tired and forced smile. The shock and horror of what had happened was still very much with them, and it was time to say something.

Purcell said to them, 'Edmund Gann was a very brave man.'

Mercado said, 'He was a soldier and a gentleman ... a knight.'

Vivian said, 'I know that he is with Miriam now.'

'Indeed he is,' Mercado said.

Vivian put her arm around Purcell and squeezed him closer to her. '*You* are a very brave man, Frank Purcell.' She told Henry, 'He threw himself over me when the hand grenade exploded.'

Mercado nodded.

Vivian put her hand on Mercado's shoulder. 'What did you say to Getachu in Amharic?'

'The usual – that his mother was a diseased prostitute who should have smothered him at birth.'

Vivian said, 'A bit rough, Henry.' She smiled.

Mercado said, 'I hope he is now burning in hell.'

No one spoke for a minute, then Mercado asked Vivian, 'Do you still have Father Armano's skull?'

'I do.'

'Well, we are going to take him where he wanted to go.' He stood. 'Ready?'

Vivian and Purcell stood, and Vivian assured them, 'The stream is ahead of us.'

They continued on.

The ground was rising now, and the marshland was again turning to tropical jungle. What looked like a beaten path began to materialize in front of them.

Vivian suddenly stopped and said, 'Listen.'

They stopped and listened, but neither Purcell nor Mercado could hear anything.

Mercado asked, 'What do you hear?'

'Water.' She moved to her right and the men followed.

Running down the slope was a small stream, choked with water lilies and vines. It was, Purcell thought, a stream from the hills that emptied into the marsh basin.

Vivian knelt down and put her hand into the flowing water. She turned to Purcell and Mercado, silently inviting them to do the same.

They knelt beside the stream and let the water run over their hands.

Vivian said, 'This is the stream. Do we follow it? Or do we follow the path?'

Purcell thought the path and the stream seemed to run parallel, but they might diverge.

Mercado said, 'Ruscello. He said it twice. Il Ruscello. The stream.'

Vivian nodded and stood. They all stepped, still barefoot, into the cool, shallow water and walked upstream.

Without looking at his watch, Purcell knew they had been walking about five hours, and it was close to noon – a half day's walk from the meeting place of the monks and the Falashas. And it had been mostly due west, even through the meandering path in the swamp. It seemed simple enough, after you've done it, and he tried to imagine Father Armano on his patrol with the sergeant named Giovanni, walking from the black rock – which the priest and the soldiers had no way of knowing was a meeting place of Coptic Christians and Jews. Giovanni had then taken his patrol to the giant cedar, and through the jungle, to the swamp, and to the stream, all of which the sergeant had found by accident on a previous patrol. And they had arrived again at the black monastery – but this time they entered by the reed basket, and only Father Armano came out of there alive.

And when the priest was healed of his wounds – by nature or by faith – he was given over to the Royalist soldiers and taken by the same route, or maybe another route, to his prison in the fortress, and there he remained for nearly forty years. And whatever he had seen in that monastery had sustained him, not only for all those years in his cell, but also for the hours he walked with a mortal wound on his way back to where he had experienced something so remarkable – or miraculous – that he had to return to that place, even as he was dying. He never made it back, but he had made it as far as the ruined spa, which was not even there when he had last been that way. And what he had found in the spa were three people who themselves were trying to find something. Trying to find the war. And Father Armano had asked them – or asked Vivian – *Dov'è la strada?* Where is the road?

Indeed, where is the road? There are many roads.

The jungle became thicker, and the stream became more narrow, and they could see smaller streams feeding into it from the higher ground. They also noticed more clusters of palm trees. None of them doubted that the black monastery was ahead, and that they were walking toward it. It was just a matter of hours, or maybe days, but it was sitting there, still hidden from the eyes of men, still unwelcoming to visitors, yet hopefully ready to receive them with a basket made of reeds.

The sun was setting ahead of them, and the few patches of sunlight were becoming dimmer. It was harder to see more than twenty or thirty feet ahead, but the stream guided them.

The jungle looked somehow different, Purcell thought, and it was more than the changing light that made it seem altered. Purcell noticed date palms and breadfruit trees, and trees that bore fleshy fruit, and other trees that he thought bore nuts, and black African violets covered the ground. This was tended land, a tropical garden such as Purcell had seen in Southeast Asia, barely distinguishable from the untamed jungle. He said, 'The monastery is just ahead.'

Vivian, who was in the lead now, said, 'I know.'

The stream bent sharply to their right, and they followed it for a minute, but then Vivian stepped out of the stream and walked between two towering palms.

Purcell and Mercado joined her.

To their front, about thirty feet away, rising above a twenty-foot-high thicket of bamboo, was a black wall.

Vivian stared up at the glossy stone. She said simply, 'We are here.'

CHAPTER 55

Purcell had no image in his mind of what the wall would look like, and he saw now that the black stones were the size and shape of brick, laid without mortar, piece by piece, until the wall reached about forty feet, the height of a four-story building.

The sun had sunk lower, and the east side of the monastery where they were standing was in dark shadow, but there was a sheen to the wall, and the bamboo thicket and surrounding palms seemed to be captured in the stone.

None of them seemed to know what to do or say next, but they all understood, Purcell thought, that the road that had taken them here was strewn with betrayals and death — but also with acts of courage and caring, and memories that would last them a lifetime — no matter how short or long that was.

Mercado asked, 'Do you think anyone is here?'

Vivian replied, 'Let's find out.'

They pushed their way through the thicket of bamboo to a narrow path that ran along the base of the wall and they went to their right.

They walked along the wall for about two hundred yards to the corner and turned along the north side, then around to the west, and to the south side of the long wall, then back to where they had started. As Father Armano had said, the monastery was built in the style of the Dark Ages, without an opening. But sitting on the ground now was a large basket attached to a thick rope.

Purcell was about to ask if they were sure they wanted to climb into the basket, expecting some hesitation or discussion, but Vivian threw her revolver on the ground and stepped into it without a word. Mercado dropped his AK-47 and followed. They both looked at him. Purcell said, 'Maybe we want ... a potential survivor.'

Vivian said to him, 'That is your decision, Frank.'

Mercado said, 'Don't wait for us too long.'

Purcell hesitated again, then threw his Uzi on the ground and climbed into the basket, and held on to the rope that Vivian and Mercado were holding.

The basket began to rise.

They didn't bother to look at the top of the wall – there would be no one there.

The basket came to a halt, and they were now able to see the roof of the church that Father Armano had described.

They climbed over the parapet onto a wooden walkway that surrounded the walls, and they looked down into the monastery below. It was as the priest had described – a fountain, gardens, eucalyptus trees, palms, and a pond. The peaked roof of the large church was made of a translucent material, also as the priest described. There seemed to be no one there. But of course, there was.

Again without hesitation or comment, Vivian led the way along the wooden walk until they came to a staircase, which they descended.

They all walked toward the closed doors of the church, which were covered in silver that had obviously been rubbed and polished not too long ago, and they saw the symbols of the early Christians on the doors – lambs, fish, and palms, and in the center of each door was a Coptic cross.

Vivian asked Purcell, 'Do you have any weapons?'

'No.'

'Then open the door.'

Purcell grasped the large ring on the door and pulled. The door opened easily and he went inside, followed by Vivian, then Mercado.

The inside of the large church was simple and almost crude. The walls and floors were of black stone and there was no ornamentation, and Purcell was reminded of the church of San Anselmo in Berini. But unlike San Anselmo, the altar here was a simple and crude table, partially covered by a white cloth, on which sat a Coptic cross. Also unlike San Anselmo, there were no stained glass windows – in fact, no windows at all.

But the sun was still high enough to come through the high ceiling, and a strange, prismatic light came through the translucent roof, casting rainbows over the floors and walls. The colors seemed to dance, and to separate into their primary components – red, green, blue – then blend again into their various hues.

Purcell noticed a door behind the altar, and he walked toward it. Mercado and Vivian followed, and Vivian said in a barely audible voice, 'This is the way Father Armano walked.'

This door behind the altar was open and Purcell passed through it. He sensed, but could not see, that he was in a large space. As his eyes adjusted to the darkness, he could make out that he was in a long, narrow gallery, and that two rows of stone columns ran the length of the space.

Vivian came up behind him and put her hand on his shoulder. Mercado stood to Vivian's side, and they all stood where Father Armano and the ten men of his patrol had stood forty years before. Unlike Father Armano, Sergeant Giovanni, and the other men, they did not move forward — but neither did they retreat.

At the end of the long gallery they could now see two fluttering candles, but the candlelight was so weak that they could see nothing but the flames, as though the fire radiated no light, but gave light.

They stared at the candles. Vivian said, 'It is there.' She took their hands and began walking with them between the two rows of thick columns.

As they passed each set of columns, Purcell thought that he should be feeling fear, but a sense of peace took hold of him, and he continued on with Vivian's hand in his.

As they got closer, the two candle flames seemed to give off more light, and he could see that the candles were set toward the middle of a table. As they got even closer, they could all see that it was a very long table, on which was a white cloth that seemed to shine as though it was luminescent.

Behind the table were thirteen high-backed wooden chairs, facing them, and Purcell understood that this was a representation of the table of the Last Supper, with a chair for Jesus and all the apostles, including one for Judas, though that chair was often missing in such representations.

Vivian and Mercado didn't see it at first, because it was small, and the bronze was not polished, but in the center of the table, between the two candles, and opposite the chair of Jesus, was the kiddush cup of the Passover. The Holy Grail.

Vivian stepped close to the table and let go of the men's hands. She stared at the cup. Mercado, too, stared at it, and took a step closer. He said, 'It is filled.'

Vivian said, 'It is beautiful.' She turned to Purcell. 'Frank?'

He kept staring where they were looking, but he saw nothing.

'Frank?' Vivian seemed concerned. 'Do you see it?'

He didn't reply.

Mercado kept staring at the spot. 'How do you not see it?'

'There is nothing there.'

Vivian again looked at him, then back at the spot between the candles. 'Frank … do you feel it?'

'I don't … I can't see anything, Vivian.' He looked at her, then at Mercado, realizing they were sharing the same hallucination.

Tears began running down Vivian's face. 'Frank … you must see it. Why can't you … ?'

He stepped up to the table and reached his hand out between the candles, but there was nothing there.

Vivian said to Purcell, 'Do you want to see the cup or do you want to be proven right?'

Purcell stood there, not knowing what to say or what to do. Finally, he said, 'I want to see it, and believe it.'

Mercado opened Vivian's backpack and he pulled the skull out and quickly unwrapped it.

Purcell said to him, 'Henry, what are you doing?'

Vivian replied, 'We have brought Father Armano home.'

'No, put that back.'

But Mercado had set the skull on the table, in the center, facing the seat of Christ, and Christ's cup.

Purcell drew a deep breath and reached for the skull, and he felt something touch the back of his hand. He felt it again, and he looked at his hand, where two drops of red glistened in the candlelight.

He stared at the two red drops that were now running down to his wrist, then he looked past his hand, and sitting on the table was a small bronze goblet that he had not seen before.

He kept staring at it, to be sure it was there, and he said to Vivian and to Mercado, 'I can see it.'

He held the back of his hand toward Vivian and Mercado and Vivian smiled. Mercado, too, smiled, and said, 'We were worried about you, Frank.'

Vivian said to him, 'I was never worried about you. You just needed to believe in your soul what your heart already knew.'

Purcell nodded.

The three of them looked up toward the ceiling, and they all saw the lance, suspended in air, and as they watched, a red drop formed on the tip and fell into the cup.

They heard something behind them and they turned. Coming out of the darkness of the gallery, between the columns, were figures moving toward them. As the figures got closer, they could see that they were men in monks' robes and cowls, walking two by two. The monks came closer, then separated, left and right, and stood in a line behind them, but seemed not to notice them though they were only a few feet away.

The monks all dropped to their knees, facing the long table, then bowed their heads and began praying silently.

Vivian took Purcell and Mercado by the arm and turned them around, facing the table, and they dropped to their knees. Vivian took their hands again and they all bowed their heads.

Vivian said softly, 'We have come a long way and we are not afraid.'

Purcell didn't know if she was speaking to him, to the monks, or to God. But whatever fear he felt at seeing the monks vanished, and he squeezed her hand. 'There is nothing to be afraid of.'

Mercado said, 'I told you, Frank, we have been chosen.'

Vivian said, 'We can go home now.'

Purcell nodded. He was ready for that journey home.

— PART V —

Rome, February

Journeys end in lovers meeting.

—William Shakespeare
Twelfth Night, II

CHAPTER 56

Frank Purcell sat on a bench and lit a cigarette. A cold wind blew down from the Gianicolo – the hill of Janus – and the Vatican gardens were nearly deserted on this overcast afternoon in February.

It was time to leave Rome, but before he left he wanted to see Vivian and Henry.

Henry had suggested dinner at Etiopia, but Purcell had suggested the Vatican park, after Henry left work. This needed to be short, sweet, and non-alcoholic.

It was 5:30, and Henry was late as usual, but Purcell saw Vivian coming down the path. She spotted him, smiled, waved, and quickened her pace.

He stood and they hesitated for a moment, then hugged and did an air kiss.

He said, 'I've saved a seat for you.'

She smiled and sat, and he sat at the far end of the bench. He put out his cigarette.

She asked, 'Can I have one of those?'

'You shouldn't.' But he held out his Marlboros and she took one. He leaned toward her and lit it with a match that flickered in the wind.

She inhaled and let out a stream of smoke and breath mist. 'It's cold.'

'Spring is coming.'

They both stayed silent awhile, then realizing they might never have another moment alone on a park bench, or anywhere, she said, 'He needs me.'

He didn't reply.

'And you don't.'

'I think we've had this conversation.'

'If I change my mind, can I come back?'

He was supposed to be tough and say, 'No.' But he said, 'Yes.'

'But you'll be taken by then.'

Again he didn't reply.

'Can we remain friends?'

'You don't have to ask.'

They stayed silent and Purcell looked across the dark, windy park at the Ethiopian College.

Vivian saw where he was looking and said, 'I still haven't developed any of the photographs.' She asked, 'Are you going to write about . . . our quest?'

He thought that the world did not need to know what he, Vivian, and Mercado knew. Nor did the monks need the world to know. 'I think we should all close the book on Ethiopia and move on.'

She nodded. 'That is our beautiful and sad secret.'

'Right.'

She asked him, 'Would you ever go back?'

'If I found the right photographer.'

She laughed, then asked him, 'How are your job prospects?'

'Probably better than yours.'

She smiled.

'I'm looking for something in the States.' He stayed silent a moment and said, 'It's been a long time since I've been home.'

'Let me know how I can contact you.'

'Will do.' He glanced at his watch. 'Must be a late-breaking story on the Holy Year.'

She smiled again and said, 'Why don't you come to dinner with us?'

'Thanks, but I really do have to meet someone.'

'How long will you be in Rome?'

'I leave tomorrow.'

She looked at him.

'I'm going to London tomorrow to meet Colonel Gann's family. He has an ex-wife who was fond of him, and two grown children.'

'That's very nice of you.'

'The British embassy still has no word on the body.'

'He's in heaven, Frank.'

'Right.' He asked her, 'Did Henry get that skull to the right people?'

'He did.' She suggested, 'Maybe we could meet in Berini.'

Purcell didn't know who she meant by 'we.' He said, 'I'll let you know when I'm going.'

'I'll be your translator.'

He smiled at her. They both stayed silent, then he asked her, 'Tell me again why they let us go.'

'Because they knew we were chosen.'

'So was Father Armano, and he spent forty years in a cell.'

'The Falashas are all gone from Shoan, and the monks were leaving the black monastery with the Grail.'

'Right.' It was more than the monks thinking they were chosen.

He looked again at the Ethiopian College where a group of monks were entering, and he thought back to the black monastery, which was now abandoned. The monks had packed a dozen donkey carts, and presumably taken the Holy Grail and the Lance of Longinus with them, though Vivian somehow got the impression that the Lance was spectral, and appeared by itself wherever the Grail was.

In any case, the monks had taken them – he, Vivian, and Henry – with them, and when they reached the monastery of Kirkos on Lake Tana, their three uninvited guests were put in a small boat with two oarsmen who rowed them across the lake to the mouth of the Blue Nile. The oarsmen left them, and the boat continued on in the swift current of the river with Purcell at the helm, across the border into Sudan until it reached Khartoum, where the American embassy helped get the three refugee reporters on a flight to Cairo.

Purcell had chosen to stay in Cairo for a few days to visit his apartment and see some people at the AP office. Henry and Vivian had gone on to Rome. And when Purcell had joined them, he discovered, not to his complete surprise, that Henry and Vivian were at the Excelsior together.

As he'd thought, and as he'd always known, Henry and Vivian were better suited for each other. But better is not best, and though he was angry – and hurt – he was also concerned about

Vivian. He still liked Henry, but not as much as Henry liked himself. He would have told Vivian this — as a friend — but she might think it was coming from a jealous ex-lover. So he wasn't going to say anything now.

He said to Vivian, 'I meant to ask you — what were we chosen for?'

'I've thought about it. I think we were chosen to give some meaning to Father Armano's life. I think God blessed him, and sent him to us so he could die with peace in his heart.'

'Okay. But why us?'

She smiled at him. 'There must be something special about us.'

'There was — we were the only ones around.'

'Don't start being cynical again.' She asked him, 'How can you be cynical after what you saw?'

'I'm not sure what I saw.'

'I am.'

'I envy you.'

'Open your heart, Frank.' She reminded him, 'If you believe in love, you believe in God.' She asked him, 'Do you believe in love?'

'You shouldn't have to ask that.' He looked at his watch again. 'I have to go.' He stood. 'Tell Henry I said good-bye. And tell him I'll see him next time I'm in Rome.'

She stood, too, and they looked at each other.

He thought she was going to suggest that he walk with her along the path, toward Henry's office. But she didn't.

He said to her, 'I wish you all the happiness in the world.'

'I wish you God's peace and God's love.'

'You, too.'

'We have a bond that can never be broken.'

'We do.'

There wasn't much else to say, and he didn't want it to be awkward or emotional, so he said, 'Take care,' turned, and walked away.

This was the first time his sense of loss was not made easier by a sense of relief. In fact, he felt as though he were walking away from life.

Purcell knew never to look back, but this time something made him look back. She was standing near the bench, watching him.

He took a few more paces, then turned and looked at her again, and she was still looking at him.

He walked back to where she was standing, and she came to meet him.

They stopped a few feet from one another and he saw she had tears in her eyes.

He asked her, 'Where's Henry?'

'I told him not to come.'

He nodded.

She reminded him, 'You said you'd take me back.'

He'd thought it was a moot question, but apparently it was not.

She smiled. 'Are you taken?'

'No.'

'You are now.'

He didn't know what to say, so he asked, 'Would you like to take a walk?'

She put her arm through his and they walked through the Vatican park.

She reminded him, 'You said we'd return to the Capitoline Hill.'

'Right.' He asked her, 'Are your things in my room at the Forum?'

'I'm not that presumptuous.' She let him know, 'They're in the lobby.' She also let him know, 'We have been chosen for each other. Believe it.'

'I believe it.'

ACKNOWLEDGEMENTS

I'd like to first thank Rolf Zettersten, publisher of Center Street, for taking an early and earnest interest in my idea, pitched in a bar, of me rewriting and he republishing *The Quest*. It's not often that good decisions are made during cocktails, and less often does that idea survive the sober light of day. I am grateful for Rolf's enthusiasm and long friendship.

Rolf assigned a longtime friend of mine, Kate Hartson, as my editor. Kate read the original version of *The Quest* and immediately saw what needed to be done — more sex. Or, more romance. She helped guide my fictitious characters through their relationships and emotional turmoils while nudging the author toward a happy ending. Much gratitude to Kate for all her help and patience as I missed every deadline but the last.

Many thanks to my assistant Patricia Chichester, who loved this book even while we were both bleary-eyed from late nights spent writing, typing, rewriting, and retyping. Patricia's careful and quick work on all aspects of the manuscript, including research and working closely with Kate Hartson, made this book possible.

Thanks, too, to my assistant Dianne Francis, who also burned the midnight oil to keep the office running, and who became Nelson DeMille while I was locked in my writing cell. Thank you, Dianne, for keeping the world at bay.

Another good decision, made over vino at a long lunch, was my joining up with Jennifer Joel and Sloan Harris, literary agents extraordinaire, at International Creative Management Partners. Jenn and I go back many years, and Sloan had not had the pleasure of my company until we met at that fateful lunch. We all clicked, and I'm happy and proud to be represented by true professionals.

No writer should try to read a publishing or movie contract, or try to deal with the US Copyright Office. I have been fortunate to have as a friend and attorney David Westermann, who won't let me sign my name to anything he hasn't read and revised – including his checks. Thanks, Dave, for your good counsel.

When I first wrote *The Quest* in 1975, my childhood friend Thomas Block, who was a young pilot for Allegheny Airlines, helped with the flying scenes. Thirty-eight years later, I asked the still young US Airways retired Captain Block to take another look at the flying scenes in the book, which he did. He assured me that he had gotten it right the first time, and that the principles of flight had not changed all that much in the past thirty-eight years. I thanked Tom in 1975 for his time and advice, so I don't need to do it again – but I will. Thanks, Tom.

And last, but never least, I thank my young bride, Sandy DeMille, who said to me, when I was having doubts during the rewriting of *The Quest*, 'This is some of the best writing you've ever done.' That set the standard, and I remembered those words every time I sat down to face a blank page. As Ovid said, 'Scribire iussit amor' – Love bade me write.

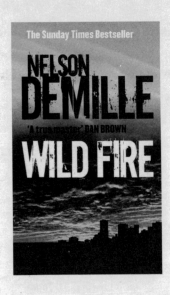

NELSON
DEMILLE

'A true master' DAN BROWN

WILD FIRE

'Wisecracking alpha-male thriller heroes don't come
much tougher, or much funnier, than John Corey'
Guardian

Welcome to the Custer Hill Club – a secret society whose members
include some of America's most powerful men. On the surface, the
club is a place to relax with old friends. But one weekend, the club
gathers to talk about the tragedy of 9/11 – and finalise a deadly
retaliation plan, known only by its code name: Wild Fire.

That same weekend, a member of the Federal Anti-Terrorist
Task Force is found dead. Soon it's up to Detective John Corey
and his wife, FBI Agent Kate Mayfield, to unravel a fiendishly
clever plot that starts with the Custer Hill Club and ends
with a terrifying nuclear stand-off ...

'A real page turner'
Independent on Sunday